"ARE YOU TIRED OF BEING THE UGLY GIRL, THE PLAIN JANE?"

It was like the stupid ad was talking to her, recounting the night's failures. Her looks *were* ruining—had ruined—her life. She *was* the original ugly girl . . . ugly enough to give lessons in it.

It didn't matter how smart you were, how funny, how great a person—the package was the deciding factor when it came to the opposite sex. Even Art Bradshaw, who Audra had thought might be just a little different, had turned out to be a full-fledged member of the club.

The commercial raced around her brain, its pitch resonating in her mind. What would it be like to look in the mirror and find not fat, black, and ugly . . . but lovely and desirable? What did it feel like to glance in the mirror and find a reflection like a movie star?

By the time the movie ended, Audra had the phone in her hand. "Welcome to the *Ugly Duckling*," a smooth, recorded voice said. "To be considered for a spot as a contestant on our show—" Audra snatched a pencil from the drawer, ripped off a clean sheet of paper, and began to write . . .

By Karyn Langhorne

KARYN LANGHORNE

Diary of an Ugly Duckling

HarperTorch
An Imprint of HarperCollinsPublishers

HARPERTORCH
An Imprint of HarperCollins*Publishers*
10 East 53rd Street
New York, New York 10022-5299

Copyright © 2006 by Karyn Wynn Folan
ISBN-13: 978-0-06-084755-5
ISBN-10: 0-06-084755-7

First HarperTorch paperback printing: July 2006

HarperCollins®, HarperTorch™, and ✦™ are trademarks of Harper-Collins Publishers Inc.

Printed in the United States of America

Visit HarperTorch on the World Wide Web at www.harpercollins.com

10 9 8 7 6 5 4 3 2 1

This book is dedicated to my husband, Kevin,
who loves me in a T-shirt, a towel, or a tiara.

Acknowledgments

I don't know about you, but I've always found something to hate about the way I look: I'm too fat, my skin looks funny, and I'm having a bad hair day that's lasted for twenty years. My hips are too big, my boobs are too small, my waist is too short. My eyes are too close together and my nose is too flat; I have this funny little ridge around my lips and absolutely no eyebrows whatsoever. Since I was about 14 years old, I've always found something to hate.

Then, last year, I came across a stack of photos taken when I was in college twenty years ago. I was so cute! True, at the time those photos were taken, I thought my hips were too big and my boobs were too small, and my eyes were too close together, etc. But looking at that girl now, twenty years and forty pounds later, I think she's adorable. Only I wish she'd known it.

The funny thing is, twenty years older and forty

pounds heavier, I'm more content with myself now than I was at 21. And that's what *Diary of an Ugly Duckling* is all about: learning to love yourself, not for *what* you are on the outside, but *who* you are on the inside.

I get weird ideas like *Diary of an Ugly Duckling* all the time . . . but they don't become books without the help and guidance of many, many people. I want to mention a few now.

First, let me thank Paula Langguth Ryan and her Art of Abundance coaching. Paula is a "life coach" with whom I've worked on and off for the past three years. She is super at helping you "uncover" your true self and she has given me some great "life exercises" over the years. I encourage everyone to visit her Web site at www.artofabundance.com. She's the best.

I'd also like to thank my mother, Evelyn S. Langhorne. She is nothing like the mother in this story! She's a lovely woman—inside and out—and one of my best friends and role models. Thanks, Mom!

As far as researching and developing this story, I have to thank Dr. Jan R. Adams. Other than appearing on several television shows dealing with plastic surgery, he wrote a book I found extremely helpful, *Everything Women of Color Should Know About Cosmetic Surgery*. Any sister thinking about having a "lift" should find a copy.

Without Esi Sogah and Selina McLemore, my editors, the story you're about to read would have made far less sense. I'm forever grateful to both of these talented ladies for their guidance—and to my thoughtful and dedicated agent, James C. Vines, who tells me I'm "shaking up" the romance genre with my weirdo ideas!

My husband, Kevin, and my daughters, Sierra and Sommer, are the greatest. They put up with the long hours of "not now, I'm writing"—and they even love my cellulite.

Last, but not least, I thank you, the reader. Thanks for reading—and I wish for you a healthy self-image and, for those of you who haven't already found him—the man of your dreams!

PART ONE

Fat, Black and Ugly

Chapter 1

Thursday, March 29

Dear Petra,

Greetings from your fatter, uglier sister! (I know, I know—but I figure starting this letter like that will get your mind off the chaos there in Iraq.)

Glad to hear that the latest violence has not affected you or Michael. Me, the same as always: work, home to help Ma look after Kiana (who, other than missing her mom and dad, is doing fine), watch a good classic movie (Double Indemnity was on last night!), sleep and back to work.

Speaking of work . . . there's a new guy. Girl . . . smooth milk chocolate skin, eyes light as caramel . . . delicious! Even a married woman like you would lick her lips! Works the same shift I do, but he's never said a single word to me. Actually, he doesn't talk much at all. The strong, silent type, I guess. No one seems to

*know much about him, so he could be married with
kids. Or he could be a snobbish jerk who thinks he's
tougher than the rest of us because he worked at
Upstate Maximum.*

*Or maybe he just doesn't like fat chicks . . . ☺ I
wonder what it would take for him to acknowledge my
existence?*

*Oh well, that's all from the home front. Let's be
careful out there,*

Audra

"**T**here's a speed limit in this state, mister."

Anyone else would have told the kid to
walk, to stop speeding through the day room
like he needed Ritalin, but Audra Marks was too
bored to do what everyone else would have done.
Instead, when the kid passed her at run, hurrying
over to a gaggle of young men hovering over a video
game rivalry, *Double Indemnity*—that great movie
classic of greed and betrayal—rose to her lips. In
a blink, she was no longer Audra Marks, a big-
boned black woman in a size-too-small uniform,
but Barbara Stanwyck—a film noir princess hitch-
ing the hem of her slinky dress to flummox Fred
MacMurray's careful cool with a shapely, ankle-
braceleted leg.

Too bad her captive audience didn't get it.

"Huh?" he offered with the eloquence typical of
young men of a certain age.

"Speed limit. Forty-five miles an hour. And you're
over it, sure as ten dimes will buy you a dollar."

Puzzlement creased her listener's face. He was

literally her captive—an inmate named Carlton Carter at the tail end of eighteen months for petty theft. He stopped short, watching her intently, his dark eyes skittering in his face, trying to decide if she was hassling him for a specific reason or just for general purposes.

Audra sighed. For the half instant before he opened his mouth, she played out a scene from her own secret fantasies—that she'd be answered with a line from one of the old classics, from *The Petrified Forest* and *Mildred Pierce*, *Desk Set* and *All About Eve*. It wouldn't matter if he was nineteen or ninety, if he was a convict or a conqueror, once he offered the words like a magic kiss, Audra would lift eyes of adoration to his face, violins would begin to play . . . and they would live together happily ever after, The End.

Clearly this kid wasn't her guy . . . Audra shifted her feet as though expecting to hear the telltale shimmy of anklet beads colliding with each other instead of the faint scuff of her orthopedic, regulation black lace-ups. She put her hand on her ample hip and leaned her sizeable frame close to the kid, tossing her head as though it were covered with Stanwyck's flaxen curls.

"Look, kid," she continued, mimicking the rapid-fire delivery of a black-and-white film as the boy's brow crinkled in deeper confusion. "There are a lot of losers in this mixed up, crazy world. Desperate people, people willing to toss over their own mothers just for a shot at the brass ring. One day soon, they'll spring you from this hole. But if you're stupid enough to commit another crime and end up back here, you'll regret it. Maybe not today, maybe not tomorrow, but one day soon, and for the rest of your life—"

Audra stopped short. *Crap, wrong movie.* She cut her eyes nervously at the young inmate, but the kid obviously didn't know the difference or much care. She glanced around, wondering if anyone else had heard the mistake.

Not likely.

Around them, the day room of the prison buzzed with the chatter of men: young ones clustered around video games, older ones gathered around card tables or the pieces for chess or checkers. Indeed, the only person close enough to have overheard any of Audra's little bit of drama was that new corrections officer—that very tall, very handsome, very built brother named Art Bradshaw—but Officer Bradshaw was staring determinedly at a table of inmates in the opposite corner. There was such a blank expression on his GQ cover-boy handsome face, she was pretty sure of one thing: Even working the same shift, in the same room, he didn't even know Corrections Officer Audra Marks existed.

When she turned back to him, Carlton was inspecting her in minute detail. Audra saw herself in the kid's eyes: He must have preferred the long, flowing, hair-weave look, because he seemed to grimace at her short 'fro. And Audra already knew her face was too full and her nose too flat—it seemed like she'd heard those criticisms every day since she was a kid—curses of a heredity she could only guess at. But the bulk of her arms, the shelf of her breasts straining against the crisp white cotton of her uniform and the thick roll of excess skin and fat beneath them, her thighs straining the fabric of her pants uncomfortably—those were her own doing. And no, Carlton Carter wasn't seeing Barbara Stanwyck . . . or any other starlet before 1944 or since, Audra realized, with an unpleasant jolt back to reality. Not for the first time this week, she wished she'd really started that diet and exercise program she'd been planning on starting since New Year's . . .

Today, she vowed, *starting at lunch. I'll just have a salad* . . .

"Uh . . . Officer?" Carlton snatched at her attention, dragging it back to him and the present moment. "You done? Can I go?"

Audra sighed. "I'm trying to teach you something here, Carter. I'm trying to teach you how to *banter*—"

"Banter?"

"Yeah, banter. It's how you win a woman with your words—"

"You mean my rap?" He shook his head, grinning. "Yo, I don't need no help with *that*—"

"Take that, you bitch!" someone behind her screamed.

Audra's fantasy faded like the trappings of Cinderella's trip to the ball, leaving neither a glass slipper—or even an ankle bracelet—to keep alive the memory. Audra leaped to her feet, one hand on her baton, the other on the service revolver snapped tight into the holster on her right hip as she whirled toward the sound. She touched a button on the walkie-talkie at her hip, activating a speaker and microphone on her shoulder, following procedures on reflex.

"Control, this is 0847. Incident in the day room. Backup requested, over," she murmured quickly into the device as the words, "Fight! Fight!" went up like a grade-school chant, filling the room.

Art Bradshaw was already wading through the sea of orange toward the brawlers and Audra dived into the commotion. "Hey!" she hollered, dropping her voice to its hardest, most authoritative edge as she bumped through the knot of jumpsuited men hyped on the sounds of fists flying. "Get back! Back, I said!"

"You heard her! Get back!" Bradshaw rumbled, echoing Audra in a commanding chorus. "Out of the way!"

The cluster of orange onlookers fell away at the power of the man's voice. Of course, it wasn't just his voice that parted the men like Moses at the Red Sea: Audra noticed, not for the first time, that the new corrections officer was very tall—at least 6 feet 5 inches in his socks, with the kind of thick muscles that usually meant a man sweated for a living. Audra glanced quickly into his face: It was smooth and rich, chiseled sharp at the cheekbones and chin. Impossibly handsome. Prince Charming handsome. Once again, he gave Audra not the slightest look or word, ignoring her as thoroughly as if she didn't exist, even though the two of them needed to act as a team to resolve the conflict unfolding before them.

Two men lay tangled in each other's arms, each trying to beat the living hell out of the other. The top man's number was stenciled across the side of his jumpsuit like a tattoo: MI 761098. Audra transcribed it in her mind to the face of a long, lean, don't-give-a-good-damn brother whose mama had named him Princeton Haines, though he was neither princely in manner nor smart enough for the college of the same name. Even with only the back of his cornrowed head visible as he wrestled with the man beneath him, Audra knew his cocoa-colored face was contorted into the sneer it always wore. Unlike kids like Carlton, there was no point talking to inmates like Haines; odds were overwhelming that not only would Haines likely return to Manhattan Men's for repeat visits when he'd finished this three-to-five, but that he'd probably one day reside at Upstate, the maximum security prison, for the rest of his life.

If the top man was Princeton Haines, the bottom man had to be a new inmate he'd been exchanging bad blood with for the past two weeks, a youngster by the name of Garcia, who was working overtime to create a bad-ass rep. An instant later, her suspicions were confirmed as the two men shifted positions and the bottom man became the top.

"Break it up!" Bradshaw shouted, grabbing at Garcia's back and lifting him easily off the floor. Audra slipped her baton back into its loop at her belt and on the impulse of her training, grabbed Haines firmly by the armpits and tugged him upward with all her might, dragging him to his surprised feet.

"Dag," one of the orange-suited men muttered from the cluster. "You see her lift him like he was nothing—"

"That's one strong-ass chick, man—"

"You sure it's a chick? Looks like a dude to me."

"Yeah man, one fat, black ugly dude, y'know—"

"Fat, black, ugly dude with tits," another voice chuckled.

Fat . . . black . . . ugly. The words shook her insides like they always had, and she was nine years old all over again, listening where she shouldn't have, hearing things that cut her to heart's core.

Fat . . . black . . . ugly . . .

She jerked toward the voice, half-expecting to see the ghost of her father, when—

Rip.

It was the most awful sound imaginable: loud and insistent, more shattering than gunfire. It seemed to echo in the room, reverberating, registering in every ear with deafening meaning. Automatically, Audra threw Haines roughly aside and heard him crash against something, hard and loud. She reached behind her, feeling for the tear and getting a nice handful of her large, white, granny panty underwear—as a flush of mortification heated her face.

Her tight blue uniform pants had given up their valiant struggle and ripped waistband to crotch down the center butt-seam . . . in front of a roomful of men.

An instant later the sound of laughter filled the room, echoing in her ears as Audra spread her hands over the tear, humiliation settling thick and hot in her chest. The last remnants of the elegant fantasy of the forties slipped from her mind as tears bubbled just beneath her eyelashes.

I won't cry. I won't cry . . . Corrections officers don't cry, Audra told herself.

"Thank you, thank you very much," she muttered Elvis-style, taking a couple of quick nodding bows around the room, blinking quickly as though it were a part of her routine and not a desperate attempt to keep her emotions at bay. "I'm here in Vegas 'til Tuesday . . ."

More laughter reverberated around her and Audra took another quick bow, her hands firmly affixed to the seat of her pants, just as four more COs joined them in the day room to help. She glanced at Bradshaw, hoping for support, but he simply stared into the space between her shoulder and the walls, as usual.

The handsome creep.

"It's okay, fellas," Audra said, taking charge of the confusion on the newcomers' faces. Clearly they'd been expecting an outbreak of prison violence . . . and were surprised to find themselves in the audience of a comedy show. "It's all over but the jokin' and the sewin'—"

"Gonna take a big needle close *that* up!" Someone quipped, but before Audra could isolate the identity of the speaker Haines' moaned.

"Shut up! Won't somebody shut her up? Fat bitch broke my ribs! She broke my damn ribs then slammed me into that table there!" He clutched at his abdomen, bent double, Audra supposed, with pain. "Y'all saw it! It's police brutality! I want my lawyer! I'm filing a claim with the warden! I want reparations—"

"Quiet, Haines."

Audra turned in surprise.

Bradshaw.

His voice was smooth, rich and deep like some forbidden chocolate treat or an expensive coffee drink. The voice of a screen legend from Hollywood's heyday, mesmerizing in its depth. She glanced over at him and found a somber expression on his face.

"You okay?" he asked at last.

Audra hesitated. He still wasn't exactly looking at her, but when no one else replied, she assumed the question was intended for her. For some reason, Bradshaw's concern made tears tremble just below the surface again, but Audra shook them aside. "Marvelous, darling," she muttered in her best diva dame voice, but with the inmates still muttering "fat" and "dude with tits" and with her fingers tight over her rear end, it was hard to keep the image alive. "Thanks for asking. I was beginning to wonder what it took to get your attention." She shrugged toward her rear end. "Now I know."

Bradshaw blinked, his light eyes shifting at last to her face. Audra felt a shock like electricity course through her body as his full lips curved into the slightest smile. "Sorry. Had a lot on my mind lately," he said, then leaned toward Audra, dropping his voice to a husky whisper. "And you confused *Double Indemnity* with *Casablanca*," he murmured in a tone intended for her ears only. "Try to get it straight next time, Marks." Then he shifted his attention to the inmates. "Recreation's over, gentlemen," he announced in a smooth baritone. "Line up! Now!"

Reluctantly, the men shuffled into a haphazard line along the wall. Bradshaw led the way back to the cell block, leaving Audra staring after him with her hands covering her bloomers and her mouth open in surprise.

Chapter 2

"If that's all you're getting from what I told you," Audra said, her voice rising to a near shout in frustration, "You are missing the *point*, Ma—"

"I ain't missing *nothing*, Audra," Audra's mother, Edith Marks snapped, her words lilting with the tobacco fields of North Carolina, as though she hadn't lived in New York City since she was eighteen. "The *point* is, you ripped your pants and showed your butt—literally—to this man—"

"Art Bradshaw—"

"This Art Bradshaw," Audra's mother repeated, more loudly than before, hammering home her point by volume alone. "What must he think of you?"

What *did* Art Bradshaw think, Audra wondered, replaying the way his eyes had locked on hers, liquid and glowing with warmth. His words betrayed that he'd been listening to her conversation with the kid, Carter. Audra wondered how many other times he'd watched her, as surreptitiously as she'd watched him.

"I think . . ." Audra began slowly, determined to say the words aloud in spite of the patter of her heart. "I think he thinks what I think. That we're soul mates—"

"Soul mates! Soul mates, my eye," Edith scoffed. "You humiliate yourself in front of him and now, you're talking some mess 'bout him bein' your soul mate?" She rolled a pair of shrewd, bright eyes carefully lined with black pencil and batted her mascaraed lashes in Audra's direction. "Honestly, Audra. If you think that man's interested in you because you can crack a joke after humiliatin' yourself, you musta bumped your head—"

"Will you forget about the pants for just a second, Ma?" Audra folded her arms over her chest like a defiant teenager and lifted her head in protest. "I think he's interested in me because we both know the movies—"

"Movies!" The older woman tossed this week's hairdo, making the strands of a sleek black bob dance. Audra knew for a fact most of the hair was fake, purchased wholesale from the inventory of her mother's salon, Goldilocks, and sewn in on a Monday or Tuesday morning when there weren't many paying customers. It looked good, too, on her mother's still pretty fifty-something head, but then most styles did. It was yet another way they were different: opposite as night is from day. "So he likes movies. Everybody likes movies. What's that got to do with the price of beans in China?" her mother concluded, as if the question were completely logical.

Talking to her mother was always like this. So many questions, so little listening. They were as combative as the mother-daughter relationship in *Mildred Pierce*. Joan Crawford played the long-suffering, giving mother to Ann Blyth's selfish, greedy, mean-spirited daughter. Only in their case, Audra was certain, it was the daughter who was the suffering one.

"It's *tea*, Ma," she corrected, infusing a touch of the movie's drama into the moment to make it more bearable. "The price of *tea* in China. And I'm telling you, that stuff with the pants, it won't matter. He knows the old movies—the *classic* movies—and he knows I know them, too. Did you hear what he said about confusing *Casablanca* and *Double Indemnity*?" Her chest lifted in a sigh of longing. "It's like we were *meant* for each other—"

"Oh, Audra, please," Edith Marks muttered dismissively. "Stop talkin' foolishness and get *real*. I can't think of anything much more of a turnoff than a woman who's let her butt get so round she rips her pants in front of a bunch of men!"

Audra rolled her eyes. Leave it to Edith to reduce things to their lowest, crudest denominator. "They ripped," she said loftily, wishing her mother would let her forget the awful mortification that had accompanied that moment, but the woman seemed determined to make it breathe again, "because I was breaking up a *fight*—"

"No, Miss Queen of De-Nial," her mother drawled. "They ripped 'cause you need to lose some weight!" She sniffed sanctimoniously. "I know that sounds mean, but it's the truth and you need to hear it. A little weight is one thing, but you're getting too fat, Audra."

"I just need to cut back a little—" Audra began.

"A little?" Edith interjected. She reached behind her, opening one of the old kitchen's cabinets to reveal its contents: a solid wall of junk foods piled on its shelves, cookies, crackers, candies and chips jumbled atop each other. "You just bought all this stuff last night and it'll be gone by the end of the weekend—"

"I'm not the only one who eats that stuff. Kiana likes it—"

"Kiana's a child," Edith reminded her, jerking her head toward the other room where Audra's niece watched animated girls cartwheeling around, solving some kind of mystery through their derring-do. Either because she was transfixed by the images, or because she was used to Grandma and Auntie A's noise, she didn't even turn toward their raised voices. To Kiana, the sound of the two of them arguing over the dinner dishes was as comforting as a lullaby.

"She doesn't need this stuff any more than you do," Edith added when Audra focused on her again.

"Okay, so I like a little something sweet from time to time." Audra shrugged. "I know in your world of high fashion and glamour, that's some kind of *crime*, but to the rest of us mere mortals, it's no big deal."

Edith sighed. "I don't understand you, Audra. Seems like you don't care about what you look like. Not at all," Edith continued. Audra was pretty sure she didn't do it on purpose, but her mother punctuated the words by striking one of her little poses, slewing out a foot and propping her hand with her waist, emphasizing her trim figure. She nodded toward a snapshot of Petra, Audra's older sister, looking like Tyra Banks doing a photo shoot for army fatigues, taped to the refrigerator. "Even soldiering in that awful Baghdad, your sister takes some time to put herself together. It's just a matter of pride—"

"I'm looking for a man who sees deeper than outward appearances. Someone who'll love me no matter what I look like," Audra muttered, tossing a dish towel on the counter and snatching at an open bag of Oreos protruding from the cabinet like a chocolate tongue.

"Men are visual, Audra." Edith grabbed the bag from her hands and tossed it into the garbage can. She dipped her hands into the sink for the next of their dinner dishes. They were a leathery brown— almost an entire shade darker than her cinnamon-colored face thanks to the harsh chemicals of her three decades working as a hairstylist. Still, dark as the hands had become, they were still three shades lighter than the lightest part of Audra's body. Audra frowned, staring at those hands.

"You want to catch one, you don't gotta be no beauty queen, but you sure as hell better work what you got," her mother continued, enjoying the sound of her own wisdom. "Why do you think Goldilocks Salon is packed from morning to night? Sisters in there pressing and curling and straightening and weaving"— the hands came up out of the water as Edith snapped a couple of soapy fingers. "Working it, that's what they doing. Working it!" She shook her head, folding her full lips in disapproval. "You keep that hair cut short as a man—and I run a beauty salon, for God's sake! How do you think it makes me look in the neighborhood, my own daughter wandering around with her hair looking like this?" She reached toward Audra's short naps, but Audra danced backward out of her way.

"You know I like my hair short, Ma," she said defiantly.

"I don't know any such thing—"

"Well, you ought to know it. We've tried every other style and none of them work any better, you've said so yourself."

Edith paused, blinking while she remembered the countless hours she and Audra had spent trying to get the thick bristles of her hair to behave. But it was no use: unlike Petra's locks, which lay down perfectly under straightening comb or relaxer—and unlike Edith's own—Audra's hair seemed to have a mind of its own.

"Well," Edith said slowly, since there was no argument to refute this, she wagged her swingy new hairdo again. "The short look doesn't do a thing for you with your face that full. I don't understand why you can't Pretty Up—like they say on the Beautify! Network—"

"Stupid makeover shows," Audra grumbled.

"Not as stupid as your classic movie fantasyland," her mother shot back, a tinge of anger in her voice. "From where I'm standing, it seems like you're going out of your way to look fat and ugly—and both of those things are completely within your control!"

Fat and ugly . . . fat and ugly . . . fat, black and ugly . . .

The words chimed in her ears, chanted by inmates and now uttered by her own mother.

Fat, black . . . black . . . black . . .

Something angry slithered and squirmed deep in
Audra's soul, and before she could stop herself she
snapped, "What about *black*, Ma. Is that under my
control, too?"

Her mother turned to her in surprise, hands pausing over the sink. "Black?" she shrugged. "Of course
not. We're all *black*, Audra—"

"No, Ma. You're not black, you're *brown*. Even *tan*.
You and Petra and Daddy—you're all *tan*." Audra
stretched out her own arm, rolling the sleeve up to
the elbow. "See this? *This* is black."

Edith blinked at her, her mouth working silently,
then she pushed Audra's outstretched arm away
from her. An instant later, she thrust her hands back
in the soapy water, fished up another plate, and began scrubbing as if her little sponge could clean up
this turn in their conversation.

"So what?" Edith told her sponge in a careful, low
voice. "I'm brown-skinned, Petra's light-skinned.
But there are darker people in the family—"

"Name one," Audra demanded.

Edith's dishwashing hands paused, the plate slipping out of them to splash audibly in the bubbly water. Her whole body grew very still, as though some
kind of spell had been cast on her, making her as
motionless as Snow White after she ate the apple.
She did not look at Audra or speak.

"I've seen the pictures." Audra pressed on. "I've
been with you back to North Carolina. Almost all of
us have the same eyes and same shape of face . . ."

Audra hesitated, and then pushed the words out with sudden determination. "Your people aren't this dark, Mama. Even Gran said she couldn't figure out where my coloring came from—"

When Edith finally faced her, her lips were folded tight and there was a funny auburn flush creeping up from the skin of her neck up to her ears.

"Really, Audra," she said, in a voice that struggled for light, bright and breezy, but ended up sounding strangled and tight. "There's some darker kin on your father's side—"

"No, Ma." Audra interrupted, shaking her head. "Remember that reunion we went to? All of his people have fair skin. Next to them, you and Petra are dark!" Audra stared hard at her mother. "No one either side of the family is as dark as I am, Ma." She swallowed hard, forcing herself to continue. "Is—is there something you want to tell me?"

Edith's eyes slid from Audra back to the plate, back to the sink. "Like what?" she asked the dish in the same constricted voice.

Audra shrugged. "Like I'm adopted . . . or . . . something else," she murmured.

Now, Edith's head snapped toward Audra in surprise. For a long moment, mother and daughter stared at each other in a game of visual chicken, each daring the other to blink first. Audra's heart pounded in her chest, banging so hard against her ribs she wondered if her mother could see it, wondering if it looked like the animated heart of an old-time cartoon character. She put a hand to her chest, pressing, hoping to still the frantic beat.

Just tell me the truth, just tell me the truth, she

thought over and over in her mind, knowing that Edith could read the words in her eyes. *For once, just—*

When her mother finally spoke, her voice was hard as a slap.

"What's this supposed to be? Some big dramatic scene out of one of your old movies? The climactic scene where all the secrets are revealed? Well, I'm sorry, but you weren't adopted . . . or anything else," she said brusquely. "I don't know why you'd want to say something like that," she grumbled. "You and Petra got the same father . . . and he's been dead two years now and you know it. Didn't leave anybody anything but bad debts and worse memories, so you're better off without him. Not that you ever needed a thing from him anyway."

"No, not a thing," Audra agreed, an ugly sarcasm taking over her tone. "After all, we always had you."

From her mother's silence, Audra suspected the woman understood fully the implications of that comment, that she could feel Audra's resentments, longstanding and desperate, flowing toward her in the silence between them.

"You need to lose some weight. Do something with yourself," her mother said in a nasty, hasty voice, giving back as good as she was getting. "Then you'll stop focusing on this crazy mess." She dried the sparkling plate herself, pulled the plug and released the water from the sink with an air of rushed finality. "Make yourself useful and go put your sister's child to bed," she told Audra abruptly. "We promised to take care of my baby's baby until she comes home from the war, and I ain't lettin' this trash you're talking keep you from doing your part." Then, with a swish of her new hairdo, she fled the room and Audra heard her bedroom door slam, locking Audra, and further conversation, out.

"This one."

Six-year-old Kiana handed Audra a thin story-book, its paper cover vividly illustrated, and then climbed into Audra's lap with a proprietary certainty that only a niece who'd enjoyed a young lifetime of considerable doting and spoiling could manage. "Read it with the voices, Auntie A. Can you do it with the voices?"

"You bet I can do it with the voices," Audra told her, letting the little girl snuggle tight against her ample chest. Kiana didn't seem to mind how tight her sweatshirt was or how her thighs spread across the surface of the old rocking chair. Audra breathed deeply, letting the girl smell of bubbles from the bath she'd just taken erase the day, snuggling her chin into the child's freshly braided hair. Kiana held Mugsy, the stuffed rabbit she'd slept with since she was a mere baby. "You read, too, though," Audra told her. "You're getting to be a big girl. Pretty soon, *you'll* be reading the whole book to *me*."

Kiana nodded solemnly, showing the smoky brown eyes that were the signature characteristic of all the women in Audra's family—even Audra had the eyes.

You ain't adopted . . . or anything else.

Her mother's words echoed in her brain, stirring memories, questions and more questions, questions she wondered if she would ever get answered. But before she could get too lost in considering the matter, Kiana was prying Audra's distracted fingers off the book's glossy cover. "The Ugly Duckling," she read, girlish and serious all at once.

The Ugly Duckling.

Great, Audra thought, a sinking feeling of dread pulling her heart down to her toes. *Of all the stories, on all the bookshelves, in all the world . . . this book has to jump into my hands.*

But all she said was, "Very good," squeezed the girl tight, and started to read.

Although it had been years since she'd given the story any serious thought, the plot hadn't changed. Separated from her own kind, a swan chick was raised by Mama Duck and her cute little ducklings, who teased and mistreated her for her ungainly awkwardness. Finally, ostracized from the duck family altogether, the ugly one went out into the world, where she met with similar treatment from other animals in both the wild and the barnyard until, after a long harsh winter of solitude, she discovered that she was never a duckling at all, but a beautiful creature of another kind.

"And, no longer an ugly duckling, the swan lived happily ever after," she read aloud to the little girl on her knee, closing the book. "The end. Now, you'd better hop into this bed before your grandma finds out you're still awake. It's nearly eight-thirty." Audra frowned, dropping her voice to a co-conspirator's whisper. "You know how she gets when she's mad."

"Gramzilla," Kiana murmured in a voice of reverent respect and immediately hopped out of Audra's arms and into her bed, her face as serious as a spanking.

"Gramzilla is right," Audra agreed. "When she sends your mommy and daddy their emails tonight, I want her to be able to give them a good report on you."

"Are Mommy and Daddy all right?"

Audra nodded. "Fine," and she added a prayer of thanksgiving in heart that it was still true. "Mommy will probably be home soon. Before you go to first grade in the fall, we hope. We'll send them another package this weekend. Now, go to sleep."

Kiana nodded and immediately closed her eyes, feigning sleep.

"That's the way." Audra laughed. She smoothed the covers around the child, kissed her forehead and headed for the door. "Good night."

Kiana sighed the deep and grateful sigh of childhood rest. Before Audra had backed out of the room, Kiana was no longer pretending and was already half asleep.

The lights were already out in the rest of the three-bedroom apartment they all shared. Clearly, her mother had emerged from her bedroom long enough to accomplish that mission, and, Audra assumed, double-check the locks on the door—all in the time it took for Audra to supervise Kiana's bath and read *The Ugly Duckling*. Audra passed her mother's room on the way to the bathroom; the light was on and Audra knew she was in there watching one of those makeover shows she loved so much, typing out her daily message to her daughter and son-in-law at war so many thousands of miles away. Audra hesitated for a moment, staring at the shaft of light seeping from beneath the door, fighting down the urge to reconcile, to beg to be forgiven.

But I'm not sorry, she reminded herself. *I'm not sorry, and I'm not wrong. Art Bradshaw might very well be my soul mate . . . and if he is, it won't matter how much I weigh, or whether my hair is done. When people connect like we did—when the connection is beyond the superficial, looks don't matter. It doesn't matter if you're fat, or ugly or—*

She pushed aside the last of it, not wanting to contemplate skin tone or her mother or the possibility that she might have more in common with the ugly duckling in the story than she ever could have imagined.

But ultimately, it was her bladder that pulled her away from her mother's door. Audra hurried up the narrow hallway of the old apartment toward the bathroom. But when the urge was satisfied and she was giving her hands some needed attention, she looked up and into the mirror.

She could see the extra weight in the roundness of her cheeks, which these days seemed on the verge of becoming part of her neck—and her hair was a wiry, unnatural helmet of brittle, black spikes. Her ebony skin was pocked and marred by the after-effects of adolescent acne—and as if to remind her that the bad old days were far from over, two new zits shined out on her chin and forehead. Audra's attention bypassed her lips and eyes—there was nothing wrong with them—to find her nose. It appeared to be a misshapen blob off-center in her face, like a lump of overused Play-Doh crudely abandoned by a bored child.

"Please let him see beyond fat, black and ugly," she whispered toward the sky. "I'm counting on you, Art Bradshaw." Then she moved quietly through the house toward her own room, where the sweeping music and opening credits of another old black-and-white film were coloring the darkness in shades of gray.

Chapter 3

Friday, March 30

Dear Petra,

She was so angry. She looked at me like I'd called her a "slut" to her face last night. I almost told her what I overheard all those years ago . . . but I couldn't do it. I just couldn't do it . . .

She hasn't said a word to me since our kitchen conversation last night. It's an early day at the salon, so she was up when I got up, but she kept sipping her coffee and didn't even look at me.

I've been up all night, watching movies, trying to figure out how to proceed with AB (Art Bradshaw, to you). We work the same shift, so there should be opportunities, right? I really want to get to know him—see if what I hope might be there, really is.

I watched Desk Set—the Hepburn-Tracy dynamic is classic, so that could be a nice opener. Lots of good dialogue. But I always have a hard time getting my Katharine Hepburn imitation straight, so I might mess it up. And anyway, I keep hearing the spirit of Mae West in my brain. She's earthier, sexier, more overt. Think that would get his attention?

I wish you were here to give me your opinion before I head off to work. As it is, I'll just have to send you an email tonight and let you know how it went. I really think he might like me, Petra. And once he gets to know me, I think he might like me a lot!

Well, I've got to go, dahling. The New York Department of Corrections awaits!

Be careful out there,

Audra

"**W**oodburn wants to see you, Audra," Darlene Fuchs, the assignment officer on duty murmured as Audra clocked in at Control and double-checked her duty assignment for the day. "Here," and she thrust a small piece of memo paper bearing the name Deputy Warden Stephen Woodburn into Audra's hands. On it, in a ballpoint scrawl, were Audra's name and the words, "See me, ASAP."

Crap, Audra thought. *This wrecks everything . . .*

On the subway on the way to the prison, Audra had decided to march into the day room, flounce right over to the handsome Art Bradshaw and blurt out a few lines of dialogue from *Desk Set*—just to see how deep the man's repertoire really was. After all he said he liked movies, but was he limited to film noir? Or was he versatile enough to do the comedies and dramas, too? And what about the musicals? Was

he man enough to admit to Gene Kelly? To Ginger
Rogers and Fred Astaire? Or would that he draw the
line at the films where they danced around, the
women's beautiful costumes swishing around them
like fans?

For an instant, Audra lost herself, caught up in the
image of herself as Ginger and Bradshaw as Fred,
swirling around a ballroom floor together—

"Marks, did you hear me?" Fuchs repeated, more
insistently. "The deputy warden wants to see you.
Now."

Ginger/Audra and Fred/Bradshaw tripped and
fell flat on their faces, then hurried, embarrassed, off
the stage and out of sight. Audra shook herself back
into the moment, almost surprised to find herself at
Manhattan Men's Correctional Facility now that the
power of her daydream had been broken.

"The deputy's here?" she asked the woman,
round-eyed with surprise. "This early?"

"Apparently," Fuchs replied without looking up.
Now here was a woman who could have done
Katharine Hepburn justice, Audra decided, taking
in the other woman's rangy, thin figure and long
chestnut hair, worn in a bun as tight as her thin lips
while on duty. Audra had seen an entirely different
side of the woman at a retirement party for a col-
league of theirs a few months back. With her hair
down and her lips loosened by a couple of apple
martinis, Darlene could have given a few of the
young women on *America's Next Top Model* a serious
run for their money. But there wasn't a glimpse of
that beautiful party girl to be seen today: Darlene
was all business this morning. "All I know is, when

I got here, he waltzed down and gave me these little 'see me' notes for you and Bradshaw—"

Heat climbed from the pit of Audra's stomach to her neck, warming her ears and cheeks. "Bradshaw?" she stammered, sounding anything but cool, calm and collected.

Darlene's eyebrows shot over her green eyes as though she knew Audra had spent most of the night and right up to twenty seconds ago rehearsing romantic scenes with Bradshaw as the male lead.

"I mean," Audra said, bringing her voice back to its normal register and adding a little casual *what's-the-diff* to the mix, "what does the dep want with Bradshaw?"

Darlene stared at her just a second longer, and Audra got the distinct feeling that, had they been out on the New York streets, or sitting in a cozy little café somewhere, she would have leaned forward and asked the most girlfriend-ly of questions, like a character on *Sex and the City* or out of one of Terry McMillan's books. But as they were in a men's prison—"Testosterone Central"—the other woman simply lifted a shoulder and said in her blandest and most professional tone, "My guess would be something to do with that skirmish in the day room yesterday," and from the look on her face, Audra knew she'd heard as much about the color of Audra's bloomers as she had about the fight between Haines and Garcia that had precipitated it all. "Don't you think?" she asked, struggling to sound innocent.

"Yeah," Audra mumbled, trying hard to smile, even though the memory of the event was the last thing she wanted to relive. In an instant, she abandoned willowy Kate Hepburn for a vampy imitation of Mae West. "I guess when you rip your pants in the line of duty, you gotta expect the tale," and she turned and wagged her behind at the other woman, "will be told."

Audra had expected Darlene to laugh . . . but instead the woman gave her a smile that mingled friendliness with pity and changed the subject.

"I'll radio your sergeant," she said, grabbing the needed telecommunications device from its slot on the table. "Tell him you and Bradshaw will be a few minutes behind schedule—"

"You mean Bradshaw's in there now?" Mae West vamoosed, and Audra heard her own voice, rising nervously into the stratosphere again.

"Well, yeah, Marks," Darlene said, in "duh" tones. "He's like a minute ahead of you." She checked a thick-banded, masculine-looking watch on her freckled forearm. "Make that two minutes, now." She looked up and winked at Audra. "If you hurry, you might be able to catch him," she finished, and Audra was pretty sure she didn't just mean in the hallway.

"Sit down, Marks. Sit down," Deputy Warden Woodburn said as Audra appeared in the open doorway of his office.

Art Bradshaw had already settled his massive collection of muscles into one of the Warden's two side chairs, but he jumped to his feet as soon as Woodburn's words indicated her presence. He didn't speak—or even turn in her direction—just stood at attention as gallant as any movie prince for the few seconds it took for Audra to navigate the room and ease herself nervously into the proffered chair beside him. Audra took a quick second to admire his profile, the breadth of his football-player-wide shoulders and the smooth skin of his shaved skull, wishing in spite of herself that he'd turn so she could see his eyes. Her heart was doing a vaudeville soft shoe in her chest: If the man had spoken to her, she might have had another kind of accident— and she didn't have any more uniform pants to change into right now.

She squared her shoulders, imagining herself encased in one of those big-shouldered suits of the 1940s, concentrated her attention on the deputy warden and sat, making a futile attempt to cross her legs, diva-style, before giving up and folding them against each other, ankle to ankle. "Sir," she said, crisply. "You wanted to see me?"

Deputy Warden Stephen Woodburn looked like he'd been at work for hours. His desk was cluttered with papers, and a huge mug, running over with coffee, sat fresh and steaming on a manila folder, making a dark stain. On a credenza behind him were pictures of a brown-haired woman and three towheaded kids dressed in their Sunday best, angled for maximum visitor admiration.

"Don't look so nervous, Marks," Woodburn said, grabbing the stained folder beneath his coffee cup. Audra read her name on a white label across its tab. "I don't think you have any real reason to be. But . . ." he paused to skim through the folder's contents, giving Audra a moment to skim her eyes over his short, graying hair, very precisely trimmed in a conservative cut, and the rimless glasses perched on a straight nose. The man's eyes left the folder and found hers again. "We do have a slight problem that impacts you, and to a lesser degree, Officer Bradshaw. That's why I've asked you both to drop by before assuming your duties this morning."

He paused the pause Audra knew came before any climactic bombshell in every movie worth its salt. Audra had just counted *one, two, three* in her mind when Warden Woodburn said:

"So yesterday, there was an incident in the day room. Or rather, a couple of incidents," he corrected, pale lips curving into something like a smile. "One involving a couple of inmates in a scuffle . . . and the other involving . . ." he coughed a little, as though suddenly uncomfortable. "Shall we call it . . . uh . . . a wardrobe malfunction?"

Wardrobe malfunction. *Am I ever going to live this down?* Audra wondered as, once again, a prickly embarrassment warmed her cheeks and neck. She could almost hear her mother in her mind (*What must he think of you?*) as Woodburn averted his face from hers as if to spare her shame. She cut her eyes toward Bradshaw, but got nothing but a stoic profile, so there was nothing to do for it but sit up a little straighter and make the most of it, the only way she knew how. She settled her fist on her hip and leaned forward.

"Both were contained according to procedure, sir," she wisecracked, wiggling a bit and keeping the Mae West purr in her voice.

Woodburn chuckled a little and Audra whipped

her head toward Art Bradshaw to gauge his reaction. Nothing but his profile. Still.

"You're funny, Marks," the deputy warden told the folder. "Humor's a helpful quality in our profession, within limits, of course. But unfortunately . . ." his eyes snapped to her face again. "One of the inmates involved . . . a Mr. Haines . . . has filed a brutality complaint. Apparently he was injured yesterday. Broken ribs, it appears . . ."

Both humor and Hollywood died the moment the word *brutality* hit the air.

"A brutality complaint? Against me?"

"A brutality complaint. Against you," Woodburn repeated. "Haines alleges you violated his civil rights and caused him personal injury when you lifted him bodily off the floor then threw him against a table—"

"Threw him against a table!" Audra shook her head, astonished. "I was breaking up a fight—a fight he probably started!" She peered toward Woodburn's folder. "Does it say that in there? Because there were about two dozen witnesses." She nodded in Bradshaw's direction. "Officer Bradshaw can tell you—"

Woodburn lifted his hand, stopping the rest of the explanation tumbling form Audra's lips. "He already has, Officer Marks. In fact, he says your conduct was exemplary, both in dealing with the inmates involved in the altercation, and in handling the . . . uh . . . wardrobe malfunction. But I'm not the one who has to be convinced," he continued briskly. "I'm sure Mr. Haines's charges will be dismissed in short order. But Haines is within his rights to file it, and, as you know, it will have to be investigated by the Internal Review Board—"

Charges? Internal Review? Me? Audra swallowed back an A to Z catalog of emotions: from anger to the zealous desire to wring Princeton Haine's sneaky, scrawny neck. *Only that* would *be police brutality, now, wouldn't it?* wisecracked a voice in her head, and for a wild half-second, Audra wasn't sure she would be able to stop herself from laughing—knowing full well that if the laughter started, the tears wouldn't be too far behind.

"But sir, it's a waste of their time!" Audra insisted. "It's utterly groundless—"

Woodburn raised his silencing hand again. "I know this is frustrating, Marks, but that's procedure and we're going to follow it to the letter," he said, and his nonexistent lips disappeared that much deeper into his face. "The rules require that any officer accused of misconduct toward an inmate be removed from duty until a cause/no cause inquiry is completed, so you're officially on administrative leave pending resolution of the investigation. Shouldn't be more than a week, I would guess." He curved the lower half of his face into a grim smile. "Try to think of it as a well-deserved vacation, not as a disciplinary action."

Audra suppressed a sigh. "I understand, sir."

Woodburn took a nervous sip of his coffee. "There's ... uh ... one other thing," he continued, licking his lips. "Regarding the ... uh ... wardrobe malfunction? That's not likely to happen again, is it? Because it poses ... uh ... all kinds of problems. I mean, this *is* a men's correctional institution and—"

"I know, sir. It's not appropriate for a woman to—"

"Oh, it's not that," Woodburn said, dismissing her femininity behind another quick gulp of his mug. "It's a question of maintaining authority and order here, Marks. This is a prison, not a comedy club. Impressions and wisecracks are fine, but they are secondary to the realities of what we do. Just lose weight or buy the right size or . . . whatever . . ." His eyes found hers. "Right?"

"It won't happen again," Audra said quickly before the man could skip down this yellow brick road any further. She cut another surreptitious glance Bradshaw-ward, but if the size of Audra's ass was of any interest to him at all, she couldn't read it on his face.

Woodburn shifted his attention to Bradshaw, too. "How are you adjusting, Bradshaw? I suspect Manhattan Men's is a walk in the park compared to Upstate, huh?"

"Yes, sir," Bradshaw said, filling the room with his mellow baritone for the first time. Audra turned toward him, reveling in the sound of his voice, but again, the man wasn't looking at her.

He hadn't spoken to her, hadn't looked at her at all, not even when she was wiggling her ample hips Mae West style . . .

Audra frowned, suddenly unsure. Maybe it was just being in Woodburn's office. Or maybe he was concerned about being involved with anyone who was accused of brutality and now relieved of duty. Or maybe . . . maybe . . . maybe her mother was right, and he didn't like the way she looked—

Audra smoothed a nervous hand over her hair and then along the crease of her new uniform pants. She licked her dry lips, wondering if she still had the nerve to vamp up to him with the lines of a movie on her lips. *Abort, abort, abort*, something in her brain was screaming, and Audra was inclined to obey.

"Anything else?" The deputy warden's eyes flicked over them both one last time, dismissing them. "If not . . . thank you, Officers."

And before she could even turn to glance at him, Art Bradshaw had unfolded his big, tall body and made a quick, silent exit.

"There's a speed limit in this state, mister—uh—I mean, ma'am."

Audra stopped short. There was no doubt who was speaking—there was no one else in this silent office corridor far from the day-to-day activities of prison life.

Relieved of duty, after leaving Woodburn's office Audra had changed back into street clothes and was about to leave the building when the big man's voice arrested her, not far from the officers' break room.

Audra whirled around, staring into the man's face in surprise.

He was so handsome, with those liquid amber eyes and perfect bow-shaped lips . . .

"There's a speed limit in this state. Forty-five miles an hour," he repeated, and then paused, clearly waiting for her response.

Speed limit? There wasn't a statewide speed limit, and in the city the limit was more like thirty or thirty-five.

"Come on, Marks," he rumbled at her, a glimmer of playfulness in his eyes. "*Double Indemnity*, remember?"

Audra cleared her throat.

"How fast was I going, Officer?" In her nervousness and surprise, her voice was less Barbara Stanwyck and more hoarse whisper, but somehow even that felt loud in this quiet corridor. Audra could barely hear herself at all over the knocking of her heart. Her fingers twitched to reach for her ankle—checking for that telltale anklet the screen legend had worn. There couldn't be an anklet—she didn't own one, but if Art Bradshaw had actually tracked her down to quote *Double Indemnity*, some kind of magic was afoot, perhaps the same kind that could produce an anklet where there had been none.

I told you, Ma! I told you, Audra thought, doing a happy dance in her head. *I knew he liked me! I knew it—*

As if reading her mind, Art Bradshaw's perfect lips curved upward into a shy smile. "I'd say about ninety," he said softly.

That was the next line. Audra knew the scene by heart. Almost without realizing it, she took a step up the corridor toward him. "Suppose you get off your motorcycle and write me a ticket?"

"Suppose I give you a warning?" he said, tracking the dialogue from the movie, word for word.

"Suppose it doesn't take?" Audra shot back, right on cue.

Bradshaw's shy smile had widened into a big grin. He took a long step toward her, narrowing the distance between them.

"Suppose I'll have to rap your knuckles then."

"Suppose I put my head on your shoulder and cry," Audra said.

Bradshaw hesitated. "Next line is Stanwyck's, 'Suppose you put your head on my husband's shoulder,' but that doesn't fit, does it?" He lifted an eyebrow over those striking light eyes. "For a couple of reasons."

Audra stared at him, the spell only partly broken now that the dialogue was his own words and not the words of a movie script. "I didn't think anyone knew that scene but me."

Bradshaw shrugged. "I love movies," he said, his deep voice soft. "Had a film noir phase. A few years back. *Double Indemnity* is one of my favorites."

"Mine, too," Audra agreed. "I love the banter. And it's kind of a love story—"

"Pretty sour ending, though." Bradshaw grimaced. "Not many people know the old black-and-whites. Nice."

"Yeah . . ." Audra said, and before she knew it, her face had gone all gaga and gushy and she was staring at him like he was dessert and she hadn't had chocolate in over a year. "Nice for me, too."

In the pause that followed, Bradshaw's eyes slid off her face and focused so steadily on a spot over her shoulder that Audra turned. There wasn't anything behind her but wall.

"What are you looking at?"

He hesitated again, and for a flash of a second, Audra feared her mother might be right. After all, he'd heard the inmates' remarks—heard the litany of *fat, black and ugly*—and he had eyes after all. For a moment her mask of bravado slipped and she wanted to cover herself head to toe like the Muslim women in the foreign land where Petra was now stationed.

"Uh . . . nothing," he said. His eyes snapped back to her face and Audra's concerns were swept away again, lost in those bright, honeyed orbs fringed by black lashes. "I . . . uh . . ." he hesitated until Audra quirked a curious eyebrow at him. "Forget Haines," he offered in his clipped, not-a-single-unnecessary-word way. *John Wayne*, Audra thought. *He talks like John Wayne.* "Warden's right: be cleared up in a few days."

"I didn't mean to hurt him—"

"You're a tough woman. Strong," Bradshaw said with a nod.

"Is that a good thing . . . or a bad one?" Audra laughed, rolling her eyes girlishly.

Bradshaw considered for a long time before replying, "Good. If you're a corrections officer," in a tone as serious as if she'd asked him to opine on death. "Which you are."

Audra stared at him, parsing through the words fifteen different ways before she decided to just mark it down as a compliment and move on. She gazed up into Bradshaw's eyes, a grin spread over her face like margarine on burnt toast, and he stared back, looking unsettled and nervous, like he was waiting for something to happen and wasn't sure it would. They stared at each other a good ten seconds past the comfortable point as Audra racked her brain, trying to think of just one of the clever lines she'd practiced all night—just one famous movie quip or quote to fill the space—but now that he was standing right in front of her, it was as if she'd never seen a movie in her life. But it didn't matter. Stupid and awkward as she felt, there was a part of her that would have happily stayed rooted to this spot, staring at Bradshaw and dreaming that Fred-and-Ginger ballroom dream all over again.

As if reading her thoughts, Bradshaw opened his mouth.

"Do you like parties?" he blurted out in a rush of words.

Yes! Audra's soul jumped to her throat, dancing, and she had to struggle to keep her feet from joining it. A prayer of gratitude sprang to her lips and she imagined herself sauntering home just as fat, black and ugly as she'd left it, and dropping this piece of news on her mother's dinner plate.

"You really came through, Bradshaw, you know that?" she murmured, beaming at him. "I knew you were different. I just knew it—"

Bradshaw blinked at her in surprise. "What?"

"Forget it," Audra said quickly. Calling upon the ghosts of dead divas, she cocked her head and met his gaze with an expression she hoped said something sassy and seductive at the same time. "What did you have in mind?"

He hesitated a little, a puzzled expression gleaming out of those honey-colored eyes. "Having a little get together. Saturday. For my daughter. Sweet sixteen."

Daughter?

"Oh . . ." Audra said, feeling a little like she'd been doused in cold water. "I—I didn't know you had a daughter that old. I guess you and your wife—"

"Not married . . . and I was a father young. Too young." They stared at each other again, each apparently waiting for the other, until he said, "You'll come?" he asked sounding suddenly urgent. "I was hoping you'd . . . talk to her."

Talk to his daughter? Audra frowned. "You want me to talk to your daughter? About what?"

Art Bradshaw's amber eyes gleamed down at her. "Girl stuff. The stuff girls have to deal with," he finished hurriedly, as if just naming the things girls had to deal with were too much for him.

Audra shook her head. "This sounds like a job for her mother—"

"No," Bradshaw's voice sharpened to dangerous. "No help there."

"Is it just the two of you?"

"Just the two." He hesitated a moment, then stepped closer to her, filling the space between them with warmth and heat. "So you'll come? Saturday. Eight o'clock—"

Audra was almost swept away by the desperation radiating in his handsome face, while movie titles flickered through a mental catalogue in her brain. There were dozens of mother-daughter films—but father-daughter? The only one that came to mind was *Father of the Bride* . . . and that hardly suited the circumstance Bradshaw was describing. Audra shook her head. This was sounding less like a date and more like a babysitting gig with every second . . .

"She wanted a party," Bradshaw said suddenly,

sounding almost as though he were talking to himself. "A fancy one. To help make friends."

"I seriously doubt your daughter wants me at her party—"

"I want you there," Bradshaw said and now those lovely golden eyes fixed on her, igniting a fire inside Audra that erased all of her questions and reservations. "I need you there, Marks," he repeated and Audra stared into those eyes, seeing herself reflected in their amber pools, not as fat, black and ugly, but as a princess as lovely in the eye of the beholder as the swan in Kiana's fairy tale.

"You . . . want *me* there?" she squeaked.

"You'll come? Please?"

Audra nodded, transfixed by the image of herself reflected in the man's shining eyes.

"Sure," she heard herself mumble. "Just name the place—"

"Saturday night. Eight. Caverna—it's a restaurant in Brooklyn. She picked it. It's sort of . . ." he grimaced like he tasted something sour, screwing his gorgeous face into a wrinkled mush of lips and nose. "Trendy," he finished distastefully. "Hip."

Audra smiled. Trendy, hip. Handsome, strong, silent-type Art Bradshaw had just invited her to join him at a trendy, hip club in Brooklyn, Audra thought, skipping over the stuff about his daughter's party or that there was something she was supposed to talk to the girl about once there. The unpleasantness with Haines was forgotten, as were her own nagging feelings of doubt.

See, Ma, she telegraphed her mother in her mind,

as she lifted her chin toward Bradshaw, batting her eyes like a Hall of Famer. *Life can be like a movie . . .*

"Hip, huh?" Audra put a hand on her upper thigh and curled her lips into a Mae West smirk of a smile. "I got plenty of hip, big boy. But what on Earth will I wear?"

Chapter 4

"**S**omething fancy and hip. Fancy and hip," Audra sang the words over and over like a mantra, as she boarded the subway and squeezed into the little space between a chunky, sour-faced sister who grimaced as though Audra had attacked her and a white man who snapped his newspaper around him like a shield. Audra ignored them both, pushed Princeton Haines and the brutality charge to the back corner of her mind, and whispered, "Something fancy, something hip," softly to herself, hoping for a vision.

Fancy.

Hip.

She had to keep saying the words to keep up her courage to do what she had to do. It would take courage to do this kind of shopping: the kind that would require branching out of the safe world of elastic-waist pants and loose sweatshirts in drab solid colors. Because everyone knew "hip" meant come-hither, form-fitting, and "fancy" meant color-ful or sparkly or something more elaborate than the everyday blacks, navy blues and grays. It meant—for one evening—the chance to be a days-gone-by diva, dressed to the nines, surrounded by gaiety and laughter. It meant swishing about in too much costly fabric, with glittering jewels in ears and on neck and in hair while sipping highballs and making witty repartee with Art Bradshaw, her captivated host. Au-dra closed her eyes, letting the rocking train lull her deeper into her dream until the hard subway bench around her transformed into an elegant forties-style divan, the clattering roll of the car's wheels into the tinkling of piano keys and clinking martini glasses, and the aroma of sweaty bodies into the smell of cig-arette smoke dense in the air. Audra imagined her-self an Audrey Hepburn or a Grace Kelly, laughing a throaty, worldly laugh as she tossed her head like a princess and rearranged her gown like a woman who had a closet full of party clothes at home and a dozen places to wear them—

"Do you mind? You're crushing me!" the sister beside her hissed with some serious New York atti-tude. "Can't you"—she jabbed Audra in the side with a pointy elbow—"move over"—another jab—"a little?"

Audra opened her eyes to find herself in reality's living color once again. The woman beside her was staring at her with an annoyed expression on her face, and Audra saddled up her own 'tude, ready to give back as good as she was getting. She took an-other quick look at her adversary to make sure the sister wasn't packing something worse than a nasty mouth and wicked set of elbows. But instead of seeing potential weapons, she found herself drawn to what the woman had on her back.

The sister was a far cry from model skinny, but she was beautifully dressed in a pair of chocolate brown suede slacks and a pink cashmere sweater that suited her body shape perfectly. Audra had to stop herself from reaching out to caress the soft fabrics.

She scooted a little closer to the newspaper-reading man who scrunched a little deeper behind his paper.

"Where do you shop?" Audra asked the sour-faced sister.

"What?" The woman frowned up at her like she'd asked her what color her underwear was.

"It's just . . . you look very nice," Audra told her, smiling as if a smile proved she wasn't a psycho killer. "It looks like I'm going to a party tomorrow night and I've got to find something trendy. Something hip," she leaned toward the woman. "See, if it were up to me, I'd go to some vintage store and try to look like Ingrid Bergman in *Indiscreet*"—she chuckled a little, like she and the stranger were sharing an inside joke, but the woman just stared at her blankly. "Well, anyway," Audra continued, realizing how ridiculous she sounded. "I thought I'd better model myself after someone still alive"—the woman blinked at her in alarm—"I mean, someone who's not in an old movie," Audra corrected. "Someone who looks *good*. And when you poked me just now, I noticed your sweater, so I thought I would ask—"

"Marciella's," the woman replied, her face finally

relaxing out of its city-wise, don't-mess-with-me game face into a kindness that softened her features and made her much prettier than Audra had originally thought. "It's a little boutique on Madison, between Thirty-fifth and Thirty-sixth."

"Marciella's," Audra repeated, wondering if she should write it down. "Madison and Thirty-fifth."

The woman nodded, a pleased smile spreading over her face. She wasn't really so sour-faced after all, Audra decided. "Great stuff. Pricey," she warned, wagging a manicured finger at Audra. "Very pricey. But it's really classy stuff. You won't meet yourself coming and going."

"Pricey, huh?" The word resonated in Audra's mind. Combined with the words *Madison Avenue* and *boutique*, Audra couldn't help but feel this woman's shopping budget went way beyond her own. She wanted to follow up with "How pricey?" but bit back the question. *If I have to, I'll spend it*, she told herself firmly. *But I'll try the cheaper stores first.*

After all, Art Bradshaw had invited her to a party . . . and all was right with the world.

"The next station stop is . . . Thirty-fourth Street," the automated conductor announced in its soul-less voice. Audra thanked her new friend and rose to leave the train, freeing up a considerable amount of seating space in the process.

"Fancy and hip, fancy and hip," Audra sang aloud, moving through the pedestrian traffic on Sixth Avenue, pushing herself through the doors of Macy's and heading determinedly for the women's section, pushing aside her dread of the fitting room and

wishing for the thousandth time she'd stuck to her
New Year's Resolution diet.

Only there was nothing that said "fancy and hip"
in the way Audra defined them. Sure, there were
hip, casual clothes galore in the larger sizes (boot-
cut jeans and bohemian tops, big, fringed poncho
shawls, rhinestone-studded denim jackets) and a selection of fancy ones (dresses as wide as muumuus,
mostly in dark colors, of a cut and style guaranteed
to make any woman look like the mother of the
bride) but nothing that spoke of youthful fanciness.
Nothing in the entire store . . . and Audra traipsed
across it repeatedly, searching rack after rack with
uncharacteristic diligence.

She abandoned Macy's for Bloomingdale's and
then Lord & Taylor, and then gave up the department stores for the large-sized boutiques, meeting
with disappointment after disappointment. About
the only thing that came close was a partly sheer,
yellow chiffon shawl of a top that, with its fringe
and assymetrical cut, had a light, party feel . . . but it
showed a hefty chunk of chubby shoulder, too.

"Pork loin in a yellow blanket." Audra grimaced
at herself, shrugging it off and vowing to search on.

As the sun sank into afternoon, Audra headed
across town to where the fancy boutiques were
clustered in row after row on Madison Avenue, still
hoping to find the outfit that would capture Art
Bradshaw's imagination, the look that would kick
fat, black and ugly to the curb, if not forever, at least
for a night.

And sure enough, in the window of Marciella's
Audra found it: the perfect top, draped over the

shoulders of a mannequin. It was a sleeveless, silvery, glittering thing with a deep V-neckline that scooped just enough to show a little cleavage, but not enough to scare anybody. Like the yellow shawl, it graced the mannequin's hips in a diagonal line. Audra imagined it thrown almost casually over a nice pair of black pants and coupled with a pair of strappy sandals.

"Hello, hip and trendy," she murmured, her nose nearly pressed against the window. Only . . .

Audra could tell just by looking at it that it was expensive—probably as much as she made in a month. She hesitated, intimidated by the top, the store, and the idea of spending thousands of dollars on a single garment—but then she thought of the divas of old with their gorgeous costumes and changed her mind. Hell, even fickle old Scarlett O'Hara had known that sometimes a woman had to have a new dress to send the right signal.

"Thank God for MasterCard," she muttered, folding her lips determinedly and yanking the handle on the boutique's heavy glass door.

A series of chimes sounded as she stepped inside, her feet landing soundlessly on a spotless white carpet. The air smelled of some gentle perfume, and soft romantic music played at a volume just above noticeable. And the place was completely empty.

"May I help you?"

A skinny white girl not much older than twenty or twenty-one appeared at Audra's side like a mannequin coming to life. She wore a tiny pair of black pants and a little top with a pair of slim spaghetti straps not quite appropriate for the cool of the

March day, balancing herself atop a pair of ridiculously high heels. She looked cool and chic and completely sophisticated.

A deep feeling of inadequacy and an awareness of her own imperfection swept over Audra as she stared at the girl. The sudden irrational urge to run out the door seized her heart and she had to remind herself that any woman tough enough to stare down a bunch of convicts day after day could probably handle buying a top from a high-end Manhattan boutique.

Probably.

"May I help you?" the girl repeated, since Audra hadn't said a word yet, just stood there staring at her with her mouth open like some oki hick come to the Big City. "Do you need directions—"

"I'm looking for something for a party," Audra said, donning a crisp, arch, cosmopolitan voice that sounded suspiciously like Bette Davis in her ears. "And that top"—she jerked her head toward the display behind them—"looks perfect. Very trendy. Very hip."

"Yes . . . yes it is . . ." the girl murmured, eyeing Audra from head to toe. "Uh . . ." She licked her lips a couple of times, then stuttered, "We—we might be able to help you, b—but . . ." she looked around nervously and lowered her voice, even though they were the only two people in the store. "Well, if you don't mind my asking, what size are you?" Watching Audra's face change, she added quickly, "I ask because we only carry up to size twelve. The designer is launching a plus-size line in the fall, but right now—"

"Are you calling me fat?" Audra snapped at the

girl, her good mood quickly slipping away. Audra thought back: the woman on the subway hadn't been small . . . but now that she thought about it, she'd been a heck of a lot smaller than Audra. A sudden embarrassment swept through Audra like a raging forest fire. Of course this was a smaller-size store. What on earth had she been thinking—

But then again, the top in the window looked like it might be cut a little on the roomy side . . .

"No ma'am," the young woman was stammering in front of her. "It—it's just . . ." she hesitated, and then spoke quickly, as though the speed of her delivery would make the words somehow less upsetting. "I don't mean to offend you . . . but I really don't think it's going to fit and these are very expensive garments. If you rip it—"

"It won't rip. And if it does, I'll buy it," Audra snapped at her with a force she hadn't fully intended. The girl's eyes widened and she backed away from Audra, putting her hands up to her chest as though she were afraid she'd have to use them in self-defense.

"I didn't mean to offend you—"

"I know. I'm sorry," Audra said, and meant it. "It's just . . . I've been dealing with a lot of negativity lately about my size," she admitted. "And there's this guy at work." She sighed. "This really, really good-looking guy. The strong, silent type who knows old movies. He's got these eyes . . ." She sighed again. "And he asked me to a party. Okay, it's last minute, but still, he asked *me*, and I've got to be hip and fancy and I've been looking all day . . ." She blew out a heavy exhale. "I can't help the fat and

black parts, but . . . I just don't want to look ugly,"
she said, more to herself than the salesgirl.

To her surprise, the girl touched her arm in consolation. "I understand totally," she said gently. "The dressing room is behind the curtain . . . over there," she said, pointing to a dramatic black curtain near a platform lined with mirrors. She hurried to a counter and squatted. "Let me find the twelve . . ." she murmured, and disappeared.

Audra heard the rattling of cardboard, then the girl reappeared with a series of flat red boxes.

"Thank you, *darling*," Audra drawled and swaggered toward the curtain as though she were really Bette and this were really a movie scene.

Audra avoided the mirror as she stripped off her sweatshirt, sick of the image of herself she knew she'd find there. There was too much skin, too many rolls. *I'm not eating until after the party is over*, she told herself. *And Monday morning, I'm back on my diet*, she vowed, imagining herself svelte and sexy on Art Bradshaw's arm by the end of the summer. In the tiny fitting room, the image seemed possible, probable, attainable—but then, there weren't any Oreos lying around back here to tempt the resolution.

But Art won't care, either way. He sees the real me . . . my true beauty, she added mentally and dismissed the planned day-long fast almost as quickly as she'd embraced it.

She lifted the frothy, silvery top out of the box with a sigh of appreciation. It was so soft, so shimmering, so beautiful, so fine . . . and had no price tag—no tags of any kind—except for a tiny label stitched into the side seam with the designer's name. Eager for the feel of the fabric on her skin, Audra slipped it over her head.

She got one arm through, too, before she got stuck, her other arm wedged trapped in the seam, bound tight to a roll of flesh at her side. She struggled with it, gently, but it didn't give. She pulled harder, unwilling to give up . . . and made it worse. She was wedged into the fabric now, too in to get out, too out to get in.

"Uh . . . help!" she called. "Help!"

The curtain parted. For an instant, the girl's eyes rolled upward in an expression Audra instantly interpreted as "I told you so," making the movie-star attitude Audra had adopted now nothing more than a useless ruse. But the girl said nothing. Instead, she stepped toward Audra and began pulling gently on the fabric, trying to ease Audra's left arm through the armhole.

"Just . . . a . . . little more . . ." Audra encouraged, feeling her fingers stretching for light and air. "A little more . . ."

"I don't want . . . to rip it . . ." the salesgirl grunted, still working the fabric. "Maybe if you suck in a little . . ."

Audra complied. Her arm popped through the sleeve . . . but as soon as she exhaled the fabric stretched extremely tight over her breasts and stomach, revealing every bump and roll of flesh. Audra panted, afraid to breathe, lest the delicate side seams pop. She stared into the mirror, seeing an effect far different from the one on the mannequin. The woman in the mirror looked like a plump sausage wrapped in a casing, a silvery, gauzy wrapper.

"Oh dear," the sales clerk breathed, shocked. "I . . . I don't think it suits you . . ."

Audra wanted to agree, wanted to rip the thing off and run as fast as her legs would take her from Madison Avenue, fancy boutiques, and any hope of glamour. But that was impossible now.

"I don't think I can get it off," she admitted, no longer Bette Davis, but an embarrassed fat woman in a shirt far too tight. Her eyes found the salesgirl's, seeking assistance. "Please help me out of this . . . If I rip it"—she sighed, dropping the façade totally—"I really can't afford to pay for a top I can't even wear."

She left out that part of the story when her mother came in from her day at the Goldilocks salon—along with the details of her meeting with Woodburn—concentrating instead on the magical moment when Art Bradshaw had invited her to his daughter's sweet sixteen.

Edith stared at her for a long moment. "Sounds to me like you got a date with the daughter," she said at last.

Audra rolled her eyes, her voice rising, ready to re-enter the fray. "Didn't you hear what I told you he said? About wanting me to come? Needing me to come—"

"Yeah, but I don't know how you get a date out of that—"

Audra opened her mouth to explain, but her mother waved the opportunity away.

"It doesn't matter, Queenie D." She sighed. "I been thinking about last night . . . and I've decided I ain't arguing with you no more. You want to run headfirst into a brick wall, you go ahead. Just don't expect me to pick you up when you get your feelings hurt." She shook her head. " 'Cause I'm tired. I'm just too damn tired."

"Me, too, Ma," Audra told her, settling deeper into the couch and returning to the mystical magic of *Breakfast at Tiffany's* currently playing on the Classic Movie Channel. "And the only thing that hurts my feelings is that you don't think anyone can love me just the way I am."

Her mother hesitated a moment, then murmured, "I've never said that, Audra," and then hurried to her room and closed the door.

Chapter 5

Dear Petra,

Do you really think that I go out of my way to antagonize Ma? Because I really don't see it that way—not at all.

Besides, I don't want to talk about her, or her secrets or any of that stuff right now—not on the day of my big night out!

You'll be happy to know that after the embarrassment in Marciella's, I pulled some kind of outfit together. It's not as glamorous as I would have liked, but it's nice, I think. Of course, I'll still be the fat chick, but I'm going to try hard to look as good as I can. Fortunately, I also have my sparkling personality to rely on— along with a fantastic repertoire of scenes from Hollywood's greatest!

Still . . . I'm nervous, P. Really nervous. I think he

DIARY OF AN UGLY DUCKLING59

may really like me. God, I hope so. But the things Ma says get under my skin sometimes and make me doubt myself. And it doesn't help that I have that trouble brewing at work, either. Sometimes it feels like everything's always against me and it will take a monumental change to turn it around . . .

Or maybe I just need to eat a few more Oreos!

Wish you were here,

Ugly Sister

Too trendy for words.

That's what the place was, considering it was in a basement, sandwiched between an Indian restaurant and an art gallery in a "transitional" neighborhood in Brooklyn.

It's at least aptly named, Audra thought, studying the bright neon script spelling out the word: Caverna.

A cinnamon-skinned teenager with long, black hair, wearing a tiny beaded halter, stood just outside the entrance dragging determinedly on a cigarette and pretending not to shiver while a not-quite-spring breeze caught the smoke and bore it away. A short, older-looking white kid stood near her, talking excitedly, but the chick barely seemed to be listening. As Audra descended the five steps toward the bar's entrance, the odd couple fixed their collective gaze on Audra, making her feel self-conscious all over again: Her nicest black pants were tighter than she would have liked, and the yellow-shawl-like top from the plus-size store that had been her second choice flapped in the breeze like a tent. The pointy toes of her new shoes pinched her feet. Audra wished there were time for one last check of the makeup slathered on her face like a mask by a determined beauty consultant a few hours ago, but there wasn't. She was here now ... and acne or no acne, running mascara or lipsticked teeth, her look would have to be good enough.

Still, if she weren't mistaken, the kids were giving her that same folded-lip look her mother had given her just before she'd walked out the door ... and to make matters worse, she thought she heard the smoking girl burst into a twitter of sudden laughter in the space between the time Audra's foot crossed the threshold of the club and the second after, when the door thudded closed behind her.

She shook off the sound with difficulty and looked around her.

The owners of Caverna had taken the cave thing literally. It was dark except for a few torch-shaped sconces set strategically around the room. The ceiling dripped with stalactites and the tables and chairs were designed so they looked like stalagmites growing up from the cave floor. Audra thought she heard the sound of dripping water under the pumping rhythm of hip-hop music, but could not locate its source among the crowd of youthful bodies jamming every square inch of the place.

Sleek girls in slim, short skirts and high heels, showing brown midriffs from tiny halters danced with boys in low-slung pants and slick-patterned shirts. Other girls were more conservative in their strapless, gauzy chiffon and flouncy, asymmetrical hems, but all of them were so attractive and energetic that Audra hesitated, the worst memories of herself as an uncool high schooler returning with a vengeance.

This was a mistake, a voice from deep inside her announced, flashing back to many a high-school dance, when Audra's only companion had been her own isolation, her own loneliness. *There's nothing for you here.* Audra's feet seemed inclined to agree. They were already shuffling her backward away from the dancing and the music and the whole party scene.

This isn't high school. He invited me and we're going, Audra told her juvenile self, pulling the mantle of dead Hollywood dames around her consciousness like a shield. She strode deeper into the place, her too-round hips bumping and jostling against the sharp angles of the dancing young people, scanning the corners of the room for her host's broad-shouldered silence. She had already decided: She'd greet him with that famous line from *All About Eve*: "Fasten your seat belts. It's going to be a bumpy night!" and see what developed from there.

"Marks!"

Audra turned toward her name and saw him, standing in a dark crevice of the room where the stone bar curved toward darkness. "Marks!" Bradshaw shouted again over the music, waving his arm. "Here!"

The sound of his voice erased her carefully prepared dialogue, but the awkward memories of teenageness also dissipated, so Audra wasn't entirely mad at him. Her heart skipped a quick beat as a feeling of excitement and eagerness replaced the unease that had been there a moment before. She waved back, smiling, and began her approach, moving determinedly through the dancing bodies toward the rear of the room.

He looked delicious: like the sweetest bar of milk chocolate, luscious from the gleaming skin of his head to the tips of his toes, and Audra could imagine gobbling him up in a single serving as she took in the pure sexiness of the man. He looked like he'd just stepped out of a magazine, from his crisp seventies-style butterfly-collared shirt in a soft fabric that looked like linen, opened to the smooth mocha of his perfect throat. He wore dark slacks and shoes. But it was his face that most captivated Audra's attention: those liquid eyes, strong cheekbones—and those lips! Audra imagined herself getting a nibble of those beautiful bow-shaped lips and just the thought of it was better than the thought of a bag full of Oreos—with a candy bar on the side.

She pulled at the yellow shawl, baring a bit more rounded, ebony shoulder, and willed the butterflies in the pit of her stomach to stillness as a wide, happy grin spilled across her face.

"Hi, Bradshaw—"

"Art," he corrected, blessing her with a curve of those luscious lips.

Audra's heart did another desperate flutter up her windpipe and then down to her kneecaps before she panted out, "Art."

"Glad you could make it. You look . . ." his eyes swept over her. Audra gave the yellow top another tug, showing even more plump shoulder, before he finished, "nice."

"Thanks. So do you." She glanced around. "Looks

like your daughter has a good turnout." She peered
around the dance floor. "Which one is she—?"

A woman approached them, gliding confidently
up to Bradshaw and slipping her arm through his
with a certain possessiveness that couldn't be mistaken for anything else. At first, Audra thought she
must be Bradshaw's daughter, but in another instant
she realized her mistake.

Her skin was the shade of roasted almonds—fair
and smooth. Her hair, long and dark, burnt straight
and smooth by the latest chemical process, gleamed
off her forehead until it disappeared down her back
in a tumbling wave that brushed against the soft
fabric of her blouse. Audra's breath caught in her
throat: She was wearing the same top Audra had
struggled so mightily to fit into the day before, but
clearly, based on the delicate bones of her shoulders
and the thinness of her, in a very much smaller size.

A tiny flare sprang to life in Audra's soul, burning
with the unfairness of it all . . . and then the woman
locked eyes with her.

"Audra Marks," Art Bradshaw turned toward the
woman, his eyes shining with an emotion Audra
thought must be desire, but she couldn't be certain
in the low lights. "I'd like you to meet Esmeralda
Prince."

Esmeralda Prince. Esmeralda Prince. The name
tripped off the tongue, made little skipping sounds
through the mind. It was a pretty name . . . one that
suited her, conjuring as it did the very kind of
smoky, distant beauty this woman was in possession
of. Audra stared at her, drinking in every detail of
her features, from the perfect café au lait of her skin

to the sculpted bones of her cheeks and the way the designer blouse hung as perfectly off her shoulder as it had on the boutique mannekin. Audra realized that the top she'd wanted to buy wasn't a top at all, but a tunic—and Esmeralda wore it like a dress, with nothing beneath it but a pair of stiletto heels. Audra watched her green eyes, shadowed with dramatic makeup as they flickered with some unspoken thought and wondered if there were enough makeup on the planet to make her own face look like that.

Esmeralda Prince appraised Audra dispassionately as she quirked an exquisitely shaped eyebrow over a lovely sea-green eye, then shook her dark tresses.

"Nice to meet you," she said in a husky, sexy voice.

With a fresh stab of ugliness, Audra felt the contrast. Standing side by side, Esmeralda was like a sunrise and Audra the deepest midnight; Esmeralda was a leggy twig . . . and Audra a dumpy donut, a hole in her center where her heart should have been.

But it wasn't the voice or the woman's obvious beauty that made a sharp pain skewer her heart like a shish kebab. It was the way Art Bradshaw's hand curved over the woman's shoulder, the way his eyes locked on her face when she spoke, even though she wasn't looking at him.

Art Bradshaw was completely in this elegant woman's thrall . . . in the same fascinated way Audra was in his.

Queen of Denial . . . her mother murmured in her ear. *Queenie D* . . .

Looking at the two of them was like a rock in the face of her perfect fantasy. Audra watched her illusions fracture and shatter like so much glass.

But there they were, staring at her, waiting for her to say something. Audra suppressed the thousand needles of mortifications prickling beneath her skin, and tossed her head, diva-style.

"Charmed, darling," she purred, offering a limp hand in perfect imitation of the silver screen legend.

"Bette Davis," Bradshaw said immediately, his smooth low voice rumbling over the hip-hop beat surrounding them. To Esmeralda: "Audra's a fan of the old movies."

Esmeralda's eyebrow arched even higher as she said in a not entirely pleasant tone: "You two would be perfect for each other." She reached for a small, shimmery handbag resting on the table. "I'll be in the ladies'."

There was an awkward pause as she shrugged Bradshaw's hand from her shoulder and stalked away.

Art Bradshaw frowned. "Don't mind her," he began, his eyes following the sway of the woman's hips as she disappeared. "She's—"

"Rude," a youthful voice completed the sentence, replete with attitude.

Bradshaw turned toward the table behind him. In the dim candlelight, a teenage girl in a relatively demure black dress hunched over a soda, her shoulders drawn tight to her shoulders, as though trying to blend into the scenery.

"Cut it out, Penny," Bradshaw said, warning in his tone.

"But it's true, Dad—"

"No, it's not—"

"She only gets away with it because she's pretty," Penny insisted. "The rules are always different if you're pretty enough—"

"That's enough, Penny," Bradshaw snapped, sounding at the crust of his patience. "Now come and say hello to Ms. Marks."

"Do I have to?"

"Now!" Bradshaw barked, making it clear that that remaining crust of his patience had now been consumed. Even over the loud music, several youthful heads turned toward them.

Penny slid out of her chair, rolling her eyes. "Gee, thanks, Dad," she hissed. "It's bad enough we're throwing this stupid party in the first place, do you have to humiliate me, too?"

She was nearly as tall as her father—at least five foot eleven if not a full 6 feet—and as wide-shouldered and muscular, without being fat, also like her father. She had the man's deep, amber eyes and even, milk-chocolate skin, the kind of features that would mature into a striking kind of female handsomeness that would have its own admirers in time. Audra couldn't stop herself from thinking how much she looked like her father, which probably would have been fine if the girl had been a boy. Under the circumstances, however, Audra suspected looking so much like Daddy might be a problem.

"Audra Marks, my daughter, Penny Bradshaw."

Audra hitched the yellow shawl over her shoulder again and fumbled with her tiny new purse, pulling out the small wrapped box and stretching it toward the girl. "Happy birthday."

Penny Bradshaw blinked her light brown eyes at Audra for a long second, then turned to her father, shaking her head in dismay. "Oh, Dad," she whined in an utterly teenaged way. "Not *again*!"

Bradshaw's frown deepened. "What are you—"

"I want to go home," Penny announced, and without so much as a "how do you do" she stomped away from them, elbowing her way across the dance floor and out of sight.

"And she calls other people rude," Bradshaw muttered under his breath, before giving Audra his eyes for the brief second it took him to say, "Don't mind her. She's sixteen." He frowned toward the ladies' room, and kept his eyes in that direction as he continued, "A drink?"

I want to go home, too, Audra thought. *Right now. I want to rip off this stupid top and the silly pointed high-heeled shoes and—*

"No, I can't stay," she said quickly, before the last of her bravura evaporated and she melted into a puddle of snuffling tears. "Silly me, I forgot I had a prior engagement. A . . . friend of mine . . ." she continued conjuring a quick lie. "Bachelorette party. Wild night ahead, you know?"

Art Bradshaw wasn't listening. His head swung from the hallway where the lovely Esmeralda Prince had disappeared to the dance floor, where his daughter had vanished from view. "Uh-huh," he muttered.

Audra's heart sank like the *Titanic*, settling itself somewhere near the pit of her stomach. She felt tired

and sick and sad and lonelier than she could ever remember.

"I'll just . . . put this . . . here," she said, lowering
the birthday present to the table behind him.

Bradshaw sighed and swung his face toward
Audra.

"Sorry, Marks. She's been acting like this ever
since Esmeralda showed up—"

"No problem," Audra said, not wanting hear any
more about Esmeralda Prince than was strictly
necessary—especially since the only thing that really mattered about the woman was abundantly
clear from the expression of concern on Bradshaw's
face—and the chick had only gone to the ladies'
room. Audra made her shoulders a little more
square and her upper lip a little stiffer than she felt.
"Good night, Bradshaw." She made a perfect silver-
screen-star flounce door-ward, and even if he had
called out "Audra, wait!" romantic hero-style, she
would have been too far ahead to hear him.

"Nice meeting you, Penny."

She was leaning against the wall, in the same spot
where the smoking girl had been, her sleeveless
brown arms crossed against the night's chill. The
girl's eyes met hers, as calm and steely as any a
grown rival's.

"I wish I could leave," she said.

"But it's your party! Don't you want to—?"

"These kids don't like me. They laugh at me in the
halls. Call me Bigfoot. Sasquatch," she said angrily,
but Audra could see tears glistening unshed in her

eyes. "Not one of the guys has even asked me dance." Her forehead crumpled. "I'm taller than most of them, anyway. They're just here to dance and hang out."

"Then why—"

"It was my father's dumb idea. Same reason he invited you. He actually thought it would help," she rolled her eyes. "But nothing helps. Nothing will ever help," she finished with teenaged drama.

Audra ignored it, her own dejection forgotten in the girl's self-indulgent revelations.

"I think it's nice, your dad caring enough to throw this bash for you," she said slowly. "But what do I have to do with it—?"

"Oh don't pretend to be innocent!" The girl exclaimed. She inhaled as if gathering up all the attributes of her most grown-up self. "I know all about this plan you and my father have cooked up."

Audra blinked at her for a long second, recovering from the pure shock of Penny Bradshaw's accusations. Then she let her hand slip to her hip and shook her head. "Look, sweetie. I'm not sure what you think is happening here but—"

"I know *exactly* what's happening here," the girl spat with teenaged venom. "You think you're the first ugly woman my father's asked to 'talk to me'? You think this is the first time he's invited one of his homely co-workers or one of his 'great personality' friends to meet me?" She shook her head. "Please."

Her words settled over Audra like a shroud. *Homely co-workers . . . "great personality" friends . . .*

"What—what are you talking about, Penny?" she demanded.

"The minute I saw you, I knew he was doing it again," Penny continued, almost as though she hadn't heard Audra's question. "Trying to find me someone to talk to about being a big, ugly giant. A tenth-grade freak on the road to becoming a grown-up freak—"

Audra's heart stilled, stopped. *Homely co-workers . . . "great personality" friends . . . Talk to my daughter,* he'd asked her. *Talk to my—*

"I—I don't believe your father thinks you're a freak—" she stammered in a tiny, uncertain voice.

Penny didn't hear it. "Of course not. He's my father! He has to say that I'm beautiful—but I know what he really thinks," Penny railed on to the night, seeming barely aware of Audra standing beside her in her rage. "I know, because he keeps introducing me to the ugliest women he can find!" Her eyes found Audra's, no longer hard with fury but wet with unshed tears. "Women like you."

It felt like the last straw—the last brick—bringing down any remaining illusions Audra had about herself. *Ugly, ugly, ugly* . . . the word was coming at her from all sides now . . . and there were no movie-queen lines, no quips or character to erase it. That was the reason she was here tonight. That was the reason, of all the women in the prison, Art Bradshaw had invited her. It had nothing to do with her sense of humor, the things they seemed to have in common or even her sterling character. It was just a matter of being the ugliest woman in the prison— the ugliest woman he could find.

Fatigue, sudden and exhausting, settled over her like a garbage bag, hot, stifling.

"You didn't know, did you?" Penny Bradshaw asked, suddenly grasping Audra's arm.

Audra shook her head, not trusting her voice. A lifetime of hurt, loneliness and pain seemed lodged in her throat. Penny's image swam in her wet eyes and Audra thought she read in them the echoes of her own pain.

"God . . . I'm sorry . . . I thought . . ." Penny whispered. "Oh my God . . . you *like* him, don't you? And he didn't tell you—about Esmeralda or—anything?"

Audra cleared her throat, willing herself to speech. "No."

"It's not quite like it seems. My dad isn't a bad guy, but—" the girl sighed. "He's a *guy*. You and I both know how they are. Niceness and goodness and smartness don't matter. If you're pretty, you can be a bitch," she said, anger snaking beneath the words. "You can be dumb as dirt, mean-spirited, hurt people—and still, you'll never be alone." She shook her head. "No one cares about what you've got going on the inside—at least not until they like the package on the outside. Forget character: the thing to do is pretty up, like they say on TV. Pretty up by any means necessary. My dad doesn't get that—because it's different for him, being a man and all. But for a girl . . . for a woman . . ." she sighed, as world-weary as any sixty-year-old. "I'm sorry, Officer Marks. I'm sure you're a nice lady . . . but I don't want to be anything like you. Not ever."

Penny shuddered, whether from the cold or from

the words she'd spoken or the thought of being like Audra, Audra didn't know. But with a quickly muttered, "goodbye," she disappeared back inside the restaurant, leaving Audra very much alone.

Chapter 6

"**M**y God, Audra! Do you have any idea what time—"

Audra ignored her mother, thrust her arm deeper into the junk-food cabinet and swept a four-pack of mini-puddings, a canister of potato chips and two bags of cookies into the waiting garbage bag with a single swipe.

She knelt on the kitchen floor in her bra, the button at the waist of her tight black pants loose, her new yellow chiffon top in a puddle on the floor beside the spikey high heels.

"What on earth are you doing?" her mother demanded, standing over her in her bathrobe, her hairdo now concealed under a colorful do-rag.

"What does it look like?" Audra snapped, crawling deeper into the cabinet. "I'm going on a diet. Again. Are you happy now?" She pulled out a small bag of Halloween candy she'd forgotten was back there. She dumped it into the waiting plastic bag along with a half-eaten box of ancient crackers and then rose, letting the cabinet door slam.

"You're gonna wake Kiana—"

"I'm not gonna wake Kiana, Ma," Audra said tightly. She moved around the kitchen, opening doors and drawers, pulling out a bottle of chocolate syrup here and a package of marshmallows there until the garbage bag was too heavy to hold any more. She let it slip to the floor and turned toward Edith, breathing hard with her efforts.

Her mother stared at her. For a brief time the two women considered each other, then Edith shook her head.

"So, I'm guessing it didn't go well with your Bradshaw," she said in a tone that suggested she was trying very hard not to sound smug and failing miserably. "I don't want to say 'I told you so'—"

"Then don't," Audra snapped, dragging the garbage bag toward the front door.

"That's just how men are, Audra," her mother continued, following her. "It's not that they're not interested in the rest of the package, but they appreciate the efforts we make on the outside—"

Esmeralda Prince rose like a vision in Audra's mind. Art Bradshaw appreciated the outside, all right. That much was very, very clear.

Audra opened the front door, dragged the garbage bag of junk food out into the corridor and slammed the door on it like it was an unwelcome guest. Edith shook her head.

"So you're going on a diet. Again. Do you have to make such a production out of everything? After you lose a few pounds and do something with your hair, there'll be plenty of men—"

Audra whirled on her, angry words rising in her throat as she stared into her attractive cinnamon face.

"Will there, Ma? Is that all it takes—twenty pounds and a hair weave?" she gestured at herself, bra and all. "Look at me, Ma. When is the last time I had a date, huh?"

"Back when you were in criminal justice school, I think," her mother frowned calling up a memory. "Nice boy. Leon or Larry or something—"

"Lamont," Audra said bitterly. Her mother couldn't keep track of the names of the people in a conversation about today, but she could get within a few syllables of the name of a rotten jerk she'd had one date with years ago. "And he wasn't so nice, Ma. You know why he went out with me? To win a competition with his buddies. A competition over who could sleep with the ugliest girl."

Edith sighed a sigh that suggested Audra should have known better. "Well, he was really handsome, Audra. You can't expect a guy that handsome—"

"Why can't I, Ma?" Audra roared her anger and frustration and humiliation beyond containment. "Why can't I?

"Because that's not the way it works, Audra. An ugly man has as good a shot as a good-looking one, but an ugly woman is a sin against nature," she preached. "I earn my living on the truth of that. Do you think I caught your father with my personality?" She shook her head. "No—"

"And that great love story worked out really well," Audra scoffed. "He left you when I was nine."

"Well, there were lots of reasons for that."

"Tell me about it," Audra muttered, closing her eyes against the memory of the night her father left.

Edith hesitated, her eyes fixed on Audra's face. "What's that supposed to mean?" she asked in a low voice, that suggested to Audra that she didn't really want to know.

"It means I heard you, Ma!" Audra shouted. "I heard him, I heard you—" she paced away from the sight of her mother's horror-stricken face. "I know what he accused you of that last night."

Audra's mother's hand flew to her mouth.

"Listen, Audra . . . you don't understand. He was just angry, he didn't mean—"

"He said I wasn't his," Audra hollered bellowing out the words at the top her lungs. "He said there was no way he could have had a child as black and ugly as me, Ma—"

"Hush! You'll wake Kiana—"

"Are you ever going to admit it, Ma?" Audra swung on her, her fists clenched. "Are you ever going to tell me the *truth*?"

"Can't nobody tell you nothing, Audra," Edith snapped. "And that's what's wrong with you. Now, I'm going to bed. And if you were smart, you'd go to bed, too." She hurried past Audra toward her bedroom up the hall. "And put some clothes on. Nobody wants to see all your jiggly stuff," she hissed, a final parting, hurtful shot before closing her door and shutting Audra out for what must have been the thousandth time.

* * *

She flipped through every channel of the dial at least twice, but there was nothing—no distraction in film or otherwise. Not tonight. Sleep was impossible . . . and she knew it. If she fell asleep, if she allowed her mind to wander for even a second, she'd hear the girl's words all over again—*I don't want to be like you*—or see the expression on Art Bradshaw's face as he watched Esmeralda Prince sashay away from them. Or she'd be nine years old all over again . . .

"Why?" her mother wailed, in a voice more desperate that Audra had ever remembered hearing, before or since. "Why *now*, James?"

"Because I'm sick of the whispers and the looks, that's why! Because I'm tired of playing this game with you, Edith!" And she heard him throwing suitcases, drawers opening and closing . . .

"James—"

"That girl ain't mine," her father had growled behind the partially closed door of her mother's bedroom. "You know it, and I know it—everybody knows it. Ain't no way I could have a child as black and ugly as *that*. Get the guy you been fucking to raise her. I'm not doing it—"

Audra snapped herself back to the present, willing her mind to focus on the television screen.

"I mean, look at these pants," a slender woman in one of those tops with a single thin strap over one shoulder and full-length arm on the other was saying. She stretched a pair of what seemed to Audra to be perfectly acceptable gray sweatpants toward the camera, while gesturing to several other pairs in the closet behind her. "This is all she wears! Sweatpants!"

and the slender woman shook her straight, blonde locks in disgust.

"But they're comfortable!" Another woman stepped into the frame, clutching the sweatpants defensively. And of course, she wore a pair of dark blue sweats, matched with a faded orange T-shirt. Her dark hair was tied back in a long, frizzy ponytail. She looked just fine to Audra. Just your average-looking white girl, the sort of woman Audra might see on the subway or pass on the street a thousand times in a typical New York day. Unlike her tarted-up friend, who looked like something off a television commercial or a movie set.

"Just because I don't dress like you doesn't mean I look bad," the average-looking girl was saying, and Audra found herself nodding her head in absolute agreement.

"Listen, girlfriend," a masculine voice lisped, snatching the sweatpants so violently, Audra felt a deep sympathy for the poor girl whose wardrobe was being savaged. "Sweats have their time and place," he announced, like some kind of authority, and to punctuate that point, the words KENNY CLOSE, MASTER STYLIST appeared on the screen beneath him as he continued. "If you're cleaning your apartment, you wear sweatpants. If you're at the gym in winter, you wear sweatpants. After that . . ." and he tossed the sweats into a waiting garbage can that clearly had been placed in the room just for that purpose.

The dark-haired owner of said pants gasped in horror. Then to Audra's surprise the fashion man yanked the remaining pants out of the drawer and tossed them into the trash with glee.

"You can keep the ones you have on," he finished, slapping his hands together like he'd just finished a particularly distasteful chore, while the brown-haired girl fairly wept with dismay. "Don't worry, honey," Kenny Close Master Stylist offered comfortingly. "When we're done with you, you'll have forgotten all about sweatpants, I swear. We're gonna give you a hot new look and have men lining up outside your door!"

Then the program cut to a promotion for the next segment, through which Audra learned that the name of the program was *Recreate Me*, and that after this program ended, a show called *Style Spy* promised to update the looks of unsuspecting passersby, and that both were part of Makeover Madness Weekend on the Beautify! Channel.

"Pretty Up with Beautify!" a pleasant female voice suggested in a tone that mixed encouragement with command. Audra could almost imagine the words "or else" being added to the tag line.

Pretty Up . . . by any means necessary. That's what Penny Bradshaw had advised. *Pretty Up . . .* her mother was always nagging. *Lose weight, change your hair—then the boys will like you . . .*

"Are your looks ruining your life? Are you tired of being the "ugly girl," the "plain Jane?" a calm female voice asked from the television screen, startling Audra's attention back to the box. But there were no graphics, no stylish pictures or products. Instead, the screen was filled with the elegant image of swans, floating calm and serene on a quiet lake. It was mesmerizing in its stillness and beauty.

"We can help. Accepting audition tapes now for

Ugly Duckling, the Beautify! Channel's ultimate makeover show. Call us at 888-UGLY DUCK for details, or visit our Web site at BeautifyChannel.com. Hurry, tapes must be postmarked by Monday, April second."

Ugly Duckling. It was like the stupid ad was talking to her, recounting the night's failures. Her looks *were* ruining—had ruined—her life. She *was* the original ugly girl . . . ugly enough to give lessons in it.

Pretty Up, the words echoed in her brain, pulsing toward a moment of decision. *Pretty Up* . . . but not just with a new outfit, and some over-the-counter beauty consultant comestics. But *Pretty Way Up*, dramatically, drastically, permanently.

Because her mother and Penny Bradshaw weren't wrong. For all the platitudes the ugly girls of the world were asked to live with, accept, embody, the girl wasn't wrong. It didn't matter how smart you were, how funny, how great a person—the package was the deciding factor when it came to the opposite sex, and even this child's own father, who for just a second, Audra had thought might be just a little different, had turned out to be a full-fledged member of the club.

Her own father was certainly a member, too—if that's who the man who had raised her until she was nine really was.

The gauzy, hazy light from another dawn filled the bedroom. The last of Beautify! Network's makeovers surrendered to fresh programming focusing on home décor, and Audra flipped the channels listlessly. In another couple of hours, the apartment would come to life, and her mother would bustle out of the door for sixteen hours at the salon, pretending once again that nothing was wrong between them— nothing except that Audra needed to *Pretty Up!* Kiana would need care. There would be things to clean, errands to run . . . Audra saw her life stretch hopelessly out in front of her: predictable and safe and entirely alone.

Ugly Duckling . . .

The commercial raced around her brain, its pitch resonating in her mind. What would it be like to be totally transformed, to see yourself remade, not just in new clothes and fresh makeup—how many times had she tried that, only to be disappointed—but re-shaped from the bones outward? What would it be like to look in the mirror and find, not fat, black and ugly, but something lovely and desirable. What did it feel like to glance in the mirror and find a reflection like a movie star's, like Esmeralda Prince's, like Petra's? Could it be as close as a telephone call? As close as 1-888 UGLY DUCK . . .

But I can't do that. I couldn't possibly call some reality television show, Audra thought, flipping down the dial toward Classic Movies Channel. *I couldn't possibly call . . .*

Why not? another voice in her brain answered. *Nothing else has worked.*

I don't have time. The deadline is Monday—

And you're off, the other voice in her head reminded her. *You're on administrative leave, indefinitely, thanks to Princeton Haines, remember?*

I don't have a camera—

But at the same instant she remembered something

Darlene Fuchs had said, drunk as a skunk at that retirement party. Something about a place in Greenwich Village. A place where they help actors make audition tapes . . .

I couldn't, Audra told the voice again. *I'm no actor—*

Fine then, the insistent voice challenged. *Do nothing. Let your perfect guy date some boring, selfish woman just because of her outside packaging. Sure, you could change your own package and find happiness . . . but no. You can't. You won't . . .*

And again she saw the look on Art Bradshaw's handsome face as his eyes followed Esmeralda Prince into the ladies' room and beyond. He'd never looked at Audra like that . . . In fact, when she really thought about it, he'd never looked at her much at all if he could help it.

Not mine . . . Ain't no way I could have a child as black and ugly as that . . .

Maybe . . .

This is madness, Audra told herself firmly, shaking the idea and the insistent, challenging voice egging her onward from her mind and focusing on the TV instead. A movie was starting as Audra resettled herself under her comforter with a deepening sense of depression. Bette Davis was in the movie, and Paul Henreid . . . and as the credits faded into the opening scene, Audra knew exactly what she was watching.

Even the movies seemed to be sanctioning her course.

Now, Voyager. The ultimate forties makeover film.

Bette Davis played an ugly spinster, stuck and stifled by her domineering mother, who, after a nervous breakdown, completely remakes herself and finds love with a married man on an ocean voyage. She returns home, stares down her mother and—

Audra watched, transfixed. It was as if Bette were speaking to her . . . telling her what to do . . .

They probably won't pick you anyway . . . Why not at least find out? It couldn't hurt to find out . . .

By the time the newly glamorous Bette Davis challenged her strict mother's control and vowed to wait, forever if necessary, for the man she loved, Audra had the phone in her hand.

It couldn't hurt to find out . . .

"Welcome to the *Ugly Duckling*," a smooth, recorded voice said. "To be considered for a spot as a contestant on our show—"

Audra snatched a pencil from the drawer in her bedside table, ripped a clean sheet of paper from a notepad beside it and began to write.

Tuesday, April 3

Petra,

I've done something . . . It's probably crazy but I didn't know what else to do. It's a long shot, but with all the movies I've watched, I know a little about how to tell a story.

I told them my story, Petra—at least as much of it as I know. I didn't leave out anything—not Ma or Dad or the stuff I heard. I only had a day to work on it. While Kiana was at school Monday and I usually would have gone to work, I found this video place, made a tape and mailed it before I lost my nerve. It came out rather good, if I do say so myself.

I didn't tell Ma about it—and don't you do it. She'll just say "They'll never pick you," and tell me to stick to my diet. She's right: They'll never pick me, I'm sure of it . . . but I don't need to hear her say it.

When they clear up this stuff with Haines at work, I'm going to change my shift to graveyard. I'd rather give up sleep than have to look at Bradshaw again.

Wouldn't it be amazing if they did pick me? I'd ask them to make me look just like you!

Be careful out there,

Audra

PART TWO

Light, Bright and Beautiful

Chapter 7

Thursday, May 11

Petra,

The news reports we've been getting are kinda scary.
Are you sure you two are alright? Kiana hasn't had a
note from Michael in a long time—not since his unit
entered Basra. It's hard to reassure her that her
Daddy's okay when there's no word. She's doing okay
though. Don't worry, for all our differences, Ma and
I agree on our love for her.

Still no word from Ugly Duckling . . . Remember I
told you they called? They said they'd call back, but I
haven't heard a thing. If the show comes on in the Fall
and I'm not on it, I guess that means "no!"

Be careful out there,

Audra

"**A**udra, it's Shamiyah Thomas again, from the *Ugly Duckling* show?"

The young woman spoke fast, her voice holding a hopeful edge as though she expected Audra's immediate recognition. "We spoke last week about your tape?"

"Yes, I remember," Audra said, her own tones coming to immediate attention. "But you said there were problems—"

"Problems aplenty, girl," the young woman said. Audra pictured her: some energetic twentysomething, probably as cute as she was perky. She talked fast, in the crisp college tones of a Seven Sisters education, but there was enough ethnic in her voice for Audra to believe this child might actually be black— and not just playing black for TV. Besides, Audra suspected there weren't very many white women named Shamiyah in the world. "Is this a good time?"

"Sure," Audra said. "But I'll be getting on the subway in about five minutes—"

"Won't take that long. Listen, we don't normally do this, but the show wants to fly you out. You haven't been selected yet, understand, but the doctors want to meet you in person. To assess you as a candidate for plastic surgery. See, I been lobbying that we have at least one sister on this show—to keep the finale from looking like Barbie dolls on parade, you know what I'm sayin'?" She chuckled, sounding worldly and girlish all at once. "But the docs keep saying there's all these additional issues with black skin and plastic surgery. Make it sound like it's a plague or something." Shamiyah's voice reached a level of good-humored indignance. "Now what kind of signal is that sending in this messed-up, racist, sexist culture of ours, I ask you?"

Audra hesitated, not sure at all what the appropriate response to that question might be. In the end, she decided on diplomacy and changed the subject. "You want me to come out to Los Angeles? When?"

"Tonight," Shamiyah said. "Tomorrow at the latest. We've got decisions to make here. This show's supposed to air during November sweeps. You remember the rules—we need at least three months for the surgeries and healing time. Not to mention the weight loss and body sculpting." She lowered her voice conspiratorially. "I've heard they think you should drop about *eighty pounds*. And there's a lot of doubt you'd be able to lose that much in the time we've got—"

"I've lost about twenty since I sent the tape," Audra muttered. "Maybe twenty-five. I haven't had an Oreo in—"

"You've lost twenty-five pounds! That's great!" Audra could hear the girl scribbling down the information. "That could make a *big* difference, Audra. A big difference around here. See, I've got to tell you. We all *love* the tape you sent. So funny. The way you did all those *imitations* of old movie stars—a real smart way to play to the Hollywood crowd. You're such a *character*!"

"Yeah, well. We ugly girls strive for character," Audra quipped again, not entirely joking, but Shamiyah laughed like she was an audience of one in a tawdry comedy club.

"See? That's exactly the kind of stuff I'm talking

about. You'd be a hoot on the show. Just a hoot. And
I love that you've got a serious side, too. The story
about what the girl said to you, about not needing
any advice from any ugly woman—Oh!" Shamiyah
inhaled dramatically. "So heartbreaking! Did that
really happen . . . or do you just have the ear for the
kinds of stories people want to hear?"

Before Audra had decided whether to admit to
the truth of that encounter, Shamiyah continued
with, "It doesn't matter either way. It would work
great on the show. Really moving. Really . . ." she
paused, searching for the word to get the italics that
were so much a part of her manner of speech. She
found it in: "*emotional*. I've *got* to tell you, Audra.
You're the *definite* front-runner for the African-
American spot on the show. I mean, we just *love*
your story. The woman wearing the top you were
too fat to squeeze into at the party. The stuff about
your pants *ripping* on the *job* in front of the hottie
you had a crush on—" she enthused onward, pluck-
ing the most painful events of Audra's life with delicate enthusiasm. "It just boils down to whether the
docs think they can do a *dramatic* job on you." She
paused just long enough to inhale, then barreled on
with, "So, if we make all the arrangements, can you
catch the last flight out of LaGuardia tonight? I'll set
up all your meetings for tomorrow and we'll put you
on a plane back to New York tomorrow night. Can
you do it?"

"What do you mean you're going to California?"
Edith said slowly. She'd already slipped off her

shoes and dug into the plate of beef noodle casserole
Audra had left for her. "You don't know anybody in
California—"

"You don't know who I know," Audra told her.
"Besides, I'm not asking for your permission. I'm a
grown woman. I'm telling you: I'm going to California and we need to work out how we're going to
take care of Kiana while I'm gone."

Edith quirked an eyebrow at her and frowned.
They weren't getting along any better, but at least
things were no longer alternating between yelling
and screaming and frosty silence.

"I suppose I can ask the Quintanas to watch her
until I get home from the salon," she muttered, her
eyes still fixed dubiously on Audra. "How long you
gonna be gone?"

"Call them." Audra waved the phone under her
mother's nose and glanced at her watch again.

"What's the hurry? What's going on?" She surveyed Audra. "You're not running out to Hollywood for some old-time movie fantasy bullshit, are
you?"

"No, Ma—"

Edith peered at her, taking in her faded sweats and
comfortably ripped T-shirt before asking, "You ain't
going out there to meet a man, are you? You're on the
computer all the time these days. You meet someone
on the Internet? Is he out in California? Because if
that's what's going on, you need to watch yourself.
Just because you lost a few pounds doesn't mean
you're some Hollywood diva, ready to handle yourself around some man you've never even met—"

Audra slammed the phone back down and whirled on her. "You were always nagging on me to lose some weight. Then when I lose some, you accuse me of being full of myself?" Audra rolled her eyes. "What do you want from me? Make up your mind, Ma!"

Edith frowned. "Well, sure, the weight loss looks good, but—you know what I'm saying." She hesitated. "After that fiasco with that guy from your job I'd think you'd learn your lessons about pinning your hopes on men you hardly know." She crinkled her nose into her forehead with the effort of memory. "What was his name? Art something—"

Audra stiffened. She had barely seen Art Bradshaw since that night, now that she'd been reassigned to another shift. He hadn't made any efforts to get in touch, either.

Which was just fine, Audra told herself. One less distraction. And thinking about his daughter, Esmeralda Prince and that awful night at that cavelike bar made it easy to wolf down lettuce leaves and fruit instead of cookies.

"This has nothing to do with Art Bradshaw," she told her mother.

"I knew it!" Edith proclaimed, nodding vehemently. "Some Internet guy—"

Audra shook her head. "No guys, Internet or otherwise. I've sworn off."

"Then why you gotta go to California?"

Audra gave a noncommittal shrug that she knew would drive the older woman absolutely crazy. "You got your secrets . . . I got mine." She picked up the phone again. "Now, if you don't mind, please dial the number. I'm leaving right now. There's a cab waiting for me downstairs."

Which was how Audra ended up on a late flight from LaGuardia to LAX, ensconced in a first-class seat with only her little black bag and a stack of fashion magazines as companions. Inside the bag were a change of panties and a toothbrush.

Audra pushed any thoughts of Art Bradshaw or her mother to the back of her mind and focused on the magazines in front of her with the diligence of a law student preparing for the bar exam. Shamiyah had given her an assignment—to find the image or collection of images that would make up her ideal face and body for final "Reveal" . . . and she was determined to show the folks at *Ugly Duckling* exactly what kind of diligence they'd get if they picked one Audra Marks for their television show.

The plane touched down only minutes before midnight. A man in a black, liveried car service uniform and holding a small sign bearing the words A. MARKS stood waiting at attention as though expecting royalty.

"That's me," Audra said stepping up to him. "I'm Audra Marks."

The thin man looked her up and down, from her short, scraggly hairdo to her rumpled black pants as though he considered her highly unlikely in every aspect of the word. Audra stored up the look, adding it to the stockpile of images that was her daily fuel and waited for him to get himself together.

"Your luggage?" He asked in a voice like the obsequious servants in Audra's ancient movies. Audra couldn't help but wonder if he spent hours listening to himself on a tape recorder to get that sound.

"This is it," Audra patted her little black duffel. "I'm all set. I mean—" She attempted a jovial smile just to see if this little man would answer it with a smile of his own. "Hey, it's just one night, right?"

"Of course," he agreed blankly, reaching for the black duffel.

"That's okay. I got it," Audra told him, tugging the thing just out of his reach.

Once again the thin man looked her over with an expression of indifference mixed with disapproval. Apparently, he preferred women to arrive with a full set of luggage for him to carry and a toy poodle yapping in a handbag. But all he said was, "Very well, madam. Follow me, please."

It was after midnight Los Angeles time and even later in Audra's mind when they drove off the grounds of the sprawling airport and hit one of the city's many freeways. Grateful not to have to navigate her way to the hotel on her own, Audra sank back in the dark leather seat of the car and closed her eyes. Perhaps tomorrow she'd have a few minutes to herself to see something of the sights of L.A., but for now she wanted nothing more than to lay her head on a soft pillow somewhere and sleep.

When at last they pulled into the circular drive of the hotel, Audra understood the driver's snarky attitude toward her rumpled clothing and battered black satchel.

"Oh shit," she muttered as the driver hopped out

and hurried around the car to open her door with a bow.

"Someone will pick you up promptly at nine A.M. to take you to the studio, madam," he said in a tone that made it perfectly clear that that someone would not be himself. "As you have no luggage, madam, I'll just say goodnight and trust the hotel staff to see to your remaining needs." And he nodded with a finality Audra could not misunderstand: Get out of the car, you're here.

Audra knew instantly where "here" was.

Most people would have recognized it: It was one of the most famous hotels in Beverly Hills, pictured on television shows and movies as frequently as the Kodak Theatre or the famous Hollywood sign. It was an imposing Spanish-style structure with ornate frescoes and a sense of palatial opulence. Audra could almost see the ghosts of stars of ages past— could almost hear the sounds of today's hottest young actors cavorting within its walls.

"Oh shit," Audra whispered again, feeling like she'd landed in another world—a world to which she could never belong. "Oh shit."

She stepped away from the vehicle, forcing herself to close her mouth so that she wouldn't look even more "bumpkin" than she felt. Good thing, because an instant later an elaborately uniformed doorman stepped into the space between herself and the entrance, a wide smile on his face as he lifted the strap of Audra's black satchel off her shoulder as though he handled bags of its exquisite quality all the time.

"Welcome to Beverly Hills," he said. "Checking in?"

Audra turned back to the driver behind her, ready to question the accuracy of his choice of destination. But the man was already gone, the black car turning in the cobbled driveway and disappearing back down into the street. Automatically, Audra thought of her credit-card balance, wondering if there was enough on the thing for just one night in a hotel that was probably as swank on the inside as it looked on the outside. Hopefully, when Shamiyah said she'd "take care of the arrangements," she meant more than the airfare.

The doorman was waiting.

"I'll guess we'll find out if I'm checking in in a second," she quipped to the valet.

He laughed like his tip depended on it and led her inside.

Chapter 8

Dear Petra,

Had to log on quickly to tell you how fab this hotel is! Girl, it's beyond plush. It's like living a moment out of that VH1 show, The Fabulous Life of . . .

Still not entirely sure why I'm here, but I guess I'll find out in a few minutes. There's a car on the way to take me to meet with the Ugly Duckling people.

I'll write more later.

Be careful out there,

Audra

"**A**udra! So *nice* to *finally* meet you! Though I feel like I *already* know you, from *all* our phone conversations and of course, that *fabulous* tape of yours!"

Shamiyah—for this was surely the woman; Audra recognized the voice and the emphatic use of certain words—grabbed her by the shoulders and pulled her close, planting two quick butterfly kisses on both her cheeks.

"Let's get a *look* at you!" she said, pushing Audra away as suddenly as she'd grabbed for her, her face crunching with the effort of inspection, as though they weren't standing in the middle of a leafy sidewalk, outside an utterly unremarkable-looking Beverly Hills office complex.

Audra stared back her, conducting an inspection of her own. Shamiyah was older than she had sounded on the phone, probably as kissing close to thirty as Audra was herself. She was a petite, sepia-toned person with a heart-shaped face framed by a mass of unruly black springs of hair, held off her face by a pair of designer sunglasses. She was a little rounder in the behind than Audra expected—carrying a little of Africa in her hips and thighs—but her tight white tank T, her low-slung jeans and high-heeled mules suited her figure perfectly.

"Girl," she said in her Ivy-league ghetto voice, "you weren't *kidding*. How much have you *lost*?"

"Not sure," Audra replied, her mind racing. These people were expecting some quick-thinking, comedienne version of herself and she had no intention of disappointing, even if it cost her every line in her personal arsenal, plus a few from the old movies as well. "Fat girls don't weigh themselves, you know. Axe-wielding mass murderers don't scare fat girls." Audra rolled her eyes. "Hell, I'd probably just ask to borrow his knife to carve my chicken dinner.

But the scale?" And she made her voice like a Vincent Price horror movie from back in the day. "Scaaaarrrryyy . . ."

Shamiyah chuckled her appreciation for the performance. "Well, we'll get some *numbers* today," she said, taking Audra's arm and guiding her toward the lobby of the building. "What did you think of the hotel?"

Audra rolled her eyes. "When that car rolled up in front of it, I thought I was going to have to prostitute myself just to pay the bill. Can you see me, hanging out on the street corner in this neighborhood, flashing passing cars with a little leg?" And she struck a pose she knew looked utterly ridiculous—especially for a woman of her size and build.

Shamiyah broke into another gale of laughter. "That would be hilarious."

"Probably wouldn't make me enough money to pay for the newspaper they left on the threshold."

"You'd be *surprised*," Shamiyah muttered, her voice losing a bit of its bubbly edge. "Strange place, L.A. People literally sell their very *souls* here and consider it worth the bargain." She shook her head. "I've been here for almost eight *years* . . . and I sometimes wonder if I'm *one* of them." Before Audra could ask her any questions about herself or her adopted town, the woman frowned. "But you shouldn't have needed *any* money. The room should have been *totally* comped—"

"Yeah," Audra said. "That's what they told me when I went to check in. That everything was complimentary . . ." she grinned. "Except the tips."

"Well, there's a few things a sister's gotta handle

on her own. But for everything else"—she gave Audra a cynical eye roll—"there's an expense account. Now." She grasped Audra's arm again. "Before you meet everybody, there's some *stuff* they want you to do."

"What kind of stuff?" Audra asked, suddenly feeling on guard.

"*Medical* kinds of stuff," Shamiyah said, waving her fingers vaguely as if she weren't certain of the details. "Basically they want to do the whole exam, like you were going to be on the show. It's pretty comprehensive—takes hours and hours—so we'd better get started."

Shamiyah steered her toward the elevator and along the third-floor corridor to a glass-encased office. The words ALAN BREMMAR, M.D., and HERBERT KOCH, M.D., graced the door, each man's moniker followed by a long line of letters like a perverse alphabet soup. Through the glass, Audra could see an elegant reception desk and an even more elegant receptionist.

"These guys are absolutely the *best*," Shamiyah murmured as though it were a secret, guiding her through the glass doors with one surprisingly firm and determined hand. "They've done *everybody*. More stars than the Walk of Fame . . . Hi Maisy!" Shamiyah said with a gushing enthusiasm that Audra couldn't decide was real or fake. "Here she is, Audra Marks! The *Ugly Duckling* candidate we've been talking about?"

Maisy stretched her face into a smile, staring at Audra as though she were some interesting new species that required great analysis, while Audra stared back at her with similar interest. Up close, Maisy had the look of someone who had seen a few cuts of the surgeon's knife herself: her eyebrows were suspiciously high, her nose perfectly straight, her breasts impossibly perky. Add to that the warm glow of a paid-for tan, and the perfect lowlights of a custom dye job and Maisy looked fake right up to her enhanced eyelashes.

"Nice to meet you," she said in a voice far too high and girlish for her years, but pleasant enough. She stood up, showing them a lean figure clad in a tight black T-shirt and black pants in some clingy, sexy fabric that would have shown every bump of cellulite, if the girl had had any. "Carla—she's one of our nurses—is waiting for you in Room One. But first . . ." She pulled a thick folder full of papers from the cubby beneath the elegant desk. "Papers to sign," she said, handing them to Audra.

"Good grief! More papers?" She shook her head, turning to Shamiyah in amazement. "My hand still hurts from the stack you sent over last night. Haven't I released you people from all liability for just about every conceivable accident imaginable?"

"I—I don't know," the girl said, looking genuinely confused. "But these are the medical forms so Dr. Bremmar and the others can do their preliminary consultation. Did someone already send you these? Because—"

"No, no," Shamiyah patted the girl on the arm, reassuringly. "The forms she got *last night* were from the *Ugly Duckling* show. Consenting to her appearance on the program, for the use of her image in promotion, release from libel and slander—stuff like that. Not the same. She's got to do these, too." She cast a significant glance at Audra. "Just skip all the financial and insurance information. Write *Ugly Duckling*. They know where to send the bills."

"So basically, I'm giving these docs permission to kill me and your production company permission to film it." Audra quirked an eyebrow at Shamiyah. "Is that about right?"

For once, Shamiyah seemed to forget to smile. "Yes, that's about it," she said levelly, meeting Audra's eyes. "You're cool with that, though, right?"

For the first time, a current of the seriousness of this undertaking charged the air between them like ions before a lightning storm. Audra grabbed the edge of the reception desk, steadying herself.

The whole point was to remake herself . . . and she was actually here, in Los Angeles, to find out if—and how—it could be done. She imagined herself transformed into a swan of unimaginable beauty, and inhaled.

"Ice-cold chilly," Audra told the woman, clenching and unclenching her fist, making ready for the work at hand. She grabbed the folder, crossed the room and threw herself into a nearby chair, feigning exhaustion. "I'm gonna need surgery for carpal tunnel by the time you guys get done with me."

"Carpal tunnel?" The blonde's confusion seemed to deepen even further. "I don't think Dr. Bremmar does *that*. It's somewhere in the foot, right?" She smiled and continued before either Shamiyah or Audra could respond. "Can I get you ladies something? Espresso? Latte?"

"Double skim latte sounds great to me," Shamiyah

breathed. "You're a *life* saver, Maisy. Just a life saver! Audra?"

A Snickers bar would really hit the spot, Audra thought, but she decided against saying that out loud in this company. Instead, she shook her head, "No, thanks."

"We also have all kinds of fruit juices," Maisy tempted, as though it were specifically in her job description to make sure every guest had a cup of something. "Papaya? Kiwi? Guava?"

Audra grimaced. "No, thanks," she insisted and watched the girl's face crumple in disappointment.

"Are you sure?"

"How about just a bottled water?" she said to keep the girl from feeling like a failure, and watched a smile twitch Maisy's lean face again. "Okay, so that's one double skim water"—she slapped herself on the forehead—"Double skim water! I mean, latte—and a water." She nodded. "When you finish with those"—she nodded at the forms—"Room One is the first one on the left. Go on in, she's expecting you. I'll be back in a flash with your drinks."

"Thanks, Maize," Shamiyah said, already pulling Audra down the hall. The second they were out of earshot, she murmured, "You can do those forms later. And don't mind *her*. She's nice enough . . . but she's not here for her brains. She's a walking *advertisement* for Bremmar and Koch's work. Nose, eyes, chin, boobs, lipo—you name it."

Audra nodded. "I suspected as much."

They stopped outside a door upon which a silver *1* had been affixed. Shamiyah lay her hand on the knob, then paused, staring hard into Audra's face.

"I'm not supposed to tell you this," she said at last, "but I really want you to have this chance, Audra. The rest of the candidates won't do this step until we bring them here in three weeks. We're doing this now for you, because, of all the tapes we got from African-American women—and there weren't that many, I'm sorry to say—yours was *absolutely* the *best*." She lowered her voice. "But these docs, they've got real *concerns* about whether they can make your transformation work. The only way I could convince them to consider you was with this advance consultation to work out the . . . details. But you can *never* tell anybody about it and . . ."—she leaned closer, her eyes intent—"it will *really* help if you show them that you're willing to do whatever it takes. *Whatever* it takes," she repeated. "Okay?"

Whatever it takes. The words echoed in Audra's brain, sounding suddenly dark and dire, as if some kind of shadow had suddenly engulfed this sunny office space. In the movies, this moment would have been accompanied by music so tense and ominous that Audra shivered a little, just imagining it. For a second, running back out into the California sunshine and finding her away aboard the next flight back to New York seemed like the wisest course, even if she had to walk all the way to the airport. But then she imagined herself a finished swan of a woman, as pretty as Petra, able to silence her mother's criticisms with a single bat of a perfectly mascaraed eyelash. She closed her eyes, carrying the fantasy further, imagining herself running into Art, Penny and Esmeralda Prince—his long-haired, long-legged, fat-free Esmeralda Prince—and heard herself saying:

"Art? Art Bradshaw, is that you? It's me, Audra Marks!" and watching their mouths fall open in amazement as she tossed her hair, and struck a pose for their admiration. She could almost hear him stuttering out his "hello," could almost see the expressions of interest and desire competing on his face. In the fantasy, the two of them walked on together, chatting about old times while poor little Essie stood on the sidewalk with her vapid little mouth hanging open in surprise and disappointment.

"Okay," Audra said grimly. "Okay."

Shamiyah's small bosom heaved in relief and she ran a café au lait hand through the wiry strands of her kinked-up hair. "Great. Sisters in Lala Land—or anywhere else for that matter—really need to stick together, Audra. Remember that."

Nurse Carla was another athletically thin woman, with red hair and a real-looking nose, but suspiciously plump lips. She greeted Audra warmly, then commanded her to strip to her underwear "for the examination and the photos." Audra did as she was told, glad she'd brought her newest matching pair of skivvies. The examination part made sense—but photos?

"What are these for?" she asked as the nurse used a digital camera to take front, side and rear views of her body, then close-up profiles of her face at several different angles.

"The doctor uses them in a software program to get an image of what your body can look like after surgery." Carla snapped the camera again and again until Audra felt like some kind of super-sized model doing an underwear shoot. "They're also our before and after shots. We'll send copies to Shamiyah and the other producers of *Ugly Duckling*. No doubt they'll be a part of the package when your show airs," Carla replied.

"You sound like you know quite a bit about this TV stuff."

Carla laughed. "Drs. Bremmar and Koch consult on about half a dozen of these makeover shows. It's a solid half of their business!"

"And the other half?"

Carla shrugged. "Celebrities and celebrity spouses."

Shamiya had said as much. Audra wondered if she would recognize the names of the stars if she heard them. "Like who?"

Carla just shook her head. "We never tell," she said lightly, then lowered her voice a little. "Out here, just about everyone has a 'little work done' . . . but no one admits to it. This office is the repository of some of the best-kept secrets in Hollywood, believe me. Okay, Audra," she said in her normal tone again. "Hop up on the scale, then we'll do the blood and urine work. Then we've got to get downstairs to the pool—"

"Pool? Why?"

"To test your fat-to-muscle ratio, of course. How else are we going to figure out exactly how much weight you have to lose?" She grinned. "You don't actually think we just use one of those silly height-weight charts, do you?"

"Uh . . . no . . . of course not," Audra mumbled,

not wanting to admit that that was exactly what she had thought.

"Then hurry up. You're meeting with the other experts at noon—"

"Other experts?"

"Didn't Shamiyah tell you?" Carla's reddish hair bobbed from side to side again. "Between the show people like Shamiyah and Camilla, the fitness people and the doctors, you've got a whole baseball team!"

"Camilla? Who's that? Shamiyah's assistant?"

Carla barked out a short, bitter laugh. "The other way around. Camilla Jejune's the producer. Shamiyah works for her. The whole show was Camilla's concept, and she's the one who did all the leg work to bring it into being—not an easy thing, no matter who you are—and until last year, Camilla Jejune was a nobody. I guess that could explain why she's so protective of it. A real micro-manager, if you ask me. She's gotta okay every contestant personally. Make sure each one of them has a concept that will sell the show to the network . . . and hopefully kill all the competition in the ratings."

Audra blinked at her, stuck on an earlier thorn in her words. "B—but I thought Shamiyah was the producer—"

"She's *a* producer. The show has three or four of them who work on creating the package for each woman featured as an Ugly Duck. Shamiyah's *your* producer. But Camilla's the executive producer—or one of them anyway." She sighed. "Lots of people have the title 'producer' on these programs. Camilla's the executive producer who does the work."

"I don't know anything about television. I'm a classic movies chick myself."

"The titles of the producers should be the last thing on your mind, honey," Carla said, swabbing a streak down Audra's arm with a cotton ball.

"Oh yeah?"

"Yeah," she gazed earnestly into Audra's face. "I just hope you're not sensitive to criticism." She shook her head again, before gazing at Audra with a look of such intensity the odd, nervous feeling of grave importance fluttered in Audra's belly again.

"Why?"

The woman hesitated, and then sighed. "I've only had to sit through one of these kinds of sessions . . . and"—she paused again, her eyes finding Audra's— "they really know how to take people apart, body part by body part. It's a little creepy—like sitting down with Dr. Frankenstein while he assembles his monster . . ." She shuddered until she felt Audra's eyes, wide and nervous, fixed closely on her face. "But of course, instead of a monster what they end up with is a beautiful woman. Right?" she added, struggling to resume her former brightness. "Now let's find a good vein and draw this blood."

Chapter 9

"So which one was it? The Atkins or South Beach?"

Shamiyah thrust a deli box of salad greens into Audra's hands, along with a massive bottle of water. "Never mind, this should work with either one," she continued before Audra even could process the words.

"You're talking about my diet, right?" Audra said. "I really wasn't following any particular plan. It's not like I've been living on salads or anything. I just . . ." and she stopped short, not sure that she wanted to admit that she really had only given up candy bars and Oreos, along with the late-night habit of snacking to the dramas of Betty, Joan and Barbara. "Cut back. Started lifting a little weight—"

"Well, girl, you better *like* salads, because if you come on this show, that's the bulk of what you're gonna be eating for a good three months—"

"Just salads?" Audra spat. "I'm down with the

slice-and-dice plastic surgery, but salads every day? That's near inhuman! What about jerk chicken? What about fried chicken and macaroni or—"

"Just salads." Shamiyah said with such finality that it made Audra's heart sink. "Remember what I told you? About being willing to do anything?" Shamiyah's eyes searched Audra, assessing her sincerity again.

Audra nodded slowly.

"Just salads," Shamiyah repeated, then glanced toward the door, an edge creeping into her voice. "They'll be here in a second . . . and a few of them won't like seeing you eating, even if it's only a salad. Hurry up, all right? Have you got the pictures from the fashion magazines? The features you like?"

Audra nodded, pulling a wad of ripped pages from her back pocket. "I got 'em. But I gotta tell you, Shamiyah, I don't see how I could ever look like any of those girls. But I brought a picture of my sister Petra—" Audra reached for her wallet, flipping to the wedding photo of Petra and her husband. "I really think—"

"It's okay," Shamiyah said, not even glancing at the picture. "They probably won't ask you for that input today . . . but making sure you're prepared is a part of my job. Now, hurry up!" She glanced at a sporty wristwatch in a candy apple shade of red. "I swear, she's fanatical about time . . . and we don't have much more of it."

When the salad and water were consumed, Shamiyah seated Audra at the head of a long table, so dark and highly polished that Audra could see her reflection in its gleaming surface. At the other end of the room, a large-screen plasma television hung from the wall, a small laptop computer resting on a stand just beneath it. Audra glanced around the rest of the room, but for the most part it looked like a conference room she might have found anywhere—nicer than many, but still just a conference room.

Or it would have, had it not been for the light poles dotting the carpet, angling their theatrical lighting implements toward the table from every conceivable vantage point.

"Are there going to be cameras?" Audra asked, raising her eyebrows in surprise.

"Is this *Hollywood*?" Shamiyah shot back and this time there was no mistaking the anxiety in her voice. "You read the papers you signed, right? We tape just about everything—"

"But I thought this was preliminary?"

"If you're willing to do what they want, it won't be," Shamiyah said cryptically, then took a seat far away, leaving a gap of at least a half dozen chairs between them.

Cameras. Audra let the idea sink in. Somehow, from what Shamiyah had said, she hadn't expected there to be cameras at this extremely preliminary stage . . . but then, as Shamiyah had also said, this *was* Hollywood, and *Ugly Duckling* was a television show.

"Most of this footage probably won't get used . . . but you never know," Shamiyah said as if she realized the coldness of her earlier comments. "I'd rather have it than wish I had it, you know? Besides, you signed the papers." She shrugged her shoulders. "We own your image and your story now . . . at least for a while."

Audra nodded like she was in the know, even as another creepy feeling, like a footstep on her grave, crept down her back. Even the image of her transformed self wasn't enough to dissipate it. She shuddered in spite of herself, searching for an anchor to banish fear and root her in the present moment.

"Why are you sitting way down there?" Audra asked, focusing all of her attention on the other woman. "Did my deodorant quit or something?" She sniffed at her pits, tossing a smile at Shamiyah. "I know it's been a tough morning, but Carla did douse me in a pool of water just before I came back up here."

Shamiyah smiled and opened her mouth like she was about to answer, but then the door opened and the sound of other voices filled the room.

The first to enter was a smallish, wiry-looking white man with dark hair on both his head and his chin, and a white lab coat over a dress shirt and tie. His lips quirked into a quick smile as he spotted Audra at her place at the top of the table, but he said nothing, just quickly took the first seat on her left. Three more lab-coated professionals followed: a blonde woman who looked more like a TV soap-opera version of a doctor than most of the actual ones Audra had met, then a gray-haired older man with a tough action-hero physique, and last, a stocky, barrel-chested black man whose shaved dome of a head instantly reminded her of Art. All of the white-coated figures looked familiar . . . but it was the black man who locked eyes with Audra in a protracted stare, as if he could see through to her skeleton.

She didn't have time to explore that feeling, however, because following the white-coated figures was a whole crew of others. A rangy, muscular woman wearing the kind of crop top that only a woman with a flat six-pack of a stomach could carry off swept in, fussing with a straight mass of shoulder-length black hair. She was followed by another trim woman, her short, gray hair worn close to her head, who seemed more interested in the sheaf of white paper in her hand than her fellow human beings in the room. Two more women followed her: a petite brunette woman wearing a pair of expensive-looking eyeglasses and a sober blue suit who smiled at Audra as she took a seat by Shamiyah on the left side of the table, and a Hispanic-looking woman with a mass of henna-colored hair streaming down her back. She carried a thick clipboard jammed with paper and was talking a mile a minute to someone behind her. That "someone" turned out to be not just a single person but an army of young-looking men and women holding devices of all kinds. Two black professional cameras rested on the shoulders of two of the men, while two others carried some kind of sound devices that looked like sophisticated amplifiers. A set of young women carried what appeared to be microphones dangling from a couple of long silver poles. To her surprise, there were several younger men holding nothing at all, and what appeared to be a small army of young women holding little black boxes Audra did not recognize until they plopped themselves in front of each of the white-coated figures and proceeded to open them, revealing a bigger collection of makeup, makeup brushes and makeup paraphernalia than Audra had ever seen outside a department store in her life.

"Shamiyah!" The Latina shouted the name, an edge in her voice that made Audra jump in surprise. The woman sounded like a furious drill instructor on a bad hair day. Shamiyah popped to her feet like an automated soldier, an expression of out-and-out fear on her face that didn't jibe with her earlier confidence.

"Yes, Camilla?"

"I thought I told you to arrange the chairs so that the cameras can get the entire panel at once—"

"I tried but—"

"I don't want to hear that! I want to see the chairs arranged so the camera can pick up the entire panel at once!" Camilla nearly shouted, snapping her fingers with impatience.

"But—" Shamiyah began again until Camilla shot her a withering look. Shamiyah folded her lips.

"That's my fault," the black-haired doctor said mildly, rising. "I asked if we could hold this meeting here because my schedule is so tight . . . but the table's not long enough for us to get that kind of shot, Camilla. Do you think we can figure out another way to get what you need?" His eyes flickered around the room again. "I see you've got two cameras, so, maybe we can station one guy at each end of the room and—"

"Thanks, Alan. I'm sure we'll figure something out," Camilla gave him a warm enough smile, shot

Shamiyah another evil glance, then addressed the production crew. "Maybe if we can station cameras at both ends of the room?" She offered, repeating the good doctor's suggestion verbatim. "Don't worry about the images on the TV, we can edit them in later. And for the most part, let's not worry about shooting the subject. If we use this footage at all, it will be for the segment when the panel of experts discusses the necessary changes, so what she says won't matter—"

"Camilla!" Shamiyah hissed, jerking her head toward Audra.

Camilla stared blankly at her like she had no idea what Shamiyah's problem might be.

"Uh . . . *this* is Audra Marks," she offered in a prompting sort of tone as if to remind the woman that her "subject" had a name.

Audra prepared her face for greeting . . . but the woman never even turned in her direction.

"I know who she is," Camilla said, taking the first seat on Audra's right and leaning back to allow a young makeup artist with blue dye spiking her hair to do her thing. "We'll tape an introduction when she arrives for surgery," she muttered as the girl dotted and dabbed and swiped colors over her face. "That's supposed to be our first meeting, and it'll be more authentic that way."

"But—"

Camilla waved her fingers in impatient dismissal. "She's just here for us to look at today," she snapped. "If she doesn't agree to the proposal, we're not going to take her anyway, so—"

"So, the sooner we get on with the discussion

process, the better for all involved," interrupted a sonorous male voice.

The entire table seem to turn as a group toward the speaker. Audra knew without having heard it before that the voice belonged to the black doctor.

"You're absolutely right, Dr. Jamison," Camilla said, using her deferential tone again. She shoved the makeup girl aside and tossed her mane of thick hair again before opening her notebook. She snapped her fingers, shooing the makeup crew out of the room, and summoning Shamiyah to her side in a single gesture. Taking her cue, Shamiyah proceeded to dole out several small folders to the men and women seated around the table as though she were the secretary, and not a producer in her own right. Audra watched in confusion, feeling once again that nagging uncertainty, but she kept her mouth shut.

"I trust you've all had a chance to review the data from the examination, but we thought it would look good to have the folders on the table, in the event any of this footage makes the final cut." She glanced at the young man kneeling beside the amplifier device. "How's sound?"

"I need a quick vocal of everyone to be sure," he muttered, sounding like he, too, was eager for this session to begin and end.

"You heard the man." She glanced at Audra, looking her full in the face for the first time since she'd entered the room. "Say something."

"Something."

Laughter filled the room, cutting some of the tense atmosphere Camilla's attitude had created.

"That's it, Audra," the doctor to her right—whom Audra had decided must be Alan Bremmar, one of the plastic surgeons whose offices these were—chuckled. "I, for one, really do hope this works out. It's always nice to work with women with personality."

"Yeah, but once you make me beautiful, I won't need a personality anymore, now, will I?" Audra quipped. "Like I said on the tape: The uglier you are, the more personality you need—"

"We are not rolling yet, people!" Camilla interrupted, her eyes flashing angrily. "If we could just do the sound check? Please?" And she glared at Audra like the whole thing was her fault.

"Fine," Dr. Bremmar said good-humoredly enough, as though the woman's shrewish rudeness meant no never mind to him. "I suggest we check by introducing ourselves to our guest. I'm Alan Bremmar."

One by one, the experts announced themselves. The blonde doc was actually a cosmetic dentist named Katherine Martin, the athletic white man, the plastic surgeon Herbert Koch, whom, Audra realized with a shock, she recognized from another of the Beautify! Channel's many makeover shows. The only African-American expert was a clinical dermatologist named Dr. Reynolds Jamison . . . and from the way he stared at her, she suspected that he thought she might be just to the left of crazy, and that she needed far more than a new nose to correct what ailed her. Audra felt the man's eyes still trained on her face, even after he'd introduced himself and the process had moved on to the next person.

The rangy young woman was Julienne Rapista, the celebrity personal trainer—also vaguely familiar to Audra for her various TV projects. The bespectacled woman was a shrink with an expertise in body image named Anna Goddard. Audra had the feeling she'd seen her on the talk-show circuit recently, but she couldn't be completely sure.

Audra stared at each one for a long moment, committing their names and responsibilities to memory. It was weird: on the one hand, she felt like she'd been asked to audition for an important role, and on the other hand, she felt like a woman pleading for a pardon.

How do I play this scene? she wondered. *What exactly is happening here?* She tried to ask Shamiyah with her eyes . . . but the woman had her face in her own copy of the file and didn't look up.

"Good," the sound guy said, showing Camilla—who still hadn't introduced herself—his thumb.

"You guys ready?" Camilla's steely gaze swept over the cameras and lights, and receiving affirmatives, she smiled sweetly. "Roll cameras, please." She paused, and then spoke as smoothly as if reading from a teleprompter. "This is a preliminary meeting of our expert panel on the case of Audra Marks, a candidate for *Ugly Duckling*. Each of our experts has reviewed medical and personal history information provided by Audra with an eye toward determining if she is the right kind of candidate for our unique makeover program." She paused, shooting Shamiyah daggers until she jumped up and hit a key on the laptop, filling the TV screen with Audra's underwear-clad image.

"Dr. Bremmar, let's begin with you."

* * *

Carla was right: They were brutal. Even Dr. Brem-mar, who, Audra's intuition told her, always tried to be kind, had very little positive to say.

"We can do the surgery before you lose the rest of the weight—to reshape your thighs—" He drew on the keypad in front of him, tracing a slimming purple line that appeared over the bulges in the image of Audra on the screen. "And your tummy." More lines. "And your derriere." Still more lines. "But you wouldn't really be able to see the effects of the liposuction until you lost a substantial amount of weight. Probably about, what? Sixty more pounds—"

"I'm thinking more like seventy," the nutritionist piped up, bending back over the sheaf of papers in her hand. "And even with a fairly low-calorie diet and a pretty strenuous exercise regimen, I'm not sure she could lose that amount in only three months. She'll lose some fat in the process of the surgery, but as I calculate it, even on only 1200 calo-ries, it comes out to about three or four pounds a week, or"—she scribbled—"between thirty-five and forty-five pounds overall." She shook her head. "Any faster than that, and I'm afraid we'll be court-ing a host of nutritional deficiencies—"

"But it says here that Audra's got a pretty decent ratio of fat to muscle," interjected Julienne, the fit-ness chick. She popped a lazy bicep, admired it, then continued in a low, calm voice. "Let's say she loses forty-five pounds of fat and builds up her lean muscle mass. She could easily look sixty or even seventy pounds slimmer than she appears today.

And she's already in pretty good physical shape, by nature of the kind of work she does."

"That's one of the things that argues in favor of her as a candidate. Her excellent overall health," Dr. Koch interjected.

"For the body, I agree," Dr. Bremmar nodded. "But the face . . ." He shook his head and sighed.

Dr. Koch echoed the sigh. "Yes . . . the face," he repeated, and said no more, letting the room lapse into a prolonged silence.

Audra stared from expert to expert, but suddenly no one in the room was looking at her . . . except Dr. Jamison, whose velvety brown eyes had never once wavered from her features since he'd entered the room, even though, since his introduction, the man hadn't said a word.

"Well?" Audra looked around the room, forcing her voice to its most jocular tone, even though her heart was pumping loud in her chest, and her ears were ringing with ugly phrases like *dude with tits* and *not my daughter*. "Don't tell me my face is too ugly to fix. I mean, look at me," she gestured toward the screen. "Almost anything you do will be an improvement. How can you lose?"

This time there was no laughter, and still no one, not even the staring Dr. Jamison, spoke. Shamiyah cast a quick look at Audra that conveyed nothing but her nervousness, but she said not a word.

Finally, Dr. Bremmar cleared his throat. "See, the thing is, darker skin poses some . . . particular problems," he began, cutting his eyes at Dr. Jamison, as though, as a black man he should be the one to speak. But Jamison just kept staring at Audra, wordless and soundless, his expression as blank as the gleaming surface of the conference table. "And while your medical history doesn't suggest any particular predisposition for those problems, we can't be sure—"

"He's talking about keloid scarring," Dr. Koch interrupted, seeming impatient with the other man's gentle, hesitant style of speech. "Do you know what that is?"

Audra frowned. She was about to reply when Camilla jumped into the silence with, "Big, ugly, raised scarring." She grimaced. "We do your face and you heal badly and—"

"I wouldn't sue you, I promise—"

"Of course you wouldn't. The releases you signed would completely bar any type of lawsuit. That's not the point. The *point*," she continued dramatically, "is that the entire show is on the line. The show may be called *Ugly Duckling*, but we make swans here. If you're not going to come out a swan, then we're not gonna spend production dollars on you—" She cut her eyes at Shamiyah. "No matter how much 'character' you have."

Audra blinked at the woman, assessing her quietly. She wasn't unattractive, but from where Audra was sitting, she certainly wasn't good-looking enough to get away with this kind of crap. Still, no one seemed to take any position to correct her bad behavior, and Audra got the feeling, today wasn't the day for her to take on the job.

"I've gotten cuts before—some of them pretty bad ones—and they didn't heal badly," Audra offered. "I mean you guys have inspected almost every inch of me. You don't see anything that suggests that this surgery would be any different—"

"Unfortunately, Audra, it could be quite different." Dr. Bremmar sounded a little like a school-teacher, patiently giving a lesson to a resistant audience. "We're talking about a fairly serious and dramatic surgery here with the possibility for infection and serious scarring under the best of circumstances. Darker skin, as I indicated earlier, often tends to show darker, more noticeable scarring, even if it's not the keloid variety." His purple marker reappeared, as a close-up of Audra's face dominated the screen. "See, what I would want to do—and I'm sure Herb has similar ideas—is liposuction here to create a stronger jaw line." He drew purple lines on the skin beneath Audra's chin. "Restructure the cheekbones and the nose"—more lines—"to give the face more definition, then pull some of the fatty deposits from beneath the eyes and the brow bone . . ." He kept drawing until Audra's face looked like it had been scribbled over by a two-year-old with a new crayon. He stopped abruptly, surveyed the screen and shrugged. "Every one of these lines is a potential scar—a black line on your face, at best. At worst—"

"It doesn't help that you don't have any family history from your father's side. That information might help us determine if it would be wise to go ahead—"

"No, there's no paternal history," Audra interrupted, shrugging aside the feelings that simply mentioning the subject brought to the center of her consciousness. Out of the corner of her eye, she saw

Dr. Goddard make a move for her notebook and begin scribbling animatedly, but the shrink's notes were the least of her concerns at that moment. "Why don't we do a test, then? I mean just do a cut and see what happens?" Audra offered. "I mean, I could even pay for it—"

"There's no reason to put you through that," Dr. Bremmar said, just as Dr. Koch murmured, "That's really not necessary."

"Your acne suggests you might be prone to a certain amount of scarring, Audra," Dr. Bremmar said, cutting his eyes in Dr. Jamison's direction again. "I'm no expert, but I do know there are drugs that could make a substantial difference in that condition—even minimize the scarring you already have, but they won't have the same effect on post-surgery scarring unless—"

"Then I'm not sure why you even had me come out here," Audra interrupted, staring at the purple-marked images of her face and body. "Sounds like you've already decided it's hopeless."

"No, not hopeless. Far from it."

Audra turned toward the heavy bass of the man's voice. The room became quiet, the kind of quiet of a dozen people listening eagerly for an important man to make an important speech.

"There's a way to do this kind of extensive facial surgery that can minimize the risks of scarring to the same level as a light-skinned or Caucasian patient," Dr. Jamison continued softly. "But it's highly controversial. Not everyone believes it should be done. And some people even find it offensive—"

"But it could be great for ratings for both of those

reasons," Camilla interjected, her eyes gleaming. "Your transformation is sure to be one of the most watched ones we've ever done if you agree to Dr. Jamison's treatments—"

"Treatments?" Audra stared at the man, meeting his even gaze with curiosity. "What kind of treatments?"

Dr. Jamison's lips curled into the faintest of smiles. "There are a variety of methods, actually. Usually a combination of medications taken orally and applied topically." His gaze narrowed, searching her face. "In your case, we'd also have to work in medication for the acne, but that shouldn't pose any serious additional detriment. But you'd have to begin immediately to hope to achieve any significant lightening effect before the surgery begins—"

"Lightening effect?" Audra frowned. "What are you talking about?"

Dr. Jamison gazed at her, his liquid eyes seeming to penetrate right to the heart of who she'd always thought she was and what she'd always thought she wanted. "You said on the tape you sent you were sick and tired of being called 'fat, black and ugly,' " he said in his slow, sonorous voice. "Diet and exercise will eliminate the fat, Drs. Bremmar and Koch can eliminate the ugly." He shrugged. "That leaves only 'black' to be addressed."

"Black," Audra repeated. Her eyes circled the room, searching for clarification, but she found nothing in any of the other faces, except rapt interest. These people were clearly waiting for something. Something monumental. "Black," Audra said again, forcing out a strangled little laugh. "Don't tell me you can turn me into a white woman!" She coaxed the laugh into a chuckle of merriment. "You can't possibly—"

Dr. Jamison's voice rose above hers, drowning it out with force and clarity. "The drug is called hydroquinone. If you apply it daily between now and the Big Reveal, you'll start this process a dark-skinned African-American woman . . . and end it as a much, much, much lighter-skinned one." He wiggled his fingers in something like a wave. "Goodbye fat, black and ugly. Forever, if you like. There's only one catch," he added a second later. "You have to decide today. Right now."

Chapter 10

"**H**e's kidding, right?" Audra swung her face around the room, then fixed her eyes back on Dr. Jamison. "You're kidding, right? You can't actually—"

"I assure you, Ms. Marks, I can." His voice was calm and level, but his eyes danced as though he found the conversation highly amusing. "Actually it's not all that uncommon in the entertainment world. Surely you've noticed how some African-American performers start their careers one shade of brown and, as they become more success-ful, seem to become a lighter shade of brown? True, some of that may be attributed to lighting and makeup . . . but in other cases, that shift in skin tone is very much a direct result of our pro-cess."

He touched the keypad and cleared all of the purple markings Dr. Bremmar had made on the close-up image of Audra's face. "First of all, we address the recurring acne itself with isotetrinoin—it's been proven to have a fairly decent success rate in minimizing the occurrence of acne scars, even in darker skin." As he spoke, the picture was altered and the clusters of bumps faded from Audra's cheeks, chin and forehead. "If all we were concerned about was the acne, we'd address laser treatments to the upper dermis—the visible layer of skin"—Audra's image's skin became clearer with the words—"but that's not the effect we're going for. What we want is lighter coloring on all of your skin—or at least on all the visible surfaces. The result is—well, obvious."

As Audra watched, the image of herself lightened on the screen, from the deep, bitter chocolate color she was used to seeing in the mirror . . . to the color of coffee beans . . . and onward up the color scale until the woman staring out of Audra's eyes and nose and lips was framed in a warm cinnamon. She gasped. With the lighter tone and the lack of scars and bumps, she saw her mother in her own face.

"Audra, are you all right?" Shamiyah's voice reached her from far away, in a universe without fat, black or ugly.

"Yeah," she muttered, emotions tumbling and swirling inside her. She turned back to the doctor. "How . . . ?" she began.

"A drug. It's called hydroquinone and most often it's prescribed in a four-percent solution." Dr. Jamison's eyebrows lifted. "We'd start you out on at least twice that, applied topically twice a day to the entire body. We'd increase or decrease the dosage as needed to get the result we need . . ." He paused for dramatic effect. "But you'd have to begin applications almost immediately in order to have reached the desired skin tone by your Reveal."

"That's why you've got to decide right now." Camilla injected herself back into the discussion. "Because if you don't want to do it, we'll have to choose another candidate who fits the concept."

"Concept? What concept?" Audra asked, remembering the word from Carla's brief education on the making of a television show. "Is there a particular concept you're working with—?"

"Don't worry about that. The most important thing about the concept is that we have an African-American woman," Shamiyah interrupted, cutting her eyes toward Camilla with a frown. "A real woman who could give voice to some of the frustrations some black women feel." Her voice grew earnest, persuasive. "We see this show as more than entertainment, Audra. It's education. There are women out there who need to know there are *solutions*. There are women out there who need to see their options beyond a lifetime as fat, black and ugly. Women who need to know that—in a world gone crazy for beauty—there's more for them than second-class status." She tossed her head, eyes wide and eloquent. "That's the concept—message, really. And I've known since I first saw your tape, you are the messenger."

Audra barely looked at her. She stared at her features on the screen. The image was still a black woman's face—but a totally different shade of African-American womanhood than Audra's present version. It was . . . weird . . . like catching a glimpse of her double in a store window or seeing some twisted photographic mishap. But it was one thing to complain about her dark skin . . . and something else to erase it altogether.

"Wild," she murmured, more to herself than anyone else. "Just . . . wild . . ."

"You want to see wild?" Dr. Bremmar spoke up, his pleasant voice brimming with enthusiasm. "Look at this . . ." and he began tapping wildly on the little keyboard in front of him.

While Audra watched, the light-skinned face in front of her shifted and changed. The double chin melted away, the eyebrows lifted above the smoky black eyes. The bone of the nose rose and straightened, while the nostrils were narrowed and reshaped. Sculpted cheekbones appeared out of jowly cheeks.

With a few strokes of his computer program, Dr. Bremmar had created a woman that Audra recognized.

"Petra," she breathed, staring at the image. "Except for the hair . . . that's her. That's Petra . . ."

Dr. Bremmar turned toward her. "Who?"

"My older sister. She's in the Army. Stationed in Iraq." Audra frowned. "You know that also sort of looks like . . ." *Esmeralda?* Audra shook the resemblance from her mind. "Never mind," she said quickly, pushing aside thoughts of Art Bradshaw and *Double Indemnity*, of movie-style romance and soul mates. Instead, she stared hard at the image one more time before turning back to the row of doctors, her heart thumping wildly in her chest. "You can really do this? You can really make me look like *that*?"

"Well, there are no guarantees with this kind of surgery, but"—the polite doctor gave her another of his wide grins—"if Dr. Jamison's treatments achieve the coloring and eliminate our concerns about scarring . . . I'm reasonably confident you'll look at *least* that good. Depending on Koch's aim that day, maybe better." And he gave the other man a playful wink.

Dr. Koch rolled his eyes like he was sick of the joke, but seconded his partner's comments with a morose, "I completely agree."

"Wow," Audra muttered. "Wow. It's like . . . magic."

"Hardly," Camilla snorted. "It's a ton of work!"

"I can do the work," Audra snapped at her. "It's just . . ."

"A question of cultural identity." Dr. Goddard made her first appearance in the conversation, interrupting with her clipped and intelligent-sounding voice.

"Yes," Audra said quietly.

"There are potentially serious ramifications of this kind of decision. In addition to radically changing her appearance through plastic surgery, she'll be altering how she's perceived as an African American." The doctor sounded as though she were reading from a textbook, but she had the gist of it right. Color resentments in the black community ran strong and deep, Audra knew. As a dark-skinned woman, she harbored more than a few of them herself.

"And unlike celebrities, when this show is over, Ms. Marks will be returning to a real world, where people who know her as she is now might not receive the changes in her appearance in a welcoming way. This sort of change will be controversial—"

"Controversy is a good thing. It'll make her a star," Camilla interjected.

"But it will also impact her relationships with others in her life," Dr. Goddard warned. "Her friends and co-workers, family and lovers . . ."

Friends and co-workers . . .

Audra couldn't think of one person in this category whose opinion would affect her in any serious way. She imagined herself walking down the corridors of the prison in the face and body of the woman before her. There would be no more "fat, black and ugly," no more wardrobe malfunctions, no more "dude with tits," she realized, and couldn't help but smile.

Family . . .

Audra stared at the image on the screen across from her again. Just the coloring of this virtual woman alone made her look like her mother and sister in a way she never had before. And if these doctors could give her even a tenth of the image's beauty, there was no doubt in her mind: She'd finally look like them. She'd finally look like she belonged, like part of the family and not like a swan chick left on the ducklings' doorstep, out of sync and out of step with everyone around her.

Lovers . . .

She thought of Art Bradshaw for a moment and saw his broad face, amber eyes and full lips in her mind.

But Art Bradshaw had only been interested in her for the lessons she could teach his daughter about getting along in an ugly world. And since the girl had no desire to learn, there wasn't much reason to think of him as friend or co-worker anymore.

"The truth is . . ." she said slowly, "I don't think I have any family or friends, co-workers or lovers whose opinions matter to me." She glanced around the room. "So really, this decision is mine and mine alone." Her eyes strayed to the two images of herself on the screen across from her. The "before" of herself Carla had just taken a couple of hours ago. The "after" shot was, for now, a computer simulation. But it could become real. It could be hers in only a few months' time, if she said the word.

But she hesitated still, staring at the images, unsure if she could surrender herself so completely. Audra Marks, as she knew herself, meant a certain way of being in the world . . . a way that was so tied up in her physical body they could not be easily separated. How would Audra Marks behave in the world if she were beautiful? What would it mean to be Audra Marks, light-skinned woman, instead of dark?

Audra didn't know.

"It's a part of my responsibility to help you integrate these changes in your physical appearance with the rest of your identity," the shrink said quietly, as though reading Audra's mind. "If you choose to become an Ugly Duckling, we'll talk through what these changes might mean in your everyday life."

Audra nodded at the woman, then let her eyes stray to the black folks in the room.

"Shamiyah?"

"I think you should go for it, Audra," she said earnestly, a pleading expression on her face. "Think of all the pain your looks have caused you. The insults and the humiliation . . ." she said, tapping into the rich mine of Audra's greatest motivator. "Do it for yourself, Audra. For yourself . . . and for the thousands of women like you." She paused, fixing a pair of determined eyes on Audra's face. "But if you're gonna do it, you have to do it all the way. The weight, the surgery and the color."

Audra let the words flow over her but said nothing. She cut her eyes toward the other person of color.

"What would *you* do?" she asked Jamison in a low voice.

The man shook his head. "It's your decision, Ms. Marks," he said in his rumbling radio voice. "No one else can make it for you." His eyes rolled toward Shamiyah. "No matter how much they might *like* to—"

"Great, so what's the word?" Camilla snapped

impatiently. "You gonna stay fat, black and ugly . . . or do you want to do light, bright and beautiful? Because if you're not gonna do it, then I'm pretty sure Shamiyah's got a stack of tapes of other homely sister girls who'd jump at the chance—"

"I'm in," Audra announced. "I'm in."

Shamiyah's face broke into a big, happy smile tinted with more than a little relief, and even Camilla looked satisfied. Only the bespectacled psychiatrist didn't meet her eyes; she was too busy scribbling in her notebook.

"Besides, you said controversy's good, right? Me, I'm down with that. I live with people saying all kinds of nasty things about me right now . . . so what's the diff?" Her eyes found Dr. Jamison's. "So, doc. When do we start?"

"Immediately." And the man slid another clump of papers at her. "You'll need to sign those—"

"More signing?"

"It's a consent to the dermatological treatments that will lighten your skin, as well as an explanation of the various side effects and precautions—"

"Side effects? Precautions?" Audra frowned. "What—"

"Nothing serious," the doctor said easily, rumbling over her objections in his calm, melodious voice. "You have to spread it over your entire body—everywhere, if you want the tone to be even. And you have to avoid the sun. Completely. Hat, gloves, sunglasses, long sleeves. Completely, unless you want to look like a checkered tablecloth," he said, his eyes pinioning hers. "I'll provide you with a prescription for the hydroquinone, which you will use faithfully on your entire body from now until I tell you otherwise." He glanced at Camilla. "Even on an accelerated dosage, it will take several months. Can you schedule her surgeries for last?"

Camilla consulted her clipboard and nodded. "She'll be last. Scheduled for surgery in late June." She shook her head. "But that's the latest we can go and leave time for editing and distribution for shows scheduled to air in October."

Dr. Jamison nodded. "That's long enough to see a significant difference . . ."

"I'll give you a diet to follow," piped in the nutritionist. "If you could lose another twenty pounds before we start the process here—"

"Without sacrificing any muscle mass, of course," interjected the trainer.

"No, of course not," the nutritionist said, sounding peeved. "I'll fax it over to Dr. Jamison's office this afternoon."

"Great, great." Camilla was all bustle and energy again. "Thank you all. This has been very . . . informative. I've got to get with our marketing folks and give them the go-ahead on the promos for this color-consciousness stuff, but I believe we've all made a good choice, so—"

"And Camilla,"—Shamiyah's voice had a new edge of confidence in it, as though she'd conquered something—"since it looks like Audra's *in*, I think I should take a crew and go to New York next week. Shoot the 'surprise selection' segment. You know, catch her off guard, at home. See her with her family and friends. Maybe even a couple of shots at the prison, if that can be arranged. That way, we'll have some good shots of her in present life . . . and in her present look, before Dr. Jamison's treatments take hold. It makes for a more dramatic before and after—"

"All right," Camilla agreed, but her voice had lost some of its nastiness, as if she, too, knew something had shifted in the power and energy of the room. Her steely eyes fixed on Audra again as she jabbed a finger at her in admonition. "And, you'd *better* act surprised. I'm talking Academy-Award-winning surprised. You got it?"

The woman clearly didn't know who she was talking to.

Audra summoned tears of gratitude to her eyes and grabbed Camilla's hand.

"Thank you . . . thank you so very much," she said in a hoarse whisper, straight out of Ann Baxter's acceptance speech in *All About Eve*. "You don't know what this chance means to me . . ." She murmured, and then, right when Camilla seemed about to buy it, she smiled. "Psych!"

The room exploded with laughter, but Camilla didn't seem amused in the slightest. "Yeah, exactly like that," she muttered, slamming her notebook shut. She barked to the cameras to wrap for the day, then she turned back to Audra, her voice sicky sweet. "I'm Camilla Jejune, executive producer for *Ugly Duckling*." She leaned close. "You belong to us now—and don't you forget it."

"Sure," Audra said glibly enough. But the truth was, this woman wasn't nearly as scary as the conversations waiting for her back in New York.

Chapter 11

May 31

Dear Petra,

When we heard about the bombings in Basra, we were scared to death. Things actually thawed out enough for Ma to talk to me, she was that scared. I can't tell you how relieved we all were to hear that Michael is still safe and that you're still in Baghdad, far from that tragedy. The minute we learned you all were okay, Miss Frosty came back out. I don't think she's said more than "pass the peas" in three days.

I don't know what she's mad at. If anyone should be mad, it's me. I'm not the one with some deep, dark secret . . .

Okay, I guess I do have a secret.

I know, I know, I really should tell her. But after talking to Shamiyah about it, we felt that it might be better to just let her find out when they shoot the "surprise" footage of me being notified that I've been selected. Since I'm not supposed to know I'm going to be on the show anyway, Shamiyah thought it would be better if I didn't tell anyone (except you, of course). And all that's fine with me: I don't want to hear Ma's mouth until I have to. She's not stupid, though. She knows something's up—that's why she's mad at me. She's been needling me with questions since I got back from California . . . but all I do is smile.

Shamiyah and the camera crew will be here either today or tomorrow, so I guess my days of silence are about to end with a scene that would shame the campiest dramatic moment in Hollywood. I wish you were going to be here to see it!

It's only been a couple of weeks, but people are starting to tell me I look "different." Of course, I'm still losing weight, but they always say, "No, that's not it," and just keep staring at me, like somehow continued inspection will answer the question. Ma does it a lot. I just stand there and smile. I don't really see any difference yet, if you want to know the truth. I scanned a picture in—you can tell me what you think.

I hope your detail doesn't have to make that supply run you wrote about. Sounds dangerous. Really dangerous. I know it's what you're trained to do . . . but maybe you could call in sick that day? Just joking . . . ☺

Be careful out there,

Audra

"You want to bring some cameras into it, fine with me!" Edith shouted, signing her name in a broad flourish across the bottom of the paper

Shamiyah proffered, then slamming the pen down on the kitchen counter. "Just don't expect me to put all my private business on TV just because *she* wants to"—she gave Audra the kind of hard, gangsta stare Audra saw all the time at the prison—"because that is *not* the kind of woman I am!"

"No, no, of course not, Mrs. Marks," Shamiyah nodded as though she were in vigorous support of Edith's position, then gave Audra a quick wink the second her mother turned her head. She looked exactly like she had the last time Audra had seen her, only now she wore a teal camisole in some shiny, lingerie fabric over her demin jeans and seriously pointy, black high heels. "We want your honest reaction. That's what makes it a reality show."

"Oh, you'll get my honest reaction," Edith snorted, glaring at Audra in disbelief. "And I honestly hope you're kidding about this whole idea, Audra. I hope this is one of your weirdo jokes, right? That you watched *Now, Voyager* again on TV, and now you're poor, put-upon Bette Davis, treated badly by her family until she gets beautiful and runs off on an ocean cruise with Charles Boyer—"

"Actually, it's Paul Henreid," Audra corrected, ignoring the wheeling, circling motions of the cameraman as he angled himself into position just a foot from her shoulder. Edith's tone dug at her, tingling her most sensitive spots and goading her toward response. "I'm impressed, Ma. I didn't know you knew that movie—"

"Oh, stop it Audra!" Edith snapped, shaking her head so hard, Audra knew she missed the extensions she'd just taken out a few days ago. Now she

was experimenting with a look that featured heavy
bangs and razored short sides that Audra thought
made her look a little too much like a Marine. "You
can't be serious, right? This is why you went out to
California? You aren't actually going to—"

She stopped, staring hard into Audra's face. "Oh
my God . . . that's it. I knew there was something
different about you! You've already started it. What
did you have done to your face?"

"Laser treatments for the acne . . . though the
doc says I'll need a few more. And . . ." She hesitated, steeling herself for Edith's next explosion, as
Shamiyah nodded vigorously, urging her toward
confession. "And a drug to lighten my skin tone."

Edith's mouth fell open. "Lighten your skin!" she
repeated, peering close into Audra's face. "You're
actually going to lighten your skin? Why? What's
wrong with the color you are now?"

"Nothing . . ." Audra began slowly, "but . . ." Her
eyes swung toward Shamiyah, whose head was bob-
bing furiously with encouragement.

"Go for it," she mouthed, silently stretching her
lips so that there was no mistaking what she was
trying to communicate. "Go for it!"

"Nothing . . . except that I'm darker than everyone in my family," Audra said quickly, pushing the
words out with more difficulty than she had antici-
pated. After all, she'd said them a thousand times
before. Only there hadn't been cameras before. "I'm
darker than everyone in my family," Audra repeated.
"Darker than Petra and Kiana. And you. Everyone
I . . . love," she concluded, as unexpected emotion
sprang to her throat.

Edith frowned, then tried to turn away from the cameras, but they followed her, recording both the sudden softness and the fearful nervousness that flushed into her face. She mastered them an instant later, and swung on Audra, choosing once again not to ignore the family resemblances—or the lack thereof. Instead, she fired back with a sharp, "Are you nuts?" And before Audra could respond, she had launched into, "I've seen these shows. They turn women into—into—Miss America look-alikes, whether that suits them or not." She eyed Audra dubiously, shaking her head. "I should have known something was up. I should have known when you finally started getting serious about losing that weight. But don't tell me you're *this* pathetic, that your self-esteem is so low, you'd actually do something as crazy as *this*. That you'd be willing to put yourself through all *that*."

Audra swallowed back her tenderness in a single bitter gulp.

"Oh, I'm absolutely going to put myself through it, Ma." Audra twisted her lips into a determined grin. "I'm going to put myself through all of it."

"But *why*, Audra?" Edith's voice rose in exasperation, and if Audra wasn't mistaken, she threw up her hands as extra emphasis just for the benefit of the cameras. "You've lost some weight and I think that's great. But surgery and—and"—she struggled with the words as though they were choking her— "skin bleaching. Why would you do something like that?"

"To be something different, Ma," Audra replied calmly. "To see something different—something other than fat, black and ugly when I look in the mirror—"

"You still gonna be the same person on the inside," Edith said, as if that weren't obvious. "And if you don't like yourself now, you won't like yourself any better, just because you see something different when you look in the mirror."

"I like myself just fine," Audra declared. "It's a matter of making the outside match the inside."

"Audra . . ." Edith muttered. "Audra, Audra, Audra . . ." she repeated, then folded her arms about herself and stared at her daughter with an expression Audra was certain she'd never seen on the woman's face before. Amazement, fear, anger and contempt seemed to have blended into a single arch of eyebrows and pull of lips. Audra waited, staring back at the woman, feeling she wouldn't have been surprised if her mother reached out an arm to hug her or a palm to slap her face. But in the end, she did neither: just kept staring at her with that strange look frozen on her face.

"There are also some amazing prizes offered to the contestant with the biggest transformation." Shamiyah interjected. "A modeling contract, cash, a part in a movie—just a walk-on part, but still." She grinned so wide Audra could have counted all her teeth. "It could lead to all kinds of opportunities."

"A modeling contract," repeated Edith, her eyes still fixed on Audra's face, her lips in a tight line. The eyes seemed to say, "don't do this," but the lips carried a different message, one of determined distrust. "Is that what you want?" her mother asked at last. "You wanna be a model? A movie star?"

Audra shook her head. "I just want to look like Petra . . . and you," she said quietly, speaking to the woman's eyes, trying hard to ignore the judgment in the rest of the face. "I just want to fit in . . ."

Edith lowered her eyes, then turned away entirely. The camera crew might have picked up her expression, but Audra got nothing, nothing but a bit of her shoulder. Edith sighed and that shoulder lifted nearly to her earlobe. Audra waited, feeling the weight of the air between them. Would she finally admit it now—now, to stop Audra from going to California, to stop her from erasing her skin tone as an Ugly Duckling?

Audra held her breath, feeling a confession swirling between them, the explanation for the words she'd overheard all those years ago: *She ain't mine . . . She ain't mine.* She glanced at Shamiyah: the woman was following the scene between them with such intensity, she looked like all she needed was some popcorn.

When Edith spoke there was a sadness in her voice that hadn't been there before.

"Fine. Do it," she said tersely. "It's your body, your skin, your life. Who knows? Maybe you'll be better off."

Audra stared at her, her heart sinking deep in her chest with disappointment. Clearly, her mother intended to take her secrets to the grave.

"She'll be in California for the surgery from the end of June through September," Shamiyah said when the silence became loud and unbearable. "You—the whole family—are invited to the Reveal at the end of the process. We're already working with the Army to get permission for your other daughter and son-in-law to join us and I'm optimistic. But that's just the taping. You won't see the episode on TV until the end of November. If Audra gets enough audience votes, she comes back to do a special show with the other top three Ugly Ducklings," she continued, grinning again as if the power of her smile alone could diffuse the tension in the air. "That's a real cool show. The UDs—the Ugly Ducks—will get a crash course in modeling and take a screen test. We're going to be using this really cool interactive tool to let people vote online and use cell phones to crown a winner that very night—"

"So you're gonna be gone."

Audra shrugged. "Three months. I only go back if the audience votes for me—"

"They will," Edith muttered. "You got a black woman turning herself into a white woman? They will . . . just so they can keep talking about you."

Audra opened her mouth to object, but her mother changed topics before she could speak.

"And just what are you gonna tell Kiana about this?" she said at last. "She looks up to you. She thinks you're the strongest, most wonderful person in the world—and she always has." Edith studied the floor as though the effort of paying Audra this compliment had cost her something. "I sometimes think she loves you more than she does her own mother. Or me." The woman's smoky eyes pinned Audra's in query. "How do I tell her that her beloved Auntie A is actually a shallow, superficial mess?"

The words stung, but Audra did her best not to let her hurt show. "You give with one hand and take with another, Ma," she said, as a wry smile lifted her lips.

"What's that supposed to mean?"

"It means, don't tell her anything," Audra replied. "I'll tell her myself. In my own way, in my own time. Probably the next time we read *The Ugly Duckling*." And she leveled her most penetrating gaze on her mother again. "Anything else?"

Edith gathered herself up like an affronted Queen. "Else? What else is there? You made up your mind. Me and Kiana will get by those three months somehow." She turned, head up, lips turned down, and marched toward the doorway, batting at the surrounding cameras. "Get away from me, now. I've said all I'm gonna say about it, so you can turn those things off."

"You realize we may end up showing some of this on television, Mrs. Marks—" Shamiyah began.

"Yes, I realize that," Edith snapped. "But I ain't the one who's done something she ought to be ashamed of," and she swept herself from the room.

Chapter 12

June 5

When I get back—if I come back—I'm moving out. I know I've said it before, but this time, I mean it. Even if I have to move to one of those tough-girl neighborhoods where you need a switchblade to go out for your morning newspaper. Or maybe I'll stay out there in Los Angeles and live among the "beautiful people." Maybe I'll even be one of them!

And no, I'm not avoiding your questions about Art Bradshaw. I just don't have anything to report. I haven't seen him at all since his daughter's party and I don't plan to—not until after the surgery. Then I might just call him up and treat him—and his daughter—to a nice meal. I guess I owe them "thanks." If it hadn't been for their one-two punch I probably wouldn't have called UD.

But then, again, maybe I would have. I don't know . . .

*Anyway, it's great news that you might be given leave
to come to the Reveal—and even better news that one
or both of you might be home for good in December. Is
Michael seriously considering re-enlistment? Is he
insane? You're not going to re-up, are you? Kiana
needs you guys.*

So do I.

Be careful out there,

Audra

"**M**arks!"

His voice rumbled through the air toward
her, low and smooth as the bass line of a soul groove,
and Audra stopped short, struggling with the competing emotions that welled up inside her.

Bradshaw.

She sighed. It was bound to happen, she knew it
as soon as she saw his name on the duty roster. For
whatever reason, Bradshaw was working the graveyard shift tonight, and Audra knew that tonight, after all these weeks and months, the thing that had
been opened with movie flirtation and the invitation
to his daughter's party would finally, at last, be
closed.

She turned around slowly, searching her mind for
the angle, the character, the stance to play this
scene, feeling the need of the protection of a role,
the safety of an imitation.

"Well, well. Look what the cat dragged in," she
drawled, slewing out a foot and lifting her chin,
dead diva style. "How are you, Bradshaw?"

He was as handsome as ever, every tall, muscled

inch of him. There were smudges of fatigue under them, but his amber eyes glittered a little and a bit of a smile twitched the corner of his still-delectable lips.

"Heard you were cleared," he said, as though that answered her question. "Woodburn make you switch to nights?"

No, you did, Audra thought, but kept the words in her mind. Instead, she shook her head. "My idea," she said quickly. "How about you? What are you doing here?"

But he appeared not to have heard.

"You look different, Marks." Art Bradshaw squinted down into her face, a puzzled expression on his handsome face. "New makeup?"

Audra ignored the question, though she knew it was true: She did look different. After some initial irritation, Dr. Jamison's dermabrasion, along with her continued efforts with dieting, seemed to be fading the acne and its scarring. And the daily application of the doctor's lightening cream was definitely beginning to show its efficacy. Her skin had more browns and reds in its tone than blacks or charcoals.

But unlike the weight loss, which brought comments almost daily, to most people, the skin changes weren't really noticeable yet—only people who paid regular attention to her face had commented on it: her mother, mainly, and to a lesser degree, Kiana. Audra was a little surprised that the tall man had commented first on it and not on the fact that there were nearly forty-five pounds less of her—especially since she hadn't seen him in over two months.

Instead of launching into a detailed explanation she wasn't sure he needed or deserved, she pulled the cool mantle of an aggrieved dame around her and quirked an eyebrow at him, lifting her foot off the rickety break-room seat so the man could settle into it across from her. "You're the disappearing man, Art Bradshaw," she quipped, sounding exactly like wisecracking Eve Arden in her own ears. "I haven't seen you since . . ." she furrowed her brow as though trying hard to remember, as if the whole incident weren't as fresh as today's bread. "Since . . . Penny's party . . ."

Bradshaw's tawny skin seemed tinged with red. "Penny's party . . ." he grumbled, lowering his luminous eyes from her face. "Sorry, Marks. About Penny and the way she acted that night," he finished quickly. "Been meaning to make her apologize, but . . ." He sighed. "We've been dealing with so much shit lately—"

"No need to apologize. Doesn't really matter much now anyway, does it?" she said lightly, managing to sound almost like she meant it. "Actually, I guess you and your daughter did me a favor that day. It was the last straw . . . just the last straw. I mean, I've heard all that stuff before . . . but to hear it from a sixteen-year-old girl . . ." She shook her head. "It helped me to decide to send in my audition tape. And now look what's happened . . ."

"What stuff?" Bradshaw stared at her, puzzlement creasing his face. "Audition tape? What did Penny say?"

Audra quirked an eyebrow at him.

"She didn't—didn't you just say you wanted her to apologize—?" she began.

"I heard her being rude," he said slowly, frowning at her inquisitively. "Was there something else?"

Audra opened her mouth to explain, then closed it. There was no reason to get the girl in trouble with her father for telling the truth—a truth that had sparked so much change in Audra's life. Instead, she smiled at him and said, "No, of course not. You haven't heard my news? You must be the only one in the whole prison—"

"I had a—a family emergency." Bradshaw's brow curled into a frown of concern. "Had to take a few weeks off to try and deal with it. Just got back today."

"Emergency?" Audra sobered immediately, dropping the aggrieved routine to stare up at him in concern. "What's happened? Nothing with Penny, I hope?"

Bradshaw shook his head. "Not Penny. Her mother. "

Audra blinked at him in surprise. "Her mother? She showed up?"

"Showed up?" The frown deepened. "No, she's always been around."

"But I thought it was just the two of you. You and Penny."

"It is, for all practical purposes," he muttered, sounding bitter and defeated. "We've been divorced for years. I take care of Penny. But she's around . . . when she wants to be. Like the birthday party."

"She was at the party?" Audra said in surprise. "Penny's sweet sixteen?"

Bradshaw's face scrunched together like Audra had said something ridiculous. "Course she was. You met her! Remember?"

"I didn't meet anyone but Penny and that Esmeralda woman—"

The instant the words left her mouth, she realized who he was talking about, understood the depth of her mistake. Esmeralda Prince wasn't just his fabulously gorgeous *date* for the evening. She was much, much more. The room suddenly felt stuffy and Audra had to tell herself to breathe slow and deep to keep her lightheadedness at bay, while her memories of the party played in her mind. *Esmeralda Prince was Penny's mother?* she thought, with a sudden desperate wave of pity for the girl. *No wonder she's got issues . . .*

"Oh my God . . ." Audra murmured, covering her open mouth with her hands. "And here I was, thinking Esmeralda Prince was your girlfriend . . ."

"Prince is her maiden name. She took it back when we split up." Bradshaw peered at Audra as though her thoughts were written on her face for him to read. "When Penny was two. She's been in and out of our lives ever since . . ." He winced as though the words caused him pain. "And now she's gone."

"Gone?" Audra repeated.

Bradshaw nodded. "Again. And this time, I don't think I can let her come back."

Audra stared at him, waiting for the rest, but he

folded his lips tight and stared at something just over her shoulder like his life depended on maintaining his focus. Finally, Audra snapped her fingers beneath his nose, recalling him brusquely to the present. "Down here, Bradshaw!" she snapped at him, annoyed by his inattentiveness. Apparently a girl had to be Esmeralda Prince to get—and keep—his attention. "Can I get the rest of the story please?"

"You don't know the rest of story?" he snapped, frustration rising in his tone. "You can't tell by looking at her what a sap I've been?"

Audra almost shot back something about how thinking with his "little head" had obviously gotten him into a world of trouble, but before she could offer that unhelpful comment, Bradshaw continued with, "Well look at her! Can't you tell by how she looks? How thin she is?"

"You like light-skinned, skinny women who wear great clothes." Audra lifted a shoulder like it wasn't the tiniest skin off her nose. "If that were a crime, most of the men in America would be guilty. That's one of the reasons I'm doing what I'm doing—"

"Esmeralda's got a drug problem, Audra," Bradshaw murmured. "A bad one."

Audra blinked at him. "A drug problem? She can't have a drug problem! She's too gorgeous to have a drug problem."

"Gorgeous," Bradshaw rolled his eyes, his lips hard with suppressed fury. "I used to think so. She used to be beautiful." He paused, remembering. "Curveaceous figure . . . womanly . . ." He shook the image away. "But is it gorgeous to steal your daughter's presents and run out on her on her birthday?" he asked, and seeing the shock on Audra's face, he added, "Yeah, it's true. She stole all Penny's gifts, most of the money in Penny's bank account and disappeared. We haven't seen her since."

"Said she was clean." Bradshaw pulled a photograph from his wallet and flipped it toward her from his seat across from her in a bustling diner not far from the prison's entrance. The sun was rising over Manhattan, but his handsome faced was etched with a pain so deep Audra had to turn her head to stop herself from reaching out and grabbing his hand, or stroking his face—anything to reassure him that it would be all right.

But instead, from their booth near the window, Audra pulled the photo toward her across the table and glanced down at it.

It was much-fingered, dog-eared, clearly carried and treasured for many years. In it, Audra recognized Bradshaw, Penny and Esmeralda all looking impossibly young. Audra knew the crisp uniform Bradshaw wore as the dress blues of the Marine Corps, and his face blinked out of the photograph with an almost adolescent innocence. Penny was a happy toddler on his lap, grinning wide, showing a mouthful of baby teeth.

But it was Esmeralda who captured Audra's attention. She still had the fair skin and that long russet hair curling against her shoulders, but her face and arms were rounded with soft, voluptuous flesh. From her pose behind her husband and their daughter, Audra could make out the curves of fleshy hips.

At the very least, she was pleasantly plump. Some might even have called her fat. Indeed, the Esmeralda of this picture was certainly as heavy as Audra herself was right now. Audra glanced from the photo to the man before her, a sudden feeling of hopefulness combined with uneasiness settling in her stomach.

"Nice," she murmured sliding the photo back to Bradshaw, who returned it lovingly to his wallet.

"She said she'd been clean for a year," Bradshaw continued in his thrilling low baritone. "Wanted to apologize to Penny and me for . . . leaving us. Apparently she got a job here in the city—typing for some law firm . . ." He sighed. "But she didn't have a place to stay."

"And you let her move in with you," Audra finished.

"She's Penny's mother, for Christ's sake!" Bradshaw exploded, slamming his fist against the table so that their coffee cups jumped in their saucers. "She seemed better! What was I supposed to do?"

"I'm not judging you, Bradshaw," Audra said as gently as possible. "I'm just trying to understand what happened."

The man took a big gulp of air and offered a pained smile to her shoulder. Audra was turning her head toward it when she remembered: Except on rare occasions, Bradshaw seemed to prefer her shoulder to her face. After the picture, it was a sharp reminder: Even if Bradshaw didn't mind a woman with a few extra pounds, Audra was still no Esmeralda Prince . . . at least, not yet.

"Sorry," he muttered, and Audra focused her attention on the man again. "I'm furious with myself. And her. Penny was already all confused and crazy—"

"How is she? Penny?"

"Miserable. Says she hates Esmeralda, but . . ." His handsome head wagged from side to side. "Truth is she wants to be just like her and can't figure out why Esmeralda treats her the way she does." His eyes found Audra's again. "I took a few days off, let her skip a few days of school. Took a little road trip. Out to the Poconos. To clear our heads."

"Did it help, you think?" Audra asked, feeling a strange empathy replace her annoyance with the girl. "She was already dealing with a lot of stuff—a new school, being sixteen and tall—she needed this like a hole in the head."

"You're right about that," Bradshaw agreed. "Don't really know what to say about any of this anymore." His eyes searched hers. "I want to tell her mother, 'That's it. Stay away from her. From us. We've given you enough chances . . . but there's another part of me"—he shrugged—"believes people can change. Stupid, huh?"

"Not stupid . . . but . . . Bradshaw," she began slowly, "can I ask you something?"

"Shoot," he said, focusing his amber-eyed interest on her.

Audra hesitated, searching for the best way to ask the questions burning in her heart. "Penny shared something with me as I was leaving. She thinks you think she's . . ." she began hesitantly, "too tall. You know . . . ungainly." She paused. "Ugly." Her eyes found his. "Do you?"

Bradshaw was silent for a long moment, his big fingers curving protectively around the coffee mug. Audra imagined those fingers, cupping his newborn daughter . . . and then imagined the feel of them stroking her own skin.

"I think she's beautiful," he said bluntly, and Audra read emotion in his eyes. "Just beautiful." He frowned. "She knows that. Did I say something? Something she misunderstood?"

"I'm sure it was something like that," Audra said quickly, pretending ignorance. "What about Esmeralda?"

"What about her?" Bradshaw growled.

"Well, as angry as you are with her, you have to admit you think she's beautiful. I mean, you were married to her once."

"Yeah, I thought she was pretty, once. But now . . ." He shook his head. "Penny says her mother is ugly on the inside . . . and she's right." He locked eyes with Audra. "Why?"

Audra shrugged. "No reason." Apparently Penny hadn't shared anything of her *I don't want to be like you* conversation with her father. With her mother's betrayal, Audra suspected the whole incident had been blown to the furthest corners of her mind. Somehow knowing that Art had no knowledge of what had transpired between them and the true reasons for his absence erased the last residue of her anger toward him. She debated with herself for a split second, then decided, turning her face up to the man with a broad I've-got-a-secret smile. "You've heard my news, right?"

Bradshaw shook his big head and waited.

"You didn't hear about the television crew that was here yesterday?"

"Oh yeah," Bradshaw nodded. "One of the female officers is going to be on some reality show, right?"

Audra let her grin widen across her face until realization dawned in Bradshaw's eyes.

"You?" The big man sounded awed, impressed. "What for?"

"I've been selected for one of those makeover shows," Audra said proudly. "It's called the *Ugly Duckling* and basically they take ugly women, do a lot of plastic surgery and—and—other stuff and change them into beautiful ones who compete for a grand prize. I'm leaving in a few weeks. Off to California, where I'll be *transformed* into a swan. Isn't that a kick?" she said impishly. "Me, a beauty queen. Can you believe it?"

The smile drained bit by bit from Bradshaw's face.

"Ugly Duckling?" he said, his brow creasing with confusion. "Transformed? You? Why? You're beautiful the way you are—" He stopped, chewing on his lips like he'd revealed a deep secret.

Audra's mouth dropped open in surprise. *Beautiful* . . . Had she actually heard that word fall from the man's lips . . . with herself as its intended subject?

"But I thought . . . didn't you want me to talk to Penny because . . . I mean . . ." Audra tripped over the words, trying to find her way through her conflicting understandings. "I always thought you thought I was ugly."

"Never said any such thing," Art bristled. "And as for Penny, why wouldn't I want her to know a woman who carries herself with grace and humor? And that's what makes you—or any woman for that matter—beautiful."

Audra stared at him. "Is—is that from a movie?"

"No. Sorry," he murmured into his big hands as though too embarrassed to meet her gaze. "I shouldn't have said that." He pulled a few crumpled bills from his pocket, threw them on the table and rose, suddenly as nervous as a geeky band nerd. "I have to go. Gotta make sure Penny gets to school okay." He turned toward the street, then turned back, eyes on a spot just under Audra's chin. "You're . . . good to talk to, Marks. I mean about stuff other than movies. D—do you mind if I call you sometime? Maybe we could . . . do something?" And the remarkable amber eyes slid upward from her chin until they captured her eyes.

Audra's heart skipped, irregular and undisciplined, doing a sweet-and-low-down in her chest.

"Sure . . ." she said breathlessly. "That would be great."

He nodded, and gathering up every millimeter of his handsomeness, he strode out of the diner and into the Manhattan morning, disappearing into the foot traffic of the beginnings of the traditional workday.

It took Audra a solid twenty minutes to get herself together, processing everything she'd learned about Art Bradshaw, Esmeralda Prince and Penny. When she finally slid out of the booth, thrust her baseball cap on her head and stepped out into the cool light of dawn, her hands stuffed deep into the pockets of her too-hot-for-the-weather jacket to conceal them from the bright morning sun rays, a new feeling had crept into her heart.

Chapter 13

"**S**hamiyah . . . it's Audra."

It was about 5 A.M. in California, and the young producer seemed to take calls on her cell phone no matter what the hour.

"Hi Audra." She sounded sleepy, but not even a little annoyed. "What's up?"

"I'm sorry to wake you . . . but . . . there's something I want you to do for me, if you can," Audra said softly into her cell phone. "Someone else, I want involved with this show. Someone other than family I want on my contact list . . . and to be invited to the Reveal—"

"Shouldn't be a problem," the woman said pertly, and Audra could imagine her dark curls waving over her face as she nodded. "Go."

"His name is Art Bradshaw . . ." she said, suddenly hesitant. "He's a guy I work with—another corrections officer—"

"Consider it done," Shamiyah said, and Audra

could almost see her scribbling away in that note-book that seemed to be joined to her body at the binding. "Bradshaw . . . sounds familiar. Didn't you mention him in your audition tape? Wasn't his daughter the one who—"

"Yes," Audra interjected before they could go tripping down that path again. "But it turns out there's a whole lot more to that story. But I'm sure it's way too early—"

"Never too early for you, Audra," Shamiyah said, sounding fully awake. "Tell, tell, girl. I want to hear it all."

With a sigh of relief, Audra spilled the story from start to finish, sparing no detail. She spent some time describing the picture of a much heavier Esmeralda—she felt like she'd memorized every detail of the woman now—to Art's compliments, to his last remarks about getting together. Shamiyah listened, interrupting only for questions of clarifi-cation, and when the story was told in its entirety, she absorbed it in silence for a long moment before asking, "Anything else?"

Audra hesitated. "Tell me I'm doing the right thing again," she said, a little surprised by the plaintiveness of her own voice. "Tell me I'm doing the right thing . . . by becoming an Ugly Duckling. Maybe . . . maybe . . ." Audra struggled with the words. "Maybe I'm okay the way I am . . . maybe I shouldn't be doing this after all."

There was a second's hesitation on the other end of the phone, then Shamiyah said, "Why? Are you having second thoughts?"

"Well, yes," Audra admitted. "I mean, he said I

was beautiful. He said I had grace and humor. Me! Maybe—"

"You're doing the right thing," Shamiyah said reassuringly. "You're building yourself a brand new future, Audra. I mean, look at the confidence you've gained already. A few weeks ago, would you have had the nerve to invite this Bradshaw guy to the show? Would you?"

Audra considered. "I don't think so . . ." she said at last. "No."

"See what I mean? The changes you're making on the *outside* are giving you the courage to make changes on the *inside*!" she enthused. "Imagine what you'll be like when you've completed the whole process. You'll be a powerhouse, Audra! An absolute *powerhouse*!" Audra imagined her nodding so hard, her head full of springy curls were dancing a jig. "Don't let any of this stuff he said confuse you."

"But maybe he's right. I mean, I have lost weight. It's been really hard, but I know I look better. Besides . . ." She swallowed. "This lightening thing makes me nervous. Maybe I've done enough already. Maybe I should just quit."

"All because some guy said you were 'beautiful just the way you are,'" she said, pitching her voice in a mincing imitation that made the words sound shallow and lifeless. "Come on, Audra. That one's right up there with a 'good personality.' It's code for 'not my type.'"

Audra frowned. "But he asked if he could call me sometime—"

"He asked you to his daughter's party, too. Had he talked to you since? No." Shamiyah answered herself before Audra could get her mouth around the word. "Heck, he wasn't even looking for you today. You said yourself he just happened to work a double shift. If it hadn't been for that, you still wouldn't have heard a word from him—"

"But he's been dealing with a lot of family problems. With Esmeralda and—"

"Yeah, yeah. You've got some things to *learn* about men, Audra." Shamiyah sounded like she was rolling her eyes. "Let me lay some *knowledge* on you, sister girl." She paused for dramatic effect, using the silence as well as in any movie scene. "When a man is really *into* you, he can *find* his way to your telephone and your workplace and your front door. It doesn't matter what *else* is going on his life. When he's really interested, he'll find a way to make *sure* you know it." She let that sink in a second before adding in her worldly, know-it-all way, "I bet when he first met Esmeralda, *she* didn't have to spend three months guessing what was going on with him. I bet *she* didn't have to wait until she *happened* to run into him at work. No way. I bet he was sniffing around after her with his nose wide open!"

"What you're saying makes sense, Shamiyah," Audra agreed. "It's just . . . I don't know. I believed him, I guess—"

"You believed him," Shamiyah repeated the words, her voice heavy with skepticism. "Well, I guess we'll just have to wait and see what he does next, then, right? We'll have to see if he calls. He's got your phone number, right?"

Audra squirmed a little. "I don't know," she admitted. "I don't think so."

"Let me get this straight. He said he's going to call you, but he doesn't even have your phone number? Gimme a break, Audra!"

"I said I didn't know, Shamiyah," Audra exploded in frustration. "He might have it. Just because I didn't give it to him doesn't mean—"

"Did he look you in the face this time?" Shamiyah interrupted. "Did he look you in the face . . . or did he spend most of the conversation staring over your shoulder, or at your chin—anywhere but dead on?"

Audra sighed. She would have given anything to be able to contradict her—to offer evidence in Bradshaw's defense. But there wasn't any. She could count on one hand the times Bradshaw had shown her his eyes in the course of their conversation, and those had been startlingly brief.

"You're doing the right thing, Audra," Shamiyah said in the silence, her tone returning to calm reassurance. "You are absolutely doing the right thing!" There was another short pause before she continued with a slight giggle. "And even if you're not, you've signed a contract, so that's pretty much that. Now, get yourself over to the gym, sweetie. When your Art Bradshaw sees you again, he'll be eating his heart out with regret!" She paused a moment and when she spoke again, her voice had assumed a very different tone. "How's your mother? How's Edith?"

Audra rolled her eyes. "Don't ask."

Chapter 14

June 24

Dear Petra,

It's my last day here in New York. Tomorrow I fly to Los Angeles and the process begins.

I'm a little nervous, but mostly, I'm ready to go. Ma's been driving me crazy—scolding me one minute for being a fool, and pleading with me the next. She knows the only chance of stopping me now is to come clean, but she still won't do it. I'm beginning to think she never will.

And Shamiyah was right: I haven't seen Bradshaw since that day. He hasn't even called. She seems to think he just needed someone to talk to that day, and I was convenient. Just like he needed someone to buffer for his daughter on the night of her party . . . and I was convenient. That's me: Miss Convenient. Shamiyah's really becoming a good friend—almost

*like another sister. I would buy her explanations for
AB's behavior lock, stock and barrel if it weren't for the
movies. It's weird he watches the same TV I do. It just
seems like we'd have so much in common . . . if only
he'd take the time to find out.*

*But anyway, on the whole, I'm ready. The only
person I'll really miss is Kiana. I haven't talked to her
about it much, but I think she understands.*

*I'm using up all my accrued vacation and sick time
and taking an extended leave from work. I won't miss
it. I don't think I want to be a model when all this is
over, but I wonder how much longer I want to work in
corrections. I feel pulled to try something new . . . but
I don't know what. Maybe when I look into my own
eyes in a new face, I'll know.*

*Sounds like you're going to be on the move soon
yourself. Maybe things will have settled down in the
southern part of the country by the time your detail has
to make its deliveries. Keep emailing me—I bought a
laptop computer to take with me to L.A. just so we
can stay in touch.*

Be careful out there,

Audra

Shamiyah stood at the baggage claim when Audra
arrived, looking fresh and fashionable in a red
top with delicate flounces of lace hanging low
enough to be seductive but high enough to avoid being too sexy for everyday, another pair of low-slung
jeans and high-heeled red-tipped slides. Audra
took her in from tip to toes, deciding in an instant
that when she was finished with her makeover, she

would adopt Shamiyah's exact style, right down to the dangling earrings hanging from her perky brown lobes.

The woman was staring intently at her. "My God! You've lost another what? Twenty pounds?" she asked, nodding her approval.

"Only ten," Audra admitted. "I followed the diet to the letter but"—she grinned sheepishly, donning a Southern accent—"I loves Ma's fried chicken."

Shamiyah laughed. "Well, you won't be getting any of it out here." She appraised Audra again, this time with the cool eye of her profession. "It definitely looks good. For real life, I'd say this is the perfect weight for you. But for television, you'll have to lose about thirty more," she added, her inspection continuing. "And you really *are* lighter. There's a lot more red in your skin now than there was when we shot the New York footage a few weeks ago." She squinted as if that would make the differences more plain. "You've definitely gone from dark chocolate to milk chocolate . . . but it's not as dramatic as I would have expected. From what Dr. Jamison said, I thought you'd be"—she shrugged a pretty shoulder—"graham cracker brown or something by now."

"I was a little worried I might be white chocolate, myself," Audra joked. "He says he's going to up the dosage a bit now that I'm here and he can watch for side effects."

"Good." Shamiyah nodded, shaking her mountain of springy curls. "We want this makeover to be as dramatic as possible. That's the best way to ensure that all the sistahs from Maine to Honolulu tune in."

She squeezed Audra's arm, showing a few tastefully manicured fingers, then flipped her sunglasses down from the top of her head and started walking and talking at a speed many a New Yorker would have envied. "And that gives you the strongest chance to be voted Top Three," she said, leaning toward Audra conspiratorially, and Audra felt like the two of them were united in a common, secret mission. "I wouldn't count on winning the whole enchilada— that's probably going to go to one of the white girls— but I definitely think we can make the Top Three, if you keep working it. Now," she said, resuming her normal voice, "I've got a car waiting. Let's grab the rest of your stuff"—she grabbed the black duffel out of Audra's fingers and slung it over her shoulder by its strap—"and I'll take you where you'll be living for the next three months, and then—"

"Girl, we can go to the car now. There's no more luggage," Audra interrupted. "There's nothing of my old life I need with me that didn't fit in this little bag—underwear, toothbrush, deodorant and work-out clothes—that's it. When the surgery is over and we have the Reveal, the first thing I want to do is go on a shopping trip. Already set aside a budget."

Shamiyah draped her slender brown arm around Audra's shoulder. "If we play the marketing right, someone will be *giving* you that wardrobe when we're finished. Promise me you won't spend a dime without talking it over with me, okay?"

Audra nodded.

"Good girl." Shamiyah gave her another girl-friendly grin, then reached into the little red satchel slung casually over her other shoulder. "And speaking of gifts . . ." she pulled a little black case out of it. "Here you go."

Audra accepted the package, her mouth open in surprise. "What is it?" she asked the box, inspecting it from all angles.

"Open it, silly," Shamiyah laughed. "That's the best way to find out."

Audra pried open the case. Nestled inside were a pair of sunglasses identical to the ones Shamiyah wore.

"Wow—"

"They're really hot right now. Everyone's wearing them."

"Shamiyah." Audra shook her head. "I don't know how to thank you."

"Don't thank me." She leaned close. "The company is one of the show's sponsors, so I got them for free." She flipped her own pair down over her eyes and nodded for Audra to do the same.

Audra settled the glasses on her nose and pulled her baseball cap down low, then shrugged back into her long-sleeved jacket. It was so loose now, the sleeves easily covered her fingertips, blocking their exposure to the sun. Shamiyah studied these preparations, shaking her head. "You're gonna burn up out here, dressed like that!"

"Dr. Jamison said no sun—"

"But he didn't say no *style*. We'll work on it." The arm dropped around Audra's shoulder again. "Welcome to L.A., girl!"

"This is it." Shamiyah swung wide the double doors of a building in the same neighborhood as the offices where Audra had met the *Ugly Duckling* show's experts a few weeks before. "Home, sweet home. You're on the third floor. Letter J."

The letter J belonged to an apartment near the back of the building. Shamiyah opened the door and then handed her a set of keys, nodding her into the room.

The place was small but adequate. The horseshoe of the kitchen opened out into a living room, whose sofa, Shamiyah explained, converted to a sleeping area. "For the nurse," she explained. "The first few days after the surgery." Down a short hallway were a small bedroom, a small bathroom and a little closet. Completing the space was a ledge of a balcony reached by a sliding glass door that was covered with fake bamboo shades.

"And we've made sure you have the Classic Movie Channel, so you'll be well entertained." Shamiyah turned the TV on and off as Audra yanked on the cord to lift the bamboo. She had expected the room to flood with sunlight, but instead, the shady leaves of nearby palms clustered around the window like a jungle, allowing barely any additional light inside the apartment. The little place seemed like a cave. Audra was about to comment on it when Shamiyah hustled her into the kitchen.

"Your refrigerator is fully stocked with foods allowed on your plan," she said, showing Audra the contents with a quick jerk of the handle. "And there are some basic implements in the drawers if you want to cook."

"Where's the light switch?" Audra joked. "It's awfully dark in here, isn't it?"

"That's what the doctors wanted," Shamiyah explained with a shrug. "But the lamps should be working . . ." She crossed the room quickly and snapped a switch on the base of a lamp on the sofa-side table. "Yep. We double-checked everything yesterday when they brought in the food and took out the mirrors."

"Took out the mirrors?" Audra stared at her.

Shamiyah grinned. "You bet. Look in the bathroom," she offered, jerking her springy head toward that alcove. "You'll see."

Sure enough, where the mirror should have been there was nothing but a smooth brown patch of drywall.

"It really wasn't necessary," Audra called, wandering from the dark mirrorless bathroom to the dark mirrorless bedroom. "I hardly ever look in the mirror anyway."

Shamiyah's laughter floated back to her. "Liar! I saw you checking out how those sunglasses looked in every gleaming surface from the baggage claim to the front door of this building!"

"Yeah, but that's different," Audra murmured, returning to the living area, where she found the woman on her knees on the floor, rifling through Audra's bag like an addict looking for a fix. When she saw Audra, she flashed her quick smile, then pulled out a multicolored stack of undies and set them on the coffee table, to make it easier for her to peer inside.

"What are you doing?" Audra demanded, and for the first time Shamiyah got a taste of her corrections-officer voice. Her little body jumped, and for the fleeting second that her eyes met Audra's, she looked intimidated and afraid.

"Looking for contraband!" she said as though that should have been perfectly evident. "You read the stuff I sent you, right? About how you're not supposed to bring any mirrors?"

Audra relaxed. Of course, mirrors had been on the list of "no-nos"; she remembered that now. No mirrors, no makeup, no jewelry, no beauty products—

"There's no mirrors—or anything else that shouldn't be here—in there," she told the other woman. "Trust me. I don't even own much of that kind of stuff to begin with."

"I have to search, Audra," Shamiyah said in a voice that had suddenly gone flat and professional. "There will be no mirrors anywhere for you for the next three months. Not anywhere: doctors' offices, hospital, gym . . ."

"What if I want to go to the grocery store, or out to a restaurant? Or to do some sightseeing—"

Shamiyah shook her head slowly.

"You won't be doing any of that, Audra. No sightseeing. No eating out. No shopping—"

"But what—"

"You're here to completely change your appearance, and between doctors and trainers, shrinks and coaches"—the black curly head wagged a little harder—"your days should be pretty full."

"Are you telling me I can't so much as go for a walk unless you guys have cleared the route for mirrors?"

"Worse," Shamiyah said, grinning uncomfortably

now. She busied her hands with placing Audra's undies into one of the drawers of the cabinet. "I'm telling you can't take a walk at all—unless we say so. I know there's a lot of stuff in those contracts, but"—she sighed—"them's the rules and we've actually asked women to leave the show for breaking them."

"You've kicked people off the show?"

"You bet."

"But why? I mean, is this *really* necessary—"

"Two reasons." She held up a finger. "First, we want the cameras to capture your first reaction when you see for the first time how beautiful you are at the Reveal, and"—she hesitated a long second—"two, we want to make sure you look as"—she hesitated again, as if afraid of Audra's reaction to her next words—"unattractive as possible in all the scenes before the Reveal."

Audra stared at her for a second. "Like an ugly duckling," she said at last.

Shamiyah nodded. "Exactly." She patted Audra's bag. "You're clean, Marks," she said, trying her best to recover some of the jovial friendliness that had existed between them out in the sunshine, but the room was such a cave, even Shamiyah seemed to be finding it difficult to turn on the high-beams. "Two more things to tell you, then I've got to dash. We're in the middle of post-production on one of my other subjects—the first Ugly Duckling, actually. Her Reveal was absolutely stunning!" She gushed, reaching into her purse again, this time producing a thick letter, sealed with some kind of embossed sticker. "Your schedule and instructions for the first couple of days.

Open them after I leave ... and feel free to talk to yourself, mumble and grumble, lie on the floor and kick and scream ... whatever feels right to you."

Audra chuckled. "Now, why on Earth would I want to do all that?"

Shamiyah pointed to the ceiling, where Audra could make out several recessed openings filled with lenses and wires. "Because the *cameras* are rolling, Audra ... and of course, we'll be recording all your phone calls. That's why we had to have a phone list—and get the permissions signed by any potential callers in advance. And camera crews will accompany you on all your appointments, and of course we'll film the surgery as well. Pretty much every move you make and every word you say will be recorded for the next three months."

Audra blinked at her. "Every move? Every word?" Audra shook her head. "I'm not sure America needs to hear every word I say. Some of them might be a little ..."

Shamiyah took Audra by both arms, staring her hard in the face as though she were the mother and Audra were a child. "You're a student of the glory days of film, Audra, so you ought to understand what this is about—that's one of the reasons they *picked* you. You need to give the people a *show*, girl." She gave Audra's shoulders a determined little shake. "Remember what I told you the first day we met, about being willing to do anything for this chance?" She waited until Audra gave her a single, slow nod. "Then don't edit yourself. Let yourself be yourself. I'm counting on you." She shrugged. "Besides, you'll forget about the cameras soon enough. Until you do, just try to pretend they aren't there."

Audra nodded, tried to smile and cast a nervous glance at the ceiling. Right now—at this very moment—she was being recorded. Of course she was, she'd known that from the beginning . . . but the reality of it made her feel a little sick.

You've lost your marbles. Those had been Edith's parting words. And right now, it felt like her mother might just be right.

"You've got Dr. Jamison in"—Shamiyah glanced at her watch—"about an hour. The skin stuff is really important—it's a great visual effect—so you'll have a lot of sessions with him." Shamiyah squeezed her shoulders in a quick hug. "I've got to go, but the car service will take you there and bring you back—in fact, they'll get you to all your appointments. I'll let you freshen up a bit," she said gathering up her purse and notebook. "You smell like New York."

"Hmm."

Dr. Jamison put a finger on either side of her cheeks and turned her face from right profile to left. "Hmm," he said again, releasing her. He stepped away from her, stroking his chin and staring at her like an artist contemplating a masterpiece gone seriously awry.

Audra tried to forget the bright light being shined over them, and the presence of the two men—one resting a heavy-looking camera on his shoulder, the other supporting the light—which was exactly what she'd been instructed to do. Pretend they weren't there. Pretend she didn't have a microphone taped to her back and that she was just sitting in the privacy of her doctor's office having a heart-to-heart . . . which was easy enough with the man frowning and stroking his lips like she'd done something wrong. Before she could stop herself, a nervous chuckle escaped from her lips and she'd wisecracked in her best Bugs Bunny voice. "What's up, Doc?"

If Dr. Jamison were amused in the slightest, it didn't show in his mien. His critical expression didn't change, nor did his continual chin stroking, and still he said not a word. There was a lot about him that reminded her of Art Bradshaw—his sparse use of the English language, for one. But there was no point of thinking about Bradshaw, she reminded herself. No use at all . . .

"Yes, yes." The doctor nodded. "It's coming along fine. I think you haven't been taking my warnings about sun exposure seriously enough—but now that you're here, we should be able to address that."

"I don't spend any time in the sun, Doc, I swear," Audra averred, raising her hand for an oath on an imaginary stack of Bibles as if the gesture added instant credibility. "And I switched to working nights, so I could stay in days. And I wore hats, like you suggested. See?" And she waved the floppy baseball cap at him as proof.

Dr. Jamison fluttered his fingers dismissively. "Not enough. The medication you're taking depresses the melanin in your skin. Sun exposure augments it." He frowned. "In order to get the full effect of the medication, you must not just avoid the sun. You have to consider it to be your enemy."

Audra nodded. "Okay, so what do you want me to

do? Hire someone to shade me under an umbrella every time I step into the street?"

She'd thought he might laugh, might crack those thin lips into something she might recognize as a smile. But the doctor just blinked at her and said in a calm, quiet deadpan way: "Yes. That would help. As would a very wide-brimmed hat, along with a scarf to cover the neck and gloves for the hands and arms—"

"Gloves?"

The good doctor's bushy gray brows shot up. "Gloves. You must cover your arms and any other part of your body exposed to sunlight. That is, if you want to achieve the coloring we've discussed." He peered at her closely. "Is that still your intention?"

He seemed to almost be offering her the opportunity to back out, to change her mind, to reconsider— and in that instant a nervous fluttering of images swarmed around her like bees. Her mother and Petra, Art Bradshaw and Penny. Esmeralda Prince and Kiana's Ugly Duckling book.

Audra swallowed hard. "What color will I be when it's over? Graham cracker brown?" She reached into her duffel for the worn leather wallet and pulled out a picture of Petra, little Kiana astride her knee. The two of them grinned up at her like a two-person cheering squad. "Like them?"

The grim doctor's lips curved into a smile as he gazed down at her family. "Graham cracker brown?" he repeated, showing a set of well-shaped teeth that somehow made him look more intimidating, not less. "Yes, graham cracker brown. I think that's exactly what you'll be."

Audra nodded. "Then, yes. That is still my intention."

"I'll ask Shamiyah to see about that umbrella-toting personal servant . . . though I confess it would surprise me a great deal if that were in the budget." He paused a bit. "Your surgery is next week, I believe, so we'll begin an increased dosage immediately." Then he excused himself, leaving Audra alone with the film crew and the sick feeling she'd just offered up her first official, not exactly flattering, sound bite.

Chapter 15

Tuesday, June 26

Dear Petra,

Well, I'm here . . . and I guess there's no turning back now. The first of the surgeries is in a couple of days and I'd be lying if I pretended like I wasn't scared to death. If I didn't know what was on the other end, I think I'd back out now. Go home and live with Ma hollering, "I told you so," for the rest of my life.

Well, maybe not.

Please write to me as often as you can. I know things are heating up for you there, but it means a lot to have your support.

Be careful out there,

Audra

"**S**o, Audra." Dr. Anna Goddard crossed then uncrossed her legs as though she couldn't quite get comfortable. In fact, everything about the woman said "discomfort": the way she balanced her notepad on one precarious knee to the occasional glance she took in the direction of the ubiquitous cameraman. Which was weird, considering that his presence couldn't be a new experience for the psychiatrist. Audra knew for a fact that she was the twelfth woman made over on *Ugly Duckling* . . . and every single one of her predecessors had been required, as she was, to sit down for twice-weekly meetings with this body-image shrink. If anything, this woman should have been an old hand at being on TV and acting like she wasn't at the same time.

Dr. Goddard crossed her legs again, glanced at the camera nervously and picked at the fabric of her black slacks before flipping her notebook open and fixing her eyes back on Audra. "So . . . Audra," she began again.

"Relax, Doc," Audra joked. "I'm sure they'll make you look great."

The woman smiled. "It's not that." She rolled her eyes. "At least, it's not *just* that," she admitted, chuckling a little. "It's . . . well, I've been studying body image for twenty years. And to be honest, in my prior works, I've never really addressed the issues that affect women of color. I've been doing a great deal of reading and research to prepare for my sessions with you . . . and I'm hoping that I can be of help, without being"—she hesitated—"offensive in any way to . . . uh . . . your brothers and sisters of color." She offered Audra another nervous smile. "The last thing I want to do is come off as patronizing or unsympathetic when this is such a delicate topic. So if, I say something . . . you know . . . *wrong* . . . I'd really appreciate it if you'd correct me."

"Uh . . . yeah," Audra agreed, not certain of exactly what that meant, or what she was supposed to do.

But with that agreement, the doctor's face became serious and the last of her nervousness seemed to drain away. She clicked her elegant black pen into working order and zeroed in on Audra with target-shooter eyes.

"So . . . Audra," she began a third time, and this time Audra heard the shift in her voice. Whatever had come before was prelude, but this sentence was the real thing. "When exactly did you start to hate your skin tone?"

Audra's mouth fell open. "What?"

"You know, when did you look in the mirror and decide, "I'm too black.""

"Never," Audra shook her head vehemently, feeling her anger rising. "I never even thought about lightening my skin until I came here."

"I find that difficult to believe, Audra," the woman said. "In your audition tape, you called yourself fat, black and ugly repeatedly . . . and indeed compared to our American standards of beauty, you're quite different from what our culture considers to be the ideal." She pushed her glasses higher up her nose and peered at Audra knowingly. "In my readings about black American culture, there does seem to be historical preference toward lighter skin tones and straight hair dating back to the days of the Reconstruction, when it was somewhat easier for lighter-skinned blacks to assimilate than darker-skinned ones. And even earlier, to slavery. The conflicts between the 'house negro' versus 'field negro'—correct?"

Audra stared at the woman, too stunned by what she was hearing to speak.

"I know that black women are usually more satisfied with their body image than white or Latin women . . . at least as far as issues like weight go. But the skin-color issue is a very different image factor."

"Oh, really?" Audra muttered, not bothering to conceal her sarcasm. "Don't tell me we'se going back to the plantation now, is we boss?"

"Well, yes, we are." Dr. Goddard smiled a professional little smile. "Darker skin was associated with ignorance and poverty, lighter skin with education and affluence. Fairer-skinned women were quite sought after—at least until the 1970s and the Black Power movement," Dr. Goddard continued, sounding like she was dictating a chapter of her latest book. "And even now, biracial people are attributed with a certain comeliness, but their darker companions are not. I'm assuming that's why you want the lightening—to be perceived differently. Would that be correct? Have you incorporated the negative stereotypes of dark skin? And what was the first memory you have of being told something negative about your dark skin tone?"

As long as I can remember, as long as I've been alive . . . a voice whispered in the back of her brain, but Audra silenced it with a blink, assumed some Foxy Brown and snapped back, "All I remember being told is that black is beautiful, baby."

Dr. Goddard seemed unfazed by the attitude. "Which, of course, is true," she agreed. "But you know what I think?" The shrink leaned toward her and placed a gentle hand on Audra's knee. "I think a long time ago, someone said something. Something you carry deep in your heart to this very day. And you know what else? Whatever other reasons you might have had for joining us on *Ugly Duckling*, I think there's a part of you that wanted to do this show because you know it's time to get rid of that image of yourself. You want to erase it in any way you can."

A flood of pictures and voices filled Audra's brain. She was nine again, overhearing her father's "she ain't mine"; she was fourteen, enduring the merciless teasing of teenage boys and girls alike; she was twenty, in the criminal justice program and the ultimate "dog date" candidate; it was three months ago, and inmates were whispering "dude with breasts" in voices too loud to be considered talking behind her back. It was last week, and Art Bradshaw was looking over her shoulder rather than directly into her eyes.

These were embarrassing things, private things. They weren't things she could just blurt out, with cameras rolling, to a psychiatrist she'd only met once before.

"Uh-oh, sounds like a personal problem to me," she

quipped instead. "Wrong for the show. Not at all entertaining."

Dr. Goddard's lips lifted in another small smile. "I've worked with many women with terrible self-images, Audra. And a good number of them develop ways to compensate—sometimes overcompensate—for what they perceive to be missing. Some women work hard to be extra 'nice,' extra helpful. Others concentrate on being wildly successful. Their prominence or money becomes their shield." Her eyes found Audra's. "And some women use humor. Their weapon against the hurt is being the jolly fat woman or the prankster or the clown." The good doctor shrugged. "Some women also escape . . . into novels, movies. They create a beautiful fantasy life, imagining themselves to be Halle, or Joan or Bette. But it's still a shield. A way to hide the hurt." She raised an eyebrow. "What do you think?"

The woman's words resonated, buzzed and echoed inside her as though all of her thoughts and feelings had evaporated, leaving her hollow and empty. The room was suddenly too warm, too crowded, too small. Audra forced her lips into a smile. "I think . . ." she began, striving for lightness, for cheerfulness, and all the while feeling as if her mask of certainty and competence had slipped beyond easy repair. "It's not the sort of thing a funny woman—who would like to stay that way—would talk about on national television."

Dr. Goddard must have practiced her piercing stare for hours in front of a mirror somewhere, because she had that sucker down pat. She focused her super high beams on Audra with the expression of one who would not be denied. "Unless, of course, that woman was ready to lay those feelings aside . . . and become an inspiration to millions of women in the process." She glanced at her watch, closed her notebook and sighed. "Think about it. That's all for today . . . We'll talk day after tomorrow."

It was like living in *The Odd Couple*: Dr. Bremmar's upbeat-and-smiley-little-man routine, his white lab coat neatly buttoned to reveal a blue dress shirt and tasteful red tie; Dr. Koch his polar opposite: grouchy, sloppy, frowning and sipping at a cup of coffee as he stared at Audra through eyes so bleary that Audra wondered if he'd just crawled in from a wild night on the town.

The humiliation of another examination was over—an examination that had basically amounted to Audra standing pretty much naked in a sterile room, with a silent nurse for female company, while the two men took turns making marks on her body with a purple pen as though she were their very own living canvas . . . which of course, in a way, she was. From time to time, one or the other of them would direct a question in Audra's direction, or ask her to lift her arms or turn around. But for the most part, their conversation sounded like the pages of a medical textbook.

Audra stared down at her own body. In the places where the sun never shone, her skin was far lighter than in the places presented to the world, giving her an odd two-tone appearance. Dr. Jamison was right: There was work to be done. Whether it was for this reason, or because of her near nakedness, the cameras weren't allowed in the room . . . and this was something for which Audra found herself deeply grateful.

But as soon as the examination was over, there were the cameras again, stationed in Dr. Bremmar's office, already in position to record the discussions to come. There was no conversation at all for the time it took for each of them to be fitted with a microphone—both docs submitted to the procedure like old pros—and no conversation while Dr. Koch and Audra took seats behind the desk, as though this were just another doctor-client pow-wow. Dr. Bremmar stood, leaning against the corner of his desk, the better to gesture toward another computer screen showing front and rear images of Audra in a pair of gray workout shorts and tight-fitting Jogbra.

"We're scheduling your first surgery for Friday," Dr. Bremmar was saying, bouncing slightly on his toes, as though the prospect were the most exciting thing to have happened to him in weeks—perhaps months. And as if his body language weren't enough, he actually said the words, "Your case presents some fascinating challenges and opportunities and I have to tell you, I'm very, very excited about it. Both of us, right, Dr. Koch?"

Dr. Koch muttered something that sounded like an affirmative and took a loud slurp of coffee, staring first at Audra, then toward the cameras.

"Because of the variety of procedures to be performed, we've decided to stretch them out over several days. We'll begin with the liposuction. First I have to tell you how pleased we are with your weight loss and"— he turned toward the cameras a little, as though offering his next comment specifically for their benefit—"with the restructuring we'll perform surgically, when you lose the remaining weight after the procedure, you should see some dramatic changes in the shape of your body." He nodded a bit as though satisfied with himself, grinned big and fixed his attention fully on Audra again. "We'll do the legs, tummy and hips first. Dr. Koch will perform that surgery. Then the following day, he'll begin work on the breasts and upper arms. Then finally, we'll do the face: nose, chin, cheekbones, eyes." He stretched a forefinger lovingly toward her face, as though already imagining the finished project. "You'll be under general anesthesia for each procedure and there will be some risks associated with the process, you understand. But there are greater risks with trying to perform this many complex procedures simultaneously, so all in all, we think breaking the surgery into segments is the smartest protocol, isn't that right, Koch?"

Another grunt.

"In all the procedures, we'll work to disguise any scarring that might occur by working with the natural folds of the skin. We're counting on your continuing . . . uh . . . therapies . . . with Dr. Jamison to further prevent any other dark scarring in the process, but it's still a risk. Now, do you have any questions for us?"

Audra blinked at them. *Three days of surgeries. Three days under the knife . . .*

"You want to do three separate surgeries . . . in three days," she repeated slowly.

Dr. Bremmar nodded. "Actually, we'll do several different surgeries on each of the days. But basically, that's right. But don't worry. We've done this sort of thing before. Not often, of course. But given the time constraints of the show—"

It sounded like a hustle, a con. It sounded like something an inmate would say to shift responsibility or conceal the truth. An inmate . . . or a child.

"How long would you take to do that much surgery if there were no . . . time constraints?"

Dr. Bremmar's smile slipped. "Uh . . . well . . . it would vary, depending on the patient and scheduling and uh . . ."

"I'd wait at least six months. If there were no show. But like he said, we've done it before. With good results," Dr. Koch interjected in a flat monotone of a voice, then took another sip of his coffee and looked at them as though he'd never spoken at all.

"Very good results," Dr. Bremmar seconded.

"I'm sure," Audra murmured.

"Of course, there's greater patient discomfort when multiple surgeries are performed in quick succession—" Dr. Koch began.

"Sometimes," Dr. Bremmar corrected, as though this were an important distinction.

"Sometimes," Dr. Koch agreed.

"Discomfort, huh?" Audra rolled her eyes. "Sometimes, huh?" She shook her head. "Come on, guys. You can't kid a kidder, all right? What you're really saying is that this is going to hurt like hell, right?"

The two doctors exchanged a glance, and Audra waited, expecting their insistent denial. But to her surprise, Dr. Koch broke into a deep-throated laugh and Dr. Bremmar's ubiquitous smile spread wider across his face.

"Pretty much," Dr. Koch said.

"You betcha," Dr. Bremmar agreed. "Any other questions?"

"I wasn't expecting you." Audra held the door open wider so that Shamiyah could enter the small apartment. It had to be close to midnight, and instead of being shocked or disturbed by the sound of the doorbell, Audra felt an unexpected relief. She was used to the noise of life in an apartment filled with the drama that was her mother. By comparison this space was lonely, empty. "I was just considering shutting off the TV and going to bed—"

"Sorry. This won't take long." Shamiyah sank onto the foot of the bed and lay back, kicking off her strappy black sandals with a sigh. "That feels good. I'm beat, I tell you, *beat*."

"But you came by just to see how your favorite Ugly Duckling was adjusting?" Audra lay the back of her hand against her forehead and gave her a sappy, Hollywood diva-style sigh. "How touching."

"Well . . . not exactly," she said, suppressing a yawn. "I spent the day putting together another Ugly Duckling episode. Camilla just finished viewing it. She hates it. Says it's all wrong . . . lacks drama and interest." She sighed. "So I'll have to re-edit the sequences tomorrow. Put in a bunch of stuff about the rape—"

"The woman was raped?"

Shamiyah nodded. "Yep. She's kinda pitiful, actually," she said sounding almost casual in her fatigue. "But she had a beautiful Reveal." Her mouth stretched wide as she bit back another yawn. "God, I'm tired," she mumbled. "Camilla's a real slave driver."

"Slave driver?" Audra shook her head. "Honey, that woman sounds like a first-class bitch to me."

"No doubt." Shamiyah sat up. "But she's also the best at what she does. She created this show out of nothing, found the backers, got it on the air. That's not easy." A bit of ambition glinted in Shamiyah's weary eyes. "I intend to learn everything there is to learn from her. But that's not why I came to see you." She focused on Audra, suddenly alert. "I saw the tape from your session with Dr. Goddard today." Her eyebrows shot heavenward. "You were awfully coy. Why didn't you tell her anything?"

"Tell her anything?" Audra frowned. "Like what?"

Shamiyah frowned. "Don't play that with me, Audra," she snapped, in a hard, cold voice Audra wasn't used to hearing come from her mouth. "You know I need that footage."

"Footage? What footage?" she asked. "Remember me, Shamiyah? Audra from the golden days of film? I don't speak TV."

Shamiyah did not appear amused. "The stuff you

said on your audition tape," she said impatiently. "About what your father said. About the stuff the inmates call you at that prison. About what that girl— your friend Bradshaw's daughter—what she told you. All of it. I want that footage for the actual episode. I *need* it."

Audra waved her comments away. "I'm not comfortable talking to the doc about that stuff."

"Why? You've got something against psychiatrists? Don't like shrinks?"

"I've got no problem with psychiatry—"

"But you think you don't need one, is that it? Because—"

"I might need one," Audra muttered. "My mother certainly thinks so . . . but then, she's a fine one to talk." She lifted her fingers to her face as though holding an imaginary cigar. "Takes one to know one," she offered in her best Groucho Marx imitation. "Right?"

Shamiyah must not have ever heard of him, because she didn't even smile. "I need that footage, Audra," she repeated in a voice sharp as steel.

"You've already got it," Audra reminded her. "Like you said. On the audition tape—"

"The audition tape is crap!" Shamiyah glared at her, sounding annoyed that Audra had even bothered to mention it. "We can't use that!"

"Crap? Wait just a second," she muttered, not really liking Shamiyah as much as she had. "You've spent the past few months telling me how great that tape was, and now—"

"What's on the tape is great, but we can't use it. The production quality isn't what I need to make

this show look right. And besides, I need to feature
Dr. Goddard in this episode or she won't renew
with us for next season." Her eyes narrowed as
she fixed another determined glance on Audra.
"You were the perfect candidate to put her skills
and abilities to use . . . and what do *you* do? You
stonewalled—"

"I didn't *stonewall*—"

"You didn't tell her anything! You just pulled out
some tired old jokes—"

"Tired?" Anger crept into Audra's voice. "Whose
jokes are you calling *tired*?"

"Honestly, Audra. I don't know what kind of mo-
rons you deal with at home, but it's patently obvious
to everyone *here*"—and the way that she spoke
made it perfectly clear that in her mind, L.A. was
the hub of the civilized world—"that you're using
humor and fantasy to compensate for what you lack
in self-esteem."

A vein ticked in Audra's forehead. "First of all, it
isn't that obvious, since clearly you had to watch
Dr. Goddard on tape to come up with it," she told
the girl, hearing her voice rise with her emotions.
"And second, my self-esteem isn't as low as you
seem to think it is. And last, even I were willing to
put myself out there and discuss my dirty laundry
with the world, what makes you think I'm gonna do
that to my family, huh?"

Shamiyah wagged her kinky-curled head. "I
thought you were ready, Audra. That's why I lob-
bied so hard for you. I really stuck my neck out, you
know? Put it all on the line with Camilla." She
paced away from Audra, gathering up her things as

if preparing to leave. "She really didn't want you on the show. She didn't think you had what it took. But I insisted that you did. That you were worth the thousands of dollars in surgeries and consultations . . . that you were willing to stand up and be a real example to millions of women—"

"Shamiyah . . ." Audra sighed. "There are things here that I'm not sure I want to share with the whole world—"

"Then why are you here?" Shamiyah snapped, irritation palpable in her voice.

For an instant the two women stared at each other: irresistible force and immovable object. Shamiyah's face had lost its usual cheerfulness and in the blank expression she presented, Audra read a grasping hardness she'd never noticed before. Then, just as suddenly as she'd glimpsed it, the hardness was gone. Shamiyah stepped close to Audra and took her hand. For a second, Audra thought that the gesture was one of support, one of solidarity, but instead, she studied the skin on the arm carefully, then lay her own arm beside it, comparing skin tones.

Audra followed her eyes. When they'd first met, Audra's skin had been the color of molasses—deep, rich and dark—while Shamiyah's was a tawny red brown. But now, Audra's coloring had brightened to match the girl's almost exactly. It was the most striking evidence of the changes the drug had wrought that Audra had seen, and she stared at the two arms, as if understanding for the first time the process she'd set in motion.

"If you're willing to do *this*," Shamiyah said, gesturing toward their still-touching skin, "then you sure ought to be willing to tell the world at least some of the reasons why." Her eyes found Audra's. "Talk to the doc," she said calmly. "We need that footage . . . or the audience is just going to decide you're some self-hating black woman who wants to look like a white girl—"

"It's not going to come across like that!" Audra exclaimed. "No one's going to think—"

"They will if you don't tell your story!" Shamiyah nearly shouted. "Come *on*, Audra! You know how sensitive we are about color in the black community. If you just show up one color and leave a different one without saying a word about it, what else are people gonna think! But"—Shamiyah continued in a voice that regained its reassuring calm—"when you tell your story, you come across differently. You're . . ." She paused as if gathering steam to present her argument. "You're a person who doesn't like the hand she was dealt and has decided to use the resources available to change it. You're not filled with self-hate. You're . . . courageous," she said, nodding as though she heard a choir of *amens* in her head. "Personally, I think you're brave as hell to do this—and to tackle it on TV." Her smile vanished again. "But you got to give it to the shrink straight. We're gonna need that footage to help explain your reasons for making such radical changes. Okay?"

Audra's chest felt tight, as though her heart were being squeezed in a vise. The idea of delving into the depths of the pain of the past made her head hurt . . . but the possibility of being perceived as one of those black folks who hated her blackness was even worse. "I don't know," she muttered, rubbing at her temples. "I'll . . . I'll have to think about it."

Shamiyah hesitated, as though debating the wisdom of lengthening her pep talk a bit. But ultimately, she just nodded. "I'm beat, how about you?" she said, filling the space between them with a final elaborate yawn that seemed a little fake. "You should get some rest, too. You'll be meeting with the dentist tomorrow morning and Dr. Goddard again in the afternoon, I think—"

"And the nutritionist in between," Audra said, trying to laugh, but her heart wasn't in it.

"Right, right," Shamiyah said, but her tone made it clear that she was about as interested in the nutritionist's comments as she was in the current condition of the polar ice cap. "Oh, I almost forgot. I got you these." She pulled a wide-brimmed straw hat with a red ribbon around its base, an elegant red scarf and a pair of long, red gloves from her bag. "Throw away that baseball cap and jacket. These are much more hip."

"Wow . . . it's so . . . so . . ." Audra settled the hat on her head and wrapped the scarf around her throat, wishing for a mirror for the first time since Shamiyah had admitted her to this small apartment. "Audrey Hepburn."

"Exactly," Shamiyah nodded. "I thought you'd like it."

"I do. Thank you."

"No problem. And talk to Doc Goddard. Let's get the situation on camera for all the sisters and brothers out there to see, okay?" she said and waved her good night.

Chapter 16

Thursday, June 28

Dear Petra,

Thanks for the email. I got a little scared when I didn't hear from you . . .

It's funny, isn't it? I don't mind letting them cut me up (well, maybe a little) and I haven't minded Dr. Jamison's treatments. To me, those were meant to help me be more like you and Kiana . . . and even Ma. I don't mind knowing that at this Reveal there will be a huge blowup of me in my fat, black and ugly glory beside my new reality: something light and bright and slender. I know people will draw whatever conclusion suits them and I'm fine with it.

I don't mind inviting the public to watch all the external stuff . . . but I do mind the idea of talking to this body-image consultant and having my most personal doubts recorded for public consumption.

But I don't think there's much I can do about it now.
Maybe Shamiyah's right: Maybe it's better to explain
myself than to leave it alone and let people reach what-
ever conclusions about me that they want to. Or maybe
it's not other people I'm worried about at all. Maybe it's
just that I don't want to talk about any of that stuff. I
don't want to go there. It's one thing to beat Ma over the
head with it . . . It's something else to really think about
it, what it means to me, who I am, my relationships . . .

I keep asking myself WWPD: What would Petra do?
Enlighten me, oh wise one!

Be careful out there,

Audra

"**S**o. It's tomorrow." Edith's voice was heavy
with the lateness of the hour. She sounded
tired and defeated to Audra's ears . . . but it could
have just been a by-product of the thousands of
miles between them.

"Yep." Audra forced her voice to bouncy enthusiasm she didn't feel. "Tomorrow's the big slice and
dice. Or at least it's the first of the three days of slic-
ing and dicing."

There was a long pause. Audra could almost see
her mother's face: her cinnamon skin a little gray
without her makeup, her latest hairstyle tied down
tight in a colorful do-rag. She would be sitting in her
room by now, maybe on the bed, maybe at the little
desk that housed her computer, where she faithfully
typed an email to Petra every night, just as Audra
herself did, every morning. The image gave Audra
an unexpected sense of comfort.

"I don't suppose you're gonna back out now? I don't suppose you might change your mind before they knock you out and do what they're gonna do . . . because . . ." She hesitated for the briefest moment, before rushing on to say, "You can still come home. I know there's been some harsh words between us. But"—her mother spoke faster still, as if expecting Audra to rain anger upon her before she could finish—"like it or not, you're still my daughter and you can still come home."

But instead of prompting anger, a surprising feeling of gratitude welled up in Adura's heart.

"Thanks, Ma," Audra said softly. "But it's really too late. I've come this far." She shrugged. "I guess I'll see it through."

Edith was silent for a long moment and Audra half expected her next words to be in the "you're out of your mind" vein the woman had been mining for the past month. But to her surprise, her mother asked, "You scared?"

"A little . . . I guess."

"Well, I am," Edith declared with a little more of her usual fight and fire. "I got one daughter in Iraq and the other on a reality show." She made an odd strangled noise that sounded like a laugh gone bad. "From where I'm sitting, I got two children in the crosshairs and there's nothing I can do about it but pray."

Audra wanted to respond, to reassure her that all would be well . . . but with thoughts swirling in her head like the debris picked up by a tornado—each thought more confusing than the last—she knew there wasn't much she could say that would be credible. It was one thing to submit a tape, visit with doctors, smear some cream on your skin. It was something else to spend three days in surgery with only a picture generated by a computer to guide your expectations of what you'd look like when it was all done. It was something else to let people start picking and prying into your most private of memories and motives . . . and something else yet again to try to go home again after the picking and prodding— both physical and emotional—was through.

"All the ladies down at the shop can't wait to see you when this is done," her mother was saying. "I keep telling them they won't know you, but I don't go into the details. I mean," and again she spoke quickly as if to prevent interruption, "no one really knows how all this is gonna come out. Let 'em see for themselves, that's what I say—"

"Ma—"

"I don't want to talk about none of that, Audra," her mother's voice rose to strident. "You already said you're gonna do it anyway, so what's the point?"

"Ma—"

"Aren't you listening? I said I don't want to talk about any of it, so don't even try to—"

"Shut up, Ma, and listen!" Audra shouted into the phone. She inhaled deeply into the silence that followed. "I just wanted to tell you . . . in case something happens to me—"

"Nothing's going to happen to you. Nothing's going to happen to you or Petra—"

"In case something happens to me," Audra repeated loudly, drowning out her mother's words, "that there's a little document box under my bed—"

"Yeah, yeah, I know about the box under your bed."

Audra frowned. "How do you know about it?"

There was an uncomfortable silence, then her mother said, "I found it when I was . . . cleaning . . . one day."

"You haven't cleaned my room since I was thirteen, Ma," Audra said skeptically. "Now what were you doing—"

"Okay, okay," Edith sounded annoyed. "I was snooping, I admit it."

"Well, it doesn't matter now, I guess," Audra said smiling in spite of the violation. It was so typical . . . so Edith. And from three thousand miles away, there really wasn't anything else *to* do but smile.

"It's late," Edith said abruptly. "Thanks for calling, but you really should be getting to sleep."

"Yeah . . ." Audra agreed, but her heart wasn't in it. Any other time she would have been glad to escape from the nagging that was Edith, but tonight, she wanted her mother, could have talked to her mother all night long.

"Well, then," Edith inhaled, gathering herself together to perform a difficult task. "Good night."

"Good night, Ma."

But neither of them hung up. The connection stayed open, recording their breathing, each for the other to hear.

"I love you, Audra," her mother said at last, and her voice had the tight, strangled sound of a person who was trying very hard not to let anyone know she was crying.

"I love you, too, Ma," Audra replied, her own eyes filling with tears, and it was only then that she heard the light click of the receiver and knew that her mother had finally hung up.

Audra sank down on the bed, her mind reeling. The doctors had advised her to get a good night's sleep . . . but that seemed to be shot to hell now. There was too much to think about, too much to worry about . . . too much to regret.

With the touch of a button, the television sprang to life and Audra was transported, mid-story, into another time, another place. Gene Kelly was dancing . . .

She must have fallen asleep, because when she came to herself again, the phone was ringing. Audra almost pulled the pillow over her head to block out the sound, until she remembered where she was and grabbed for the phone.

"Officer Marks?"

Audra sat up, alarmed. The voice was female, youthful, formally polite, unfamiliar. A thousand thoughts swarmed through her mind as she came fully into consciousness . . . but only two had names.

"What is it? Is it Petra? Michael—"

"No, Officer Marks . . . it's me. Penny Bradshaw."

Penny Bradshaw?

"How did—" Audra began, but the girl intercepted her.

"My Dad got a call from the show. Asking if we would come to the Reveal . . . and for permission to use my name and . . . uh . . . comments."

Of course. Audra rubbed her forehead. "They

certainly are thorough, aren't they?" she muttered. "How much trouble are you in?"

The young woman at the other end of the telephone line twittered a nervous little laugh. "I'm calling you, aren't I? To apologize?" Her tone changed into one flat and carefully rehearsed. "I was very rude to you, Officer Marks, and I apologize. I hope you'll forgive me for what I said to you"—she lowered her voice to an eager stage whisper—"but I think what you're doing now is totally cool. Are they going to use what I said? Is that why that woman called my dad—"

"Hello?"

Penny's soft tones were replaced by a heavy masculine voice. "Marks?"

A thrill ran up and down Audra's spine, but she mastered it and managed a perfectly calm, "Hello, Bradshaw," like his call wasn't out of the ordinary in the slightest.

There was an awkward silence before he said, "Seem to be constantly apologizing to you," in that slow drawl of his. "Penny told me what she said to you. I'm beyond sorry—I'm appalled. She's totally wrong: I've never introduced her to any woman for the purpose of educating her on ugliness or anything like that. You believe that, right?"

Audra hesitated. Shamiyah started talking in her brain, reminding her of things done and not done, things said and things not said in the "Art Bradshaw" account. And again, the result was mixed: On the one hand, he'd called. On the other, the call was more of a matter of parenting than anything suggesting interest in one Audra Marks. At this point, Audra concluded, she really didn't know how to rate the man. She sat up a little straighter, tied on the breeziest of Bette Davis routines and said, "Don't come down too hard on the kid, Bradshaw. It's hard to be a girl, believe me. Especially if you're too tall, or too fat or too short or too smart—any 'too' is too much."

"This is no joke, Marks," Bradshaw grumbled. "I'm trying to teach her about character—about the things that really matter. But all she cares about is what her silly little girlfriends think and whether a bunch of dumbo teenaged boys with their balls in their brains think she's cute. Her rudeness to you is just—just—"

"When you were sixteen you had balls for brains, too," Audra interrupted, keeping her chin high and enunciating every syllable of every word as was the style in the films of Bette's era. "You may still have them, for all I know. The point is, she wants acceptance from her peers like most teenagers. Hell, like most people."

He was silent for so long Audra suspected she had offended him in her frankness.

I don't care, she told herself. *I'm sick of tap dancing around, trying to get this man's attention.*

"You don't sound so good," Bradshaw said at last. "You doing okay?"

Fat lot you care, Audra almost replied, but she stuffed the words back. "I'm having surgery in the morning . . . and . . . I'm a little scared," she answered truthfully. "That's all."

"Hell, give me a prison fight any day," Bradshaw muttered. "I hate needles and knives." He sobered a little to ask, "You changing your mind?"

Audra shook her head. "No. I'm going to do this."

"Okay," Bradshaw said quietly. "Then I guess what you have to do is keep telling yourself that you'll be fine. Say it over and over in your mind until you believe it."

"Do you think that will work?"

"Know it will. Got me through Iraq War, Part One," he said solemnly. "That and picturing myself getting home in one piece. When things got tough, I'd imagine that Kodak moment at the airport."

"Kodak moment . . . ?"

"You know it, Marks. When the soldier steps off the plane and his family comes running to meet him. See, Penny was just a baby then and I'd imagine holding her in my arms and hugging my wife—" The sentence came to an abrupt end at the specter of Esmeralda. "Anyway," he continued in his brusque military way, "just picture yourself getting what you really want. Feel the joy of it. You'll be fine."

"Joy?" Audra repeated. "Wait a minute . . . Is this Art Bradshaw? Hardboiled corrections officer? Talking about joy?"

"Joy is the only word for it—the only word I know for the feeling," he said softly. "The word for loving something so much, it comes alive with feeling. If this makeover does that—gives you that feeling—that's great. But if it doesn't, you gotta keep searching until you find that thing. That thing that gets your heart and soul involved with the daydream. That's what you want to think about and think about and think about . . . until it happens." He paused. "Listen Audra, I just wanted to apologize, okay? Hear that you're okay out there. Don't want to keep you up too late . . ."

"I'm fine, really."

"I'm not. I'm working the seven-to-three tomorrow. I've got to go to bed," he said, yawning, and Audra imagined him stripping off his shirt to reveal a sculpted chest. "I'll call you again in a few days . . . after the surgery . . . to check on you."

"Sure," Audra thought, wondering how many weeks were bound together under his "few days." "If you want . . ."

"Then that tears it," he said, using an idiom of a bygone era. "Good luck tomorrow," he said quickly as though he didn't like talking to her and didn't care to continue. "Good night." Then he hung up, leaving Audra with one more thing to contemplate.

She lay back on the bed, searching through the swirling images in her brain, looking for the one that sparked the emotion Bradshaw had talked about, the one that made her long for its fulfillment above all others. The one that connected mind and body with the power of emotion.

Of course the Reveal was there, and she saw Petra's and her mother's faces, shocked into stunned admiration. There was a sort of weird triumph in the moment, but behind that a surprising emptiness. She took the image deeper, imagining every detail . . . seeing her mother, her sister and Michael, little Kiana . . . but there was no joy there, just the discomfort of so many issues and hard feelings still yet to be resolved.

Joy, joy, where are you? Audra thought. *Come out, come out, wherever you are!*

She closed her eyes again, searching for joy along the streets of New York, and finding nothing but the sad reality of life without its presence . . . until the image of Art Bradshaw, walking at her side along the dim corridors of Manhattan Men's Correctional Facility filled her mind's screen.

Her body relaxed, her mind cleared, her lips curved into a smile . . . and she drifted back to sleep.

Chapter 17

July 5

Dear Petra,

Are you okay? No email in over a week . . . I'm getting worried now. Please write as soon as you can.
  Be careful, please . . .

Audra

One big, oozing incision.

That's what she felt like when she came fully to herself again about four days later, covered in bandages from what felt like forehead to foot. For the first few seconds, she had no idea where she was, even though it was the third time she'd woken up to the sounds of beeps and buzzes in the little recovery room, the third time an oxygen mask had made her face feel heavy and stiff, the third time for the pulse oximeter clipped to her finger and the EKG wires feeding from her chest. And for the third time, there was an odd sense of anxiety—a nervous impulse that bordered on absolute panic, that only subsided to manageable when, for the third time, a recovery nurse leaned into her face and said sharply, "Audra!" as though she were in trouble or something.

And it was so cold in the place, just like the other two times. Cold enough to make her want to beg for a roaring fire, or a trip to Phoenix in the middle of July. "Cold," she managed to force out of her numb lips, hoping the nurse would understand the word. "Cold . . ."

"From the anesthesia," the nurse said matter-of-factly. "I'll get you some extra blankets in a bit, but first we've got check on some things. Make sure you're all right . . ."

Then, for the third time she started the poking and prodding that went part and parcel with the whole experience. Audra lay still, focusing on nothing, still struggling to make her brain function.

"Looking pretty good, considering everything," the woman said, her examinations complete. "I'll tell Dr. Koch. He'll want to come in and look you over himself, but it's all over, Audra. You did it."

All over . . . you did it.

The words echoed in her mind, fraught with significance. *All over . . . you did it.*

But what have I done? Audra thought, the panic flashing fresh in her mind. At this moment, thick with bandages, drainage tubes in her belly, her thighs and buttocks encased in some kind of tight-fitting girdle that probably would have seemed sadistic even by medieval standards, she wasn't entirely sure what she had done. It might have been her imagination, but she could have sworn there was a camera in the corner of the room . . .

It was all too much to think about right then.

"Think . . . think about it . . ." she murmured.

"Hmm?" the nurse asked. "What are you trying to say?"

"Think about it . . . tomorrow . . ." Audra mumbled, closing her eyes.

"Why, of course, dear," the woman replied. Audra couldn't see her face, but there was a smile in her tone. "Like Scarlett O'Hara said: Tomorrow is another day."

"It's probably going to take three to four weeks for you to feel well enough to resume normal activities." Dr. Bremmar smiled as though this were a particularly wonderful thing, then did his little toe-heel bouncing bop like he was pirouetting for the camera behind him. "But I have to tell you, Audra, the surgeries went wonderfully."

"Better than I thought," Dr. Koch added, sounding like he really wished for a cigar and ice-cold beer. He was unshaven and tired-looking, as if her extended surgical procedures had taken something out of him as well. "I'm still a little concerned about the potential for scarring, but we'll keep a close eye on it. The pressure garments—"

"You mean the girdle?"

He nodded. "That should help . . . but if necessary, we may have to look toward the corticosteroids to break down keloids if they form. If that doesn't work . . ." He shrugged as if to say, "there's not much more I can do."

"Goodbye Ugly Duck, hello Frankenstein's monster." Audra managed to say it cheerfully enough, but the words stirred her deepest anxiety—especially as stiff and bloody and bandaged as she appeared right now. What if the surgeries had done nothing more than make things worse? What if—she thought quickly of her mother, of Petra, even Art Bradshaw and his daughter crossed her mind—she really became some kind of monster? What if, in her bid for beauty, she'd only made it all worse? And there were no mirrors, no way to check—

She shook the grim thoughts from her mind, fighting with a sense of depression bordering on despair.

As if reading her thoughts, Dr. Bremmar offered his optimism once again, and Audra received it with a tidal wave of gratitude. "I really think we'll be fine. Especially the face," and he stretched his fine-boned fingers toward her bandaged features as though he could already imagine the end results. "I was able to work toward the hairline for everything but the nose," he said, brushing at the air around her face in demonstration. "You may have to style your hair more toward your face in the future. Maybe some bangs?" he suggested with the happy hopefulness of a wannabe hairstylist. Audra could almost hear her mother grumbling, "Don't know what he's talking about," as the man continued, "And I'm optimistic that Dr. Jamison's treatments will minimize any scarring from the nose."

The nose. Audra couldn't understand why he was

so excited. She could barely breathe out of the thing, packed with cotton as it was. But Dr. Bremmar kept bouncing and smiling, then clapped his hands together. "I've got to say, I'm excited about this Reveal, Audra. Very, very excited."

"Doc, I got a feeling you say that to all the girls," Audra quipped, her voice sounding nasal and flat in her ears, like she had a very bad head cold.

Dr. Koch snorted.

"You're right," he deadpanned. "He does." And before Dr. Bremmar could object, he continued with, "So now it's time for the fun part."

"The fun part? More fun than I'm having right now?" Audra lifted her arm to gesture toward her heart, disturbing the incisions from the liposuction of her upper arms and all along her chest from her newly-lifted breasts. Even hopped up with painkillers, it hurt with a wrenching ache just bad enough to make her wish she hadn't attempted it. "You want to talk about fun, guys, my last trip to the bathroom was more fun than I think I can handle. I've resolved not to drink anything else for the next three weeks."

"It's good to get moving, Audra. I know it hurts, but—"

"Do you?" Audra would have liked to quirk a doubtful eyebrow at him, but she wasn't sure if she still had any . . . and if she did, where they were. "And tell me, Doc. Just how much plastic surgery have *you* had?"

Dr. Bremmar's cheeks went a little pink. "My experience with my patients gives me a pretty good idea of how you're feeling at this point," he said quickly, evading the question. "Anyway, what I wanted to tell you was, you can go home this afternoon."

"Home? You mean back to New York?"

Confusion twisted Dr. Bremmar's face for a moment before he laughed. "No, no. To your condo."

"That little joint ain't anybody's home," Audra reminded him.

"True," Dr. Koch weighed in. "But it's better than this little joint, isn't it?"

Audra turned toward the man with fresh appreciation. "You know something, Doc? You're absolutely right. When do I go?"

"Just as soon as we get all the prescriptions filled. You'll have a home nurse for the first week—mainly to help with the drainage from the tummy tuck. We'll see you back here in three days."

"What a relief! I've spent so much time with the two of you over the last few days, I was starting to feel like we should all get married."

The faint outlines of a smile ghosted Dr. Koch's lips. "I hear Shamiyah's laying in a supply of classic old movies on DVD, to ease your recovery. *Now, Voyager* tops the list."

"Along with *Imitation of Life*," added Dr. Bremmar. "She said to tell you she has both versions, 1934 and 1950. I've never seen it, but I hear it's appropriate."

Audra hesitated. *Imitation of Life* was the story of a light-skinned black woman desperate to pass as white in the days before desegregation. Not for the first time, a sense of unease stirred deep in Audra's heart, along with the deep desire for a mirror.

I've got to talk to Dr. Jamison, she thought with a panicked determination. *I don't want this lightening to go too far . . .*

"Did you hear me, Audra?" Dr. Bremmar was saying, looking concerned. "You're not in any discomfort, are you?"

"Just thinking," Audra wisecracked. "And usually that doesn't hurt. Much."

"And what were you thinking, may I ask?" Dr. Koch's wry eyebrows drew together in anticipation. "You got such a funny look on your face."

"Like you could tell with all these bandages," Audra quipped back. "I was thinking . . . never was a woman more blessed than I." She considered laying a dramatic hand over her forehead . . . but the memory of her prior attempt at that gesture kept her from moving more muscles than it took to speak.

Dr. Koch's expression made it clear he didn't believe her, but he chose not to press the point. "Well," he continued in his dry monotone, "if you thought it was fun going to the bathroom . . . the process of getting you in and out of the car is going be a trip to the Comedy Store."

He wasn't lying. Who knew that the process of bending to sit in an automobile used every single muscle in the body? It hurt four times as much as her legendary trip to the bathroom. Audra's new-sculpted thighs screamed, her reshaped arms ached and every muscle in her recently tucked tummy protested with every nerve ending in their entire surface. By the time she was settled in the front seat beside the driver, there were tears rolling down Audra's face.

Oh, God, she prayed. *Let me stay in this car forever . . . because I don't think I can stand the process of getting out.*

"It's normal to feel depressed after surgery, Audra. You know that, right?" Dr. Goddard sat in the chair at the edge of the bed, staring at her from behind her square, black spectacles.

"I'm not depressed," Audra muttered. "I'm in a funk. Literally. I haven't a shower in almost a week."

"Clever," Dr. Goddard nodded, acknowledging the pun. "But you know there are some very good reasons for that. The doctors don't want you to change those bandages for at least forty-eight hours to help prevent infection—"

"I know, I know. They've explained it a thousand times," Audra said irritably. "It's just annoying."

"It's a disruption of your routine. That's part of what makes people depressed after surgery—that they can't do what they would normally do. And the fact that, at first anyway, you don't look better. You look worse."

"I wouldn't know," she gestured around them. "No mirrors, remember?"

"Which is also depressing." Dr. Goddard seemed determined to diagnose depression whether Audra wanted to admit it or not. "Not having control of something as basic as being able to see yourself in the mirror."

"Well, I guess, then, I'm what you'd call 'surrendering to the process,' right?" Audra quipped, knowing full well she hadn't done any such thing with this talking-to-the-shrink part. She heard

Shamiyah's admonitions in her mind, heard her own promise to make every effort . . . but time and time again, she found herself vehemently resistant. She wanted nothing more than to get through this fifty minutes and be left to her too-dark lair in peace.

"It's got to be difficult. Especially for a woman with a job like yours. A woman who's used to being an authority figure. Used to being in charge of others."

"I don't really see it that way," Audra mumbled. The bandage packing in her nose from the rhinoplasty made it hard to talk and breathe, but this woman didn't seem to care about Audra's comfort. She wanted to talk and wasn't going to quit until her time was up.

"Then how do you see it? Why did you choose such a masculine profession, Audra?"

"I've always been interested in criminal justice," Audra answered quickly. "There's nothing deeper to it than that!"

Dr. Goddard was silent for a long time. Audra felt the woman's eyes on her, studying her carefully.

"I don't entirely believe that," she said at last.

"Well, whether you believe it or not, it's the truth."

Another long silence punctuated the space between them, the woman said in a low and careful-sounding voice, "It seems to me you've got all kinds of issues around your femininity, your appearance . . . even your identity."

Audra froze. *Oh shit*, she thought. *Oh shit, oh shit . . .*

"How long have you suspected your mother's former husband wasn't your father?"

That child's too ugly to be mine . . . The words echoed in Audra's brain and she closed her eyes tight against them. *Too ugly to be mine . . .* At the time, it had seemed like a good idea, but now, she regretted having used those words in her audition tape. These people seemed too determined to make a big issue out it.

"You've seen the pictures," Audra replied, her jaw clenched tight. "The differences in coloring . . . in body type . . ." She opened her eyes, fixing the other woman with a determined stare. "Look, doc. I know what you want me to say—and I know this is going to bring the powers that be down on me big time, but . . ." She shook her head. "I'm not outing my mother like this. I might be mad as hell at her, in my way. But I'm not accusing her of adultery. Not on national television."

"All right," Dr. Goddard said, as though she weren't disappointed in the slightest. She uncrossed and recrossed her legs. "So how did it feel to grow up the darkest one in the family?"

"Listen, Doc, I'm really, really tired. I don't want to talk about this right now."

"That's why we're talking about it, Audra. It's at the core of what's driving you—"

"All that's driving me right now is pain!" Audra snapped. "I can barely *breathe*. Everything from my neck to my kneecaps hurts—"

"And so does everything inside you, Audra." Dr. Goddard leaned forward again, giving Audra her most concerned doctor look. "Listen to me. You will never be happy with what you see on the outside if you're constantly running from the wounds on the inside."

"It's not painful," Audra shot back and crossed her arms over her chest, ignoring discomfort so intense that it made her eyes water. "These 'wounds'—if they ever were that—healed a long time ago. There's no point to re-opening them now—"

"Then why are you here, Audra?" Dr. Goddard's eyebrows shot up with an infuriating significance. "If you recreate yourself—if you completely reshape your face and body—aren't you erasing your parents, your heritage, your past?"

If she could have gotten up and stormed out of the room, she would have . . . but as achy and tired as she was, that was damn near impossible. Besides, this was her space. Let the doctor leave.

"I hate that you listen to my private phone calls," Audra hissed instead at the woman. "Don't you think this would be more productive if you let me bring up what I want to bring up on my own time?"

"But that's just it, Audra. You're an Ugly Duckling. You have no privacy . . . and we don't have any time." She sighed. "Look, Shamiyah told me about your reluctance—"

"Great," Audra muttered. "That's just great."

Dr. Goddard waved Audra's indignation away. "It doesn't matter. What matters is that you acknowledge that this decision—this life change—goes deeper than wanting a boyfriend, more than wanting to know what it feels like to be one of the 'pretty girls.' You don't know who you *are*, Audra. And unless you're willing to explore that question, all you're accomplishing is moving from a very plain, very lonely and very insecure woman to a very pretty, very lonely and very insecure woman."

Audra glared at her. "You know, I really don't like you."

Dr. Goddard pushed her severe glasses higher up on her long nose and smiled. "Yes. I get that a lot. Now, I think a journal might be helpful here, so . . ." She thrust a book covered in a plain dark fabric into Audra's hands. "Talk to it—"

"I don't have anything to say."

Dr. Goddard sighed. "Just try it, Audra. It won't bite you."

Audra eyed her suspiciously. "Are you going to read it, Big Brother . . . or should I say, Big Sister?"

"It depends. Are you going to talk to me?"

Audra frowned, but didn't answer. Instead she stared at the book and the neat gold-leaf pen the woman had clipped to its surface.

Dr. Goddard rose. "Why don't you write down all those caustic things that are going through your brain right now? Get them out on paper, if you don't want to say them." She patted Audra on her foot as if she knew it was the only safe part of her whole body. "You're doing well, Audra. Do you realize you haven't cracked a joke or mentioned a movie in this entire session? I consider that progress."

She reached for a large leather carry tote, nodded at the nurse and paced the few short steps toward the door. "Oh, Audra . . ." She leaned back into the room. "I almost forgot. Who is Art Bradshaw?"

Audra felt a flush coming to her cheeks and for the first time felt grateful for the bandages.

"Just a co-worker," she answered. "Why?"

The good doctor smiled. "No reason," she said

sweetly, then opened the door and disappeared into the hallway.

"I think it could be a good idea." Bradshaw's voice rumbled over three thousand miles to her, offering calm support. To her surprise, he'd actually called back, a couple of times. He usually didn't say much, just asked how she was doing and then, after a long, painful silence, hung up.

But tonight, Audra was boiling over with anger, and the bubbles spilled over onto Bradshaw. She let the whole story of the session with Dr. Goddard come tumbling out . . . or almost all of it. For some reason, she still couldn't tell Bradshaw about the lightening drugs.

I don't want them using that stuff on TV, she told herself, thinking of her mother, of Petra and Kiana. *I don't want to give them any more ammunition than they already have* . . . But she knew it was deeper than that.

She didn't want Bradshaw to know . . . at least not yet.

"Might turn up something," Bradshaw was saying. "Something that really helps you get a new handle on your life," he said.

"It seems kinda . . . stupid to me. Writing down my feelings and stuff. How's that going to help? I already know how I feel about"—she paused, editing herself before she mentioned anything about skin lightening or her parentage—"being the family ugly duckling. And . . ." She sighed. "I'm not much of a writer, Bradshaw. Or a feeler if you want to know the truth."

"Not all that crazy about it myself," he offered after another of his signature pauses. "When you're a guy of my size, people think you're invincible. A big block of flesh that don't feel nothing. They say all kinds of things, act all kinds of ways, because you're supposed to be so big . . . so tough . . ." He paused for a long moment, as though reliving a memory he chose not to relate. "Bought that bullshit myself for a long time. Too long. But the truth is, I'm human too." Another silence, but this time, Audra heard hesitation in the pause, as though he were looking for the words to say something he wasn't sure would be well received. "I've heard some of the things people say about you. You'd have to be deaf to miss them," he muttered in a low voice. "And I can understand why you want to do what you're doing. So you won't have to feel that hurt anymore. But people say nasty things about all kinds of people: big ones because they're big . . . fat ones because they're fat . . . beautiful ones because they're beautiful, ugly ones because they're ugly. Point is, you're gonna get your share of hurt from other people one way or the other . . . and you got to learn to deal with it."

The dude was more than just handsome . . . He was deep, Audra decided. And since she was protected by miles and miles and miles, she felt completely comfortable saying, "Thank you, Dr. Bradshaw."

This time the pause at the other end of the phone stretched and expanded into something almost large enough to have a life of its own. Audra felt something palpable taking shape between them, something that might mean something. Something exciting and different. Something world-changing and terrifying.

"Whistle if you need me," he rumbled, a bit of a sexy chuckle in his voice. "You know how to whistle, don't you, Marks? You pucker up and blow."

Chapter 18

July 15

Dear Petra,

I hope you're okay. I'm not sure I am. They tell me I'm depressed . . . I guess I am. Maybe I just miss my sister. I miss home. I even miss Ma.
  Be careful out there,

Audra

"So what color are you now?"
  Edith's voice had a familiar edge to it, like she was trying to sound like she was joking, when almost anyone with half a brain would be able to tell a joke was the last thing on her mind. Audra closed her eyes and pictured her: dramatic eyeliner and lipstick, her hair in some fashionable, youthful style.

"To what do I owe this pleasure?" Audra shot back, trying not to grunt in pain as she resettled herself on the bed. Reaching for the phone had been an uncomfortable stretch that jangled all the nerve endings in her torso, but to admit to pain would give Edith ammunition that Audra didn't want her to have. "It's two in the afternoon. Aren't you supposed to be at the salon?"

"I am," her mother replied. "But I own the joint, remember? I can take a break if I want to and make a few phone calls. Besides, I got something to tell you. About Petra."

A tingly feeling of anxiety coursed from Audra's stomach to her mouth, drying up every bit of moisture between them.

"You heard from her? You got through?" she stuttered over a tongue that felt like a dead leaf. "Is she all right? Michael, too?"

"She called," Edith said, sounding bright and relieved. "She's all right. Michael, too. Her detail's on the move, that's why she hasn't been able to write. They're going to be manning a new supply station."

Audra exhaled relief and inhaled a breath of fresh suspicion. Edith thought she was a decent actress, but Audra knew every nuance of her mother's voice too well to be fooled.

"A new supply station?" she repeated. "Where?"

"I don't remember," her mother lied.

"You don't honestly expect me to buy that, do you, Ma? You and I both know you memorize every word Petra says! Now tell me where the new supply station—"

"Well, I wasn't sure you'd want to know, considering you're out there in California trying to change yourself *into* your sister. I thought you might be more worried about how much you weigh, or the shape of your nose or whether your skin tone is closer to coffee or toffee—"

"Nice try, Ma. If we were talking about anything other than Petra, I might be distracted by those insults. But I love her, too, Ma, so I'm just going to have let all that bullshit slide." Audra sighed. A pounding headache started behind her eyes, a headache she would have liked to have blamed on the healing pressure of her face-lift, were she not certain its cause was a certain attractive hairstylist on the isle of Manhattan. "Now, where's the new supply station? Where's Petra now?"

"Well . . ." Edith dawdled. "I *think* she said a camp set up in the southern part of the country—"

"Fallujah," Audra said, feeling the hairs rising on the backs of her arms. "Is that where she is? Fallujah?"

Thousands of miles away, Edith heaved a little sigh that Audra knew instantly signaled the affirmative. "Shit," she muttered, knowing fully well that the Iraqi city was one known for violence and a high number of U.S. casualties. "Shit."

"She said she's fine," Edith continued quickly, covering her own concerns with annoyance at Audra's reaction. "No need to panic. She's fine. She even said to tell you her superior officer got a call from that girl—Shamya—"

"Shamiyah."

"That's the one. About her coming home for the

show. She said she'd email you as soon as they get the infrastructure set up."

Infrastructure. Audra nodded to herself. That was a word straight from Petra's mouth, *infrastructure.* Army-speak.

"Thanks, Ma." Audra sighed, feeling a week's worth of tension drain from her body in a single breath.

Her mother didn't reply right away, and when she did, she took the conversation in a different direction altogether: "I guess I should start getting ready, shouldn't I?"

"Ready? Ready for what?"

"I ain't stupid, Audra. You're up there, erasing yourself, erasing me and your father and our entire family—"

"I'm not erasing you, Ma," Audra told her. "I'm going to look more like you, not less. And as for my father, it's kind of hard to erase someone when you're not sure who he *is*—"

"His name is Andrew Neill." Her mother blurted out the name in a tumbled rush of syllables. "Andrew Neill. Not James Marks."

Audra caught her breath. "Ma," she began in a low voice. "You know this call is being recorded . . ."

"His name is Andrew Neill . . . or it was. He's dead now. Been dead, almost as long as you've been alive."

The words stretched around Audra like a swath of cotton, swaddling close, blocking out light and air.

"Ma—" she began again.

"He was a good man . . . a good man," her mother's voice rose, defensive and angry. "And you are so much like him. If he'd lived, I would have left James Marks—I would have left Petra's father for him and you would have known him, Audra. Then maybe you'd be proud to look like him."

"I look like him?" Audra repeated. "He's where the dark skin and bumpy nose come from—"

Edith sighed.

"All these years every time I looked in your face . . . I could remember . . . you don't know how many times I looked at you and felt—felt—"

"Ashamed?" Audra muttered. "That's what I read in your face over and over, time and time again every since I was a child." Audra heard her voice rising and swallowed hard, struggling to keep it down. "And you know something else, Mama? I'd bet every cent I'll ever have that we wouldn't even be having this conversation if it weren't for this surgery . . . if it weren't for *Ugly Duckling*. You'd have been happy to keep staring at me like you didn't know where I came from—like you wished I'd never been born—"

"Not true, Audra."

"Then why now, Mama? Why *now*?"

From the other end of the phone, a long painful silence, but no words. Audra felt her anger crest and subside in that silence, making her insides hollow and dry, as though every drop of feeling inside her had been wrung out.

"That girl Shamiyah. She said they need it to help you. That you need it to . . . move on. She said they'll keep it confidential . . ." Edith continued. "I been thinking a lot. And maybe I should have told you a long time ago, but I didn't. I thought it was for the best." Her voice had an edge of nastiness to it as she said, "I suppose now you blame me."

"Well, who else is there?"

"Fine, then, blame me," Edith said tersely. "But while you're blaming me, you ought to understand. It's not so simple. I was a young woman with two little girls. In the time James Marks and I stayed together I was able to get this salon up and running. Provide for you two. That's something, isn't it?"

Questions swirled in Audra's mind by the dozens: angry questions, sad questions, practical questions, dumb questions. But before she could stammer out the first of them, her mother muttered, "Shit, my customer's here. I told that girl Shamiyah I won't be coming out there. You do what you gotta do. I don't need to see it," and Audra could hear her proclaiming to someone in the distance, "Well, girl, I know why you're early. Your head is a *mess*—" then the connection was severed and Audra was alone with the information she'd waited a lifetime to hear.

"Andrew Neill." Bradshaw repeated the man's name slowly. "That's it? That's all you know? Just his name?"

"That's it." Audra repeated.

She wasn't sure why, but he was the first person she'd called.

"This is pretty heavy, Marks," he began.

"I guess that's not even my name," Audra interrupted, trying to laugh it off. "My name should probably be Neill, too . . ." She stopped, her voice faltering. She was silent for a long moment, trying to master herself and failing. Tears slipped from her eyes and rolled unchecked down her face.

Art Bradshaw seemed to know what was going on. For the longest time, he didn't say a word, and in a way, his silence just made it worse. Audra dabbed at her face, still bandaged at the brow and around the chin, her nose still packed with cotton. She snuffed in a ragged breath through her mouth and muttered, "I'm sorry," in a shattered voice.

"It's okay," he murmured and Audra heard the words as license to sob in earnest.

"I don't understand her," she stammered. "How she can just drop this on me . . . then go and do some woman's *hair*"—she gave a wild chuckle— "Have you ever heard anything like it?"

"Beats any movie I've ever seen."

"You got *that* right." Audra sniffed, struggling to bring herself under control. "Of course, they pretty much didn't do story lines like this back in the thirties and forties. I think that's one of the reasons I like those movies so much . . . Everything was so . . . squeaky clean."

"This isn't your fault . . . uh . . . Audra." Bradshaw sounded uncomfortable in a way Audra hadn't expected. Not with the information, but with her pain. Like he wished he were closer or something. "Might not be hers, either. Your father—at least the man you thought was your father—he doesn't sound like much of a guy if he walked out on you guys all those years ago."

"He did . . . and he wasn't. I—I—always felt like that was my fault, too . . ." Audra whispered, feeling her fragile control slipping away again. "Like . . . they might have stayed married . . . if only . . . if only . . . I'd never . . . been born . . ."

And then the tears were there again, drowning out any hope of speech. Audra covered her eyes with one hand as if that would somehow stop them, but it was like a damn had burst inside her and now there was nothing to stop the flood of feeling from its release. And Art Bradshaw kept murmuring, "It's okay, it's okay," in a gentle, encouraging voice that made it that much harder to stop, so she kept crying and crying . . . until finally there was a big empty space in the pit of her stomach where the tears had been.

"Andrew Neill . . ." Art said when Audra had calmed herself enough to listen again. "You say he died the same year you were born?"

Audra nodded. "That's what she said."

"In New York?"

"I—I think so. Why?"

"Maybe we can find out about him. At least something. Maybe there's some records. Maybe a photo. You might even have more family, Audra. Got a buddy from Gulf War One whose a P.I. now. I could call him. See what he can find out. Dude owes me a favor anyway—"

"You'd do that?" Audra interrupted.

"If you want me to. If it would help. Do you want to know?"

"Yes," Audra said, not needing to think about it. "Yes, I want you to. Yes, it would help and yes, I want to know."

"Consider it done then. Just don't get your hopes up. He might not be able to find anything, and even if he can, it might take a while."

"Thanks, Bradshaw—"

"Better make it Art."

"Thanks . . . Art."

"No problem. But you've got to promise me you'll do something."

Audra felt her heart banging hard in her chest. He'd only made one other request of her since she'd known him—and that had been the fiasco at Penny's party that had had its role in bringing her here, to *Ugly Duckling*. So this moment she wasn't entirely sure she was as happy about it as she had once thought she would be. "W—what?" she stammered. "What do you want me to promise? What do you want me to do?"

"Promise me you'll talk this through with that therapist—what's her name again?"

"Goddard."

"That's the one." Audra could hear the smile in the man's voice. "Remember in *Now, Voyager*, Bette Davis had Dr. Jaquith? Well, she's your Dr. Jaquith, and if you're any kind of Bette, you'd better use her."

"I don't know . . ." Audra protested. "I really don't want them using this stuff in the show . . ."

"Didn't Shamiyah promise your mother all this was off-limits?"

"Yes, but—"

Art silenced her with the force of his voice. "You talk to her, and I'll talk to my friend. Deal?"

Chapter 19

"**I**s that it?" Dr. Goddard nodded toward the thick brown mailing envelope Audra held pressed to her chest by a single brown hand.

Audra nodded in the affirmative, unsure that she could get her vocal cords to cooperate. Art's friend, the private investigator, had worked amazingly fast and now she was holding in her hands an envelope from his office. An envelope that, she knew, held both the keys to her past, as well as, in many ways, the hope of her future.

Shamiyah had shown up to deliver it personally, handing it to her just a few moments before Audra had arrived for this appointment. She stood in the hallway, just outside Dr. Goddard's office, turning the thing over and over in her hands.

"I assume you've been waiting for this," she said with an eagerness that didn't match the vibe of the moment, and she held the package toward the cameras for a second too long before she stuffed it into

Audra's hands with a quickly murmured, "Oops." "I'm dying to hang around and see what's in it, but I guess I'll just have to wait," she said, squeezing Audra's shoulder. "Good luck!" Then she set off down the halls, humming a little to herself, swinging her round hips in yet another pair of designer jeans.

"Would you like me to open it, or would you like to do it?" the good doctor asked gently, when Audra had done nothing more than turn the envelope in her hands a few times. The cameraman had taken a spot across from her and she felt the light on her face, but she'd become so accustomed to him, it was like he wasn't there.

All that mattered was the envelope, and yet, Audra realized with a sudden jolt of fear that shook her to her heart's core, she was absolutely terrified of knowing what lay inside. Instead, she focused her eyes on the doctor.

"Do you think she loved him?" she asked at last. "That it was more than just . . . Oh, I don't know. Some kind of cheap thrill?"

"Oh, I'm certain she loved him," Dr. Goddard said without hesitation.

"How can you be so sure?"

Dr. Goddard smiled. "You're here, aren't you?"

"Yeah, but—"

"There's no 'but.' That she chose to have you is love. She raised you and kept you and took care of you—"

"I know all that, but . . ." She shrugged. "Maybe she felt like she had to. Maybe—"

"Even *that's* a kind of love, Audra," Dr. Goddard

said, sounding suddenly ancient, suddenly wise. "She loves you, doesn't she? You fight, you misunderstand each other, you drive each other crazy . . . but you've never *really* doubted that she loves you, have you?"

Audra considered. Dr. Goddard was right: Whatever else stood between them, however odd the form it took, Audra had never doubted that Edith's love for her was genuine. But still she paused, stroking the envelope, pinioning the doctor with, "She didn't deny that when she looks at me . . . she feels ashamed."

"Of *herself*, Audra. Not of *you*."

Audra shook her head, her eyes filling with tears. "No."

"Yes." The doctor handed her a tissue from a very full dispenser placed on the coffee table between them. "Close your eyes, Audra." Audra complied. "Now, think about it, Audra. Put yourself in her shoes if you can. You're a married woman and you've fallen in love with another man. You're pregnant by this other man, but before you work up the nerve to tell your husband and leave, he's killed in an accident—or at least that's how much of the story we've been able to piece together so far." She leaned into Audra's space from her armchair. "Now if that were you—and I personally think you and your mother have to be a lot alike—if that were you, how would you feel? Would you be mad at the baby—"

"Of course not—" Audra began, but Dr. Goddard kept speaking right over her.

"Or would be mad at yourself? And every time you looked at that child, you'd be thinking, *Why didn't I act sooner?* or, *I wish I'd done this differently*, or even, *God, why did you take him?* But you wouldn't be mad at the child. Sad, maybe. Maybe you feel bad. For yourself. For the child . . ." She let her voice trail off and for a long second there was silence in the room. "But you wouldn't be mad. And meanwhile, that child would be watching your face, thinking she's the thing that's making you feel sad, bad and mad. And that would be just wrong. Dead wrong."

Audra couldn't form words to respond. A huge lump rose in her throat, choking off everything but an odd feeling of release. It was like a golden key had been slipped into a secret lock somewhere deep in Audra's heart.

"I think it's time you met your father," Dr. Goddard said gently, nodding toward the envelope. "When a young woman makes peace with her father, she opens herself up to have loving relationships with men. Open it. There's nothing but love for you in there . . . if you're willing to see it."

Audra nodded. Through a haze of tears, she positioned her fingers at the lip of adhesive running along the top of the brown paper and tugged.

It ripped easily, sending a small stack of miscellaneous papers spilling out over the coffee table in a sudden disorganized jumble. Later, Audra would know the investigator had included his report, a few official documents, and a folded letter, handwritten on what appeared to be paper torn from a notebook. But at first her eyes followed the snapshot as it floated from the envelope to the floor, landing face down on the doctor's thickly carpeted floor. Audra bent to retrieve it.

Her own face stared out at her, only it was settled on a thick chunk of masculine body, leaning against a land yacht, a two-toned Cadillac from back in the day. He had deep chocolate skin, smoky black eyes and full lips, and was smiling a smile that seemed tailor made for this moment of reunion.

"Hi, Dad," Audra whispered as fresh tears streamed down her face. She stroked the photo with her fingertips. "It's nice to finally meet you."

Chapter 20

July 25

Dear Petra,

Glad you were able to get a message off to Ma about
your deployment. I was pretty worried, not hearing
from you for so long.

I'm doing okay. Starting to heal. Been doing a lot of
thinking . . . a lot of self-discovery. Or rediscovery, as the
case may be. It sucks . . . but it's easier than worrying
about how I'm going to look when all this is over with.

I stopped using the lightening cream. I told Dr.
Jamison that now that I'd met my father, I thought I'd
had enough. He didn't argue—actually he didn't say
much of anything about it, except to remind me to stay
out of the sun unless I want to look like a checkerboard.
Apparently once you start using this lightening cream,
weird things can happen to your skin when you stop.
But it seems to have done the job: I don't have any

keloid scars. In fact, I don't have any scars at all. I guess that's why Dr. Jamison let me stop without a word. Even Shamiya hasn't said a thing. Which, in a way, makes me more nervous than if they'd all lined up in the hallway, trying to persuade me.

I'm not quite as light as you are . . . but I think this is enough.

I have a lot of conflicting emotions about this whole thing, now. On the one hand, I want to see it through. But I wonder, if Ma could only have told me sooner . . . would I have still wanted to go through with it? I look just like him, Petra. Or I used to. Would I have wanted to bear the face of a man I never even knew?

I have no way of answering that . . . and it's too late now anyway. Most of the bandages are off and I'll be starting the exercise regimen soon. Talking to Bradshaw helps. Did I tell you he calls almost every night? No, it's not like that. Nothing romantic (though I confess, I still have some pretty hot dreams about him). It's weird. He's turned out to be kinda like my best friend. I wonder if he still will be when I get back to New York.

Anyway, write when you can.

Be careful out there,

Audra

"Bradshaw . . ."

It was one of those conversations that began with a focus and lapsed into an easy silence before picking up and sailing into fresh waters. They'd been lulling for a while, enjoying each other's silent company, when the question tickled at the back of Audra's brain.

"Can I ask you something?" she said before she changed her mind.

"Can I stop you?" Bradshaw quipped, then chuckled, sounding completely at ease. Audra couldn't stop a little trill of desire from chasing through her, but she beat it down with a mental *We're just friends* and pressed on.

She backpedaled a bit, trying to think of a way to phrase the question that wouldn't sound either too angry or too desperate and ended up with, "Well, you're a man, right?"

Bradshaw's mellow basso chuckle deepened into a hearty belly laugh. Audra imagined his handsome face turned up with laughter and wished for the ten thousandth time she were in New York, enjoying the pleasure of his laughter face-to-face. "Yeah, Audra, I'm a man. Or at least I was last time I checked. You want me to verify it again before we go on?"

"Never mind." Audra rolled her eyes in exasperation. "I didn't mean it like that and you know it. I meant—"

"You need a male perspective," he finished for her. "I get it. Ask away. But perspectives are like . . . uh . . . armpits. Everyone's got 'em."

"Armpits?" Audra squealed. "That's a new one."

"Well . . . I'm too much of a gentleman to say something disrespectful or profane in the presence of a lady."

"I work in a *prison*, Bradshaw. I've heard every kind of disrespect and profanity imaginable and you know it."

"Not from me you haven't. And I'd like to keep it that way. Now, ask your question. And if my armpit doesn't please, well," he said, "there's another aroma, right?"

Audra giggled in spite of herself. Armpits . . . ridiculous. But the silliness made it easier to ask.

"I don't get you men," Audra admitted. "Do any of you know what you want?"

Bradshaw let out another of his booming chuckles—and in the background, Audra heard Penny exclaim, "Dad!" Audra imagined her rolling her eyes at him in dramatic mortification.

"We men! Do any of you *women* know what you want?"

"Okay." Audra nodded. "That's fair. Nobody knows what they want—"

"I didn't say that, either. Or at least, I didn't mean it that way," he corrected. "I just mean that most *people* don't know what they want, or how to get it . . . or even who they are. Which makes the ones who do that much more likely to succeed. Take you, for example. You knew what you wanted—"

"Whoa." Audra shook her head. "It wasn't so much that I knew what I wanted. More that I knew what I *didn't* want."

"And what was that?"

Audra hesitated. For some reason, it was always hard to talk to Bradshaw about the physical aspects of her *Ugly Duckling* transformation. Hard to say fat, black and ugly . . . hard to explain about the face-lift and the dieting—and impossible to mention the skin lightening at all. It just all seemed so superficial, when time and time again, Bradshaw had proved himself to be more than handsome, but smart, compassionate and kind.

"I knew I felt unattractive," Audra said carefully. "And I knew I didn't want to feel that way any more." She shook aside the words before they demanded further analysis. "Besides, I don't want to talk about me. I want to talk about you, Bradshaw. Do you know what you want and how to get it? Do you know who you are?"

It would have been hard to miss the earnestness in her tone, and she wasn't surprised when Bradshaw paused to consider carefully before answering.

"I know some things I want . . ." he said seriously. "And I know some of the steps I can take to get them. But a lot of what I want involves the wants of other people. And unless those other people want what I want, short of some heavy persuasion, there may not be a lot I can do."

Something—whether it was the intensity of his words or the expression that she imagined accompanied them, Audra didn't know—sent Audra's internal temperature toward the heat of August. She fanned herself in her dim California hideaway, feeling almost like something inside him was speaking directly to something directly inside her.

"Thanks for that non-answer," Audra murmured, still trying to sound flippant light, even though there were deep currents of attraction racing though the phone lines. "Now, would you please tell us ordinary, plain-speaking folks what the hell you're talking about?"

There was a characteristic hesitation before he spoke.

"I'm looking forward to seeing you again, Audra," he said simply. "Why don't we talk about that more when we can sit down face-to-face. When you're back in New York. Okay?"

Audra's heart skittered to the pit of her stomach. It sounded almost like—like—"Yeah," she murmured. "We can do that, but . . ." She hesitated. "Suppose they've botched this surgery. Suppose—"

"Do you really think I'm that shallow?" he asked, sounding deeply offended.

"No," Audra responded, hoping it was the truth. Then she let the silence engulf them again.

Chapter 21

July 30

Dear Petra,

I have a whole other family I never knew about. Most of them live in the Caribbean, scattered around the Virgin Islands. I guess I've got an "in" now on St. Thomas, St. John and St. Croix.

As soon as she heard the news, Shamiyah wanted to invite them to the Reveal. I had to remind her that she'd agreed not to air any of this paternity stuff—she gave Ma her solemn promise. She looked really disappointed. Art thinks she had already written the script to one of those reunion shows in her mind. He's probably right. I don't know what I would have done without him the past few weeks. It's funny: My being here is letting us get to know each other in a way we probably never would have if we could see each other face-to-face.

So, of course now I worry about the face-to-face. What if he doesn't like the outside, Petra? He didn't before . . . he couldn't even look at me. But what if in person, there's still no chemistry for him (girl, you know I got chemistry for him—always have!)

Speaking of Ma (I know, I wasn't. But she's always just beneath the surface, isn't she?) Dr. Goddard says the next step in my healing is to forgive her. I feel like I already have, but she thinks Ma and I still need what she calls a "clearing." (She doesn't know our Ma!) It's kinda hard to have a clearing with a woman who won't even allow you to bring up the subject . . .

I guess that's going to take some time.

Speaking of time, mine is up. I'm going to the gym today—for the first time since the surgery. Looking forward to it.

Be careful out there,

Audra

"**N**o excuses, Audra. It's time to take this seriously—as seriously as your surgeries or your diet or any other part of the process—"

"I'm not making excuses. I'm just telling you that I was just cleared for normal activities yesterday, and this is hardly a normal activity—at least not for me."

Audra spoke from a position of precarious balance atop a bright red exercise ball.

"It's perfectly safe, Audra." Julienne had the hard, no-sympathy voice of a drill instructor. "Now quit your bellyaching and lay back like I told you—" Audra felt a pair of pincer-like fingers curl over her shoulder and proceed to gently force her into compliance.

Audra resisted, feeling an uncomfortable twinge in her abdominals with the effort. By far, of all the surgeries the tummy tuck and the nose job were the worst. And probably, for the sheer gross-out factor—what with tubes stuck inside her to drain the excess fluid resulting from the procedure—and for pure, unadulterated pain, the tummy tuck won the close race between the two. Having just gotten to the point that she could get in and out of bed without feeling like her guts were going to start spilling out between her fingers, Audra wasn't about to take any chances, bossy personal trainer or not.

"I'm telling you, Julienne, I'm not ready for—"

Julienne's face appeared beside Audra's own, pink with righteous, zealous anger. "I'm telling *you*, if you keep resisting, you'll never be ready for your Reveal. All of you Ugly Ducklings are the same: You don't want to take responsibility for yourselves. You think the surgery alone will fix you. But I'm here to tell you, the surgery only goes so far. The rest is hard work, diet and exercise, and more hard work! You have to get some discipline or—"

"Look," Audra hissed back at the woman. "Don't accuse me of having no discipline, because I've got as much of it as you! And I was in good shape when I got here! I have to be, to keep my job, okay? But I think I know my own body well enough to know—"

"Do you?" Julienne challenged. "Really, Audra, do you?"

"Hell yes!" Audra practically shouted at the woman, giving her anger its head. She felt her fingers curling into fists, her jaw locking tight. "Now cut it out, before you make me really, really mad!"

The journal Dr. Goddard had presented to her was now filled with page after page of meandering, sometimes petty vituperativeness—and her encounters with the woman seemed always to find Audra on the very edge of her seat, sitting on her hands to keep from slapping the shrink hard enough to make her taste yesterday. Even Shamiyah was beginning to work her last nerve, and mirrors or no, Audra would have to have been ignorant of her own body not to be able to tell how loose her sweatpants had become or how light the skin on her legs, arms and body was, even though she'd stopped using Dr. Jamison's cream.

The thought of a mirror was almost scary. In another six weeks or so, she'd be looking into one . . . and it was pretty clear she probably wouldn't recognize herself, probably wouldn't have a clue who the woman in the mirror was. And that gave her another reason to feel angry: Since while everyone in her daily life here could see the change in gradual bits, she, the actual subject, had no such luxury. She'd started out a heavyset, dark-skinned black woman and her whole identity was bound up in that image. What would it be like to look in the mirror and see this new person, with fair skin and a slender, shapely body? Would her dark-skinned insides see her light-skinned outside and run screaming for the hills?

The weirdest part was, the nastier she got, the happier everyone around her seemed to be. It was happening again, right now, with Julienne.

"I'm making you mad, huh, Audra? Good. Forget the ball, then. You know your body, right? You know it so well, you've taken care of it by stuffing it with foods it didn't want and didn't need. You know it so well that you've overdeveloped the muscles in your arms and thighs, but left your stomach so weak you're afraid you won't be able to sit back up if you lay back on a rubber ball. All of that, and yet you expect me to believe you know your body?" She shook her head. "You don't know a thing about your body, Audra. No, excuse me. You do know one thing about it," she continued in a no-nonsense tone of voice, all the while glaring at Audra like she'd offended her personally. "You know you positively hate it. You hate it, and you hate yourself—"

"Why do you all keep saying that!" Audra bounded up off the ball and yanked her towel off a nearby rack fast enough to use it as a weapon. But Julienne barely flinched. She just kept staring at Audra, every rangy muscle in her thin chest and upper arms flexed and ready.

"You can hit me if you want to," Julienne said, her voice calm, her face a mask of earnest sincerity. "It won't change anything, though. What *will* change things is for you to challenge your body—challenge yourself—beyond what you think you are capable of. See, Audra, it's all one!" And she cupped her hands together, making them into an irregular circle. "Your mind, your body, your emotions, your spirit. When things don't work here"—she touched her head with a fingertip—"or here"—she touched her heart—"it shows up here." She lay both hands on her stomach. "Or here." She patted her behind. "Or even here." The hands moved down to her thighs. "Some people think you have to start at the head or the heart before you can fix the body issues"—she shook her head—"but I personally believe you can enter the continuum anywhere." She returned her hands to her circle again. "You can start with any one of them, and if you keep going, the others will follow." Her stern expression broke into a sunny smile that made her thin face suddenly open and approachable. "You're doing great, Audra. Everyone thinks so."

"Great? I'm mad as hell," Audra muttered. "What's so great about that?"

Julienne's smile broadened. "It means you're ready for the gym. It's a great place to work on anger . . . and a few other things, if you're so inclined."

"I don't want to hurt myself. I've been hurt enough!" Audra sputtered, shocked by the violence of the unexpected admission. "I mean . . . with all the surgeries and stuff . . ."

Julienne stared at her for a long, silent moment. "It's going to hurt, Audra," she said quietly. "I'm sorry, but it just is." She patted Audra on the arm, a soothing sisterly gesture that made Audra long for Petra's presence so deeply, she had to swallow hard to keep from crying. "You know my story, right? I used to weigh almost three hundred pounds. You think I don't know about rejection? You think I don't know about hurt? Making it better hurts, too. But it's a different kind of hurt . . . and when it's done, you'll be able to see the results. And feel them. If you'll just—"

"Surrender to the process?"

She nodded. "It's a circle, Audra. Your body, your mind, your heart. Start changing any one of them and you open the door for changes in the others. That's why I don't put much stock in people who criticize shows like this one. What difference does it make if some people start with their outsides first? They'll get to the insides soon enough. They have to. It's—"

"A circle," Audra finished. "Got it." She rubbed the still sore muscles of her belly and donned her best Eliza Doolittle in *My Fair Lady*. "All right, guv'nor. You gonna teach me to walk and talk and act like a reg'lar laaaa-dy, you is."

Julienne patted her shoulder. "No, that's not my job. But I can help you *work* that Reveal dress, girl," she said snapping her fingers like a sister. "Now, I'll let you hold off on abdominals one more day"—she showed Audra a single skinny finger—"then it's over. We've got to work those muscles pretty hard to see the kind of results you're going to want for the Reveal. It'll also throw your metabolism into gear and make it easier to drop the last twenty-five or thirty pounds. Okay?"

No. No it's not okay. I don't want to I don't want to I don't want . . .

Julienne must have read it in her face because as added incentive she said, "I think you've got a shot to win this thing: the money, being in the film, the modeling contract, the whole Ugly Duckling she-bang—"

"Okay," Audra agreed. "Okay. Tomorrow. Right now, I just want to hit the showers and—"

Julienne rubbed her shoulder, in a gesture that Audra interpreted as pride and support. "Sure, the showers. But give me thirty more minutes on the treadmill first."

"Yeah, I can dig what she's saying," Art rumbled reassuringly into the phone. "I never thought of it quite like that—that the mind, body and spirit work like a circle—but yeah, I can dig it."

"I thought you would," Audra murmured. "Seems like you should be here, not me."

Art chuckled. "If I wanted to come on a show that transforms you into a beautiful woman, I'd have some pretty big issues, don't you think?"

"But at least you know what they're talking about. I mean, all I wanted was to come here and get made over. Try to win that Grand Prize package. The money and . . . the part in the movie. I could even get *discovered*—"

Art laughed. "Discovered? You mean like Lana Turner in Schrafft's drugstore?" Audra could almost imagine his shaved head wagging from side to side. "Money, I can understand . . . but discovered?" Another gale of booming laughter filled her ears. "You wouldn't really want that life, would you?"

"Why not?" Audra bristled. "You like movies as much as I do."

"Yeah, but I don't want to be in them."

"I bet it's great."

"I bet it's not. I've heard it's really boring. Lots of standing around . . ."

"There's a lot of standing around at the prison, too," Audra shot back.

"Touché."

Audra considered. "You mean you really wouldn't want to be a film star, if you had the chance? To live out your fantasy—"

"I don't have those kinds of fantasies," he said in strangely seductive tone, and in an instant, Audra's mind went to a place lit by candles and strewn with rose petals, and with Art Bradshaw's long, powerful body laid out a like a feast . . .

"Audra? You still there? I asked you more about your workout today—"

"Lots and lots of abdominal work," she said quickly. "And lots of fat-burning cardio. I must have walked the treadmill an hour and a half . . . and it was just the first day . . ."

And she kept talking, keeping it easy and breezy while the image of those rose petals and herself in Art Bradshaw's strong and powerful arms swirled in her brain.

That night, she dreamed of him.

In her dreams, she covered his long muscular legs and thick proud chest with kisses, pausing to suckle his manhood with her lips. It was as long and strong as thick as she would have expected from a man of Bradshaw's size and as she engulfed it in the cool of her mouth, she heard him groan his pleasure as though he were right there in the narrow bed beside her. His breath grew ragged but he whispered her name, guiding her with one massive hand while the other stroked her breasts, bringing her nipples erect, igniting an even deeper desire inside her.

"Enough," he muttered gruffly, pulling her slowly

up the long length of milk chocolate skin until her face was level with his own. Audra read fire in his eyes and an instant later, her lips were covered by his own and she was drowning in a sensation she'd never felt before, as every nerve in her body strained toward unity with his. Shameless with desire, she straddled him, pointing herself at the center of his need, filling herself with him.

Art lifted his hips, as she gripped his chest, riding him like a bucking bronco, a smile coursing over his face. "Take what you want, girl," he said. "Take it! All of it!"

"I'm taking it," Audra breathed, as a dizzying sense of pleasure tightened inside her. "I'm—I'm—"

She came awake with a start, gripping the sheets between her fingers, her heart pounding in her chest, an uncomfortable tension wet between her legs.

"My God," she muttered in the darkness of the tiny bedroom far away from New York, far away from the familiar, far away from Art. The dream floated before her eyes, playing itself out again in vivid detail, and she could see Art's body, imagine its smell and feel and taste—

But of her own body's appearance in the dream, she could recall nothing at all—not the size of her breasts or the length of her hair or even the color of her skin. It was as though she were making love to the man without a body of her own at all . . . just making love with her spirit and soul.

"But he likes you, right?"

"I guess so."

"Let me get this straight. He's called you almost every day for nearly six weeks, offered you support above and beyond the call of duty ... but you're not sure he likes you?"

Audra sighed. "Okay, I know he likes me ... but does he *like me* like me?"

Dr. Goddard rolled her eyes. "Please don't do this to me," she sighed. "I'm too old ..."

"Okay," Audra admitted, letting a grin crease her face. "That was juvenile. But you know what I mean."

"I don't see—"

"He didn't like me before ... before I came here ..."

"He didn't *know* you before you came here. You were co-workers, but you really didn't know anything about each other."

"We had the movies."

"Yes, you had the movies. But you still didn't really know anything about each other." She shrugged. "Now you do."

"But he didn't like the way I looked."

"How do you know that?"

"He wouldn't look at me if he could help it."

"And how do you know why that was? Did you ever ask him: 'Hey Bradshaw, why don't you ever look me in the eye?' Ever say that?" Her eyebrows shot up, giving her serious, bespectacled face an almost comical air. "Maybe he's got a lazy eye."

"He doesn't have a lazy eye."

"The point is you don't know *what* he's got. Because you didn't ask. And you didn't ask because you'd rather guess. You'd rather assume you know the reason than find out the truth."

"And what if I'm right? What if he didn't like the way I looked?"

"All right." Dr. Goddard uncrossed and recrossed her legs. "I'll bite. What if he didn't? What if he thought you were the fattest, blackest and ugliest woman he'd ever seen? Then what?"

Audra blinked at her in surprise. "I—I don't know—"

"Well, would that change or explain or erase all the help and support he's given you?"

"No."

"Would that mean he couldn't like you—or even love you?"

Audra shook her head. "No."

"And what if you were the most beautiful woman in the world? Would that change or explain or erase all the help and support? Would he suddenly have ulterior motives? Would you say he was only being your friend because you're beautiful and he's hoping for something more from you than just friendship—"

"No!" Audra exclaimed.

"Then maybe, just maybe, this doesn't have anything to do with what you look like, Audra. Maybe—just maybe—you finally dropped your defenses long enough for the man to get to know you—really get to know *you*, beyond the movie lines and diva dames. And maybe he's found something he values in the process."

Audra considered. "I don't know. You should see

Esmeralda. I mean, I know she's got her issues but . . . " She sighed. "She's really pretty. And he's really pretty. I can't see what a man who was with a woman that pretty would want with—"

"Audra." The doc leaned forward to pat her on the knee. "Don't you get this yet?" And when Audra shook her head, she continued, "The people who really love you—the people who matter—love *you* for who you are on the *inside*—"

"But—" Audra interrupted. The whole light-skin, dark-skin thing was swirling in her brain again.

"Yes, I know it's a cliché. And I know you don't believe it. And certainly people are attracted to beauty, there's no denying that. But at the end of the day, what makes one person beautiful and another ugly?" She tapped her forehead. "Perception, Audra. Beauty is the ultimate head game. I might find a person gorgeous—a person you think of as homely, or utterly unremarkable in every way. But when I look at him, I see stars. Why? Because I see something you don't, or I see through the lens of love."

"Beauty is in the eye of the beholder," Audra muttered.

"More than that. Beauty is in the *brain* of the beholder. What you think dictates how you see it. So, back to Bradshaw. The question isn't really what he sees . . . it's what he thinks. And that's an easy one to answer." She settled herself back into her armchair and beamed a warm smile at Audra. "All you have to do to find out what a man thinks is screw your courage to its sticking place."

"Screw my courage . . . ?"

"*Ask* him, Audra," Dr. Goddard said. "Not as Bette Davis or Mae West. As yourself. Just ask him."

Audra fixed the doctor with a small smile. "Easy to say, doc. Easy to say, hard to do."

Chapter 22

August 30

Dear Petra,

Things have settled into a rather dull routine: workout, sessions with Dr. Goddard and other experts, phone conversations with Art, emails to you. Other than that, I watch TV, work in my journal, try to get my head around all the changes I can expect when I get home.

I think I'm close to your coloring, skinwise. And I know I'm pretty thin. Even without mirrors, some things are hard to miss. I know I must look really different . . . but I feel really different, too. I'm trying hard to "be myself" as they say. It's surprisingly difficult. Who knew? I'm still scared of all kinds of things—like working it out with Ma, figuring out how to handle Bradshaw face-to-face—but at least I know why I'm afraid. The truth is Ma loves me and I love her, so no matter what, we'll be okay. And if Bradshaw's meant for me, he'll let me know. If not . . . I guess I'll have to dust off my evening gowns and make like a starlet until I find Mr. Right.

No . . . that's a lie. The truth is I'll be crushed. I really like him, Petra. I haven't even been able to work up the nerve to ask him if he likes me. And I never told him about the skin lightening. I don't think he'd like it . . . and it makes me feel . . . ashamed of myself.

I know I should tell him . . . but I can't. I just can't.

Anyway, it's only a few weeks until the Reveal, and I guess I'll have to deal with all of these things soon enough. I'm really hoping you'll be able to be there—that would be the best part. I can't wait to see all of you—even Ma. No matter how I look, it's good to know that I have you guys.

Be careful out there,

Audra

"**O**kay, I've got good news and bad news."

Shamiyah bounced into the gym specially set up for *Ugly Duckling* participants and stood near Audra as she pounded out her second hour on the treadmill in front of a dull gray, mirrorless wall. "Which do you want first?"

"Good, always the good news first," Audra panted, grabbing her towel to wipe the sweat rolling down her face.

"Okay . . . God, Audra." Shamiyah leaned closer to her. "You're starting to look . . . really, really good."

"Oh yeah?" Audra panted. "According to Julienne I've got about fifteen more pounds to lose." Audra looked down at herself. The rolls of skin were long gone, replaced by taut flesh. "Though I can't imagine from where—"

"I can," Shamiyah said, peering toward Audra's rear end. "Let's just say all of your troubles are behind you." She shook her mass of curly hair off her face, dismissing the subject before Audra could object. "Anyway, I'm talking about your face! I mean . . . you look—you look—" The curls wagged. "Gorgeous. I can't explain it. Really different and yet still *you* . . . and that's before we even get to makeup."

Her face. Audra felt the sudden twinge of high anxiety that any mention or thought of it always brought these days. It was looking good, all the doctors and experts kept saying. No, *good* wasn't the word they used. The words were usually *startling*, *beautiful*, *amazing*. She had the feeling that the surgeries had exceeded their expectations by more than the doctors were willing to admit.

"Well, that's about what we were going for, wasn't it?" She glanced at the peanut-butter skin of her hands and arms. "There's still a lot of dark scar tissue in some places, if you know where to look."

"Your evening gown will cover it for the show—"

"And there are places where I'm a couple of different colors." Audra huffed on. "I look like a patchwork quilt on my stomach and legs—"

"The evening gown will cover it for the show."

"Yeah, but—"

"Do you want to hear the good news or not?"

"Fire away, Shamiyah." Audra gave her a devilish grin. "What's stopping you?"

Shamiyah sighed frustration. "Audra, you're a piece of work."

"Glad to hear it. I was beginning to worry my outside had changed my inside more than I wanted it to." She sighed in mock relief. "Now what's the good word?"

"I've gotten you Ishti!" Shamiyah said, doing a happy dance around Audra's treadmill. "Ishti! Ishti! Ishti!"

Audra tugged on the pin in her sweatpants, making sure they wouldn't slide off her newfound hip bones and give the world a free sneak peek of the doctors' and experts' hard-won efforts. She wiped her face with the towel draped over the handrail of the treadmill and rubbed her head, feeling the wiry springs of her too-long hair rough against her fingertips. Whatever other changes, her hair was still nappy as it ever was, and long, too. Too long for the short Afro style she had been accustomed to wearing it in. Thank God today's schedule included fittings for gowns and, at long last, a trip to a beauty salon.

Audra stared at her companion. "Her name is *Ishti*? What kind of name is *Ishti*? You expect me to put myself in the hands of someone named *Ishti*?" *God help me*, Audra thought, conjuring the image of hair arranged like a tribal headdress, with a built-in altar in the center. Doubt welled up in her heart and mind as the memory of her many trips to salons back in New York surfaced. Every trip began with the hopeful promise of a "beautiful new Audra" . . .

and every trip had ended with the crushing weight of heavy disappointment.

Just because this was a ritzy salon in Beverly Hills didn't mean she couldn't end up with the same near-disastrous results. "Who's Ishti?" she asked.

Shamiyah laughed. "'Who is Ishti?'" she mimicked. "It figures you don't have a clue. Just don't let Ishti hear that. She takes herself very, very seriously. Ishti . . ." she said, pausing for dramatic effect, "is only *the* stylist for African-American celebrities!"

Audra thought of her mother trying time and time again to tug a straightening comb through her unruly naps and smiled. *Good luck, Ishti. You're gonna need it.*

"And there's more," Shamiyah was saying. "I've just finished making the final arrangements. Your mother's changed her mind: She's coming to the Reveal."

Audra stumbled a bit on the treadmill as her legs seemed to stop pumping of their own accord. She recovered herself and her stride and jogged on, staring at Shamiyah in silent expectation.

"It's great, isn't it?" Shamiyah squealed, practically jumping up and down with pride in her accomplishment. "We're going to fly her and your niece—"

"What about my sister? You got the Army to let Petra and Michael come home, didn't you?"

Shamiyah sighed. "That's the bad news. They won't be coming. The military wouldn't grant them leave. They say it's too close to their discharge date or something." Another shake of the head. "It sucks, really. Nothing like a couple of good-looking folks in uniform to boost ratings." Audra turned toward her, a hard glare on her face, and Shamiyah immediately continued with, "Well, of course I know what it meant to you, but you know what I mean." She smiled, as if that erased her earlier callousness. "But Art Bradshaw and his daughter are coming."

Audra forgot all about the treadmill and stopped short. A second later, she found herself flat on her bottom on the floor, staring up at a startled Shamiyah and, a second later, a concerned Julienne who must have sprinted a new world's record to get across the room that fast.

"Are you all right?" they asked simultaneously.

Audra ignored them, their concerned faces and outstretched hands. "Bradshaw's going to make it?" she demanded from her seat on the floor, feeling her cheeks flush hot with something more than exercise.

Shamiyah and Julienne exchanged glances.

"Why are you surprised? It was your idea to invite him, right?" Shamiyah put a hand on her curvy hip and twisted her neck, girlfriend style. "You talk to him almost every night. Looks to me like now that you've taken matters into your hands, you've finally gotten his attention—"

"I wasn't trying to get his attention, Shamiyah." Audra spat out.

"Don't kid a kidder," Shamiyah laughed. "Besides, I was there, remember? Listening to you whine about he'd promised to call, but he hadn't.

Well, look who's calling now! Another *Ugly Duckling* success story, I'd say. Clearly he's dying to see your finished product," she gushed. "I have a feeling that he's going to take one look at you and you're finally going to have a boyfriend."

"If that's the only reason he's interested, I don't want him," Audra declared. "I swear I don't."

Julienne grinned, elbowing Shamiyah like she had a secret. "Methinks the lady doth protest too much."

"Oh, shut up," Audra muttered, pulling herself off the floor with a wince. She rubbed her behind absently. There was a lot less back there to cushion a fall than there used to be, and she suspected she'd find a nasty blue-purple bruise on her tailbone later on.

Art Bradshaw. Coming Here. For real. A shivery feeling, one part anticipation, one part fear tingled along her spine. When she left New York, the man had been just a co-worker she'd built a fantasy around, a co-worker she'd dreamed of knowing better. Now, he was a friend—but in the form of a disembodied voice of someone who knew her as she had been. And in her dreams—and every now and then in her realities—he'd say something to make her hope he could be something else. Something warm and real and permanent . . .

Still, bringing him here was like inviting her old fears into this safe and mirrorless existence and making them breakfast.

Shamiyah and Julienne were still staring at her, waiting for her to say something.

Audra shrugged her shoulders with the nonchalance of a forties film star and climbed back aboard the treadmill as though she were already wearing an evening gown. She gave them a dismissive smile. "So when do I meet the famous Ishti?"

The overpowering smells of relaxer, hair oil, hairspray and the distinct aroma of hot hair on the boil met Audra's nose the second Shamiyah steered her into the spacious salon overlooking a Beverly Hills corner. To Audra's surprise, the place was bustling with attractive black women—more of them than Audra had seen in her entire visit to L.A.—but then, she had been so cloistered, she hadn't seen much of anyone.

Toward the center of the shop, Audra counted six stylists in long, black aprons bustling around customers in every chair. They were all beautiful, stylists and customers alike, all carrying themselves with the comfort and ease of those who knew they were pearls of great price. They ranged in tones from sepia to mahogany, weights from slender to thick, hair in every style and color from Afro puffs to sleek. Audra looked around. Two more women—older than most of the others in the room, but both exquisitely dressed—sat in the small, cool reception area set in a small alcove away from the window opening to the street. They were flipping the pages of fashion magazines and chatting amicably.

"A *lot* of celebrities come here," Shamiyah whispered, guiding her into an empty seat. She needn't have bothered: Even Audra recognized a few of the faces as familiar from television commercials and movies. Audra felt on edge in their presence—in the presence of all these women. They were confident in their beauty, sure of themselves. But in spite of the baggy clothes, the vanishing scars and the light color of her skin, Audra knew nothing of her own ranking in the beauty department. It was still sight unseen.

Snippets of beauty-shop conversation floated toward them from the main salon.

"Girl, no he *didn't*," a woman roared, laughter on the left edge of her tone.

"Yes, he *did*!" her stylist exclaimed, and the two of them fell against each other, chuckling in a way that reminded Audra of New York and the Goldilocks salon. She thought of her mother with a sudden longing.

"Looks like the joint is jumping." Shamiyah sounded neither disappointed nor surprised. "Hope we won't have to wait for too long."

Audra glanced at her watch. "I thought you said we had an appointment."

"We do! But Ishti's an artist, Audra. She has to make every style perfect, and perfection can't be constrained by anything as mundane as time!"

"I don't know, Shamiyah . . ." Audra said slowly. "Are you sure this Ishti—"

Shamiyah jabbed her in the ribs hard enough to make Audra wince and muttered, "Lower your voice. Ishti's a diva—talented as hell, but a diva from the old school, trust me. If she hears you—"

At that very moment, the voices around them suddenly dropped from raucous to whispers. Shamiyah's head snapped toward the center of salon with the energy of a young Marine coming to attention in the presence of a commanding officer.

A tall woman with a pair of the highest cheekbones short of Native America strode into the waiting area. Her hair was piled atop her head in a high, sleek beehive of a style, its natural black colored by streaks of bright blonde. Her skin was dark: past mahogany, past ebony, almost as a dark as night itself. She had fringed her dark brown eyes with lashes so long and carefully curved there was no way they could have been real, and spangled the space between lid and brow with a shimmering silvery eye shadow. Added to the dark shade of lipstick, Audra quickly surmised that very little about this woman was natural . . . if indeed she was a woman at all. There was something very "drag queen" about the look . . . right down to the silvery platform shoes peeking from beneath the hem of a pair of carefully frayed jeans.

"Shamiyah!" Ishti's voice was a mello contralto that didn't help Audra make any kind of final determination of gender. Audra found herself staring at the base of the woman's dark throat, searching for the telltale lump of an Adam's apple instead of listening to the woman's words, when she stretched out a much be-ringed hand and said, "And you must be Audra."

Shamiyah's demanding elbow lashed out again, prompting Audra to tear her thoughts away from contemplating Ishti's throat long enough to accept Ishti's hand. The fingers felt fine-boned but the skin was hardened, calloused. Over the years, hairstyling and the chemical processes involved could be hard enough on the hands to cause that, Audra knew. She sighed, making mental plans to quiz Shamiyah on it later, and accepted this unusual specter for the female it appeared to be for now.

"Uh . . . nice to meet you . . . uh . . . Ishti." The words sounded as phony as a twenty-dollar bill with Ben Franklin wearing an eyepatch.

Fortunately, Ishti wasn't listening. The moment after Audra released her hands, she reached for Audra's hairline, ruffling her slender, work-worn fingers through the soft naps of Audra's hair, making it stand in a fluffy three-inch halo around Audra's head.

"And this is totally virgin? Never relaxed?" She directed the question at Shamiyah as though Audra were too ignorant of the processes of style to know the answer. Audra noticed that she spoke with an approximation of a British accent that sounded as fake as she looked.

"I had one once, years ago." Audra answered moving slightly to get Ishti's fingers out of her head. "But I didn't have time for all the curling and primping to make it look right, so I—"

"Audra needs something elegant enough for the Reveal, but practical enough for her to work with once she gets back home," Shamiyah explained. "She's a corrections officer at the city prison, so—"

Ishti waved the rest of Shamiyah's explanation aside with a flutter of her fingers and an impatient, "of course, of course," while she reached again for Audra. This time the woman grabbed her shoulders and spun her around. Audra felt the woman's breath on the nape of her neck as she inspected her scalp.

"Color first, then extensions," she pronounced in a tone Audra didn't care for at all, but before she could open her mouth in objection, the woman was whirling Audra back around. "Thank you, Shamiyah," Ishti said. "This is a worthy challenge. I accept. But next time," and she narrowed her eyes at Audra as if her penetrating gaze were sufficient force to make any point. "Tell your friend how we dress here." She locked her eyes on Audra, then patted her cheek condescendingly. "Style, my dear. Style!" She pulled a long piece of black fabric from a pocket of her jeans, and waved it at her. "Are you ready?"

"What's that?" Audra asked skeptically.

"Blindfold," Shamiyah said, spinning Audra around. "This place is crawling with mirrors."

"I think this one . . . and this one . . . and this one. Jewel tones will really sparkle on your skin tone," a little man wearing a fussy peach ascot said as he ripped gowns off the racks so fast, Audra barely had time to lift her sunglasses and register their colors before she was being pushed into a fitting room . . . which, of course, had no mirror.

It was getting frustrating now: to be able to see the lightness of her skin all over her body and to feel Ishti's long, blonde-streaked extensions brushing against her shoulder blades, but to not be able to get even a glimpse of this final effect that was so "breathtaking," so "beautiful" for herself. Audra found herself running her fingers along her chin, her cheekbones, her nose, trying to create a picture. But it was useless. She needed to *see*.

Audra sighed, slipping the sweats off her hips again without disturbing the pin at the waist. As she bent for the first dress, a long, curled lock of Ishti's hair extensions, in a golden brownish color that defied easy description, fell over her shoulders and brushed the beige skin of her arms.

Tomorrow's tomorrow, she thought, holding the curl between fingers she barely recognized as her own. *Tomorrow's tomorrow, I meet the new Audra. Tomorrow's tomorrow, I get to wipe the slate clean, and start all over again. Art Bradshaw is coming . . . day after tomorrow*, another voice, even more eager, added, and Audra shivered a little in a strange blend of anticipation and fear.

"My God! What did you do before you came to us? Drive trucks? Work construction?" The woman threw back her head and laughed a deep-throated laugh that many a forties-style actor would have paid dearly to learn to imitate.

Her name was Freda Jasper and her job was simple: teaching Audra how to walk and talk and act like she was born gliding around Beverly Hills in four-inch heels and evening gowns.

"I'm a corrections officer."

Freda nodded. "That explains much. I bet you usually walk around in those awful black shoes with laces, don't you?" and she wrinkled her nose. She spoke with real humor, not in the condescending way of so many of the people Audra had met with in these final days of the process.

"Give me a pair of regulation blacks and I can climb stairs with a book balanced on my head." Audra smiled, deciding to like her.

"By the time I get through with you, you'll be able to balance your 'regulation blacks' on your head in stilettos. I'm going to teach you how to cross those shapely legs of yours in a way that will make men stammer and women turn green. I'm going to teach you how to sit with the grace of a queen. On the stage, for the Reveal, you're going to move like something ethereal—like a goddess come straight down from heaven." She fluttered her fingers a little, creating the image for both of them with a sprinkle of fairy dust. "But first, we have to teach you the basics. And the first of the basics is posture." She snapped her fingers. "Stand up straight, Audra."

"I am!"

"Not like that. Like this. Shoulders," and she grabbed Audra's shoulders and forced them back, thrusting her breasts forward in a manner that reminded Audra of a Barbie doll's outrageous figure. "Stomach in." She patted Audra's flat belly as though there were something that needed to be sucked in. Audra did her best to comply. "Head up," she instructed and Audra raised her head to a height that felt downright conceited. "Now," she concluded. "Walk."

Audra strode across the woman's studio, eyes on the space where a mirror should have been across the room. But of course they'd covered it with cardboard and Audra could see nothing. From her point of view, as weird as it felt to walk this way, it probably looked pretty good and she was about to say as much, when Freda shook her head.

"You're lumbering, Audra."

Audra stopped.

"Lumbering," Freda continued. "Like an elephant." And she imitated—a little overdramatically, Audra suspected. "The posture is fine, but the steps . . . you're shifting your entire weight from foot to foot with each step."

"What do you want me to do?"

"Close your legs, to start with."

"What?"

"Close your legs! Bring your thighs together and take smaller steps. You're walking wide-legged! It makes you look a sailor on shore leave, still rolling with the wake of the waves—"

"Hey, I'm enjoying having thighs thin enough *not* to rub together and now you're telling me that's a *good* thing—"

"I didn't say give yourself a chafing. I said to close your legs." She nodded toward the studio floor. "Try it."

Audra brought her feet together and concentrated on her thighs. She took a couple of small steps toward the mirror before Freda called out, "Posture!"

She remembered her stomach, head and chest and took another couple of mincing steps. "Toe first. Toe . . . heel, toe . . . heel . . . toe, heel . . . stop!"

Audra froze. She turned her head slowly toward the woman, awaiting her next instruction, but the woman simply handed her the shoes she'd just selected and nodded. "Okay. Put 'em on and let's see what happens."

Audra walked the room again, her legs moving slowly to the time of a single word repeating itself over and over in her brain . . . tomorrow, tomorrow, tomorrow . . .

Chapter 23

September 21

Dear Petra,

Today's the day. I'll finally get to see myself top to toe. I'm excited and scared and a whole bunch of emotions. I wish you were going to be here . . . but I console myself with knowing you'll be back home to stay by the time the show airs.

Thanks for listening. You've been the one person I knew would be supportive from the very beginning. I can't tell you how much that means to me . . . how much you mean to me, Petra. You're the best sister— the best friend—I've ever had.

Now, enough mushy stuff: I've got a job to do! I've got to get to makeup. They're going to slather on whatever it takes to finalize the effect for the TV cameras . . .

I'll be sending you a picture of the new me in my next email, girl.

Be careful out there,

Audra

"Two minutes," the stage manager hissed, taking Audra's gloved hand and dragging her to an X marked in fluorescent tape in the center of the stage.

"Hold still," the makeup artist hissed, brushing what felt like the thousandth coat of powder over her nose and cheeks, while the hairstylist fluffed Ishti's extensions and smoothed the bangs over the few remaining dark marks of scar tissue on her forehead. The two seemed almost at war for the same space on Audra's face, while somewhere behind her, a third black-clad and nearly invisible person fussed with the hem of her sapphire gown.

"One minute!"

Audra stared at thick red curtain in front of her. In less than sixty seconds, she'd strike a pose and the curtain would be pulled back, revealing her to the experts who had helped to create her and a small audience that included her nearest and dearest. Within a few minutes thereafter, pauses for commercial breaks notwithstanding, she'd be placed in front of an ornate mirror and finally allowed to see herself for the first time.

From behind the curtain, she could hear the voices of her doctors, coaches and trainers.

"Special concerns of African-American features—" she heard. The voice sounded like Dr. Bremmar's happy confidence, but she lost the rest until Dr. Jamison intoned something about "skin lightening medication used to minimize scarring and obtain the desired beauty effect."

Desired beauty effect? Audra let the words wash over her, hearing them but not hearing them, knowing she would see it all later—much later—after the Reveal and the lengthy process of editing Shamiyah was already complaining about.

"Thirty seconds."

More tugging on her hair, more swishing of the dress, another swipe of lip gloss, while from behind the curtain she heard her own voice from her Audition tape, saying: "Just once I'd like to not be the tough broad, one of the guys. Just once, I want to be the beauty queen. I want to be the one who—"

"Ten seconds! Curtain ready? Strike your pose! Spotlight in five, four—"

Audra's right foot shot out behind her, lifting the heavy weight of the gown as she pointed her toe and balanced seductively on one foot. One gloved hand found its way under her chin, the other stretching forward, supplicating an unseen lover: Audra Marks as Audrey Hepburn blowing a kiss . . . with a tan.

A spotlight hit the curtain, and Audra knew her pose was visible in silhouette on the other side. A roar went up from the small audience that she knew included her family and Bradshaw, but God only knew who else.

"Curtain in five . . . four . . ."

Audra bent her lips into a smile, a smile it seemed like she'd been practicing her entire life. Her heart fluttered nervously, and for a second she wondered if after all she'd been through, she was going to have a stroke and die now, now that it was almost over. It would be the ultimate irony to pass out and die right here without ever seeing what she'd starved and sweated for, cried and wished for . . .

"Pull curtain!"

It started to move, slowly at first, in mere inches, then more swiftly, until Audra was blinded by the spotlight and deafened by a collective gasp of surprise, followed by the noise of applause.

"Go!" someone hissed from behind her, and she dropped her pose and started to walk, kicking down the long red carpet of the stage like a runway model, adding a little Bronx-born something something, just to make sure the people watching at home wouldn't forget when it got time to make that big vote for the Top Three winners.

Seated at a long table at the end of the red carpet were her experts, and when Audra glanced in their direction, she saw they were all on their feet, applauding, nodding with approval and pride. Even stern Dr. Jamison was bringing his big hands together, and it looked like grouchy old Dr. Koch had paused to wipe away a tear.

The hostess, a willowy-looking blonde chick whom Audra had only seen once before—at the dress rehearsal yesterday—stepped up to hug and kiss her like they were old pals.

"Audra, you look mahvelous," she exclaimed in an odd accent. Audra couldn't place her: it sounded like an English accent by way of the prince of Denmark. Something about it made Audra suspect the girl was totally perpetrating and that between the funny way of talking and the fact that she made her red side-slit evening gown look more elegant than whorish were the sole reasons she had gotten the hostess job. "Absolutely smashing!"

"Thank you," Audra said, returning the woman's hug. It was a little like squeezing a collection of bones in a soft skin sack.

"The audience seems really impressed with your makeover." She pronounced the word "mackovair" and it took Audra a brief, blinky second to decipher it and respond.

"Thank you, audience," she said, executing a slight, Miss-America-style turn and waving at them. "I love you!"

More applause, whistles and even a little laughter greeted her. Basking under the lights and the love, Audra couldn't resist hamming it up. She turned fully toward the audience and struck a Marilyn Monroe, blowing airy kisses at the audience and the cameras between them and her.

"You're enjoying this attention, aren't you?"

"I've lived most of my life in the shadows," Audra said, using the sentence she'd practiced almost since the first day of her arrival in L.A. "It's time for me to step out into the sun ... uh ..."—what was this chick's name again?—"Cassandra."

"I know you've worked very hard," *veddy 'ard.* "And it shows. You're an Ugly Duckling no more. And now it's finally time for you to see yourself at long last." She gestured toward the end of the stage where a black curtain covered a long rectangular shape Audra knew concealed a mirror. "When you're ready, cross the stage, stand in front of the mirror and say the word *Reveal*. The curtain will fall away and you'll see yourself at last. Are you ready?'

Am I Ret-tay? Audra mimicked the woman in her mind, but aloud she simply said:

"Girl, I was *born* ready."

Hostess Cassandra gestured toward the black-draped mirror. "Then off you go."

Audra didn't need to be told twice. She turned, balancing carefully on the stiletto heels they insisted were a must with a dress like this—a gleaming sheath of blue, beaded with sequins from breast to hem, the scarf draped dramatically around her neck as much to hide the slight mottling from the lightening drug as for effect, and strode across the stage toward the mirror.

She paused before it, like Shamiyah and the others had coached her to do, but their words had been utterly unnecessary. Audra felt the dramatic weight of the moment nestle around her like a mantle as the crowd noise settled down to a hush and her own heart beat loudly in her ear. She couldn't compare it, it was unlike any movie scene she'd ever known.

She knew what her body must look like—she could tell by looking down at her legs and her breasts, at the color of the skin on her arms and over her body. She knew she was thin from the way her old clothes fit, and from the SIZE 4 sewn on the inside of every gown she tried in that designer shop. She knew her hair was long and light-colored, swishing on her shoulders like a horse's mane. None of these things would be a surprise.

The face. Only the face was still a mystery. Until

now . . . when all that stood between her old self and her new self was a canopy of black cloth and a single word. She spoke it now.

"Reveal."

It was the moment in *Meet Mr. Jordan*—or its many remakes—when the dead boxer sees the face of his new body in the mirror and realizes he's no longer his old self, but his old self in someone else's skin.

Audra stood, stunned, her mind unable to process the image in front of her, even as the cameras rolled and the crowd cheered.

The woman was lovely: caramel skin stretched over high cheekbones and a neat little nose, in perfect proportion to the sculpted brows of her forehead and the luscious red bow of her mouth. Only the eyes seemed familiar, still a smoky black but circled now with false eyelashes and some kind of midnight eye shadow Audra knew she'd never be able to duplicate at home.

Her eyes traveled down her body: her boobs had never stood so high, her waist never seemed so long, or her stomach so flat. As though she were home alone, she turned sideways toward the mirror, examining her profile, then again, to inspect her round, firm rear end and shapely thighs, before turning back to examine the front view once again. She didn't know whether to laugh or cry, to shout or shiver, and so she contemplated herself without making a single sound of dismay or approbation.

"Well?" Cassandra was at her side, draping an arm around her shoulder, and Audra realized all of the experts were crowded around her now. "What do you think?"

"I think . . ." Audra said, finding her voice again, thankful for its familiarity, at least. "I think . . . I'm beautiful."

And then, at last, a smile spread across her face.

She had the vaguest recollection of what happened after that.

She remembered hugging each of the doctors and experts in turn, thanking them for their efforts.

She remembered her mother and her little niece coming out from behind the stage to gawk and gape and make pleasant comments about the drastic change, even while Audra read in her mother's eyes her uncertainty about both Audra's look and its impact on the days to come.

She remembered bending close to Kiana. "Don't you have a hug for your Auntie A?" she asked, with her arms wide.

"You're not my Auntie A," the girl said decisively and refused to be persuaded otherwise.

She remembered Penny Bradshaw squealing in her ear as she embraced her, her young face a mask of teenaged amazement.

And she remembered Art Bradshaw: lifting her off her feet in a bear hug she doubted would have been possible at her pre-Ugly Duckling weight. Audra loved it: loved the feeling of being swept off her feet princess-style, of being enveloped and protected. She held him a little tighter, feeling as though she had stepped out of herself and into a fairy tale with Art Bradshaw cast in the role of the prince.

He released her, bit by bit, and Audra tilted her face toward him, expecting to see happiness shining in the bright amber of his eyes and in the broad gleam of his face.

And it was there . . . along with something else. Something she hadn't expected to see:

Disappointment.

PART THREE

The Final Package

Chapter 24

"It's amazing . . . amazing . . ." Penny Bradshaw kept saying the word over and over again, until Audra was on the verge of snapping something not very nice about needing to work on her vocabulary. "Just . . . amazing . . ."

Audra, her family, Art Bradshaw and his daughter Penny sat in a limousine, hurtling toward the airport in a thick, nervous silence.

Just like that, it was over: the ugly duckling had visited the wide world, time had passed, and now she was returning home. Only she was no longer a duckling, inside or outside or on any side. She was a prettied-up version of Audra Marks on her way to the airport in the company of her irritated mother, her confused niece, the silent Art Bradshaw and his awestruck daughter.

Audra washed her eyes over him again: He was massive, taking up almost half the long backseat of the limousine, and Audra had to talk to herself to keep from snuggling up beside him and thanking him for his help and support in a far more intimate way . . . if he'd let her. For all their conversations— and all her erotic dreams, day and night—Audra had to admit she had no idea what the man's feelings were. But that embrace . . . that hug . . .

Ask him, just ask him, Dr. Goddard whispered in her brain.

As soon as we're alone . . .

Of course, there was also something she was supposed to have told him . . . something about skin lightening procedures and the shift from dark to light . . .

It's a little late for that now.

She peered at him closely, but the confident man she'd been talking to on the phone for the past three months was nowhere visible at this moment. He was sweating a little, patting his hands on his thigh nervously, glancing around the car like a lost man.

"Amazing," Penny Bradshaw breathed again, and her father patted her on the arm in a futile effort to silence her, but an instant later, another soft "amazing" escaped from the girl's mouth.

Art cleared his throat. "Good dress," he rumbled, interjecting a few new syllables into the silence. He didn't sound like the well-spoken man she'd come to know—or even like John Wayne. He sounded more like a Neanderthal struggling to navigate the modern world. "Green. Color." He seemed to put a little emphasis on that last word . . . but Audra couldn't have sworn to it. It might have been a trick of her own guilty conscience.

"Thanks." Audra flashed a smile in his direction,

hoping to ease him back into the connection that had lived so vibrantly between them on the phone for the past several months. "It's a present from Dr. Koch—the plastic surgeon who did the body work." He said he picked it because it reminded him of the dress Barbara Stanwyck wears in the beginning of *Double Indemnity*. He rented the movie after he watched my audition tape; he'd never seen it." Audra chuckled. "I seem to have introduced a lot of people to the glory days of film."

"*Mmmfph*," Edith muttered, making her first sounds since they'd left the studio. "I thought *they* was supposed to be changing *you*, not the other way around."

"That's the funny thing about people, Ma. We all impact each other in ways we can't always anticipate."

Edith rolled her eyes. "Here we go! Here goes the blame game. I swear, Audra, if this is how it's gonna be with you day after day, I am *not*—"

"What? I didn't say anything!" Audra shot back. "Don't be so—"

"If this is how it's gonna be—" Edith repeated even louder and more stridently than before.

"Okay, okay," Audra said briskly. "Forgive me. I only meant—"

Her mother looked up at her, smoky eyes agitated. "No, never mind. I guess I'm . . . just not used to seeing my daughter this way," she admitted. "They did a good job on them extensions. Is that the same stuff Oprah got?" But before Audra could answer, she turned her head toward the window, pulling the shade and closing her eyes as though she were exhausted. "I thought sure that girl Shamiyah said they would at least put us up for the *night . . .*"

"Are you really my Aunt Audra?" Kiana asked, staring at her with big eyes from her place beside her grandmother.

"Really," Audra said, leaning toward her with a smile on her face.

"You sound like her . . . but you don't look like her," she said with a frown. "You don't look like her at all."

"Don't you like the way I look?" Audra asked.

The little girl stared at her for a long while. "You look nice . . . but you just don't look like Aunt Audra. Aunt Audra had skin like midnight and eyes like fire. And she was soft all over when she hugged me." She sighed. "I miss her."

The words stung like a lash and Audra felt tears prickling behind her eyes. She was about to say something, something reassuring and familiar that might regain Kiana's trust, when Penny Bradshaw interrupted with, "Did he give you the shoes, too?" She nodded at the emerald green pumps on Audra's feet. "The plastic surgeon—"

"Oh . . . no. The shoes were from Dr. Bremmar. He did my face. They work together—they're partners. I guess they must shop together, too!" Audra laughed like maybe someone else might find the image of the two doctors shopping together amusing, but got no takers. They didn't know either man . . . and you had to know them to get the joke. "No," she said not bothering to explain. "I'm sure they had their assistant shop for them or something. Actually I got gifts from all of them—all the experts," and she proceeded to tell them about how her old black duffel had been emptied of the things she had brought at the beginning of her Ugly Duckling journey and every item replaced by a trinket from each of the people she had worked with over the past three months. There was a pair of tiny black yoga pants and three crop tops in different colors from Julienne; a lovely wide-brimmed hat and gloves from Dr. Jamison; the clingy silk dress and shoes from Drs. Koch and Bremmar; the black handbag she was carrying from Shamiyah, and a gold necklace from Camilla. But the most unusual gift by far was from Dr. Goddard: a delicate hand mirror, edged in gilt, on which the word BEHOLDER was engraved in filigree.

"Beholder?" Edith frowned. "Why 'beholder'? What kind of message is that?"

"It's a reminder," Audra said quietly. "That beauty is in the eye of the beholder . . ." She glanced in Art's direction, but to her dismay, he lowered his eyes almost as soon as she captured them. "And that my own perception of myself is the most important one of all."

"Amazing," Penny Bradshaw breathed again, in the same tone of absolute wonder. Then silence reigned in the car again.

"I want to know all about it . . . everything. Did it hurt? How much of the hair is yours? What did they do to your skin to get it so . . . so . . ." Penny Bradshaw settled herself into the seat Audra had been hoping her father might take and started talking a blue streak. "Light?"

They had first-class seats . . . which should have provided a prime opportunity for them to talk, but Art must not have wanted that. Audra glanced at him: he leaned over the seat ahead of them, helping Kiana buckle her seat belt. With that accomplished, he excused himself for the lavatory, keeping his head down.

Audra stared after him, confused and let down, a vague feeling of depression replacing the elation of only hours ago. For months, she'd been at the center of her own little Ugly Duckling universe, where everything and everyone had been about her. Cameras had followed her every move . . . and everyone in her life had been focused on one thing: her transformation, her Reveal. And now, with the flash of a bulb and the yank of a curtain, it was over. No cameras, no Shamiyah, no experts to question and annoy. Not even Bradshaw was acting right.

"So did it?" Penny was asking, and Audra turned to find Art's deep-set amber eyes staring back at her from his daughter's face. "Did it hurt?"

"What do you think?" Audra smiled. "Like hell."

"What was the worst part?"

"Being away from home." Audra answered immediately. "I was pretty lonely. Bored, too."

"No, about the surgery!" Penny corrected, waving aside Audra's loneliness and boredom aside with a slender brown hand. "What was the worst?"

Audra frowned with the effort of remembering. Now that it was behind her, none of it seemed so bad anymore. "I guess the nose job," she said slowly. "But the tummy tuck wasn't a picnic either."

"Yeah," Penny reached over and turned Audra's

head, inspecting her nose at every angle like a surgeon. "But they did a really good job. I'd love to get my nose done—"

"There's nothing wrong with your nose, Penny."

The girl pinched at her nostrils. "They're too wide, and here . . ." She rubbed at the bridge. "It should be higher here—"

"There's nothing wrong with your nose."

Penny's lips scrunched together in disagreement. "I wish I were eighteen. Then I could send a tape to *Ugly Duckling* and—"

Art Bradshaw emerged from the lavatory at that moment and began making his way slowly towards them. Audra smiled up at him, but he kept his head turned in the other direction, taking a seat ahead of them on the opposite side of the plane. He slid close to the window and reached for a pair of headphones, blocking the sound of Audra and Penny as well as the sight.

"What's wrong with your father, Penny?"

The girl shrugged.

"Is he feeling okay?"

Penny glanced toward the seat ahead, her eyes sweeping over the man's inert form as if looking for danger signals. Finally she lifted her shoulder in another shrug. "Looks fine to me. Why?"

"He's barely said two words to me—or anyone else, for that matter."

Penny whipped a fashion magazine from one of the pockets of the heavy-looking shoulder bag she carried and began turning the pages quickly as if looking for something. "I guess he's pretty surprised. I mean you do look a lot like *her*," Penny told the magazine. She stopped abruptly, thumping her finger against the image of an emaciated-looking white woman modeling clothes in a high-fashion spread. "I like her nose. Think it would look good—"

"Like who?"

"What?"

Audra made the girl look at her. "You said I look a lot like *her*. Who's *her*?"

Penny stared at her for a long moment as though she were wearing a loincloth. "Who else? My mother."

Audra blinked at her, shock reverberating from her ear drums to the tips of her toes.

"Your mother?" she sputtered. "B-but I don't look like your mother. I look like my sister, Petra—"

"*And* like my mother. Or like she looked the last we saw her. At my sweet sixteen party." She fixed her eyes on Audra, running through a checklist from top to toes. "I noticed it as soon as that curtain lifted . . . and I'm sure he did, too. Whatever else she is . . . or isn't," she said the words with a kind of dark unpleasantness, "she's always pretty. Always." She shrugged. "Of course, up close you can tell your face is different. But the hair and the skin, and you're awfully skinny now. Really *thin*—" Her voice had a tone of great admiration that made Audra suddenly sick to her stomach. "Well, I think Dad thought you would look like you did before . . . just a little thinner and with prettier clothes and more makeup, or something. I kept telling him this was different, but . . . you know how *men* are," she said breezily, as though she'd had a lifetime of experience. "Even I was a little surprised by your color, though." She touched Audra's forearm gently, dragging her fingers against the skin as though she expected something to rub off. "How'd they *do* that? Is it some kind of makeup or—"

"Where is your mother now, Penny?"

The girl shrugged again, but her eyes hardened and her lips seemed to disappear into her face. "Don't know, don't care."

"Is he . . . upset . . . ?"

"Dad?" Her lips collapsed onto each other in an expression of teenaged disinterest. "Who knows? Ask him."

Ask him. Dr. Goddard was sitting on her shoulders like the little Martian character in a cartoon she used to watch on Saturday mornings many, many years ago. *I told you to ask him . . .*

"No . . . not now." Audra sighed, administering a swift mental kick to her own taut, round behind. "If I'd asked him when I should have, I wouldn't be in this mess."

Chapter 25

Monday, September 24

Dear Petra,

I feel like I've been suddenly dunked in cold water. Dr. Goddard warned me that coming home would be a shock to my system after all these months. She said I'd had an experience that no one back home had shared, that no one would relate to. She also said some people would be resistant to the change and treat me differently. They'd project their own ideas about what they believe is beautiful on me . . . and not all of it would be positive.

Is that what's happening with Bradshaw?

Ma is tiptoeing around me, walking on egg shells. I know she hasn't gotten used to looking at me: She starts a little when I walk into a room, and I've caught her just staring at me when I'm not looking. We still have a lot to talk about, her and me. I'm just not ready yet.

Kiana's a little distant still. It's okay: she's a child. But it's almost like starting over with her from zero. She's called me "Mommy" a couple of times. I consider that the highest compliment I can get.

I'm not any more used to "me" than they are. I keep catching glimpses of my reflection and it always surprises me. I have to remind myself that it's me I'm looking at and not someone else.

Today is my first day back on the job. I know it's going to be a little weird to take my new look and my new awareness back to a place where people were used to dealing with me as a totally different person, inside and out. I have to say, I'm nervous. But I'm pretty sure no one will call me a "dude with tits."

Are you still on track to be home in November? They're not going to delay your homecoming again, are they? I hope not. You've done your time, now it's time for the Army to honor its end of the bargain and bring you home. Michael, too. Enough is enough.

I've gotta go or I'll be late. Not a good thing for my first day back.

I'll let you know how it goes.

Be careful out there,

Audra

"You're gonna need a new badge, Marks," Darlene Fuchs said when Audra clocked in. "That's the only way anyone's going to know you."

The uniform was brand-new, in some tiny size called only "petite small" on the uniform sizing chart, and it fit her trim hips and brand-new bodacious behind in a way that the designer probably never intended the drab fabric to do. She wore a crisp, white, fresh-out-of-the-box shirt with every button flat, including those outlining the high peaks of her new breasts.

"Real or fake?" she asked, quirking an eyebrow at Audra's hair.

"Extensions," Audra answered, checking over the duty roster. There was only one name she was looking for . . . and it wasn't there. "Where's Bradshaw? He's still working this shift, right?"

"Called in sick," the other woman said, still eyeing Audra interestedly. "How much weight did you lose?"

"In all?" Audra calculated. "About eighty-five pounds of fat . . ." She made a mental note to thank Julienne as she made a bicep pop for the woman. "But I've built up a good deal of muscle, too, so it looks like more."

"Amazing. I wouldn't have known on the street if I fell on you, seriously, Marks." She stretched the bare forearm emerging from the short sleeve of her uniform blouse toward Audra. "You and I are nearly the same color, since it's summer and I have a tan. How did they do that anyway?"

"Do what?" Audra asked innocently, grinning broadly.

Darlene laughed. "You don't actually plan to pretend like you were born that color, do you?"

Audra shrugged. " 'Hey, if it works for Michael Jackson, it might work for me." She paused. "Did . . . did Bradshaw say what was wrong?"

"Nope," Darlene shook her head casually enough, but her expression said she was quickly reaching conclusions about the reasons for Audra's interest. "You're doing day room patrols today . . . in fact, all week. Next week you'll switch back to the night shift. That all right?"

"Fine," Audra said, checking her weapon and strapping on her holster and trying most unsuccessfully to feign the most casual of interest as she asked, "Bradshaw still have that detail? When he gets back, of course . . ."

"Of course, Marks," Darlene said sweetly. She leaned close and smiled. "The way he's been talking about you for the past three months, I'd say you'd have to screw up big time to keep from reeling him in," she whispered. "Congratulations."

Audra felt her face go numb. Darlene was congratulating her, but Art was evading her, it was obvious. It was beginning to look like she'd *already* blown it, big time . . . right when she finally had a chance. "Thanks," she mumbled in Darlene's general direction and turned away with a heavy heart.

"You boys are going to lose all your privileges if you don't cut it out," Audra shouted, but it was hard to keep the ghost of a smile from the corners of her lips with the hoots and catcalls answering the swing of her hips as she strode ahead along the line of convicts moving in a slow formation toward the day room. "Keep it up and you'll all be in your cells for a week with no rec time at all."

They reached the day room and Audra counted them in, watching the men's faces as they passed her, registering their appreciation. Some addressed her in low voices—she heard "baby," "flower," "sweet thing"—while others addressed her with their eyes, clearly enjoying the carefully crafted arrangement of flesh. Not one of them seemed to know her, even though—with the exception of a few unfamiliar faces—Audra knew she could call each one of them out by both number and name. Even Haines sauntered by her, his lips losing their habitual sneer of disdain long enough for him to look her over and leer something that in his twisted universe was probably considered a smile. Audra doubted he'd have given her more than his usual cursory glare if he had recognized her.

Nothing like that was ever likely to happen again. She'd worked too hard to lose the weight to ever risk gaining it back, and instead of brute strength, she'd already signed up for refresher self-defense classes to insure her skills were still sharp enough to subdue a prisoner if necessary. And fortunately, she still had brains . . . even if she'd lost a bit of her brawn.

"Officer," Haines greeted her in his sneering way and there was a touch of awe in his voice that Audra had never heard before. Apparently, there were other ways to subdue a man, Audra realized. Ways that had nothing to do with force.

Pride swelled inside her, along with an intense hopefulness. This is what it felt like to be beautiful— to have the appreciation of men and the envy of women. She inhaled deeply, drinking in the feeling, bursting to share it with Bradshaw . . . if he'd ever come out of hiding long enough to let her.

The last man came through the doorway, all slink and slither, pimp rolling along like he thought he owned the joint.

"Hey there, mama," he murmured, batting his curly black eyelashes at her. "You new here? Be happy to show you the ropes—"

"Carlton?"

He blinked, hearing his given name come out of Audra's mouth.

"Listen, sweet thing, only my mama calls me that—"

"You were paroled in March, Carlton," Audra snapped, ignoring him. "It's mid-September! What are you doing back in the joint that fast?" Audra shook her head. "I tell you what, boy. I've got an ass-whipping with your name on it."

The kid's face vacillated between titillation and confusion.

"Baby, do you know me?" he said in a voice full of sweetness.

"Yeah, I know you," Audra muttered. She nodded to her fellow CO as he brought up the rear and closed the day room's doors behind him.

"You been checking me out, huh, pretty lady?" Carlton muttered, all seduction and zero seriousness. "That's all right—but when do I get to know *you*?"

"Not so fast, Casanova. There's a speed limit in this state," Audra said, for a moment forgetting about the surgery and the changes in her look since she'd last laid eyes on this kid. She jerked her head at Carlton, nudging him toward a chair in the corner of the room. "It's forty-five miles an hour and you're doing ninety. Go sit down over there and—"

He was staring at her like she had suddenly sprouted horns. Audra watched recognition dawn in his eyes. A second later he burst into laughter.

"Holy shit! Holy shit—" he cried, laughing. "I don't believe this shit! You're—you're—that butt-ugly chick—"

"Yeah, I'm the ugly chick."

His laughing and pointing was attracting attention in the room. Audra glanced around and found the noise to have stolen some attention from the television show some of the men were watching, along with several checkers games and more than a few of the quieter conversations around the room. Only the video rivalry continued without interruption.

"Damn, girl! What did you *do*!"

"What I did is irrelevant. The point is what did *you* do to—"

"I mean I can understand losing some weight . . . fixing your hair up a little . . ." He squinted at her, unsure of how to explain the other changes he was seeing. He dismissed them anyway by guffawing and pointing. "But you've changed yourself into a white woman!" He must have felt the eyes of the room on him, because he shouted out, "Hey y'all, check this. Remember that fat, ugly chick that used to work here? One that threw down with Haines and ripped her pants—"

There were a few nods and murmurs of assent.

"Settle down!" Audra roared over the little swell, grabbing Carlton's shoulder. "That's enough now—"

"This the *same chick*!" he said jabbing a finger in Audra's direction. "Remember how dark she used to be? Nappy hair, big old tits and big old butt? This the same—"

"All right, all right," Audra repeated, feeling increasingly uncomfortable as the men stared at her, some laughing, others shaking their heads in disbelief. Audra thought she heard, "Like the King of Pop!" and "That's messed up!" along with other less-than-flattering comments.

"Remember when she threw Haines? Threw him like a rag doll!" Carlton all but cackled. "Broke two of his ribs—"

Audra's eyes shot to Haines, who was staring her down with a venom that couldn't signal anything but bad news. She let her eyes stray to the other COs, but they seemed content to let Audra handle the ribbing in any way she chose.

"That's enough!" Audra roared, as the murmurs reached higher decibels. "Back to your recreation . . . or all of you will be back in your cells with plenty of time to think about it—"

"Oh yeah?" In the few months since she'd seen him last, Carlton had gained a nasty swagger that didn't become him in the slightest. "You said you was gonna kick my ass. Look at you. You couldn't kick—"

Audra whipped out her baton, grabbed his right arm behind his back and pressed the baton tight against his throat. She jerked him to his feet, feeling the strain in her body at his weight.

"I told you to shut up, and I mean shut up!" she hissed, dragging him toward the door, thanking God and Julienne for the dozens of extra repetitions of upper body exercises she'd been forced to endure. "And if you can't shut up then—"

She stumbled against something unseen—something that felt like someone's foot and leg. She righted herself quickly, but in the tangled moment of regaining her equilibrium, Audra lost her grip on Carlton. A second later, he'd whirled around, ducking free of the baton and facing her with a little smirk on his face, while she looked around for the obstruction . . . or the obstructor. Princeton Haines stood nearby, his eyes locked on hers and his usual sneer curling his features into ugliness.

The other COs converged on the situation now, and Carlton was handcuffed in an instant, all the while loudly complaining that he hadn't done anything, hadn't said anything, hadn't been anywhere near anything ever in his entire life.

"You want to take him back or—"

"Yeah, I'll do it," Audra muttered, feeling a sudden sense of shame suffusing her skin, praying that her cheeks weren't flaming with the emotion, but knowing with her paler complexion, it was highly likely that the entire room was witnessing her discomfiture at being bested by an inmate, if only for a second. She pulled her features into her game face and let her eyes skim the room one last time, taking in every face. The room was silent now except for the blaring TV and the crashes and whines of the video games. Most of the men were staring at her blankly, unwilling to risk the possibility of being ejected in the same undignified manner as Carlton. But Princeton Haines was watching her with a funny little smile curled on his snide lips . . . and Audra had to talk to herself to keep from shuddering under its scrutiny.

She called Bradshaw that night, but Penny said he was "out" and launched into her own conversation, starting into a long-winded series of questions about her time in Los Angeles, ending with the request to bring a few of the girls from school to Audra's apartment to watch *Ugly Duckling* on the night of Audra's Reveal.

Chapter 26

October 4

Dear Petra,

He's not talking to me.

Okay, he's talking to me a little. When Penny calls (which is often, the girl has adopted us!) he'll come to the phone for a minute. He answers my questions "yes" or "no" . . . or he'll ask me about some movie that was on the Classic Channel. He called in sick every day I worked the 7-a.m.-to-3-p.m. shift; didn't come back until I was back to nights.

He's avoiding me, Petra. He's avoiding me right when we have so much to talk about . . .

I know I should have told him about the skin lightening. I don't know why I didn't.

Okay, so that's not true: I do know why I didn't tell him. If he'd only let me explain! All I wanted was to

*look like you and Ma and Kiana . . . I might not have
done it at all if I'd known about Andrew Neill . . .*

*Speaking of my father—it's weird to be saying that
and not mean Daddy—he has a niece here in New
York. I'm going to meet her this afternoon, just before I
go to work. Ma is jittery about it, but she won't talk to
me, either. Just keeps fussing and mussing, critcizing
and complaining . . .*

*I think it's her way of telling me she's scared of
where all my discoveries might lead. I think she's
worried I'm changing so much, I won't love her
anymore.*

*Do you think Ma could need reassurance? Seems
impossible, doesn't it?*

Wish me luck,

Audra

Audra knew the woman before she entered the
diner.

It was the same little place near the prison where
she'd sat with Art months and months ago, a different woman from the woman she was now, both inside and out. For one thing, she was almost half the
size she used to be. For another, her street clothes
were now designer jeans worn over Shamiyah-style
heels and a trendy little T-shirt covered by a form-
fitting jacket. And of course there was the hat, scarf
and gloves she wore to protect her skin from the
mottling effect Dr. Jamison had told her about.

Audra stared out of the window of the booth, ignoring the good smells of the place. Dieting was so

much harder now than when she was locked in a mirrorless room: there seemed to be temptations everywhere. Audra tried to ignore the smell of fresh bread and sizzling bacon fat and focused on the window, watching the sidewalks fill with evening foot traffic and the streets line with cabs as the sun sank between the skyscrapers. She glanced down at the piece of paper where she'd written the name and the woman's cell phone number, along with today's date and the time, both records of this appointment set by Audra with Art's private-investigator friend's help.

Laine Neill. That was her name. Audra's father's brother's daughter. Her cousin on her father's side.

Audra glanced up and out the window again as a butterfly of nervousness soared upward from the pit of her stomach. Outside, a woman crossed the street and began walking up the block toward her.

She was around Audra's age, with dark brown skin, of medium height and on the chunky side—carrying at least thirty to forty extra pounds, mainly around the middle and in her butt and thighs—yet she wore a fashionable pair of the same kind of low-slung jeans Audra wore and a pair of spike-heeled boots. She wore a tan suede jacket over a black tank top. Her features were utterly unremarkable in anyway: not unattractive, just not particularly striking or memorable, but she walked with the easy grace of a runway model, confidence speaking in every step.

Audra slid out of the booth as Laine Neill stepped into the diner and looked around. She walked toward Audra with a bright smile on her face and open arms—and as Audra realized she was staring

into a face very much like her own had been many
months ago, tears began to roll down her cheeks.

"Hey cuz," she said, wrapping Audra in the
warmth of her hug. "Welcome to the family."

"Audra! W—what are you doing?" Edith hissed as
Audra grabbed her arm and dragged her out of the
Goldilocks salon. "I'm in the middle of a process—"
and she jerked her arm free and waved her gloved
fingers at Audra.

"Get someone else to finish it for you."

"But the client asked for *me*—"

"If the choices are have someone else finish it or
watch her hair fall out, I think she'll let someone else
finish it!" Audra snapped. "I have to talk to you, right
now! And either you come outside with me, or I'm going to start talking in front of this whole salon."

Edith cut a fearful glance around her. It was a Friday evening and there was a woman in every chair,
plus a few waiting in the little alcove toward the
shop's front.

"All right, all right," Edith grumbled, pulling her
gloves from her fingers. "I'm sorry, dear," she called
in a bright voice toward her client. "Jasmine will finish you up and I'll be back before it's time to style!"
Then she followed Audra out onto the street.

"Aren't you supposed to be at *work*?" she demanded as soon as they were on the sidewalk. This
side street was fairly quiet, but Audra could hear the
rumble of the subway in the distance.

"You know I'm not due on until eleven."

"Well, I can't believe you would come here on a
Friday, one of my busiest nights, and—"

"And I can't believe you would lie to me all these years!" Audra snapped at her.

Edith's face froze for a moment, as her brain absorbed the words. "Honestly, Audra!" she rolled her eyes dramatically and shook her head. "I know you like to have your little movie scenes, but there's a time and place for everything." She turned back toward the salon. "I am not about to stand out here in the cold and—"

"You *are*, Ma. You are, because I've waited long enough to hear your explanation. And I'm not waiting anymore!"

Her mother blinked at her, her composure ripped away like a cheap Halloween mask. Audra read fear in her eyes now, even as she struggled for self-control.

"There ain't no reason to shout, Audra."

"I just met my cousin, Ma. My cousin! She looks just like me—just like I used to look. Do you have any idea what that means to me? Do you have any idea what it would have meant to know her—to know the truth about myself—all these years?"

"Well, I didn't know 'Drew had any family in New York. Last I heard they were all still on St. Croix—"

"Don't change the subject, Ma," Audra shot back. "Why didn't you tell me about him? Why didn't you tell me about my father! Why didn't you tell me before I went on the *Ugly Duckling*? Before I—" she gestured to herself. "Why did you wait until it was too late?"

"Because I didn't actually think you'd go through with it, that's why!" her mother shouted. "Right up to the very last minute, I was sure you'd back out. I was sure you'd come running home like you always did and I could save myself some shame—" And she burst into tears, hard jagged sobs that had Audra not been so determined to hear the story, it would have been impossible to listen to.

"He was a good man . . . a good man," her mother cried. "Why do you have to look so much like him? Why—"

Audra sighed, her anger draining from her with every word her mother spoke. "I need to know how it happened. I need to know . . ." She rubbed her forehead. "How and where and when . . ."

But her mother just paced away from her and sobbed, her face in her hands.

"Here, Ma—" Audra approached her gently and led her to a spot at the edge of the curb. "Sit down . . ."

Her mother sat, but kept sobbing, her face hidden. Audra stroked her shoulder gently, murmuring over and over, "It's okay, Ma. It's okay . . ."

"I—I—was a young wife. Petra was just over a year old. Your—her father was always gone—always running the streets with buddies or . . ." she hiccupped a little, "some woman or the other. I was from the boonies . . . I didn't know no one. I was so lonely . . . so miserable . . . scared to death of this big city. B—but I couldn't go back." She looked up at Audra with wet, red eyes, her lips twisted with anguish. "There wasn't nothing for me in North Carolina. Nothing at all . . ." she whispered. "I knew I had to make it work here somehow for myself. For my daughter . . ." She snuffled and wiped her face with the long black smock she wore over her clothes. "I met Andrew at a soul food restaurant. I was feeling low, wishing for home and I ended up drowning my sorrows in a plate of fried chicken and collard greens. Petra was sitting beside me, giving me pure D hell and I just . . . started crying." She smiled through her tears. "I guess I'd just had it or something . . . but he was sitting at a table nearby, and he saw I was losin' it. He distracted Petra while I got myself together and then"—fresh tears formed in her eyes—"he asked us both to the Central Park Zoo. I almost said no. I was a married woman. True, I was married to a man who acted like he wasn't a married man—James Marks wasn't faithful to me a single day we were together—but I knew I didn't have to act like him. But 'Drew was so kind . . . He was so nice to me . . . and Petra had never been to the zoo." She sighed. "I said yes."

Audra waited while she paused, smiling a little to herself.

"I don't want you to think I just fell into bed with him, 'cause I didn't. He and his brother were setting up a Caribbean restaurant and he was working very hard. But when he could, he would call or come by and take me and Petra somewhere. Anywhere. Sometimes we went to movies, or sightseeing in the city. But most of the time I went with him to restaurant supply stores and to City Hall when he got the paperwork for a restaurant license. I didn't care. I just . . ." She swallowed, pressing back her emotions so that she had the breath to continue. "He talked all the time about how important it was to 'do your own thing'—it was the seventies, you know. That's how people talked. And when I told him I liked to do hair, he encouraged me to get my cosmetology license. Even gave me the money to take the test."

She paused again.

"I fell for him, mind, body and soul," she whispered. "And one thing led to another . . ." She turned to Audra. "We had it planned. I was going to get a divorce from James and we were going to get married and raise Petra—and our own children—together. I was going to open this salon"—she gestured behind her—"and we were going to be happy. And it would have happened, too, but . . ."

"He was killed," Audra finished. "I read it in the stuff the private investigator sent me. Hit by a car over on Ninth Avenue. April fifth—"

"And you were born in December," her mother finished with a sad and heavy sigh. "I know I should have left anyway . . . I should have divorced James then and gone on." She shook her head. "But I was a different woman then. I didn't have any money. I had a cosmetology license but no experience using it. I wasn't sure I could make it on my own. And when I found out I was pregnant, I really wasn't sure who . . ." She let the sentence die with a hard swallow. "It wasn't until you were born that I knew . . . and so did James. He'd suspected anyway. Some of those no-good buddies of his had seen me and Andrew together. But when you were born—"

"Because I was so much darker," Audra finished. "I always knew my coloring didn't fit with the family palette."

"I don't know why, but James's suspicions made me deny it that much more. Insist he was wrong and you and Petra were full-blood sisters in every way.

Stay with him even though..." She shrugged. "I don't know. Maybe I thought that's what I deserved. And when he finally walked out on me"—her face swung toward Audra's tear-streaked one in the dim light—"I thought I'd paid my dues."

"But he's been gone for years, Ma. You could have told me any time—"

"No." Edith shook her head. "No. You were getting older, smarter. At first we were all dealing with the aftermath of James's leaving, and I couldn't add this other burden to it. And then you were a teenager, a teenager always on the verge of rebellion because you were so different. I could see how you and Petra needed each other, kept each other from getting into too much trouble. And I was afraid if I told you I'd mess that up. And then you were an adult, and . . ." She sighed again. "I should have told you, but I couldn't bear to see that look in your eyes. That judgment for all the mistakes I'd made"—a fresh wave of tears misted her eyes—"so I just kept on denying it and denying it and denying it, even though every I time I looked at you, he was there and I'd feel like maybe I wasn't so"—her voice cracked—"alone."

"Ma—"

"I wish I could undo it—I wish all kinds of things, but I can't!" her mother cried. "The past is past. If you have to hate me for the rest of your life, I suppose it's no less than I deserve but—"

"Ma, I don't hate you. At least . . . I don't want to hate you anymore. I want—" She hesitated, struggling with the words. "I want to understand. I want to be able to talk to you about this . . . and I want to know about him. I want to know what he was like. Am I like him . . . at all?"

Her mother grimaced. "Audra, I really don't see the sense of—"

"Please, Mama," Audra grabbed her hand. "Am I like him?"

Edith stared hard into her face, then sighed, her shoulders collapsing in on each other as though she were a much older woman. "No, Audra . . . you looked like him, but you're not much like him. But . . . you're an awful lot like me . . ." Her walnut brown hand covered Audra's beige one. "And you always have been." She gave a faint smile. "I know that isn't what you want to hear, but—"

"No, Mama," Audra squeezed her mother's hand. "It's exactly what I wanted to hear."

There was just a moment, when the two of them stared at each other, each rooted to her spot by uncertainty. Audra didn't know who moved first—and didn't care—but in another moment, her arms were locked around her mother's body and she felt the woman's embrace tight around her back.

"I was going to tell you the night before your surgery," Edith whispered, clinging tightly to Audra's shoulders. "I tried and tried, but I couldn't get the words out. And then, you started talking about dying and loving me and all that. Even after you hung up, I couldn't get it out of my mind, so I called back. Got a busy signal." She pulled herself out of Audra's arms, wiping her face again. "I called and called and called . . . until finally I dug up that girl Shamiyah's number. And I told her 'I got to tell Audra something really important about herself and you gotta help me.' I told her, 'Once she hears what I have to say, she'll stop talking about all this surgery and skin bleaching and come on home.'" Edith shook her head. "She said she'd try to get you a message, but that the phones were being disconnected in your apartment there. For a whole week, to help speed your recovery—"

Disconnected? That didn't ring true. Not at all . . .

"Phones disconnected?" Audra asked, frowning. "The phones were never disconnected. At least not that I know of."

"Well, that's what she said. She said she'd try to get you a message before your surgery, but it might be too late, since they were going to start the first procedure so early in the morning."

"I never even got a message from Shamiyah that you'd called . . ."

"She wasn't able to get to you. At least that's what she told me." And when Audra turned toward her in query, she continued. "She called me back. A couple of times. To tell me how you were doing after all that cutting . . . and to give me an idea of when I'd be able to call you. She kept asking 'Is this about her father? Is this about her father?' until finally I broke down and told her yeah. That's when she got all excited and started talking about how much it would mean to you, and when she promised not to use it on the show." Edith smiled. "She's a nice girl. Seems to really like you."

Audra's frown deepened. It all sounded right, sounded logical and feasible enough, and yet, something nibbled at the back of Audra's brain like an unwelcome pest.

"What is it? What's the matter?"

Audra shook her suspicions away. "Nothing . . . I hope." She pulled herself up from the curb. "I've got to get to work, Ma—"

"Just a minute. I got something else to say," Edith announced, giving her face one last treatment with the smock's sleeve before facing Audra. "About Bradshaw—"

Audra sighed. "He's not talking to me, Ma."

"Well, what did you expect? He sends his girlfriend off a thick slab of dark chocolate and she comes back a ladyfinger!" Edith exclaimed. "That's enough to unsettle any man—"

"I'm not his girlfriend," Audra interrupted.

"Yes, you are, Audra. And the two of you are the only ones who don't know it. Now, shut up and listen, Audra, because I'm only going to say this once." Edith paused, chewing on her lips as though what she was about to say hurt her more than any of the prior confessions.

"You were right," she said slowly, at last. "He's your soul mate."

Chapter 27

Her mind was spinning with a million thoughts: Ma, Andrew Neill, Art, Laine, Shamiyah and the *Ugly Duckling* show . . .

Fortunately, it was the graveyard shift and she had the perfect assignment: patrolling the quiet cell-blocks, making sure inmates were safe and quiet, if not asleep. Other than double-checking doors and peering into cells to insure that "lights out" rules were being strictly complied with, she expected a quiet-enough night.

Which was a good thing, with the world flipped upside down.

Her mother confessing to a long-ago passion of which she was the product; meeting Laine and finding, for the first time, the beauty in her old image, now that it was nearly impossible to retrieve it for herself; Art suddenly turning evasive and quiet, treating her with a courtly arms-length distance and sudden formality that seemed particularly strange after all their intimacies. It was as though she'd gone on the *Ugly Duckling* show to turn the tables, but they'd all ganged up and spun the tables on her.

"You know how to whistle, Audra . . ."

His voice sounded so near, Audra started, peering down the dimly lit hallway, half expecting to see his tall, broad form emerge from the shadows. She thought she heard the echoes of footsteps— there were several other COs on the floor, patrolling at intervals through the sleeping prison. Art worked nights from time to time, so it could be him . . .

But the sound died as she concentrated on trying to decipher it. Instead, another sound, like a faint whisper, seemed to taunt her through the rails of a cell halfway down the hallway.

She moved along the corridor toward the sound, straining her ears to translate it into words—if indeed it was words. It sounded more like the moan of an inmate in trouble or pain.

She touched her communication device, reporting quickly the nature of the sounds and her location, according to procedure.

"Find out which unit it is, then wait for backup," came the expected response from the Central Control. Audra acknowledged, then crept down the hall toward the sound.

It came to her again, a low moan, a definite sound of sickness or pain. Audra pulled her flashlight from her hip belt and peered into cell after cell, looking for the source of the sound until she saw him, curled up in a tight ball on his bunk, holding his stomach.

"*Ugghhh . . .*" the man moaned. "*Ugghh . . .*"

Audra shined her light along the cell number, reaching for her walkie-talkie again.

"Officer . . . Officer . . . Marks?" the inmate stuttered, breathless with pain. "Oh . . . thank . . . God. Help me! H—help—*ahhhhhh!*"

If she'd thought about it or been focused enough to be suspicious, she might have wondered how he knew it was she. But between her own distractions and the man's howl of pain, Audra was swept away by concerns for the man's well-being.

"What's the matter?" she shouted into the cell. "What's wrong?"

The man let out another low moan . . . and then fell silent. Audra could hear nothing, not even the ragged sounds of breath.

"Hey!" Audra shouted, already reaching for the card key that would open the cell door. "You okay in there?"

Silence was the only response. Audra hurriedly slid the card key through a slot on the cell panel, and punched in her code, wishing that the lights weren't on a central system at the other end of the hall. But still, the door slid open quickly and she stepped inside, hurrying toward the room's single bunk.

"Hey! You okay?" she began, bending toward the man.

He was on her in an instant, pouncing catlike as he grabbed her arms, pulling her down on the narrow bed beneath him. Before she could struggle or cry out, he'd clamped a sweaty palm over her mouth and slid her gun out from its holster, pressing it tight against her temples.

"Thanks for making this easy, bitch," he hissed in her ear. He paused and she felt his fingers groping her breasts. "You're half the woman you used to be."

Haines. Audra knew the voice, even if his face were barely visible in the low light.

"Yeah, a man might actually like to fuck you now. And trust me, I will. But first you gonna help me walk right out of this prison, okay?" He jabbed a knee into her abdomen, hard enough to take her breath. "That's for busting my damn ribs," he muttered, then raised himself off her, still holding the gun's cold metal against the skin covering her skull and her brain.

Audra lifted herself slowly off the bunk, her brain racing. Central Control had already dispatched other officers, based on her report, but it was pretty clear that Haines intended to hold them off, using her as shield. And as if he'd plucked the thought out of her brain, the man grabbed her, thrusting her in front of him, his fingers tight around her neck just as they heard footsteps approaching.

"Don't you dare say a word." He tightened the grip around her neck. "Not one fucking—"

Audra thrust out an elbow, jabbing the man so hard in the solar plexus that the gun slipped from its station against her temple. In the fraction of the man's surprise, she bent forward at the waist suddenly, working with his headlock to flip him over her shoulder, like she'd been trained to do in the inmate restraint workshops and the self-defense classes that were the cornerstone of a corrections officer's training.

The maneuver just barely came off before *bang*! the report of the gun filled the air, echoing in Audra's ears in the darkness, followed an instant later by the sound of metal hitting the hard surface of the floor. She dropped to her knees, her eyes acclimating to the darkness, feeling around for the weapon. Her hand closed around something smooth and hard . . . just as Haines grabbed her ankle and yanked, pulling her away from it and tighter into his wiry arms.

They both heard the footsteps clattering toward them; they both heard the voices.

"Help!" Audra shrieked, bellowing the words at the top of her lungs as she struggled and kicked— not only in the hope of freeing herself, but in the hope of kicking the gun away in the process, making it impossible for Haines to retrieve it without releasing her. "Help!"

"Shut up!" Haines hollered, hoisting her to her feet like she was nothing and shoving her against the bunk again. With catlike grace, he stooped, feeling the floor in the low light, furtive and determined, even as the footsteps pounded closer and Audra heard clearly, "Officer needs assistance! Shots fired, Block C, Cell 1211! We need the lights!" She heard a familiar heavy voice growl from the hallway and then the crackle of response from Control.

"Bradshaw!" she cried. "Don't come in! He's got my gun!"

She heard the footsteps hesitate, knew they were right outside the open cell door. Haines was still feeling along the edge of the bunk, his eyes focused on the entrance, where Audra could hear the COs whispering to each other as they took their positions for containment and rescue.

Crap, Audra had time to think. *This is exactly the kind of incident that gives female COs a bad name—*

Then the lights came on, flooding the room with fluorescent light. Audra blinked, her eyes shifting painfully with the abrupt adjustment from dark to light. Then she saw it.

The gun.

Lying between her feet at the foot of the bunk, tantalizingly close and yet so far away. Haines saw it, too—it wasn't two feet from where he knelt, and an easy sweep of the wrist from being once again in his hand. Audra heard the music of the great western classic, *High Noon*, playing in her ears as Haines's eyes locked on hers, his lips curving into that trademark sneer of his. Then the two of them made their move: Haines for the gun and Audra for Haines.

Her right foot connected to his jaw, just as he stretched out his fingers for the weapon. But her left foot had already connected to that too, kicking it like a soccer ball for a goal toward the bars.

"Bradshaw, weapon on the floor!" she shouted. "Coming to—"

Haines's fingers went around her throat, squeezing, choking out any further hope of words, let alone breath. Audra grabbed for his hands, but the man leaned into the work now, forcing her down, weakening her with every second that passed until

Haines's murderous face was replaced by bright lights popping behind her eyeballs.

Then, as suddenly as they appeared, the lights faded. The pressure on her windpipe eased, then lifted completely. Audra coughed, dragging in air like a drowning woman, blinking fast, trying to focus her mind, focus her thoughts enough to understand what was happening now.

"Stupid bitch!" she heard Haines's screaming. "Fat, skinny, bright, dark—you still ain't nothing but a stupid, stupid—"

"Enough!" Bradshaw roared, and Audra could finally see him, towering over Haines, who lay face-down on the floor while two other officers handcuffed him. Art held Audra's service revolver in his hand and his walkie-talkie in the other. He gave a quick "all clear," indicated that Haines would be transferred to a holding cell in Solitary, then signed off, looking at Audra, concern writ in capitals on his face.

"You all right, Marks?" he asked almost gently.

A smart remark, that's what the situation demanded. Something funny that would diffuse the tension of violence circling the room like a buzzard waiting for the kill. Audra knew the words were inside her somewhere, the perfect quip that would make this another one of the stories COs swapped around locker rooms and at shift change. Something movie-star clever . . . something . . .

But the words wouldn't come: not with Art Bradshaw looking at her with that mix of concern and care. Not when all she wanted was to run into his arms and tell him about Laine and her mother, and apologize and beg to be forgiven until she could stay enclosed in those arms forever . . .

Audra rubbed her throat, which felt like it had been caught in a vise, swallowed once and felt a fresh pain twist her face into a wince. Tears sprang to her eyes.

"No," she whispered, shaking her head while Art's deep amber eyes bored into hers. "No . . . I'm not all right . . ."

"I was afraid something like this might happen," he muttered in his low voice.

He had insisted on seeing her home, but she wasn't ready to face Edith. So he offered his place, after the appropriate paperwork was filed. The supervising sergeant placed Audra on administrative leave until the whole encounter could be investigated and dealt with, warning her with the words, "I'd expect a call from Woodburn—and maybe even the Warden—tomorrow." They stopped once, for breakfast from a nearby deli, but didn't speak beyond the necessaries. The process of filing the incident report and realizing how close she'd come to being a participant in a serious attempted prison break had dried her tears. But now, sitting here in his apartment, they were right beneath the surface again.

"I screwed up," Audra said as Art pulled their eggs and toast out of the paper bag and settled their Styrofoam containers on the coffee table in front of her.

"Big time. You know the protocol. You're supposed to have backup, no matter what."

"I'm not talking about Haines," Audra said slowly. "I'm talking about with you."

Art joined her on the couch, his eyes on the Styrofoam. "With me?" he rumbled slowly. "What makes you say that?"

"Oh, I don't know," Audra said with barely concealed sarcasm. "You haven't said a word to me since the Reveal. Hiding out and changing your shifts around and generally acting like I've got the plague or something! It's still me, Art. I've just got long hair, a smaller nose and I've lost some weight— and yes, I'm a little lighter—"

"A *little* lighter!" Art exclaimed, his voice a rumble of distress. "Audra, you're a completely different woman!"

"So what? I didn't exactly see you chasing after the old Audra. You couldn't even look me in the face." She shrugged. "Not that much has changed. You can't look me in the face now, either. Look if you're not interested, you're not interested, but if this is just because you don't like my skin tone—"

"You look just like Esmeralda," he muttered, turning away from her. "What did you do? Take a snapshot of her with you?"

"And if I did, so what?" Audra challenged. "What if I deliberately set out to make myself over in the form your ex-wife, a woman you pursued and sacrificed for, a woman who you still follow with your eyes when she leaves a room—"

"Only to make sure she's not leaving with my wallet."

"That's bull. You found her beautiful and you still

do—admit it! And what's so wrong with me wanting you to find me beautiful, too?"

"I did! I do!" he roared.

"You couldn't even look me in the face—"

"Because of your eyes!" he shouted.

"My eyes?" Audra repeated, dumbfounded. "What about my—"

"You've got the most beautiful eyes I've ever seen," he grumbled as though the admission was hurting him. "It's like you're really seeing me. Seeing through to the heart of me. It's unnerving and wonderful and . . ." He paced away from her. "Every since that day in the day room, when your pants ripped and the inmates were laughing . . ." His amber eyes found hers. "You handled that with such grace, and then when I saw your eyes and saw the hurt"—he sighed—"I lost part of my heart then and there. I knew I had to keep my head down or you'd know . . . and I wasn't ready for that. I had too much other stuff to get rid of, to sort out . . ."

"Like Esmeralda?" Audra prompted.

"We'll never be completely rid of her," he muttered. "But yeah, it had to be sorted out. She was living with me at the time and I knew . . . I knew I'd lose you forever if you found that out. And Penny had to be prepped. When a child's been used to the sole attention of a parent, introducing someone new can be tough. I wanted you to talk to Penny . . . get to know her apart from being her dad's girlfriend, but that didn't go right, did it?"

"No," Audra agreed. "She thought you wanted me to meet her to give her an ugly duckling pep talk," Audra said. "And after seeing Esmeralda, so did I."

"This is just one miscommunication after another," he said ruefully. "Because by the time Esmeralda left us, you were gone. Or at least you'd made the decision to go. Off to California to be made over. I wanted to stop you . . . but I thought it was being selfish, so . . ." He trailed off. "But it turned out to be a good thing. It was so much easier then, because I could talk to you without having to worry about those eyes of yours."

"But when I came back . . ."

"When you came back and I saw those eyes I loved in a face so like my ex-wife's . . . a face I've grown to hate"—he shook his head—"I've got to tell you, it really freaked me out. That, and . . ." His amber eyes pierced her face. "Why didn't you tell me, Audra? Why didn't you tell me about the skin-tone stuff? All the talking we've done over the past few months . . . I can't understand how you could keep something so important from me."

"I'm sorry," Audra said. "I knew I should tell you . . . but I was afraid."

"Afraid? Of me?"

"A little," Audra admitted. "Not because I was trying to look like Esmeralda—I wasn't. I just wanted to look like the women in my family: Petra, my mother. Only now I've met the other women in my family, too . . ." She struggled to regain her focus. "I didn't want you to think I was so shallow. I didn't want you to think I was some self-hating black woman whose ideal of beauty was a skinny, white girl. That's not me. I may be a silly, self-hating

black woman"—Audra's eyes filled with unexpected tears—"but my ideal of beauty is my sister
Petra . . . and it always has been. I wish she were
here," she whispered. "I really, really do."

She felt Art Bradshaw's arms encircle her, just as
the first tear slid down her cheeks.

"I know," he murmured into the side of her neck.
"I've just got to get used to seeing those eyes in
that face. You're a beautiful woman now, Audra. I
came out there—to California—ready to profess my
undying love like the hero in a classic Hollywood
drama." He gave her a sad smile. "And then I realized how unfair that was. I've got to get used to seeing how other men look at you. I've got to deal with
the fact that you're a beautiful woman. And one day
you might decide you can do better than a guy like
me—"

Audra spun around to face him. "Never. I knew
from the very beginning you were my soul mate.
When you knew the difference between *Casablanca*
and *Double Indemnity*."

Art's eyes twinkled.

"All we need now," he purred in his sexiest voice.
"Is an anklet."

Audra's mouth went dry, her heart got loud. She
closed her eyes, knowing what he'd say next . . .

"Don't you get it, Audra?" He shook her shoulders gently. "It doesn't matter to me what you look
like: light, dark, fat, thin. If you wear sweats or designer clothes—I could care less. Women are so hard
on themselves about the way they look. I'll be happy
as long as you're still the woman who makes me
laugh. Who can be tough and tender at the same

time. Who's smart and loyal and full—just full to her eyebrows with passion for everything she does—" He stopped short. "Look, I know I'm not what you're looking for, so I guess there's no real point to this, but—"

"Oh, Art . . ." Audra said realizing in an instant what had been right in front of her face all along.

"Yeah, I'm in love with you, Audra," he gave a hopeless little smile. "Have been from the day you flipped Haines over your shoulder and threw him against the wall."

Audra lifted her hands to his face. "There's a speed limit in this state. Forty-five miles an hour."

He lowered his lips toward hers. "How fast was I going, Officer?"

"About ninety . . ." Audra murmured as their lips met, the violins swelled and at long last, Art Bradshaw was in her arms, where he belonged.

It was hard to tell which of them was hungrier: Audra wrapped her fingers around the man's face, pulling his lips closer to her own. She felt Art's hands encircle her waist, then slide to her hips, then lift her off her feet, all the while his mouth demanding more and more and more from hers.

"I've been dreaming nasty, nasty dreams about you, boy," Audra murmured when he broke the kiss long enough for her to speak. "For months and months . . ."

Art grinned. "Oh yeah?"

"So unless skinny girls totally turn you off so bad you can't get it up—"

"They don't . . . or least not when their name is Audra Marks."

"You mind if things get . . . a little . . . freaky?"

Now Art's features relaxed again. "I knew you were the woman for me, Audra Marks."

Now it was Audra's turn to grin. "Then do me, baby. Do me, good."

"Consider yourself done," Art replied.

There wasn't the slightest bit of awkwardness between them, as though they'd been together a thousand times before and knew each other body and soul.

"Strip!" Audra commanded, laughing.

"I will, if you will," he said already rolling down the waist of her slacks.

"Hey." Audra smacked him lightly on his broad cheek. "I didn't say strip *me*!

"Well, 'scuse me," he teased back and grabbed at his own trousers, which immediately puddled around his ankles. "Better now?"

Audra had barely removed her blouse when he stood naked and proud before her, posing and preening like a gigolo earning a paycheck. At Audra's applause, he grabbed her hands and sat her down, a naked audience at the edge of the bed, and adopted a runway strut that seemed incongruent with his impassive exterior but totally in keeping with the man she knew in her heart. He struck pose after pose, some coy, some racy—all showing his total confidence in his large, masculine body—until tears of laughter rolled down Audra's face.

"Your turn," he growled into her ear.

"Oh please, I've had enough runways to last a lifetime," Audra protested, but he was already pulling her up off the bed. He pushed her toward the mirror and stood behind her, his skin dark against her bright skin. Scars, in various stages of healing, crisscrossed her naked body. Audra averted her eyes, the playfulness disappearing from the moment. "Art . . . don't . . ."

"Look," he urged gently.

"I don't want to—"

"Don't tell me you've gone to all the trouble to remake yourself, and you can't even stand to look at yourself."

"Not exactly, it's just—"

"Then *look*!"

Audra sighed and dragged her eyes to the mirror.

"What do you see?" Art whispered, planting a kiss along the side of her neck.

"I don't know . . ." Audra sighed. "I don't wear Petra as well as she does. And after finally getting the truth from my mother, I can't help but wonder if I've made a mistake."

"Forget that stuff. Find *you*, Audra. Find something beautiful."

Audra stared at herself. Without elaborate makeup—just a little mascara and lip gloss—she saw the face of a pretty-enough woman, but one she still barely recognized with her fair skin and long hair. But the eyes . . . the lips . . . those were her own.

"My eyes . . ." she said softly.

Art's arms tightened around her as he turned her slightly and kissed both of her eyelids in a way that made warmth stir from Audra's ears to her crotch.

"What else?" he murmured, his breath a hot rush of desire.

"My . . . lips . . ."

And immediately he caught them with his own, pulling a feeling out of her that left Audra breathless. But when she leaned into him for more, he turned her back to the mirror and continued in a ragged voice, "Go on."

But now that she knew that every part she named would be due for treatment from Art's lips and tongue, she closed her eyes and murmured, "My breasts."

To her surprise, Art brought her own hands up to her nipples, guiding her fingers around the curves of flesh. "Love them," he told her in that same sexy whisper that sent another thrill of desire through her, as he encouraged her timid fingers to stroke the buds hard while his own hands slid down to her belly and hips. "What else?" he murmured roughly, planting kisses along her derriere. "Here?" His big hands parted her legs, kissing the insides of her thighs. "Here?" Then his tongue found the softness of her female center, and with a single flick of it, he set her completely afire. "Here?" he asked.

"Yes," Audra muttered, barely able to speak for the sensations coursing through her body.

"You like your body . . . here . . ." he kissed her thighs again. "And here?" Another thrust of his tongue down deep where no surgeon had touched.

"Mmmm," Audra moaned, knowing she could no longer withstand the teasing torture of his touch.

"Say it!" he growled, his voice gruff with impatient command. "Say you like it!"

"I like it!" Audra shouted like a new recruit at basic training. "I like it! Just—just—"

She didn't have to say more. Art let loose a feral shout and dove his tongue into her, tasting her until Audra's legs shuddered, barely able to hold her weight. She grabbed his head, pressing him deeper between her thighs, while the mirror recorded passion and release playing across her face.

"Art . . ." she hissed, breathless and ready. "I need you . . . inside me . . ."

"Your wish is my command," he muttered, pulling her down on the floor beside him and covering her with himself. Audra spread herself wide and he plunged deep, so deep Audra reacted, arching herself to accommodate the size and thickness of him. He hesitated just a moment, but when Audra groaned, "Harder, deeper . . ." he grabbed her behind between his two hands and pounded himself into her with an energy and passion that brought her to an explosion so complete, Audra forgot everything but the feeling of the man's hardness against her softness. She was no longer a body, but a soul, in union with a kindred soul.

Art was insatiable. He bent her body in ways she hadn't known it would move, bringing waves of fresh desire with every position, every angle, until at last, he muttered, "I'm coming . . . I'm . . ." and she felt him release the last of his energy deep inside her, while she shuddered against him, accepting his passion and returning it with a passion all her own.

Audra didn't remember later how they moved from the floor to the bed. But she remembered the feeling of complete satisfaction and the comfort of their two sweaty, spent bodies, entwined.

I love Art Bradshaw, she thought as his arms slid around her and she felt his breath on her neck, even and slow with sleep. *I love Art Bradshaw . . . and he loves me.*

Chapter 28

October 27

Dear Petra,

My Ugly Duckling show airs tonight. I was really hoping you'd be here to watch it with us. It sucks that your discharge date has been delayed again. Kiana's miserable. I don't know how much more disappointment she can stand. She really misses you both.

Art and Penny are coming over, and so is Laine, the cousin I told you about. Penny is bringing a couple of girls from her school. In a weird sort of way I've actually helped her make a few friends. Ma has a couple of her stylists coming, and one or two of her "special" clients. It should be a regular party. This is the last episode, so there will be voting for the Top Three after my "package" airs. I really don't expect to make it, but who knows?

I called Shamiyah and asked her about her promises to Ma, and the whole telephone thing. She said the phone was disconnected briefly while I was out of it during the first few days of surgery. I asked her what to expect on the show and she laughed. She said "Nothing to do now but wait and see." Then she started on how "great" it all was, and how her "career" is "made" . . .

Somehow none of that made me feel any better. But then, I have lots of things on my mind.

After the latest incident with Haines at the prison, I've really been thinking. I'd like to do some work with girls on body image. I was thinking about asking Dr. Goddard and maybe using some of the show's publicity to help me get started. Shamiyah always said I could be the voice for some of the sisters out there who have issues. Maybe I really could be. Then it really would be like Now, Voyager *wouldn't it? Remember how at the end, Bette Davis helps Paul Henreid's daughter break out of her shell and discover her beauty? Well, just call me Bette . . .*

Be careful out there,

Audra

"**I**'m sick and tired of being fat, black and ugly," the woman on the TV was saying earnestly on an obviously inexpert video tape. There was a sort of loping grin on her face that did little to conceal her obvious pain. "Just once, I want to be the woman who everyone looks at, everyone desires. Just once I'd like to be pursued, sought after. I'd like to preen around." The woman in the video assumed an exaggerated strut, but her legs rubbed together, making a whistling sound that would have been funny if it weren't so pathetic. "I'd like to toss my hair." She shook the short curls of her natural. "I'd like to know what it feels like to be a swan."

Audra sank a little deeper into her sofa, covering her face with her hands. The living room of her mother's apartment had been lively with conversation only a few moments before, as the assembled group prepared for Audra's television debut. Now the room had gone deadly silent. Audra didn't dare glance around at any of them, didn't want to see the pity in their faces. She looked ridiculous up there: not funny or clever or amusing as she'd always imagined. Just ridiculous.

"It's okay," Art rumbled into her ear, his arm tightening around her shoulders. "That's the old stuff . . . you're a different person now . . ."

But the *Ugly Duckling* people had chosen to air a good deal of her original tape, including the embarrassing confessions about her pants ripping at the jail, and the ugly names the inmates called her as she went about her job. Even Penny Bradshaw's words were repeated, but in a voice-over as Audra emerged from a car and walked alone into the building that housed the offices of her plastic surgeons.

"Wait and see." That's what Shamiyah had said. And now Audra understood. There was no way she wanted to admit to this. No way she didn't know how angry Audra would be.

But was this Shamiyah's doing? Audra wondered,

thinking about how she'd complained about the editing ahead. *Or had she been pressured to change it by the evil, ratings-hungry Camilla?*

She pushed aside her questions and focused on the next segment and saw herself, seated at the long conference table, marking up the photographs with the experts who had become her friends.

But so little of that long afternoon had made the final package. In the end, the world saw Dr. Bremmar drawing purple lines over a hefty Audra's body, outlining procedures, and Dr. Jamison explaining the process of skin lightening, while Audra appeared to listen eagerly. But somehow, none of her questions or reservations about the process had made the final cut—not even the whole discussion about scarring— because when the man finished speaking, the cameras quickly cut to her face and the only words that fell out of her mouth were, "I'm in."

Several of her mother's customers groaned in displeasure. Audra bit back the impulse to shout out, "There was more! They cut it!" and gripped Art's hand even more tightly.

"Do you realize you'd be changing your cultural identity? That decision will impact how you will be viewed in the African-American community. Friends, family—"

"I don't think I have any friends or family whose opinion holds much influence," the Audra on tape replied, and the Audra in her home living room, surrounded by friends and family, could have crawled into a hole and died.

Then Camilla Jejune's made-for-TV-voice took over as the camera zoomed tight on Audra's face.

"And so, Audra Marks made the choice to leave behind fat, black and ugly for a new image: one she calls, 'light, bright and beautiful.' Our team of experts set to work on the most challenging of Ugly Ducklings ever."

The next scene found her in Dr. Jamison's office, learning about the application of skin lightening cream and donning her hat, scarf, and long gloves for the first time. As she left the office, Dr. Jamison spoke to the camera, explaining the risks associated with high doses of hydroquinone and expressing his concerns about the self-image of those seeking a radical skin-color change.

"I think in Audra's case, there's been a lot of hurt and trauma associated with her skin tone . . . and I'm hoping she'll address those internal concerns as well as the external ones."

"He never said that to me," Audra muttered no longer able to keep silent as the sweeping heat of anger burned from her heart to her lips. "He never said any of that shit to *me*! Every time I asked for your input you just looked at me!" she told the man.

Dr. Jamison was gone, his screen time finished. Now, she was sitting with Dr. Goddard, being lectured on the tensions between light- and dark-skinned blacks in America. It was ludicrous, watching herself, a black woman, being told about blackness by a white woman, and Audra leaned forward, remembering the conversation clearly, remembering her response, which she'd launched from her own private Africa, down deep inside.

None of it made it into the package. None of it. To

the world, she was just as passive, submissive and agreeable as the "old Mammy" characters in the movies she loved so much.

Another quick voice-over teased, "Audra gets dropped a bombshell from home that rocks her motivation. Will she complete the Ugly Duckling program or will she drop out?" Then the program jumped to a commercial, leaving Audra's angry response to the doctor's condescension on the cutting-room floor.

The silence in the room was like a weight around her neck, pulling her down into a darkness worse than any feeling she could ever remember having.

"They left out a lot of stuff," Audra told her guests in a soft voice. "There was all this stuff about keloid scarring—about changing the tone of my skin to improve the plastic surgery results . . ." she added lamely.

Her explanations were met with a few mutterings, but no one seemed to want to look at her. So when the telephone rang, Audra yanked it up, anything to escape from the awful pall that had been cast over what was supposed to be a happy, celebratory gathering.

"Hello?"

"Is this Audra Marks?" an unfamiliar female voice asked.

"Yes?"

"The Audra Marks that went on the *Ugly Duckling* show?"

"Yes," Audra said slowly. Shamiyah had told her she might get calls from people who'd seen the show, and had even suggested she make sure her number was unlisted. But Audra had forgotten about that warning until this very moment.

"I think you're a pathetic excuse for a black woman, you self-hating bitch."

"Who is this?"

"A proud black woman who's sick of people like *you*," the woman hissed furiously. "The white man said you were ugly, and you swallowed it whole, didn't you? I can't believe you went on TV with this trash. You want to be a white woman, be one. Black folks don't need you no how—"

"It wasn't like that!" Audra told the woman, but she hung up as soon as she'd said her piece. The phone rang again, almost instantly.

"Audra Marks, you ought to be ashamed of yourself, my sister," an educated male voice lectured. "And I feel sorry for you, a beautiful black sister, for giving up your power for some light, bright bullshit—"

And even as this stranger filled her ears with his lesson, the call waiting was beeping through his message, signaling another caller eager to drop more curses on her.

Art wrestled the phone out of her hands. "We'll just turn it off," he said, even as the line in Audra's bedroom jangled the steady jangle of another call. "Go—"

But the show had returned and Audra stood still, not wanting to watch and yet arrested by the unfolding train wreck that was her appearance on *Ugly Duckling*.

"Troubles from home threaten Audra's progress,"

the narrator was saying and Audra saw herself sitting in the mirrorless apartment that had been her home for months, the telephone pressed to her ear. In white letters superimposed beneath her image were the words, ON THE PHONE, AUDRA'S MOTHER, EDITH.

And suddenly she knew exactly what she was going to hear and see.

"No . . ." she whispered as her heart stopped beating in her chest and the room became suddenly as cold and dark as an arctic winter. "They wouldn't do that . . . She promised she wouldn't . . ."

"Andrew Neill," Edith's voice said over the phone with a loud beep replacing the syllable of the last name. "He's your father."

"No she didn't!" Edith exploded, jumping out of her chair as ready to fight as any boxing champion at the sound of the bell. "No she didn't!"

But on the television, the conversation continued as it had in reality: "If he'd lived, I would have left James Marks—I would have left Petra's father for him and you would have known him, Audra. Then maybe you'd be proud to look like him instead of ashamed—"

"I'm gonna kill that little bitch Shamiyah," Edith hollered. "Somebody get my switchblade. I'm hopping the next plane, train or automobile and"—she looked wildly around the room as if pleading for her guests' understanding—"She *swore* on her life they were gonna leave that out—"

"Undaunted by her mother's entreaties, Audra reports for surgery the next morning," the relentless narration continued, and the next images were of the actual surgical process, sped up like a comedy sketch, as three long, hard days of procedures were compressed into less than thirty seconds.

Audra could hear the phone, still ringing in the bedroom . . . and now the cell phone in her handbag was jangling along with it, but she couldn't make her feet move to silence either one of them. She was still staring at the TV in utter disbelief.

She'd just told the world she was illegitimate—just outed her mother as an adultress—just opened the Pandora's box of family secrets and dumped them out, soiled and foul, in front of everyone.

The cold room went hot, then cold, then hot again, and she felt herself falling.

"Sit down," Art murmured, but between her mother vowing to cut Shamiyah from curls to calf, the sound of several of their guests excusing themselves and the noise of the TV, she barely heard him, barely felt the sofa beneath her legs.

It wasn't over, the humiliation. Because there she was, swaddled in bandages from forehead to neck, talking to Dr. Goddard, denying her anger, denying her hurt when it was so plain—so plain. The woman she was looking at was the personification of anger, the pure embodiment of hurt . . . and only she was too blind to see it. But there wasn't even a minute of the subsequent breakdowns and breakthroughs—nothing that might have redeemed her in the eyes of the viewing public.

"God help me," Audra muttered. "Please . . ."

But if the prayer were granted, His help appeared in a form Audra could not recognize. The show continued, marching through the healing process, the gym workouts, the slow transformation of Audra Marks, punctuated every so often by the narrator's comments, pointing out the obvious: Audra's skin seemed a little lighter, a little brighter, in every scene . . . right down to the dramatic Reveal, where Audra kicked and strutted and simpered and pranced—and seemed just as self-centered and obnoxious as any pretty woman she'd ever disliked in her fat, black and ugly days.

"For all Audra's difficulties with relationships with men in the past, it appears that there is some possibility of a new romance on the horizon," Camilla Jejune narrated in a voice filled with high drama, as Audra rushed into Art's arms at the Reveal and some sappy music played. But at least in that one brief scene, Audra seemed like a real human being, and not some kind of—of—

Character.

The realization hit her high and hard with its truth . . . because for a good deal of the whole Ugly Duckling experience—indeed, for a good deal of her life—that's exactly what she'd been doing. Playing a character, a larger-than-life version of someone she hardly knew—someone who didn't really exist at all.

"Wait a minute . . ." Audra stared at the screen, as the thing that had been niggling in the back of her mind for weeks took form and grew. "Wait a minute!" she shouted over Edith's continued cursing. "That's not right. That's not how it happened. The order is wrong." She turned to her mother. "I'd already had the surgery when you told me that. Remember?"

"Oh they just got us all messed up on here," Edith declared. "All messed up! They make it sound like you set out to turn yourself into—into— some kind of white girl! Somebody get me my switchblade—"

On the screen in front of them, Camilla Jejune was explaining the rules of the voting for Top Three. "Give me the remote," Audra demanded and once it was in her hand, she stopped the video tape they'd been recording and hit REWIND.

There it was again, herself, talking to her mother, being told about her paternity . . .

"Ma! Look!" she pointed at the screen. "There's no bandages!"

"No . . ." her mother said slowly.

"But you didn't tell me until after the surgery."

"Well, I tried to call," Edith said angrily. "We already been through all that. Shamiyah said she couldn't reach you, and then you was too out of it to take any phone calls. She didn't call me and tell me you were ready 'til damn near a week later—"

"When there were bandages all over my face and body. They've done some major editing here," Audra announced, her own anger sharpening. "They've switched it all around to suit the story they wanted to tell—"

"I don't understand," Penny interjected.

"Audra's saying Shamiyah didn't want Ms. Edith to talk to her before the surgery," Art explained.

"You bet she didn't." Audra grabbed the phone, dialing the numbers from memory. "Because she knew if I talked to Ma, I'd back out! She knew I'd call the whole thing off and she wouldn't have a show—" She stopped short as the ringing sound from the phone at her ear was replaced by a familiar voice.

"Audra! Woman of the hour!" Shamiyah sounded breathless and excited. "My phone has been ringing off the hook. You saw the show, right? Didn't you just *love* it?"

"No, I didn't love it, Shamiyah!" Audra snapped. "It's bad enough that you made me look like some kind of self-hating color-struck *freak*." Audra let her voice rise with the word. "But—"

Edith snatched the phone out of her hand. "You lying little *bitch!* I'm gonna cut you from your ears to where the sun don't shine—"

Audra grabbed the phone away from her mother.

"You asked me to talk about the man I thought was my father, that he thought I was ugly . . . and I did. But you promised not to go any deeper than that. You promised not to tell the whole world about my mother's—"

"She consented to the release of the phone call, Audra," Shamiyah said as though that were the only consideration. "I have the paperwork right here."

"But—"

"Look, Audra, it was an important part of your story. We couldn't leave it out. Not when it's so compelling and—" There was a break in the line as another call rolled Audra's line. "You should probably get that. I told you earlier that we've been getting requests from all kinds of media. All the morning shows want to interview you and Dr. Goddard. To talk more about color consciousness in the black community and—"

"I'm not answering that damned phone," Audra snapped. "I don't want to talk about color consciousness in the black community. I don't want to be on the morning shows or—"

"I'm afraid you're going to have to, Audra," Shamiyah said in a voice that had more than a little of Camilla's hard edge to it. "I'm sorry, but you've got a contract with this show . . . and it includes participating in show promotion. These interviews are the perfect lead in to the Big Reveal in two weeks." She paused, her voice becoming steely with determination. "And you *will* do them."

"And if I won't?"

"Well," Shamiyah dropped any pretense of the enthusiastic, bubbly woman Audra had come to associate with her name. "I think you can expect some serious legal consequences. Not the least of which might be the bill for all the professional services you've received, gratis, from *Ugly Duckling*. Last I heard, the tally was close to two hundred thousand dollars in surgeries and consultations, airfare, lodging—"

"Those papers I signed can't be any good!" Audra shouted. "You manipulated me! You talked me into—"

"Nobody talked you into anything," Shamiyah snapped back. "You were all too eager to do it. You were the one calling herself fat, black and ugly . . . and when we offered you the chance to be something else, you jumped on it like a crack addict to a pipe. If you'd had even a little of the *self-respect* you're claiming we took, you'd have done what the others did and refuse to have anything to do with the whole thing—"

"Others?" Audra frowned into the telephone. "What are you talking about . . . others? I thought out of all the tapes, I was your pick. I thought you wanted me because I was the perfect messenger—"

Shamiyah's laughter echoed around her as though piped in by speakers and amplified to the point of pain.

"Oh, Audra, Audra," she chuckled. "The perfect messenger is anyone willing to deliver the message. We've been looking for an African-American woman willing to do the skin lightening procedure since last season. We must have flown two dozen women out, put them through the same procedures, offered them the same arguments—and all of them refused. They had too much pride in what they were: strong, black women." She sighed with the memory. "Camilla was ready to scrap the whole thing, but it was my concept, my idea, and I wasn't going to give up that easily!" she said vehemently. "By that time, my job was on the line and I knew if I didn't get someone to sign on, Camilla would fire me, bad-mouth me in the industry and my television career would be finished." She paused. "And then you came along . . . and saved my life. Do you realize already this show has had more buzz than all the prior episodes of *Ugly Duckling* put together? With all the press this episode's getting, we're anticipating the Big Reveal to have a shot at being one of the most watched events on television this season. And that's because of you, Audra. You've made my career—I've been pitching this success around town and I may even get my own show out of it, thanks to the controversy and the media exposure. Hell, I don't know what you're complaining for: You've got a good chance to walk away with the grand prize."

"What?"

"Aren't you watching? The votes are in. You just made Top Three! Congratulations—"

"I don't want it."

"Well you got it. See you in three weeks," Shamiyah said calmly. "And Audra, don't even think about skipping the interviews or not showing up for the Big Reveal. You'll be on the *Today* show and the others tomorrow. You'll do the interviews and, when the time comes, you'll get on that plane to join us for the Big Reveal, Audra . . . or there will be legal hell to pay, I promise you."

"But—"

"*Ciao,*" Shamiyah said brightly and hung up before Audra could say another word.

"We'll just have to bust up that contract," Edith was saying for the thousandth time.

The last of the guests were long gone, slinking out in embarrassment for Audra, Edith and the whole situation. Penny had escorted Kiana to bed with the promise of a story and now Edith and Art joined Audra in the kitchen, as she tried to sort through her options.

Audra sighed, feeling as though a big steel cage had been dropped over her head, windowless and without air enough to breathe. She wanted to protest, to argue, but mad as she was at Shamiyah, she knew well there was no one to rave her fury against but herself.

They'd had to turn off all the phones, since they were ringing incessantly—and not with well-wishers. It seemed every angry black person in the five boroughs of New York had looked up their number and decided to call. Although there was security in the building, Audra was grateful for Art's presence: There were certainly more than enough crackpots in the city to make it possible for one or two to attempt to express their anger in person.

So this was the concept, the concept Shamiyah had been so vague on from the beginning: a dramatic makeover show about a black woman who wanted to look white. And with a little tweaking and twisting of the facts, the girl had definitely accomplished her goal: Here stood one Audra Marks, once a dark-skinned woman, now a light-skinned one. And the complex personal reasons for that transformation had been completely eliminated, painted over in simple black-and-white.

"We can talk to a lawyer, but . . ." Audra shook her head and sighed. For the first time in months, she longed for an Oreo, could almost taste its creamy goodness on her tongue. "I'm not optimistic."

"Why not? What she did was out-and-out fraud."

Audra shook her head. "I don't think so. And besides, we all signed the releases. That allows them to use what we said to each other pretty much any way they want."

Edith frowned. "I'm not buying that until every lawyer in Manhattan says it," she declared. "And you're certainly not going back out there."

"I may have to," Audra muttered, staring at her perfect caramel arms, one folded against the other on her chest. Although she had stopped using the cream months ago, the color remained smooth and even, since she'd taken Dr. Jamison's advice and remained vigilant about the sun. "Just like I'm going to have to do these interviews—"

"But Audra, why? They just going to make a fool of you again!" Edith said. "These TV people. All they care about is themselves and their ratings and making money. They don't care who they hurt or what happens to them after the cameras stop rolling. It's all about the—what was the word that girl used? The concept. It's all about the concept."

Audra frowned, the beginnings of an idea tickling the back of her brain. Her mother stopped short, peering closely at Audra's face.

"Why do you look like that all of the sudden?" she asked. "What—"

"Ma, do you think you can get this hair weave out?"

"I'm sure I can!" Edith sounded indignant. "You think that Ishti's *that* much better than me? It's just a matter of what the clientele can afford—"

But Audra wasn't listening, she was too busy digging into the pantry.

"What are you—"

"The *Yellow Pages*," Audra said quickly. "Here they are. I need to find out where the nearest tanning booth is—" She looked up quickly. "Art, I need you to do something for me."

"Anything."

"Oreos, please . . . and some soda—"

"But Audra, your diet!" Penny interrupted. "You'll wreck it!"

"Exactly," Audra said, grinning into their puzzled faces. "Exactly."

It took a while . . . but little by little, understanding dawned on each of their faces. Art's booming laughter filled the kitchen.

"You're a piece of work, Audra Marks . . . a piece of work!"

"Well . . ." Audra said slyly. "I was just thinking . . . This whole concept thing . . . it could cut both ways. And as long as they get their ratings, I can't see what difference it should make to the Ugly Duckling people. And I'm in the mood to fight fire with fire. But"—she cautioned them with a finger—"we'll have to be careful. It can't be obvious what I'm doing. And we don't want it to be. Not until the Reveal."

Edith blinked at her, then a slow grin spread across her lined face. "Oh, I like the sound of *this*! You're gonna undo it, aren't you! That's a great idea."

Audra shook her head. "No, Ma. I can't undo it. I can't undo the surgery . . . and I can't get my old coloring back. My skin . . . it might be pretty messed up. In fact, I may even look worse than I did before. But I'd rather be that than a slave to someone else's vision."

"You—you're gonna go back? You're going to go out in front of millions of people looking worse than you used to look?" Penny asked, staring at Audra, her mouth slack with surprise.

Audra fixed the girl with a calm stare. "That's right." She stretched her hand toward the girl. "But I hope we'll still be friends, Penny. I'd like to think you could like me . . . even if I'm not pretty anymore."

Penny stared at Audra, her brow crinkled as she weighed the question. Then a slow smile spread across her face. "You're brave, Audra. You're the bravest woman I know. I think I know why Dad likes you so much." She crossed the room and hugged Audra tightly. "And I hope I'm just like you when I'm old."

Audra laughed. "Thanks, I think."

"How long do we have?" Art asked.

"About three weeks. The live show is November thirteenth—"

"Sweeps," Penny muttered like some old-hand industry rep. "Shows that get the most viewers during sweeps ratings period can command higher advertising fees," she explained at Audra's questioning look.

"So it's really just about the money," Art offered. "That explains why they've scheduled all this media attention. To keep the controversy alive."

"But are you sure you want to go out there like that?" Edith asked. "I can pull out that weave, but you've barely got any hair under that. And depending on what happens with your skin"—she shook her head—"Penny's right. Are you sure you want to do that in front of the whole world?"

Audra considered their concerned faces for a long moment, and then smiled.

"In the words of Norma Desmond, from that

great Hollywood classic, *Sunset Boulevard . . .*" She struck a dramatic film star pose of batted eyelashes and pouty lips. "Mr. DeMille, I'm ready for my closeup."

Chapter 29

November 13

Dear Petra,

It hasn't gone exactly as I planned . . . but then I knew that. The good news is, the live Duckling starts in a few hours. It's been really hard, but it's almost over. There's probably going to be some media—and some backlash—but unless I win, the lawyer we hired says I'm a "private citizen" again right after the show ends.

I hope like crazy I don't win.

I've decided to resign from the prison. I might go back, I don't know. But for now, it's not where I want to be. I have too much to learn about myself. Too much to figure out. Laine invited me to join her in the Islands for Thanksgiving—to meet the other side of my family—and I'm going. I'll meet my father's brothers and sister and their families. I'm also going to meet my

*grandmother. My grandmother! Laine says she's going
to love me. I hope she's right.*

*Art has asked me to move in with him and Penny. I
might. I don't know. I might look for my own place.
We'll see.*

*They're all here for the TV show: Laine, Art and
Penny, Ma and Kiana. The only thing that would make
it perfect for me was if you were here, too.*

Here's hoping you'll make it home by Christmas . . .

Be careful out there,

Audra

"**W**hat's going on with your face?" Shamiyah
asked, peering at Audra.

Hours in the tanning bed, Audra almost replied, but
she bit her lips at her recent efforts to increase her
sun exposure.

"I've had a reaction to the hydroquinone," Audra
lied.

Shamiyah's brow furrowed in consternation as
she studied the dark brown patches of skin along
Audra's jaw and cheeks. "This is terrible. Just terrible. We've got to get you to Dr. Jamison—"

"I've already spoken to him," Audra said, truthfully enough, omitting the part about how she'd
called to ask him his advice on the fastest way to re-
verse the skin lightening process or mention of his
eagerness to assist, provided she did not reveal his
role. "He sent me some medicine, but I've had to
wear more makeup to cover the worst of it."

The worst of it. As she had feared, Audra's skin
had started to transition, but not into an even brown

or beige or any other color in between. Instead, it was a mottled mess of blotches: part light, part dark, part in between. The effect was a patchwork of colors that hardly looked camera-ready. Audra and her mother had spent a good deal of time coming up with a foundation that would conceal it, but the result was a thick powdery mess in the style of the old pancake makeup worn by the grand divas of the forties. The kind of makeup that looked utterly unnatural anywhere but on a soundstage.

She would need it for all of her encounters with *Ugly Duckling* people, right up until the dress rehearsal, if there was going to be a second "Big Reveal."

"Okay, okay," Shamiyah said quickly, hustling Audra toward the airport exit. "It looks funny in person, but on camera it'll probably be fine."

Audra stopped short.

"What?" Shamiyah asked impatiently. "I've got a car waiting right out front—"

"You don't expect me to go without my luggage do you—and my entourage?" She pointed to where Edith and Kiana stood, watching the metal wheel for their bags. As a familiar piece of luggage made its way slowly around the concourse, Art Bradshaw leaned over to hoist it easily onto a cart held tightly in place by his daughter. As if feeling their eyes, Edith turned, shooting Shamiyah an evil glare and an even more evil hand gesture.

"W—what's all this?" Shamiyah stuttered, her eyes widening with shock. "Really Audra," she continued, recovering some of her careless attitude, "I remember when you traveled with a toothbrush and a spare pair of panties! I *told* you not more than two guests could join you for the Big Reveal—"

Audra shrugged. "And I told *you*, Shamiyah, if you want me, you get them. We don't mind bunking up together. We're family."

Shamiyah's brown eyes narrowed slightly and Audra read her suspicions in her face.

"Look, Audra," she hissed. "Like I've told you a thousand times, you signed the papers. If you're still mad about how you came off on the show—"

"I'm not mad," Audra said sweetly. "I just brought my family out to California for a little R and R, that's all."

"But you're here to work. The live show is in two days! We don't have time for—"

"Then do what I asked you to do and get their Disney passes," Audra told her in a steely voice that would have made the late, great Joan Crawford proud. "You won't have to see Art and the girls again until the Big Reveal. Ma's going to help me with a few things."

Shamiyah's eyes strayed back to Edith, who was still mad-dogging her with determination. "This is just *great*," she muttered under her breath. "You're not listening to me, Audra," she said when she could tear her eyes away from Edith's scowling face. "They don't have *tickets* for the Big Reveal. There's no room for them."

"Kiana can sit on Art's lap—she doesn't need a ticket," Audra said, pretending for Shamiyah's sake to care about the effects of the sun on her delicate skin by wrapping a scarf around her neck and face. "And Ma's helping me with my Reveal."

"Since when were you two close?" Shamiyah demanded.

"Since always," Audra snapped back, making it clear in her tone that if the girl said another word about her mother, she might just be tasting her own blood. "She's been helping me deal with covering up this skin issue for weeks, so I need her. Backstage. With me."

"Audra—"

"Look, according to the *contract*," she put a nasty emphasis on the word. "This final Reveal is supposed to be like a beauty pageant. The contestants are responsible for their own look—we're supposed to show how we've integrated our new appearance. How we've maintained it in our daily lives. To put it your way, you've sold the *concept* as showing the contestants as individuals, not cookie cutters pressed out of the same mold. I'm expressing my own identity here, Shamiyah. And after all the shit this show's put her through, is it too much to ask for her to be the one who helps me?"

"Audra—"

"Shamiyah!" Audra snapped back, finding a power of certainty deep within herself. "This was my makeover . . . and the Big Reveal is mine to win . . . or lose . . . my way!"

For just an instant, Shamiyah looked on the verge of launching into either a stream of questions or a vehement refusal. Her eyes swept over Audra and Audra suspected that in spite of the baggy sweatpants, she noticed the pounds Audra had gained curving in round lumps on her rear end and around her waist. She opened her mouth to comment, but didn't get a chance.

Instead, the woman's cell phone rang and she snapped it off her belt in exasperation. "What?" she snapped into the phone, giving Camilla a run for her money in terms of sheer imperious nastiness. "Okay, I'm on my way. Yes, I have her." She cast a sidelong glance in Audra's direction, then continued into the phone. "She says she has her own *stylist*— her mother." She gave the word *stylist* a dubious emphasis, but paused again for the caller's next comment. "Oh, all right. I suppose it'll be all right. We'll be able to tell during full dress on Wednesday, anyway. Yeah, see you in a bit. Bye." She turned back to Audra. "You're in luck. The stylist we hired to work with you was in an accident, so now we're in a little bit of a bind. You can have your precious mother backstage . . . but your look's got to pass muster on camera, or we're going to use one of the professionals."

"It'll pass muster. And I bought my own dress."

"Now wait just a minute, Audra—"

"Do I have to read the contract to you or—"

"But what about—"

"Don't worry about your precious ratings, Shamiyah," Audra muttered. "Even I see how you can spin this to your advantage. You tell the press something dramatic, like, 'One contestant refuses the help of professional and goes it alone,' or something cryptic like that. Hell, tell them it was me, if you think it makes a better hook. Doesn't matter to me . . . besides, you all own me for a few more days.

Right until America votes, right?" And Audra tried to smile in a way that would engender confidence and certainty.

Shamiyah wasn't paying attention to either Audra or the smile. Audra could almost see the wheels in her brain turning, trying out Audra's suggestions, testing their marketability and finding them acceptable.

"Okay . . ." she said at last. "We'll try this your way." She waved a delicate finger under Audra's nose, shaking her head until her black curls swayed. "But I'm not stupid, Audra," she hissed. "I know you're thinking up some kind of sabotage . . . especially given what I—what you *think* I did." She wagged a finger under Audra's nose. "But you won't get away with it, so don't—"

"Of course not. I wouldn't dream of sabotaging you, Shamiyah," Audra said with so much sweetness, her teeth began to ache. "You can see my gown ahead of time, and I'll be in full makeup, as promised for both dress rehearsal and the Big Reveal," Audra told her.

Again, Shamiyah's expression conveyed such a depth of doubt that Audra expected her to back up and reevaluate the whole plan. Before the other woman could speak, Audra fluttered her fingers dismissively as though the clothes and hair and makeup were the least of her concerns. "Now, on to more important matters. Disney?"

Shamiyah studied her for a long even moment, sighed, then whipped out the phone and dialed.

After checking in to the hotel, Audra was shuttled off with two other women to a small theater where the Big Reveal would be held. Camilla Jejune was there, along with Shamiyah and a couple of other young women Audra recognized as producers but was uncertain of their names. None of the doctors was present, nor were any of the other experts.

"They'll be present for the Big Reveal," Camilla said, "though they won't be featured as they were for each of your episodes. Now, this is how this is going to go."

She launched into a long overview of the program. A short clip of each woman's "journey" through the *Ugly Duckling* program would be shown, then each woman would be re-Revealed.

"You'll walk down the runway behind me, pose, pause and turn, giving our judges a chance to evaluate you on your runway presence. Then you'll return up the runway, branching off to stand upstage here," Camilla demonstrated. "Next, our host for the evening—we've got a commitment from Josh Nash, the singer—will ask you a question about life after your Ugly Duckling experience, and you will respond with the appropriate enthusiasm. The audience will clap and then you will exit, here, where you'll immediately change for the bathing-suit segment—"

A woman with a thick wave of russet tresses raised her hand. "Do we have to do the swimsuits? I mean, is it necessary?"

"Of course it's necessary," Camilla snapped. "Do you know how much confidence in your body you have to have to walk around on stage in a swimsuit? When you step out in a bathing suit, you're saying you're proud of your body . . . proud in a way that never would have been possible before the show." She glared at the redheaded woman in a way that made it clear she hadn't appreciated the interruption. "Okay, when all the contestants have been presented . . ."

Audra sighed. She knew what she had to do . . . but that didn't make it any easier. She'd be out there half-naked as far as clothes went . . . but fully naked in terms of her heart and soul.

The dress was a black sheath with a halter collar made of cowrie shells, which would have been stunning on any woman, whatever her height or weight. It fitted snugly on Audra's bottom—the first place the weight seemed to be returning—giving her figure a bottom-heavy curvaceousness.

Audra grabbed the flesh on her behind and squeezed it. "I like you, bottom," she whispered, thinking of Art and the odd therapy they'd been enjoying. "I like you, thighs."

"What are you doing, there?" her mother called. "Talking to yourself?"

"I guess you could say that," Audra agreed. "I love this dress, Ma. Thank you."

Her mother beamed. "I didn't do nothing," she said, but her thin face flushed with pride. "You look like a queen," she said, helping Audra roll gloves up her arms, covering some of the darkest browning, then grabbed a heavy pot of beige pancake makeup and started smoothing it into the exposed skin on Audra's face, shoulders and neck.

"This might bring a whole new rain of trouble down on your head," the older woman muttered. "These show people gonna be plenty mad, us tricking them this way. Two wrongs don't make a right, Audie. I taught you better than that."

"I know it," Audra sighed. "But long time ago, Shamiyah told me to give the people a show . . . and that's what I'm gonna do." She inspected her face in the mirror. "That looks good, Ma. Now I guess I'd better go take my place. It's going to be an interesting afternoon."

It was hot under the lights as they walked slowly through the stages of the Big Reveal, then again, at live TV speed, timing it down to the last second to be sure the program could be aired in its entirety in sixty minutes.

As Audra strutted her way through her paces in gown and swimsuit, she felt the heavy makeup melting on her body, staining the expensive clothing. Her mother smeared on more as Audra dashed from one piece of clothing to the next, but at the end of the rehearsal every outfit looked white-streaked and stained. In the chaos of the effort of getting the contestants here and there, no one said anything, and Audra breathed easier. They'd get the streaks out of the fabrics somehow, and later—when the cameras were rolling—it would be different.

Out front where the audience sat, waiting politely for their signal to applaud, things probably seemed calm and organized . . .

But backstage was pandemonium, to such a degree that Audra realized they almost needn't have worried so much.

As it was, Audra made her appearance in the wide

makeup room with the other women, making sure she'd been seen as present and ready . . . then disappeared to the little utility closet Edith had bribed a janitor into letting them use. It had a tiny little sink and an even smaller mirror, but it was more than enough for Audra to wash off the pancake makeup, strip off the gloves, and sit quietly, while Edith continued the laborious process of removing the extensions sewn tightly into Audra's hair.

"We should have started this before last night," she told Audra in an evil, stressed-out whisper. "I'm never going to—"

"We couldn't and you know it," Audra replied.

"If you'd just worn that wig—"

"That wig looks like a wig. They'd have figured it out in a heartbeat."

"Well, we don't got time to fight about it. Help me." Audra lifted her hands to join Edith's in releasing the extensions from the tight braids that wound around Audra's head. "We have to get them all out."

"I'll go with them half in and half out if I have to."

"You won't have to," Edith hissed. "And fix your face a little bit. You may be two toned, but doesn't mean you can't wear a little mascara and lip gloss. Pretty up a little—"

She stopped short, realizing what she'd said. Silence reigned in the tiny closet as Audra processed the words. *Pretty Up . . . Pretty Up . . .*

Then Audra laughed. Edith blinked at her a moment, as if stunned by the sound, then, shaking her head at herself, joined in, so that anyone walking by at that moment might have wondered just what kind of party was going on behind the little closed door.

* * *

"Audra! Where have you—" The stage manager stopped short, staring at her in open-mouthed amazement. "Oh my God! What happened to you? You can't go out there like that."

"I just heard someone say ten seconds, so I guess I'm going out there like this," Audra told her and hurried on to her spot behind the curtain. In a matter of seconds, a spotlight would hit, the curtain would open and Audra would show herself to the world.

"I think we've got a problem," the stage manager was already muttering into her headset. "I've found Audra Marks, but—"

"Five seconds!" someone hissed.

"What do you want me to do?" wailed the distressed stage manager, but Audra tuned her out. Her heart was fluttering a mile a minute, but Audra talked to it, reminding it of their larger purpose. *Shamiyah said I was a messenger for millions of African-American women . . . and here's my message. This is my message right here . . .*

The spotlight paused for nothing, not for distressed stage managers or nervous contestants about to make their "all natural" debut. The light hit the curtain and Audra no longer had a choice: She had to walk the walk.

And walk it she did—down the catwalk like she was to the runway born, hearing the gasps of surprise from the audience at her mottled, brown-beige skin, her cornrowed, extensionless head, her rounded, rubbing-together thighs. She struck her pose, paused for the judges, and then strode, head up, toward the host for her question.

"Audra, what happened?" he asked, opening and closing his mouth in stunned surprise, and Audra knew it wasn't the prepared question written on the little card in his pocket.

"I don't know what you mean," she replied in Bette Davis's most sweetly guilty voice.

"What happened to your skin—your hair—" the man stuttered, sounding utterly horrified. Audra glanced past him into the wings and saw Shamiyah, her eyes wide in shocked dismay.

"Oh that," she answered calmly. "I stopped doing the lightening and the long hair was too hot. I don't like living on salads . . . I missed real food. So I decided to accept myself as beautiful, the way I am right now . . . whether America thinks so or not." And she made a little bow and strode past him, making her exit right on cue, right on time as a smattering of applause reached her ears.

"That's my baby!" she heard Art shout from somewhere in the darkness of the audience. "That's my girl!"

"Go Audra!" Penny's voice joined his. "Go!"

"You missed Mickey at Disneyland, Auntie A! Can we go home now?"

Winning and losing, Audra realized almost immediately, were matters of perception, as much as beauty and ugliness.

Shamiyah and Camilla were furious at first, hollering in her face about how she'd jeopardized the show and the reputations of all involved, threatening legal actions in forty different flavors . . . but that couldn't erase the feeling of absolute freedom that soared in Audra's heart the second she stepped from the lights of the stage into the cool of the wings.

"I've got to go put on my bathing suit," she told them simply, and then swung her rounding hips at them as she returned to the dressing room to change.

And when America didn't pick her as their number one, Audra couldn't help feeling light as a feather. Tonight she was an absolute loser . . . but the happiest one on Earth.

"You did it, girl! You really did it!" Edith swung herself around her daughter's neck, hugging and jumping. "I can't believe you went out there and—"

"I'm proud of you, Audie," Laine rubbed her shoulders. "And I'm glad you're my cousin. Girl, that took a lot of nerve."

Art picked her up and swung her around and Penny surprised her with a bouquet of flowers. "I think what you did was great," she murmured shyly. "Really great."

"Me, too," Kiana said. "But is your skin going to stay that way?"

Audra shrugged. "We'll just have to see."

"Now what?" Art asked.

"Let's go home—"

"Not so fast!" Shamiyah hustled up to her, a big smile pasted across her face. "Everyone's talking about your look!" She gestured to the cell phone. "I just got off the phone with the publicity people. Every show in the country wants an interview with you."

"Sorry Shamiyah," Audra shook her head. "I'm through."

Shamiyah stared at her like she'd just said she intended to commit suicide.

"What do you mean, you're through?" she demanded. "You can't be through! How many times do we have to go over this. We own you until—"

"Until the end of 'the Big Reveal, if not selected as winner,'" Audra told her, quoting the language exactly. "I wasn't selected . . . and I'm through." Audra shrugged. "You can check with your lawyers if you want. I checked with mine."

The young producer blinked at her. An expression like anger crossed her face, then disappeared. "Come on, Audra," she said, starting out on a new tact. "This would mean a lot to me . . . to my career. You can't just—"

"Yes, Shamiyah. Yes, I can. Consider it no more than what you deserve." She nodded to her family. "Let's go."

"But what am I supposed to do about all these requests for interviews?"

There was a charged moment, as everyone waited for Audra's response. Audra put her hands on her hips, feeling every moment a grand diva—right down to her evening gown. She leaned close to Shamiyah, a smile quirking her lips.

"Frankly my dear, Shamiyah, I don't give a damn," she muttered, and swept out of the studio.

There was a car waiting near the studio, and a soldier in desert khakis stood beside it, peering toward the building like she was lost.

Kiana knew her first.

"Mommy!" she cried, breaking free of Audra's

hand and beginning to run. "Mommy! Mommy, you're home!"

Audra looked up just as Petra swept her little girl into her arms. A second later, her husband Michael emerged from the car and took his turn, swinging their little daughter into his arms.

Petra swept off her cap. She'd cut her hair short again, so that it was almost as short as Audra's, and her skin was tanned to brown from the desert sun.

"Ma . . . Audra," she said in a choked voice. "I'm home."

Audra didn't remember who ran to whom, she just remembered the three of them hugging and kissing and jumping, and talking all at once.

"You look beautiful," Petra whispered in her ear. "Just beautiful."

"You, too," Audra replied.

"Let's get the hell out of here," Edith muttered.

And Audra was quick to agree. She tossed back her head and laughed like a diva, arm in arm with the people who loved her, making the exit of a lifetime into the California sunset.